DEATH WATCH

"Scared?" whispered Joe.

"No," replied young Ben Brand.

"Don't lie, boy."

"I'm scared as hell."

"Yeah, me too. You almost wish they'd hit, and git it over with."

"Joe?"

"Say it."

"Am I a coward for feeling like I do?"

"Nope. It's a fool who ain't scairt when he should be."

Nearby, something snapped. A twig. There was a rustle in the darkness that reminded Ben of bat wings, only this didn't belong to bats.

He sat upright, Dragoon in hand. Joe joined him swiftly, facing in the opposite direction.

Suddenly, a terrible cry split the night air, and a half-naked man fell on Ben with a raised tomahawk. . . .

IRON HEART

BY WALT DENVER

ZEBRA BOOKS
KENSINGTON PUBLISHING CORP.

ZEBRA BOOKS

are published by

Kensington Publishing Corp.
475 Park Avenue South
New York, NY 10016

First printing: November 1985

Printed in the United States of America

This one's for Bob Redding, the Alaskan.

CHAPTER ONE

The old man sagged in the saddle, half asleep. The creak of leather sobbed against his eardrums, lulling his senses. His horse was old and tired, unshod after a winter's neglect. The pack mule plodded on its tether behind the horse, hooves squishing and sliding in the snow-melt wet earth of the trail. The man's new beard flourished in scraggly patches. He had shaved the luxuriant growth off three days before, but had not touched his face since. The flesh was still tender from the razor's edge. The shaving had been a concession regarding his return to civilization. The pack mule labored under the burden of beaver and mink furs smashed flat, tied down in bundles by wet leather thongs that had been drawn tight when they dried.

The smell of smoke brought the old man bolt upright in the saddle.

He drew the reins in toward his barrel belly and the pinto gelding held fast. The mule stopped, drooping its head, eyelids closing automatically, like cowls.

Wood smoke.

No mistaking the smell. Fresh.

On a morning of warm thaw?

Maybe. A cookfire, perhaps. Late, though. For breakfast, anyway. The old man squinted up at the sun. Near ten of the clock, he figured.

Late sleepers?

He didn't think so. His senses sharpened as he sniffed the air. He drew a grubby finger across his wet tongue. Raised it to test the breeze. The breeze was slight, but he could feel it. It blew straight up from the trail, down below. Carrying the scent of the smoke faintly to his nostrils. He had not come this way, going up. He tried to remember why and when he tried to remember, it came to him. There had been settlers in the foothills. He had not wanted to see them, answer their questions. He remembered seeing the cabin, the corrals, and had wondered why the settlers had decided to build here in that spot. It was a good place, but it was so far away from the settlements.

So, he had skirted the ranch and wondered about the people who had settled so far from everything. He had almost forgotten about them, but now he remembered that he had wondered about them last year, in the fall.

He was going to skirt them again, but something odd about the smoke smell and another smell with it, made him hold to his course downslope. There was something not right about the smells. Mingling like that. One of them, elusive, but vaguely familiar. His skin began to prickle. He needed time and thought to sort out this newest smell. He reached in a pocket of his shirt and pulled out a twist of tobacco. The tobacco had dried up too much and was tough. He slipped his big knife out of its sheath and cut a small portion from the butt-end of the twist. Some of the tobacco shredded and flecked his fingers. He licked the tobacco into his mouth, pushed the plug down between his gum and cheek. The saliva would soften the chunk.

The gelding began to balk. His pale sorrel ears began to twitch and twist. The old man saw one of his nostrils. It was flared, sniffing, twitching like his ears. The prickling raced across his skin, spread up his arms, to his shoulders, to the back of his neck.

Death.

That's what he smelled.

"Hoo, boy. Steady." He patted the gelding's neck, stroked its mane. His voice sounded strange to him. It was very quiet and his voice sounded loud, uneasy in the stillness. The prickling got worse.

He could separate the different smells now. One was sickly, sweetish. That was the death smell. The other was smoke, and that one was stronger now. It couldn't mask the other smell, though.

Joe Cardwell untied the thongs of the rifle's scabbard, snaked the .50 caliber mountain rifle out of its buckskin sheath so carefully the fringes did not move. He checked the nipple. It was capped. He drew the hammer back to half cock, holding the trigger in so that there was no noise.

The silence was spooky.

He slipped out of the saddle, tied the horse and mule to sturdy pines. He glided over the earth on soft, thick moccasins, traded for at the rendezvous of

11

'37, worn carefully and infrequently ever since, one of two pairs that were the best things his feet had ever known. He slung his possibles pouch over his shoulder and started off downhill.

His saliva softened the chunk of tobacco in his jaw. The juice helped to keep him calm. He spat silently as he slunk through the trees, keeping his body low, using the trees for protection, stopping every so often, his silhouette matching a tree's as he stood and listened intently for any sound.

That's what bothered him now more than anything. The awesome silence. It was not the silence of deserted places. He was used to that. Rather, it was as if all noise had been sucked away by some giant invisible force. As if something terrible and noisy had happened a few moments before and had been washed away by the wind—and by sudden death. He had felt such silences before. Once, on the prairie, he had heard the terrible cries of people in extreme pain, the rushing eerie shouts of Sioux, the crack of rifles, the deadly singing of arrows. He had heard all of this without seeing any of the action. He had ridden to the knoll where he could view the scene of attack. By the time he'd reached his vantage point, the Sioux had gone. The travelers were all dead and scalped. The wagon broken into firewood. There was a silence, then, too.

Like this silence.

Joe moved slow, still. He didn't want to walk into anything he couldn't handle.

The smells grew stronger. Overpowering.

He came to the clearing, then, saw the fence, the outbuildings, the house. The smoke rising straight up in the air, then hanging there in a pall over the entire scene.

Something else, too.

Bodies were strewn everywhere. He held fast at the edge of the woods, his eyes taking in every detail. It was as if he had come upon people and animals who had frozen to death and appeared after a thaw. His scalp prickled once again. A queasy feeling rose up in his stomach. He looked at the smoke, black and rancid, hanging there like a hideous threat. Then, his eyes went to the bodies.

The whites were all scalped, mutilated, those that he could see. A young girl, no more than three years old, was split open like a melon, bloating in the morning sun. A lad of five or six, his genitals missing, a patch of his skull stripped of hair just above his forehead, gazed up at the sky with gouged, sightless eyes.

Joe walked through the mess. There were dead Indians in the yard, too.

"'Rappyhoe," muttered the mountain man, to himself. The stench was unbearable. He walked toward the main house. There was a circle of Indians around the porch, their bodies twisted into grotesque shapes, strange fleshy balloons holding muskets, 'hawks; their teeth set in agonized grins. The house was intact, he noticed, made of hand-hewn logs. There was evidence of scorching, but the logs hadn't burned. The smoke poured, instead, from a barn out back, standing to one side. The barn, with its stable, was gutted.

The Indians had gotten the horses anyway. Cattle too, if there'd been any. Joe's mind worked quickly, assessing everything he saw, everything he surmised. He brought his rifle level as he stepped onto the porch. Something was out of kilter here. The house was not burned, the Indians had gone away. Somebody inside had stood 'em off. Who? How?

A white man lay in the doorway. He, too, had been cut up, his scalp taken. So, the Indians had gotten that far. But then someone had driven 'em back.

Joe stepped inside the room. He fought down a sickness, a rising of bile in his throat. He wanted to pinch his nose, but instinct told him to keep his rifle at the ready. He saw the woman, then, lying on her back. She appeared to be about the same age as the man in the doorway. Folks in their late forties. The lines in their faces had softened in death, but they were there. These people had not had an easy life. Right up to the end.

The woman was covered with gore. In death, her nakedness was childlike, the flesh smeared with caked blood that looked like chocolate. Blowflies swarmed around her bodily orifices, crawling out of the gaping emptiness between her legs.

Joe gagged, then, and pinched his nostrils tight, holding the rifle with one hand, a finger inside the trigger guard. He moved away, quickly, through another doorway.

Another room, more Indians. Powder was embedded around the entry holes of some of the wounds. Close range. They were Arapaho all right. Their faces were vacant, but their war paint was as vivid in death as in life.

Joe saw him then, and his finger touched the trigger lightly.

The boy stared at him, a madness in his eyes.

Joe's scalp crawled along his skull as if suddenly afflicted with caterpillars.

A pistol was aimed right at his belly. The barrel hole was black, ominous. Joe's rifle stopped its slow sweeping motion. His finger relaxed on the trigger. He knew that the boy was watching his every move. Joe hoped the lad saw that he meant him no harm.

In an instant, Joe's eyes took in everything: the boy, smeared with blood, the Indians around him, dead, the hammer of the pistol at full cock, the finger tightening down on it, and that mad look in the boy's eyes. In an eerie instant of sudden insight, Joe knew that the boy no longer knew who the enemy was, no longer cared. He had killed so much that one more would not make any difference. He was like some trapped animal. He would slash at anything.

"Hold on, chile," Joe said softly. "I mean you no harm."

There was a long moment when Joe thought the boy could not speak, had no tongue.

"Back away, then. Keep your arms out where I can see 'em."

Joe stepped back, held his arms out wide, the rifle dangling in his right hand. Only his eyes moved, gaping at the area around the boy.

The lad was filthy. No more than fifteen, sixteen, maybe. Rifles lay around him. He was hurt, too. Shot, or 'hawked. There was a wide gash in his shoulder. A tomahawk lay nearby, its blade brown with desiccated blood. Joe was sure the boy was in pain, but in his eyes there was only the blazing ferocity of defiance, of hatred.

"You kilt all these Injuns?" Joe asked, in awe.

The boy's eyes glinted slightly, but he made no other sign. His eyes were steady on Joe's. His hand held steady, too.

"Those yore kin? Outside? In the other room?" There was tenderness in the mountain man's voice. "Jesamighty, boy, say somethin', will ya? Hell, I jes' come down out'n the hills. Seed all this out here. Lucky you're alive. You need tendin' to, if'n you want to save that there arm. Don' recollec' no place here before two summers ago. 'Rappyhoes. Once't peaceful. Somethin' teched 'em off, I reckon. Hey, you gonna talk, son, or you want to hear me croak on? I'm nigh sick to death of the reek in here and you still figgerin' the whole world's agin you. Hell, don't you know a possible friend when you see one?"

The boy's eyes clouded over and a sob rose in his throat. The pistol wavered for a second, then began to sink to the floor. Joe thought the boy was going to break down and weep, but he didn't. Instead, he caught himself and took a deep breath. His shoulders spread wide and he tried to sit up straight. He was very weak. But, there was something strong in him that Joe could almost feel. It was something beyond bravery, beyond courage. It was an animal's determination to live.

"You hurt bad, chile?"

Joe put his rifle down carefully and went to the boy, helped him stand. The boy's legs crumpled. Joe held him up with powerful arms, strong hands. It wasn't as bad as he had thought. The boy was starving and there was the gash in his shoulder, a

16

bullet wound in his leg. Clean through the fleshy part.

"Come on, chile, take it easy." He helped the boy out into the sunlight, shielding him from the dead as best he could. The boy kept his gaze steady, looking at the evidence of the slaughter. He had probably seen all of it happen, Joe figured.

The boy still carried the pistol. Cocked.

"You musta scairt hell out'n them Injuns fer 'em to leave off like this and not take their dead. When did this happen? Yestiddy? Day before?"

"Yesterday," the boy said, his voice cracking, not from fear or weakness, but from his age. His voice was changing.

"Lordamighty!"

"They killed Mom and Pop, my sis and my brother." The boy's voice dropped to a low register. "They run off all our stock. They tried to kill me, too."

"You better let me look to that shoulder and get you some grub. My horse and mule's tied up slope a ways."

The boy shook his head.

"What?"

"I aim to get 'em, mister. Every damned one of 'em!"

The boy stopped, jerked away from the man's grip, looked again into Joe's eyes. Joe saw the pain in them, the madness. He nodded, slowly. The boy was holding the pistol. Joe had only his knife. He held his tongue.

"Sure, boy, sure. You'll get 'em. I'll even help you.

I know these 'Rappyhoes. Knowed ever one of 'em oncet."

The boy's eyes flared and rolled into the back of their sockets. He took a step toward Joe and then fainted.

Joe caught him before he hit the ground.

CHAPTER TWO

Joe lowered the boy to the ground gently. The heavy Dragoon slipped from the youth's hand. It hit the ground with a solid thud, and lay on its side, the black muzzle staring like an evil eye. The evil didn't scare Joe. He remembered a time or two in the last few years when he'd wished to Godamighty he'd had one in his holster.

Years of taking care of himself and others in a wilderness shunned by the medical profession, had left Joe with a certain amount of skill in doctoring. He peeled the boy's shirt off and examined the slash. The bleeding had stopped and red meat lay under a light glaze. He next stripped the lad's trousers off, examined the leg. The bullet had passed through the fleshy calf clean. In time, the two holes it made would harden into twin puckers, but there would be no permanent damage.

Leaving the boy in as easy a position as the ground permitted, Joe went for his horse and mule. As the animals neared the tragic scene, they balked, their nostrils flared.

"Come on, durn ye," muttered Joe, "I don't like this here any better'n you."

Joe had been a mountain man for a long time. He had seen killings, but this massacre made his guts churn. He felt the bile of nausea rise up in his throat. The sickly stench of the dead was heavy under the sun and he shielded his eyes against the grisly sight. He leaned against his horse and gulped for air.

Jesamighty!

A moan from the boy brought him around. He tied his animals to a tree and hurried to the youth, ignoring his own discomfort. There was another whose pain was greater than his own. The boy was still unconscious so Joe built a fire. There was a fireplace in the cabin, but he wouldn't enter that place for all the beaver skins in Jefferson Territory. He simply couldn't face all that death again. What lay outdoors was much more than he wanted to see, but at least it wasn't close to him. He busied himself digging a pan out of his gear, filled it with water from a dug well. He snugged the pan up against the fire and let the flames dance the water to a boil. A couple of soft linen kerchiefs from his duffel bag served as swabs.

He dipped one of the kerchiefs into the boiling water and washed the dried blood from the boy's lacerated shoulder. Joe had taken the habit of measuring men. A stranger, met on a lonely patch in deep woodlands, reached his eye, first, in dimensions. How square the shoulders, how big the arm, and the long legs. Thus inventoried, the stranger became less of a menace. Joe knew what he could handle . . . and what he couldn't.

The boy was big-shouldered. No more'n fifteen, he figured, the lad had the breadth of a grown man, though not yet fleshed out. His arms were lanky with the strings of immaturity, but they, too, would one day be a force. Even now, Joe reckoned, the boy could accept an angry grownup fist and send an ache shivering into its knuckles. And the youth's legs, though long of bone without much meat, were tied with tough sinew. They would also, in time, clasp a horse, and stirrups need never know the touch of the boy's feet. His legs were a vise in the making.

As Joe finished bathing the wounds, the boy stirred. He sat up suddenly, fear blazing in his gray eyes. He grabbed for his Dragoon, but Joe plucked it away.

"Naw," he said quietly, "no need for that, chile."

The lad met his gaze, held it steadily for several moments before the fear cooled. The boy nodded and asked in an adolescent rasp, "Who are you?"

"They call me Joe Cardwell. And you?"

The boy's eyes flicked around the yard, witnessing the carnage once again. His eyes grew frosty with horror, as memory pressed his mind into funnel vision. Every detail of the past twenty-four hours crammed into the funnel, etching the stark images forever in daguerreotype lines of light and shadows on his mind.

He pressed his hand to his face and moaned, "Oh, my God."

"It's over, young 'un," Joe said softly. He didn't know just how to comfort a boy who had just lost his family to fiendish murder and mutilation. "Can't

21

never happen agin," he added, "maybe that's some-thing, anyways."

The boy dropped his hands, and looked long and hard at the white, bloody bodies. As the boy looked, Joe noticed a change in the sagging shoulders. They squared up, as though propped by steel rods within. The lad's fists knotted, until the knuckles paled under taut skin, and his face smoothed into flat, expressionless planes. His eyes lost their frost, and, in turn, grew warm, then hot. They glowed with intense heat, an intense reflection from fires already flaring deep down inside.

"Maybe," he said, glancing at his wounds, "I ought to have bandages, too."

Joe was startled by the boy's voice. It had steadied some, deepened. The hysteria of moments before had been replaced by calm. There was something eerie about the boy's tone that brought a thread of memories to Joe's mind, a memory of a similar voice. Five years before, he'd witnessed another massacre, by renegade whites, not Indians. But the violence had affected the survivors the same way. Once they'd gained their full minds, after the shock had worn away, the two survivors had spoken with the same calmness. Later, each of the renegades had died violently and Joe had no doubt about who had planned their deaths.

The old mountain man shivered. As he bound the boy's wounds with the wet linen kerchiefs, he understood about the lad's state. Shock. Maybe something else besides. A hatred, perhaps, buried deep inside him, a slow-burning hate that would simmer inside him until it boiled over.

"Likely I won't have to cauter them wounds," said Joe. "See how them poultices do. We can get some yerbs and sech to make the healing go a mite faster."

The boy said nothing and the hatred crept into his eyes like coals, smouldered there naked as sin.

Joe didn't speak of it. All he said was, "You ain't told me your name yet, chile."

"It's Ben Brand," the boy said as he glanced at the bodies, "and they were my family."

His voice cracked. His chest heaved with a sob that he couldn't hold back. He looked down, caught his breath, swallowed hard.

"Jesamighty," muttered Joe, who wished he could take the boy in his arms and tell him it would be all right.

Ben began to talk swiftly, in low tones, tones suited to death and sadness.

"They were my people. Jake and Carrie, my Ma and Pa. And my little brother Billy, and my poor little sister, Elisa." Ben's voice caught in his throat. "Aunt Hattie, too—she was Ma's sister. She didn't have any family but us."

"I'm sorry, Ben."

Ben doubled up his fist as he tried to control his rage. "Why'd they do it? We weren't hurting anybody. We've been here almost two years now and we were just getting the place fixed up the way we wanted it. We liked it here in the foothills of the Rockies. My pa, he trapped in winter and we tried farming in the summer. Wasn't much of a farm yet, but we got spuds and turnips. We would have done better, too, only now . . ."

The boy paused, listened. A faint voice floated

across the air.

"Ben . . . Benji . . ." The feminine voice was audible.

Joe Cardwell turned his head, saw the bloodied, lifeless body of the woman sprawled on the ground, some twenty feet away. Her head was turned toward them and even though her eyes were open, they seemed to stare vacantly, as if glazed by the blinding frost of death.

"Aunt Hattie!" Ben cried. He pushed himself up, limped over to her. He knelt down beside her, took her hand in his and pressed it gently. Joe came up behind him, stared down at the woman.

"Aunt Hattie," Ben murmured. "I thought you were gone."

"You all right, Benji?" Hattie breathed in a weak voice. She moved her head slightly to look up at him.

Ben nodded. His face hardened. "Call me Ben now, Aunt Hattie. I ain't little Benji no more. I got a man's work to do now."

Hattie looked at him, the beginning of a smile at the corner of her blood-caked lips, as if she understood that he had to be grown-up now. And then her body went slack and her head rolled back over against her shoulder, her mouth hanging open as if she still had something to say.

"Hattie! Aunt Hattie," Ben pleaded, but he knew she was gone. He released his grip on her hand, tenderly placed it on her bloodied chest, then stood up. "I'll get them for this, Aunt Hattie. I swear it."

He looked down at her limp body, shook his head. "I guess there's nothing left but to bury them."

"You cain't do nothin' with that shoulder, son. I'll

24

take keer of it, rest their souls. You break open that wound I got to put hot iron to it."

Ben nodded, too shaken to speak. Joe found a shovel in what was left of the barn, set about to dig one large grave.

"We were a close family," Ben said when Joe stopped digging to catch his breath. "We lived close, and I think Pa and Ma would want to be close now."

"Are these all the kin you have?" Joe asked, sweat dripping from his weathered brow.

"Yes," Ben replied. "All I have is right here. There's nobody else."

When the grave was big enough, they wrapped the bodies of Ben's family in blankets. Joe marveled at Ben, who went through the ritual with the same calm he had exhibited before—the calm of suppressed rage. Joe saw that Ben's hands were gentle, a feathering over the ravaged corpses, a lingering over his mother. Ben kissed her and his father, and all of the dead, before he drew the blankets up over their faces. Then, with his good arm, he helped Joe lay them side by side, straight and dignified, in the wide hole.

When Joe shoveled the first scoop of dirt on the still bodies, he noticed the tears that rolled down the boy's cheeks. Ben wiped the tears away, stood straight. And then his body heaved with the sobs he was unable to control.

Joe stepped over to the lad. "Let it come," he said, as he put his hand on Ben's shoulder.

"It's hard," Ben sobbed.

"I know it's hard," Joe said, blinking back the

tears that formed in his own eyes.

After a minute, Ben stopped crying. Joe shoveled with renewed vigor as if wanting to get it over with as quickly as possible. When the grave was filled to ground level, Joe said, "I think we oughta stop here."

Ben looked at him, a puzzled look on his face. "What do you mean? This don't look like a grave yet."

"That's what you want."

"But why? I want to put up crosses," he said as he glared at the bodies of the Indians strewn about, "and tell how my family was killed. I'll put, 'Murdered without a chance . . . by . . .'"

"'Rappyhoes," Joe said. "These here are 'Rappyhoes."

"By 'Rappyhoes," Ben finished savagely. "By cowardly Indians."

Joe shook his head.

"You mark this here grave," he told Ben, "and other 'Rappyhoes'll dig 'em up, and them Indians'll be mad. They don't respect no white eyes' bodies, like they do their own."

The boy's eyes flashed and his cheeks flushed under the summer tan.

"You mean to tell me," he said slowly, "that I can't mark the place where my people are buried?"

"Sure, you can, chile, but hear my words—yore folks'll end up bein' coyote feed."

Ben thought that over, weighing the odds of a decent, Christian burial, complete with grave markers, against the ravages of Indian revenge. The Arapahoes had lost many braves. Their own anger and grief would run deep.

26

He sighed and nodded. "They'll see this fresh dirt we dug anyways, and still go after my family."

"Listen," said Joe. "I ain't been in this country fer over twenty years without learnin' somethin'. Jus' do what I say."

First, the two trampled the earth down as hard as they could. Then Joe brought his horse and mule and had the animals trample the dirt some more, by walking them back and forth across the grave. Then he and Ben shoveled more dirt in and repeated the process until nearly all of the fresh dirt was back in the dig.

Joe scouted the area, found a wagon in back of the house. With both shoving hard, they brought the wagon up front near the grave. Joe pitched the rest of the fresh dirt into it, along with a lot of pebble-laden surface dirt, and mixed the two thoroughly, until it all looked like surface dirt. He then did the same to the grave, until it appeared exactly like the rest of the yard. He pushed the Conestoga wagon over on top of the grave, finishing the deception.

They had done a good job of trail-covering, but Joe wasn't quite satisfied. An Arapahoe, or any Indian, would see differences. They had the eyes of eagles, and could pick out flaws in a Platte River current. He sighed. If it made the boy feel better, maybe it was worth the trouble, but only time would tell. His attention turned to the dead Indians.

"What about them?" he asked Ben.

"First, we say a prayer over my family's grave," Ben replied quietly. "I got to give them that."

Joe whipped off his broad-brimmed hat and stood next to Ben.

Ben cleared his throat, peered at the flat, unmarked grave with the wagon sprawled across its surface.

"Ma, Pa," Ben said, "little Elisa and Billy, and Aunt Hattie, I pray for you. I don't know what to say, because I never been to a funeral." He glanced up at the sky. "But, I know about God, because you told me about Him, Ma, and if you say there is a God, I believe you. He's in Heaven, you told me, and He welcomes Christians, which you always said we was. So, I hope He's waiting, Ma, like you said."

The boy was silent for a moment, dealing with a grief that insisted in breaking through the outer shell. After a moment, he said, "Amen. I love all of you. All of you."

Joe kept his tongue. He wasn't good at formal affairs, be they weddings or funerals. He had been living alone in the deep wilderness too long, in the mountains of Jefferson Territory, to speak much anyway. Sometimes, he lived alone for such long stretches, that he had to search his memory for the simple greeting of, "Howdy." True, after he got through that barrier, there was some said you couldn't shut him up, but that was only with other men like himself, and not at formal gatherings.

When Ben turned from the grave with his calm face, Joe said, "Now, how's about them Indians?"

"I'll show you," Ben replied.

Ben went into the house, returning in a moment with a sheath knife.

"This belonged to Pa," he said. "He never got a chance to use it, but I will."

Ben set to work scalping the dead Arapahoes and Joe was chilled by the boy's efficiency. The youth went at the gruesome task swiftly and with knowing. It was as if he had been lifting hair all his life.

"Where'd you learn that?" Joe asked.

"I watched them scalping my people," Ben answered bitterly. "What do you call it? The school of experience."

The boy laughed, and the sound was horrible, a skeleton rasping in a mouldered grave.

"God, chile," Joe exclaimed, "you take all this hair, it'll git you in trouble."

"Who with?" demanded Ben.

"Why them 'Rappyhoes'll come after you."

Ben nodded. "Good."

"I say you oughta stop it."

Ben turned to Joe, knife clutched firmly by the bone handle. "We friends, Joe?"

"Yeah, sure."

"Then don't try to stop me. I owe this to *them*." He nodded toward the grave.

Joe saw the point. There was some justice in Ben's remark. And, there was an attitude about Ben, a stiffness as he slid his knife across a brown forehead and jerked back on the hair, that told Joe that Ben was obsessed.

"All right, chile," said Joe.

"And something else," said Ben.

"Yeah?"

"Don't call me 'chile' no more. Like I told Aunt Hattie, I'm not a boy anymore."

Joe nodded. The boy had that right. After what he'd been through, he could no longer be considered a child. Childhood was lost when the first Arapahoe tomahawk drew the blood of Ben's kin.

"I know these 'Rappyhoes," said the old mountain man, as he wandered among the bodies. "We used to be friends, oncet."

"What happened?" Ben asked, still applying his scalping knife with skill and a frightening attention to detail.

"I don't know. I think the whites turned on 'em. They was some kind of trouble. They say the 'Rappyhoes don't like whites movin' their hunting ground. 'Rappyhoes is fightin' Indians, Ben. They fight first, last and always. What I think is they just like to fight."

"Some had their last here," grunted Ben.

The boy stood up, finished. He had ten blood-wet lengths of skin and hair clutched in his hand.

"I got 'em, Ma," he said, "and I'll get more."

Joe shivered on hearing the words. It wasn't so much the words, but the way they were spoken. Joe had heard prairie fire, he had seen and heard lightning crackle and thunder, he had listened to the grizzly bear hiss in mortal throes and the mountain lion scream. In Ben's voice, he heard all of these in one tone. Not loud, but penetrating soft. Mean, deadly.

"I know this one's name," Joe said quickly. He pointed at a scalpless Indian. "That one's Crooked Nose. He is bad—was bad."

"Why was he killing innocent people?" Ben asked. His voice had recovered its calm.

"I dunno." Joe scratched his forehead. Seeing all the Indians sprawled face upward after Ben turned them over for easier knife work, made his own scalp itch. "He was with Tall Dog, chief of a renegade band."

"Tall Dog?"

"He don't like white eyes. Figgers they's bad for 'Rappyhoe territory, but Tall Dog, he don't like nobody. Whites, Utes, Pawnee, nobody."

"He sent this Crooked Nose to kill us?"

"Tall Dog figgers he owns the Platte, son, clear to the Arkansas. Anyone uses the land thouten his permission, well, Tall Dog feels obliged to lift his hair."

Anger again erupted in Ben Brand's grey eyes, and Joe marveled at the maturity of the anger. This was man's anger, dressed in the body of a fifteen-year-old boy. What would that anger be when the body grew up to match it?

"And they killed my family when Pa didn't have his gun." Ben shook his head in disbelief. "I can't see how they can kill defenseless men, how they can cut up women the way they did. Those Arapahoes are not men." Ben spit on the ground. "They are coyotes that feed in the night on rotted guts."

Joe was suddenly aware of something else. He hadn't thought of it until now. The horror of what he had come across had driven reasoning power from his mind. He had done what had to be done, without thinking. Now, he thought about it. None of the Brand family had weapons with them. Of course the 'Rappyhoes would have taken any, but Ben had just said that his Pa had no weapon. It wasn't likely the women would have been carrying firearms, and certainly not the two children. Especially when they were all so close to the house, where they felt secure.

Then who killed all those 'Rappyhoes?

Joe's attention swung full on young Ben Brand. The boy stood tall, framed against the fire-scorched house, stained with the blood of scalps. Ben had done it alone! He had killed them all with the .44, six-shot Colt Dragoon. By God, he had done it by hisself!

"Was they," he heard himself asking, "any of them 'Rappyhoes left?"

Ben nodded. "I think there was some."

"You fought them all by yourself?"

Joe found his reasoning hard to believe. He had to hear it said from the boy who did it.

"They killed my Pa right off, and the women. It was over for them in five minutes, so there was only me left. I was in the house, or I'd been killed too."

"Your pa didn't get any of them down even?"

"He didn't have a chance to even raise his hands."

"When did you start shootin'?"

"I ran into the back room and kept quiet. There was the pistol there, and I grabbed it."

"But they come in?"

"They come in, and I kept still. They ransacked everything. They ripped up the curtains Ma brought from St. Louis. They knocked over the table and even pissed on everything. I could hear it all, and all the while they were laughing." Ben shuddered.

The boy screwed his eyes shut tight, as if trying to blot the memory, but it did no good.

"I couldn't stand that, Joe. All my folks lying there dead, and everything my mother loved being ripped and dirtied. So I stepped into the room where they were. There was four. The others were outside getting the stock, and setting fire to the house and barn."

Ben sighed, gulped, wanted to stop, but now that he had opened the gates, the flood was inexorable. He had to go on.

"I stepped around the door into that room, and the four of them gaped at me. They just gaped, and I shot them dead. All four. They dropped like stones, because I shot them in their heads. I'm a good shot, Joe. I'm good and I'm fast."

Ben stopped, the flood under better control.

"But then them rascals in the yard heard and come runnin'?" Joe asked. Four Indian bodies had been accounted for, but what about the other six?

Ben's voice was raspy as he continued.

"They came screeching and yelling like demons. It was terrible. I ran back into the other room and reloaded the pistol quick. Pa showed me how to do it fast. And then I waited.

"They rushed through the door in a bunch, shooting at me. I could hear the bullets pelting all around, and they followed those bullets like hounds on a rabbit." He touched his shoulder. "That's how I got this. They were that close, a tomahawk sliced me. I don't know when I got it in the leg. I just kept shooting and reloading and shooting. Last night they didn't come. I could hear them in the distance, but they didn't come. They came again early this morning and I shot some more, when they came to drag their dead out of the house."

Ben's voice smoothed out.

"It's all I got to say, Joe."

"You're goin' to have a big reputation with the 'Rappyhoe, Ben. A boy killin' all those warriors—includin' Crooked Nose." Joe shook his head, as if shaking off a dream. "Tall Dog is going to have to get you. No white eyes can get away with killin' his braves. Especially no boy!"

"If he don't get me, I'll get him," Ben responded.

"Meanin'?"

"You know what I mean, Joe."

"Yeah, I think I do."

Joe glanced around at the still unburied bodies of the Arapahoes.

"What we goin' to do with 'em?"

"Give their kin something to think about. Come on."

With Joe's help, Ben carted the bodies into the house. Joe didn't like it much, but if the stripling named Ben Brand could stand it, he could, and he struggled through the ordeal, sickened by the stench.

After the bodies were heaped on the floor, Ben retrieved some clean linen from an overturned dresser drawer.

"For these," he said, pointing to his wounds, "from Ma."

He next piled brush up against the cabin. Dry, crackly brush that would burn good. Joe helped, until there was a pile as high as the eaves.

"What those killers couldn't finish, I will," said Ben as he struck fire to the brush.

The flames leaped into the sky and caught the cabin in a death grip. The whole thing went up in barely an hour, while Joe and Ben watched from a distance. They smelled the burning flesh, and heard it pop and sizzle, and while they went on, Ben Brand smiled. When the roof crashed down in a fan of sparks, he turned to Joe and said, "Let's go."

"Where we goin'?"

"I want Tall Dog."

Joe studied the youth, seeing in the young eyes the light of revenge. Justified revenge. Maybe the whites were taking Indian ground. Once it hadn't been bad, but now, there were too many whites, and it was bad. The Indians were fighting to hold what was theirs, but Ben Brand wasn't thinking about that. He was not into right and wrong. His family had been cruelly slaughtered by renegade savages. His family had been murdered by people whom they didn't even know. They were innocents in a country in hot revolt, and they had been caught.

That didn't concern Ben Brand. For him, the matter was personal. His dead family had to be avenged.

"First, we have to go to Cherry Creek," Joe said. He nodded at his horse and mule. "I got furs to get rid of, and we are goin' to need supplies."

"We?"

"You don't think I'd let a young 'un bash straight into 'Rappyhoe country by hisself, do yuh?"

For the first time, Ben smiled.

"All right," he said, "it's Cherry Creek first."

"You got anything to take along?"

"Just this." Ben patted the Dragoon, which was nestled in a holster at his side. "Everything else . . ."

He shaded his sad eyes against the glare of the sun.

"Everything else we worked two years for is gone, Joe." His eyes caressed the grave beneath the

Conestoga. "Everything is gone. Let's leave."

As they left, Joe walking so Ben could ease his wounded leg, Ben made a vow.

"Tall Dog, I'll get you. I don't care how long it takes, I am going to kill you."

Joe shuddered.

He had no doubt the boy meant every word.

CHAPTER THREE

Mountain Man Joe Cardwell didn't look on himself as old. He was a "young fifty, Jesamighty!" Or, at least he thought he was fifty. Where Joe spent his life there were no calendars. There were few watches. Joe kept track of time by the seasons and the sun. Memory was jogged by signals. Pete Webb was a signal, and Joe remembered life with Pete very well. The man went insane from mountain fever, during the winter of heavy snow. Seven seasons past. He'd had to bind Pete to his horse to get him to Cherry Creek and a doctor, and the horse was ass deep in drifts for five days.

Joe carried signals in his mind, like the seconds of a minute, the minutes in an hour. There was the big fire that smoked up the hill country clean to the South Platte. That was ten snows ago, ten years. How did he remember the incident occurred ten years before? Because five winters ago was the time of early thaw. Snow melted in February that year, and dribbled down the mountains to the Platte. Ten thousand dribbles filled the Platte and there was flooding. Bad water that wiped out beaver sets in bordering ponds. He'd lost his shirt that year, because of the floods. He'd not forget that depressing experience, and it was midway between now and the fire that ate up the hillsides.

Yet, in spite of the signals, the landmarks of memory, Joe knew that somewhere he'd slipped when it came to his own age. If a man lives at the edge of the world, where there are no birthdays, he forgets about his age. A man lives till he dies, and there is no age in between. Of course, a knee might give him fits now and then, because years had worn the cartilage to the bone, and the bones rubbed. Maybe that was a sign of age. Maybe, but Joe prided himself on managing the steep slopes he called home on either horseback or on foot. He was fifty—or it was forty-nine, or maybe fifty-three? He didn't know for sure, and he didn't care. He still set his foot down as well as he did in his twenties, and that was all that counted.

He strode ahead of his horse with Ben Brand aboard. He kept his body loose, his arms swinging free. He could walk fifty miles, provided that danged knee didn't decide it wanted a rest.

"You tired?" Ben Brand called from the saddle.

"Ain't no trail too hard for Joe Cardwell in these here camel humps," snorted Joe pridefully. "Don't you worry, son."

But when they camped that night, Joe took off his boots early. He let the breeze swirl around his feet, cooling them. Actually, he had done a lot of horsebacking lately.

They made a low fire behind a boulder, and cooked

38

some coffee. Neither was hungry, for both remembered the savagery of the past twenty-four hours. Both remembered the slashed and torn white bodies, the lifeless brown skins, swelling in the hot sun. Both remembered the stench of decaying flesh, and coffee was all they could stomach. They were silent.

"You all right, son?" Joe asked at last.

"I don't know. No, I'm not all right," came the thoughtful answer.

"Gonna take awhile."

"I'll never forget. Not ever." The voice was stronger.

"No. Me neither, I guess. I seen some things, but nothin' like that."

The sun was setting, and cast a red glow over the sky. White cirrus clouds turned pink and veiled the high eastern skies. Mountain tops still carried snow in crevices, like hods of white, cracked bricks. They, too, slowly blushed roseate under the sun's vanishing rays. An owl hooted in the forest, a haunting echo that drifted to silence, then tried again.

"God, it's pretty," said Ben Brand.

"Yup," agreed Joe. "She's purty."

"None of my family's going to see it again."

"No," was the quiet reply. "They ain't, but listen . . ."

"Yeah, go head, Joe. It's all right. I'm not going to blubber."

"Well, maybe some things a man holds back, but they's just under the skin, Ben, I know that. But look at it this way . . ."

Again Joe Cardwell paused. He just didn't know how to express sympathy very well, even if he did

39

feel it.

"Say it, Joe."

"Look, those kiddies, I hate it they were killed, see? I don't know why them 'Rappyhoes done that. They don't always kill them young 'uns. Them Indians must of been pretty riled."

"Pretty," agreed Ben with an edge of hostility.

"Hey, don't get your fire up at me, Ben. If'n my tongue she's slow, well it'll git said, just hold on."

Joe placed a few more sticks of dry pine on the fire, then sat down again. His feet were not so sore now, after cooling for an hour. Tomorrow, he'd wear moccasins. Indians made the best footgear a man could get. Indians, as much a part of the country as the plains or the mountains, knew what it took. Their moccasins matched the rugged rock mountains, or the dry, flat, hard plains. A man wore a pair of dry-tanned moccasins and his feet had no cause to heat up.

"I say I'm real sorry about the kids," he went on, "an' about your folks, too, Ben, but they did have a life. They saw a lot of sunsets like what we see now. They had love for each other, man-and-wife love . . ."

"Not Aunt Hattie," Ben interrupted. "She never even had a sweetheart."

"No, but she saw the sunsets, breathed the good air, had her dreams, I'll wager." Joe capsulized his thoughts in one brief rush. "What I'm sayin', Ben, is they had some livin', and that's something, I reckon."

Ben nodded. "There was good times along with the bad," he agreed. "Some of it was pretty fine, like when we got our cabin built. Until then we lived in

40

the Conestoga. And when Pa got his first trapped mink—he didn't know nothing about trapping, but that proved he could do it, so we'd have a cash crop. And when we grew our first potatoes . . ."

The boy's voice trailed off. The memories were good, memories he'd keep all his life, but right now there was too much pain with them, and he shushed like a stream drying up under a sun too hot.

Joe came in quickly.

"I come into this here country in '28—no, '26, I think. She was different then. Indians not so bad. There weren't so many whites, only them like me that was scattered around."

Joe waved his hand in the direction of the plains to the east, and swept it back to the mountains.

"They was all this country, enough room for ever'body. The Indians, they didn't mind. We was friendly. I smoked with Comanches, 'Rappyhoes, Kioways. Yeah, it's how come I know them back." He jerked a thumb toward their back trail. "You know."

"My family came too late," muttered Ben.

"Mebbe. I don't know. All's I know is that the south country was ruint by soldiers and them devil Apaches. Nothin' was safe. Ever'body gettin' kilt. Soldiers fighting Apaches, Apaches fighting all of us whites. Up here in the north, well them gold hunters about ruint it all. Too many whites all at oncet. Buffler gettin' killed off all over the country. Yeah." Joe's voice dropped. "She was better twenty year ago. What's this year now?"

"Well, eighteen hundred and forty-eight, Joe. Where you been?"

The question was given in a teasing way. Joe liked that. The boy would be all right if he could laugh a bit.

"I been hereabout," Joe said, "but the years, well I was never good at figgers. I lost a few."

"My Pa had a watch," said Ben suddenly.

"You should've kept it."

"Them killers took it," came the ferocious response. "But," the boy added with a ghastly grin, "I got him."

He nodded at the .44 Dragoon. It was sheathed in its holster at arm's length from where Ben sat by the fire.

"That," he said, "will speak better for me than the watch, anyway."

"Yeah," murmured Joe.

He looked at the sky. The stars were brilliant, but there was no moon. The sun and pink clouds were gone and it was already night. Usually, he slept after sundown, and was up at dawn, but he felt like talking. Ben needed to hear a voice, too, to keep his mind occupied.

"An' then them big companies come in here. Eastern outfits lookin' for furs. They set up posts and hired trappers. Ha!"

Joe got up again and filled his tin cup with more coffee. He offered Ben a pour, filled Ben's cup, then replaced the pot and sat once again.

"Did you join them companies?" Ben asked.

Joe shook his head violently. "Hell no! I ain't no company man, son. I like blazing my own trail too much for that." He spat to one side. "A lot of my friends joined up." He shook his head again, but not so violently. "Mebbe they made better'n me, I don't know. I know I ain't no company man. Nobody goin' to tell Joe Cardwell where or how to trap."

"I'm glad you didn't," said Ben.

"Oh?"

"If you had, maybe you'd have been someplace else, and wouldn't have come to . . . to our place."

"Yeah, they's a fate of some kind there for sure."

After that, the two of them drifted to silence, each occupied with his own memories. After awhile, they each rolled up in a blanket and slept. Nothing more was said, but they were comfortable about that. A friendship had been born and it was maturing quickly.

The way to Cherry Creek led to the South Platte. When they reached the river, Joe showed Ben where Tall Dog had headed northwest.

Ben's interest was intent.

"How do you know it's Tall Dog's tribe?" he asked.

"They's a few sign," said Joe, "like that chile carrier they must've forgot." He pointed at a cradleboard. "See them porkypine quill designs?"

Ben did.

"That's 'Rappyhoe. No squaws in the Plains can do such a job."

The design was circular, woven with white and dark quills. It was intricate, and Ben reckoned whoever made it had much patience. He was not interested in patience, though.

"Let's go get them," Ben growled. "Let's catch them. I owe them something."

But Joe cooled his young friend off.

"Sure," he agreed, "we could catch 'em. They goin' slow, lettin' their horses feed on this here spring grass and fatten some. But what're you gonna run into? Maybe a hundred brave? Two hundred? Nobody knows for sure how many 'Rappyhoes are with Tall Dog."

"I don't care. I just want one—him."

"You would never reach him."

"There's got to be a way," Ben argued.

"Mebbe. Tell you what. Let's go to Cherry Creek, like we planned. After that, if you want, we can take up Tall Dog's trail again. We can figger out somethin' then."

"You won't go with me now?" Ben persisted, though he was beginning to see the light in Joe's reasoning.

"Not now. Later—but," Joe's eyes narrowed. "I promise I will go. I want that rascal as much as you do."

Ben had to settle for that. He knew he could never trail Tall Dog by himself. He'd probably blunder right into an ambush. He'd wait for Joe. Joe knew his way around. It would be worthwhile to wait.

"How," he asked, "did Tall Dog get a name like that?"

Joe shrugged. "Indians, they take names of things they see or do. They have names like you and me when they are born, but they can change their names. Running Horse, he likes the way a horse runs, so he takes that name. Sharp Knife, he maybe spends time sharpening his knife, or maybe he kills an enemy in battle with a sharp blade, so he takes that name."

44

"But how come Tall Dog? Did he see a tall dog someplace?"

Again, Joe shrugged. "Mebbe. Maybe he dreamed about one and liked what he saw."

"You know what I'd like to call him," grumbled Ben.

Joe chuckled, throwing some humor in.

"I know, his mother really was a dog, is that it?"

"That, my friend, is it."

That evening, beside another low fire, the two ate for the first time. Joe shot a couple of rabbits and they had fresh meat and bannock—along with plenty of coffee. Joe carried a good supply aboard his mule.

"One of life's pleasures," he admitted. "Trappers think I'm crazy to carry so much. They figger that's weight furs should be making on my mule. Yeah, well," he grinned, "we all have our weak spots."

That night Joe spoke again of the changing country.

"I don't always trap," he admitted. "Sometimes I look for that yellow dust." He squinted into his cup. "I never make much, though. I just do some pannin' and take out enough color for five, mebbe six, ounces. It's harder work than trapping, boy."

"There's more money in gold," Ben suggested.

"Mebbe, but I know trappin' better. A shoemaker, he ain't going to do so good as a baker, if you foller me."

The fire crackled. Pine sent sparks showering the night. Joe glared at it apprehensively.

"We will run out of pine country 'fore long," he observed. "Then they won't be no signals to 'Rappyhoes to come lift our hair."

"I'd like for them to try," said Ben, his gray eyes slitted against firelight. He reached for the Dragoon and patted the holster. "Yeah. I'd like that."

"I hear them Texicans use them pistols," said Joe.

"Texicans?"

"Yeah, those molasses-mouthed, wild-eyed jacks from way down south. They been bringin' cattle up north for sale to big towns and over in California. They use them cannons, I hear."

"Good pistols," responded Ben. "My Pa, he started me on this when I was pretty small." He grinned, remembering. "About kicked my hand off."

"I guess you got good, eh?" Joe questioned carefully. He remembered the ten dead Arapahoes, all head shot, but he didn't want Ben recollecting all of a sudden. Joe stepped very lightly around the subject, but he was curious about the excellence of Ben's shooting.

"I could hit rabbits between the eyes at fifty paces," Ben admitted proudly. "I could draw and hit a grouse before he flew ten feet."

Joe did some calculating. "Hey," he warned, "don't fib to me. Ten feet? Why, son, you drawed like lightning hits."

"Pa said I was pretty quick."

"Quick ain't the word."

They slept soon after and got an early start the next morning. Ben's leg was throbbing some and Joe didn't like the festering.

"I seen worse," he told Ben, "but I think they's a doc in Cherry Creek, and he oughta have a look."

They paused often for rest breaks—for Ben, Joe

said, but to himself, he admitted his legs weren't what they used to be. Too danged much horse. Hell, there was a time when all he had was a pack mule, and no horse. Then he got rich one winter—beaver was plentiful, so he bought a horse, and spoiled himself. Even so, by damn, he'd come sixty-seventy miles on foot. Another coupla days and he'd be toughened to walking again. Another two days, and he'd hike rings around a mountain lion. If that cat was perched in a tree watching him, he'd walk in circles so fast the critter would get dizzy and topple out of the tree. Joe grinned, thinking about the lion screeching and clawing through the branches on its way to meet mother earth.

Whenever they stopped, Joe showed Ben how to use a knife and tomahawk.

"Yer good with a pistol," said Joe, "and mebbe a rifle if you got an eye fer the other. But knives is different."

He showed Ben how to grasp the handle of the knife, blade out, edge up, ready for slicing. He made him practice on dummies made of willow. He hung a bunch of willows from a tree, and Ben would charge into them, knife swinging.

"You can scalp," Joe admitted, "but that's nothin' more 'n skinnin' a dead deer. When you run that deer down and kill it with your knife, then you know about knives, son."

Joe had in his possession a Comanche tomahawk. It had a long handle, dyed red, and the blade was a steel, store-bought, flared hatchet head.

"'Hawks is a deadly weapon," instructed Joe,

"when you know how to use 'em proper."

He taught Ben to throw the 'hawk, so it would strike edge first. He showed him how to use it in hand-to-hand combat, during which the whole tomahawk, handle, cutting edge and squared end of the head became a weapon.

"'Course you gotta have practice," noted Joe, "on a live target to become really good. But this here will show you how to at least grab it."

"When will I ever see a live target, much less fight one?" Ben grunted.

"Your time will come," said Joe. "Don't rush it."

Ben, whose wounds were still looking for substantial scabbing, couldn't do as much practicing as he liked. Still, he managed an hour or two every day, and he learned fast.

"Don't worry about it," advised Joe. "Just remember what I showed you . . . and practice." He grinned. "When you're healed up and haired over again, we can rough-and-tumble and I'll show you some holds."

Ben appreciated his friend's concern. He knew what the old mountain man was doing. As good as the .44 Dragoon was, firing six shots in succession, it took time to reload. The Dragoon was a front-loading, percussion pistol. Usually, a man carried an extra cylinder already loaded and ready to slip into the frame. That gave another six shots in seconds, but Ben had only one cylinder. When he ran out of shots, he could then use the knife and tomahawk. The better he could use them, the more chance of survival he had.

Old Joe was preparing him to save his life, or at

least give a good account of himself. The reason Joe was doing it was simple: Joe knew he was going after Tall Dog. When a white, or any man, went after Tall Dog, death stood in the way, and a man had to get past death.

Any damned way he could.

CHAPTER FOUR

Cherry Creek was one big store where a man could purchase almost anything if he had the currency of the day. On Blake Street, he could trade his furs and gold for cash, and head for Curtis Street.

Curtis Street was made up of a line of outfitters. A trapper could replenish his supplies, or start from scratch. For a price, saddle horses and pack animals were his. He could load up with flour, beans, rice, dried fruit, tea and coffee, and whatever else he thought would make long months of isolation tolerable.

If he wanted fun, he sashayed down Larimer Street. This was firewater-heaven, as some of the more cynical old-timers termed it. But there was more there than just drinks. There was the real pleasure a man got in meeting old friends. The talk flowed as readily as the whiskey, and a man relaxed with friends, and got six months of smothered words out in the open. If a man felt romantic, and he usually did, the saloons offered that, too. For a price.

Larimer Street was the club house of Cherry Creek. There were good men on Larimer Street. Ninety-nine percent of those who spent a little cash in the palaces of joy, were hard-working trappers and miners. Even the wanderers, who didn't know what they wanted, were neutral fellows. They worked awhile for wages, then pushed on to see the Peaceful Water, maybe, or hire out to Hudson's Bay, up north.

But every now and then, a man came along who had to prove himself. If he wasn't the Big Man in Camp, he soon made sure he was. Such a one was Pete Targ.

Targ blew into Cherry Creek from down south. It was said he'd been run out of the Rio Grande country by irate Texans, after he'd bushwhacked a rancher. The rancher didn't die, but Pete Targ nearly did in escaping.

Targ should have been satisfied. He had his life, and no Texans were on his trail, but the bully in him surfaced like the sulphur mists up on the Yellowstone. When things got too slow to suit his nasty disposition, he had a few drinks. After he was full of 100-proof courage, he bragged that he could outdraw any man alive. He had a booming voice to match a large body, and he made sure his voice carried from one end of Cherry Creek to the other. When his stentorian rasp broke over the happy town, people shuddered. Even hardened frontier men grew silent. They'd fought many times to survive, but seldom picked a fight.

For that was Pete Targ's method. He bullied a man, usually a drifter who didn't know he was being harassed by a man who liked to kill. Targ had a way, and the situation always ended with the drifter being carted off to potter's field.

Two days before Ben and Joe arrived, Pete Targ had had his fun. A young itinerant, name never known, paused for a drink at Landing's Castle, a popular saloon. Targ stood at the end of the bar, half-drunk, mean-eyed, and growly.

"Hey, you," he bellowed at the drifter, "who said you could drink here?"

"It's a public place," was the mild reply.

"Only if I say so!" thundered Pete Targ.

The young man questioned the barkeep. "Is that so?"

The barkeep, a white-shirted man, with a droopy moustache and balding head, didn't answer. He didn't want to answer. He wanted to tell his innocent customer to get out, but he dared not. If he did, he knew that, later, he would be singled out by the town's bully. And he had no skills with weapons, aside from the sawed-off shotgun he kept under the counter. He'd never reach it in time. Pete Targ was fast. He could draw and shoot like a diving falcon.

The drifter, seeing he was not going to get an answer from the barkeep, ignored the whole matter. He downed his drink and was leaving, when Targ challenged him.

"Looky that yellow belly. Runnin' out of here like a scared skunk."

Fighting words.

The young man turned. He was wearing a Colt Walker, in a worn holster. He turned, more curious than anything, but he made the mistake of touching the butt of the Walker with his hand.

Targ pulled his own pistol out, and shot the man dead. He grinned as he claimed self-defense, and his glaring eyes dared any man to contradict him. None did, and the matter was closed.

The first thing Ben did after reaching Cherry Creek was to see a doctor. What a doctor was doing in a town like Cherry Creek did seem odd, until Ben met the medic face to face. The good doctor was crocked. It was only ten in the morning, but he could barely stagger about to accomplish his duties.

He looked blearily at Ben's wounds, and suggested they were inflicted by a sharp instrument and a bullet. Ben affirmed this diagnosis.

"Indians or Pete Targ?" came the question.

"Indians. Who is Pete Targ?"

The doctor waved a hand freely in the direction of Landing's Castle, and muttered, "Local bad man."

He said no more, nor did Ben ask. He couldn't have cared less about a bully named Pete Targ. After the doctor had bathed his wounds in a solution of boric acid, salved and bandaged them, Ben left. The fee was two dollars, which he didn't have. Ben had seldom had two coins to rub together in his life, but he promised to return and pay.

The doctor waved this off with, "Sure, thass what they all say. Sure."

Ben found Joe Cardwell on Blake Street. Joe was dickering with a man about his beaver and mink. He also had two wolf, three coyote and seven fox pelts. The entire street was alive with repetitions of the same scene that Joe and his fur dealer made. For a second, Ben felt a weirdness, like he was seeing Joe reflected in a dozen mirrors. Joe's voice, however, was not a mirror. Joe's voice was not only real, it was indignant.

"You must be crazy," Joe told the dealer. "Them beaver was worth twicet that last fall."

"Prices change," returned the dealer firmly. "You gotta adjust to that, Joe."

"By damn, I don't believe it," snorted Joe. He took off up the dusty street, cautioning Ben. "You stay with them pelts, so's this scamp won't lift any on me."

The dealer flushed at the insult, but kept his mouth shut.

Ben watched as Joe wound in and out of the mass of traders and trappers, like a needle sewing thread. He was slightly embarrassed by Joe. After all, he had insulted the buyer, and left him to endure the man's discomfort.

In fifteen minutes, Joe was back. He was smiling, and he extended his leather-hard hand to the dealer.

"They's yours, Mike," he cried, as the other grasped his hand in a grip of agreement.

"I told yuh what prices was," said Mike grinning.

And then Ben realized it was a game. Joe knew Mike wasn't lying about fur prices, but he wasn't about to give in readily. He had to make Mike sweat, and Mike knew it. It was a game they played out all the way.

Cash changed hands and Joe said, "Let's go to the Castle. I got me a dry throat."

All three strode to the saloon and on the way, Joe asked about Ben's wounds.

"They're all right," said the boy, "but I have to have two dollars. Can I borrow from you?"

"Sure."

Joe dug into his trousers and extracted two silver dollars.

"You gonna join us at the Castle?" he asked the boy.

Ben nodded.

"Ain't he a little young?" questioned Mike, the fur trader.

Joe looked at Mike and said, "No. Not that chile. He ain't too young for anything."

The three separated and Ben returned to the doctor's to pay his bill and pick up more bandages.

The doctor, a bit more saturated than earlier, but still coherent, examined the two coins as if they were fakes.

"Be damned," he muttered, "you came back."

"I said I would," replied Ben, "and if you'll hand me more bandages and salve, I'll be going."

The doctor obliged and tossed in an extra tin of salve.

"Who knows," he muttered, "if you got one gun shot, you might get another gun shot in you some day."

Ben left the doctor. He found Joe and Mike hoisting their second whiskey when he entered the bar.

"What you want, son?" asked Joe. "Whiskey? Beer, mebbe?"

Ben had never tasted either in his life. His family were nondrinking people, though his father did keep a bottle of wine for special occasions. Even on those occasions, it was a short glass, and the cork popped back in quick.

Ben was curious.

"Whiskey," he said to the barkeep.

The barkeep poured with a flourish and left the quart bottle on the counter.

Ben tested it, by sipping. The stuff burned his lips, and the few drops he took in trailed down his throat searing it like liquid fire.

"Uk!" he exclaimed, and set his glass back on the counter.

Joe laughed till tears came to his eyes.

"By Gar', son, you ain't sure of this pizen, are you?"

"It's different than I figured," replied Ben. "Danged stuff burns."

"That's how come they call it firewater, kid," boomed a voice at the other end of the bar.

It was Pete Targ's voice.

Ben nodded. "I'll try a beer, if you don't mind," he said to Joe.

The bartender poured him a glass, and Ben tasted it. He grinned.

"Can't say as I like it, but at least it'll quench my thirst."

"At least it'll quench my thirst," mimicked Pete Targ. "Good God, whoever talked like that, anyways?"

Ben looked at the man fully, for the first time. He saw a burly fellow, with mean, blank eyes. The man's face was dark and flushed, and his mouth was spread in a humorless smile.

"I talk that way," replied Ben. He turned to Joe. "If

you lend me another few dollars, I'll be getting some new clothes."

Ben's clothes were still bloodied from scalping the Arapahoes. The blood wouldn't wash out, and as long as he saw the stains, he would be reminded how they got there. He didn't mind remembering what he'd done to the murdering Indians, but in remembering them, it brought back pictures of his mutilated family. He wanted freedom from that, some freedom, anyway. He would never forget, but a change of clothes would help.

Joe, without question, gave Ben some more dollars, enough for a complete new outfit.

"What's the matter, little boy?" jeered Pete Targ. "Does dirt bother you?"

Ben ignored the sarcasm and started for the door.

"What's a gray-haired old coot doin' givin' you money, boy? Can't he get a squaw? Does he have to have young boys around for his pleasure?" Pete Targ laughed loudly at his own insinuation, and glared at Joe, daring him.

Ben stopped where he was and turned toward the loud man.

Joe flushed, but didn't move. He wasn't wearing his sidearm or a knife, and he had sense enough to know that the man would use any excuse to kill him. He'd seen his kind before. The bully boys of the camps.

"Hey, Pete," cautioned the bartender, showing more bravery than he felt. "Lay off. He's just a pup."

"My name's Pete Targ," said Targ, "and I don't like what I see here."

Ben wasn't sure what it was that Targ did see. He did know that he didn't like the inflections in the man's voice. There were evil tones in it, hints of anger. Ben did realize one thing, and it came to him as a shock. The man, Pete Targ, wanted to fight him. He was deliberately provoking trouble.

"I'm sorry," said Ben, "but I don't know what you see. As far as I know, you got a lot that's empty up here." He tapped his head.

"No mealymouth brat is going to call me crazy," roared Pete Targ. He came around the end of the bar and stood in the center of the floor.

Ben didn't move.

"I see you wear a pistol, kid. Draw it," Targ challenged.

A deadly silence fell over the room. Customers scattered, seeking safety. They'd seen Targ in action before, and they knew lead would fly soon.

Ben might have been naive in some things, but he knew what Targ was up to. The man was pretending to be drunk, and maybe irrational, but Ben saw into the blank eyes, and he knew Targ was entirely sober.

"I don't want to fight you," he said. "I got no reason."

He turned on his heels, just as a shot rang out. Ben whirled around and saw the Walker in Targ's hand. Targ was aiming not at Ben, but at Joe.

Joe froze to his glass. The bullet had missed him by inches—inches that Ben knew were deliberate.

"You'll fight me, boy," raged Pete Targ, "or I'll shoot this old man for molesting you. That's agin the law around here."

"Leave him alone," Ben said, cool and not in the least afraid. "He isn't molesting me in any way. He's my friend."

"Oh, sure he is," said Targ with a nasty laugh.

"Come on, Joe," said Ben. "Let's get out of here."

He turned to leave again, when a second shot roared. The floor within inches of Ben's right foot splintered.

"Your Ma was a whore, and your Pa a pimp," howled Pete Targ. "And you are a bastard, kid."

For the first time, Ben's calmness left him. Pete Targ could have said anything he wanted, with little reaction, but when he brought Ben's mother and father into the conversation, Ben couldn't turn away. Visions of his parents' bloody and torn bodies flashed in his mind.

Once again, he turned full on Pete Targ.

"Do you want to fight?" Ben asked, his voice controlled.

"Hell, no, I don't want to fight," sneered Targ. "But this country has got to get rid of nobodies like you and this old man here." He jerked a thumb at Joe. "You bastards don't belong nowhere except under the ground."

Ben nodded. He was furious. Targ had succeeded in arousing his anger.

"Step outside," said Ben, his quiet voice barely masking the fury and revulsion that he felt. "If you want to kill me, step outside."

Targ roared with joy.

"You hear that?" Targ demanded of the onlookers. "That skinny gink is offering to fight me. I sure can't turn him down, now can I? We don't want his kind in Cherry Creek, right? It'll be self-defense, because he challenged me."

If that wasn't exactly right, nobody said a word. To have objected might have invited a bullet into one's heart, and life was sweet in Cherry Creek—even with Targ around.

Ben stepped into the street, followed quickly by Joe. Mike had long since disappeared.

"Don't, Ben," begged Joe. "The man's a practiced killer. He'll get you, boy."

"I don't see any way out of it," replied Ben, "after what he called my parents."

"The man's drunk," argued Joe. "He don't know what he's sayin'."

"Oh, I think he does," said Ben. "And so do you."

Targ banged through the door of Landing's Castle. He was grinning fiercely, his hand inches from his Colt.

Ben walked out into the street, then turned. He saw that Joe was safely to one side, and that no others were in the line of fire. Joe's expression of horror didn't move him. He knew what he had to do.

Targ stepped into the street, too, so there was less than twenty-five paces between the two men.

Then Targ's right hand dove for his Walker.

As Joe saw it, Ben didn't seem to move at all. The boy's own actions were a blur. He had his heavy Dragoon out of its battered holster, cocked and fired, before Targ even had his gun half out of the leather.

Pete Targ, bullyboy of Cherry Creek, stared at Ben

with a surprised expression. He stood perfectly still, a statue of flesh, with a widening stain of crimson on his chest. Then he dropped to the ground. His body made a loud thump as it landed, but Pete Targ never moved again.

Ben holstered his pistol, and walked over to Joe.

"I didn't want to do that," he said, but his voice was calm.

"You had to," said Joe. He had never seen anybody as calm as Ben Brand. He had never seen eyes so cold as those gray eyes of his young friend. They were the eyes of a killer, and he understood, now, how it was a fifteen-year-old youth could have slain ten experienced 'Råppyhoe warriors. The boy had not flinched. He had aimed his weapon, cocked the hammer and pulled the trigger with deliberation. And he had not missed. He had taken head shots with the Indians, a breast shot with Targ, but Joe was sure that Ben had placed his single bullet just where he'd wanted it.

For a moment, Joe felt a chill. What kind of a boy, man, had he teamed up with?

But the chill faded, to be replaced by pride in the boy. He knew he had taken up with a rare boy, a rare one, indeed.

The news of Targ's death spread through town quickly and it was then that the legend of Ben Brand began. A thin kid, with broad shoulders and a changing voice, had gunned down the most feared man in the area. The boy's hand was so fast that nobody had seen him draw. Nobody. One minute his hand was empty, the next it was full of .44 Colt Dragoon. Nobody had ever seen anything like it. Not ever. Ben Brand would not be forgotten, especially by those who had witnessed the fight at the Castle.

As for Ben, he turned to Joe and asked, "Are we through here?"

Joe nodded.

"Then let's leave. We have work to do."

CHAPTER FIVE

Though Ben was anxious to pick up Tall Dog's trail, Joe advised caution.

"Even a small breeze raises dust that can be seen a long ways," he explained. "I figger we set out for Wyoming Territory."

"Why there?" demanded Ben, his anger like a crimson flower on his face. "I want Tall Dog. I'm going to kill him."

"If'n we kin get him, we will," promised Joe grimly, "but let me tell you something. Ain't no 'Rappyhoe gonna let us within ten mile of Tall Dog. He got his scouts up front and all around. You take it from me, Ben."

Ben knew enough to keep quiet. Joe Cardwell had been more than generous with both his time and money. He was older and much wiser, and he knew what he was talking about. Joe had also become a second father to him, a father whom he respected deeply. If Joe said it was dangerous to invade Tall Dog's country, then it was. But Ben wanted that

Indian chief, and he wanted him dead. He behaved like a sullen teenager for the rest of the day, and not at all like the man/boy who had stood up and killed the bully of Cherry Creek.

Joe noted all of this, and was baffled by it. He'd had no experience with boys in their mid-teens. He'd had little family experience at all. He'd spent one winter with the 'Rappyhoes, when things were good back in '30, and he saw some family life then. But he never learned much, and Ben puzzled him. One minute he was a man, the next, a boy, pouting like a child.

By evening, when they built their camp fire next to a stream, Ben was the man again.

"What you say goes," he told Joe.

"I'm glad you see it that way," returned the mountain man, baffled once more by the change in the boy.

It was during moments like these that Joe saw clearly the change that was taking place in Ben Brand. He was a boy, yes, but his voice was steady most of the time now. It didn't crack on the higher notes so much. His gray eyes were calm, cool, and all-seeing. Those eyes were the first to spot the rabbit for supper. They saw the dark-backed trout in murky water. They noted the hawks wheeling high, and the prairie dog scamper for its hole.

Ben Brand was growing up fast, maybe too fast, thought Joe. But, then, the boy had done things that would have matured a grizzly bear cub. Ben's shoulders seemed to broaden every day. Joe could almost see their growth, like bunch grass on a hot spring day. The boy's chest was developing, thickening, and his arms were rounding out, powerful muscles finding adult strength. Ben Brand was going to be a man among men all right, because under it all was the steely determination to achieve a goal. Joe had no doubt that Ben would never let go of his avowed quest—to find and kill Tall Dog.

Joe Cardwell shook his head in silent amazement. Was the boy really growing so fast? They'd known each other for—what? Only a couple of weeks. But Ben Brand, fifteen when they met, seemed like a man of twenty-five now. Was it something to do with the spirit? Was it the inner Ben Brand that made him *seem* to grow? Did it matter? What mattered was the end result, and, to Joe, the boy was changing swiftly. The long legs were no longer tied together with sinew, but were of a piece, and they cinched the ribs of the pinto Sam, easily. Ben had no saddle, preferring bare back to hard leather.

The pair traced a dim trail northward. They followed creeks looking for trapping grounds, but the beaver were gone, and there were no mink.

"Trappin', she's movin' west," observed Joe softly. "We got to head west after we hit Laramie."

"Laramie!" exclaimed Ben. "Why are we going that far north?"

"Them soldier boys can tell us about Indians, boy. You want to know where Tall Dog is? Ask them bluecoats."

In the meantime, Ben practiced with his knife—a long-bladed sheath knife that Joe bought him in Cherry Creek, and Joe's tomahawk. He got so he could split a stump at forty paces with the tomahawk.

"That'll do you good," said Joe proudly. "You can

outdo a Comanche I'll bet my last chaw."

One day, while resting in the shade of some cottonwoods at high noon, they heard approaching wagons. The sound drifted along the river, chinking and clanking, horses snorting.

"Them ain't traders," said Joe. "Wagons too light. Traders they load 'em down, so they's no noise 'cept grinding axles."

Curious, the two stood in the shade, waiting for whatever it was to come around a sharp bend into sight.

What rambled into sight surprised them both, three wagons in a string. Several men walked alongside the wagons, and one was on horseback in the lead. Ben noticed a number of women, too. One of these, a girl about his own age, was driving one of the teams.

A gaunt, thin-faced man, wearing a suit and a tall beaver hat, held the reins on the team pulling the lead wagon.

When he saw Ben and Joe, he raised a bony hand, and called a gentle whoa to his team of two giant-footed dray horses.

"My name is Ephram Locks," he said pleasantly. "It looks cool here. May we alight awhile in your company?"

"'Course!" cried Joe in a hearty voice, a voice accustomed to raising echoes in the high mountains. "We's glad to see yuh."

The man on horseback took charge. With other men, he unhitched the horses and led them to the river. The animals were thirsty, but were allowed only a small ration of water. Too much, with still half a day's work ahead, could bring on the colic.

While he and the others were busy with the horses, the women climbed down from the wagons. There were, Ben noted, about an equal number of men and women.

"What's your business in these parts?" Joe queried.

One didn't usually ask such personal questions. A man, or a woman for that matter, might have reason to keep shush about their past or their future. But these people were different. Even Ben, as young as he might have been, noticed there was an openness about them that invited conversation and, even, questions. No offense would be taken.

"My wife," said Ephram Locks, nodding at a trail-worn woman who was overseeing the unloading of tea things, "and I are missionaries. The others are missionaries, too, but volunteers. They will serve for a year, then return to Boston. My wife, Abigail, and I intend to remain. This will be our life."

"Where are you going?" questioned Ben.

"A place called Cherry Creek."

Ben found he was glad that Pete Targ was out of the way. Missionaries were just the sort that Targ would delight in taunting. These people, with their soft hands and soft manners, would be no match for the Targs of this woolly country. Especially, the girl. Ben eyed her with stealthy glances. She was blue-eyed, and had long blond hair that hung over her shoulders. Her developing figure pressed tightly against a bodice grown too small. The party had been on the trail for months, and there had been little time for dress alterations.

She caught one of his glances, and smiled.

"My name's Martha," she said. "Would you like some of our tea?"

"Oh, well yes, sure," muttered Ben, blushing.

"Then help us get some wood for the fire," directed Martha.

Ben scuttled about and returned with an armload of driftwood from the banks of the river.

"This will burn hot," he said.

The girl looked at him with her blue eyes, and Ben found he was blushing again—hotter than the hottest driftwood fire.

"I know that," replied Martha. "We aren't exactly newcomers, you know."

"How long you been trailing?" Ben asked awkwardly. What did one say to such a beauty?

"Four long months, all the way from St. Louis."

"That's a long time," agreed Ben, and ran out of conversation.

Martha's family joined them, and she introduced them. Ben's sharp, knowing eyes sized them up at once. City dwellers, business people, probably, soft and accustomed to comforts, yet there was something gallant about them. They'd given up the known for the hazardous unknown, having no idea what they were getting into. They were carrying the word of God to the heathen, a goal of such noble aspiration that it seemingly gave them strong wills and uncommon courage.

Ben's thoughts drifted back several years. His own Ma and Pa had had the same spirit. They weren't missionaries, but they wanted a new life, and had endured much to get it—loneliness, near poverty, backbreaking labor. And just when their goals seemed in hand, along came a band of killers . . .

"Why are you scowling?" the girl asked. "Don't you like tea?"

Ben shook off his terrible thoughts and managed a smile.

"I like tea," he murmured.

Missionaries! For a moment Ben thought about asking Mr. Locks if he would accompany him to his family's grave. A real man of God saying a few words over that flat square of ground, would be something his mother would have liked. The burned cabin was not so far from where they were—maybe seventy-five miles across the South Platte.

But Ben tucked the thought into memory for future use. A one-hundred-and-fifty-mile round trip would take up much time. The trail of Tall Dog was already cold, and the delay would make it even fainter. He would, one day, get a preacher to his family's resting place, but not now. It wasn't the proper time.

The wagon people gathered around the fire, and tea was poured. The man who had been on horseback joined them. He introduced himself as Jed Black, the trail boss for the little caravan.

"Think I knowed you back in '29," Joe said thoughtfully.

The other nodded. "Mebbe. I used to set traps below Cherry Creek."

Joe nodded. "Yep, me too. Probably we met in town."

As big as the country was, Ben noted, it was a small world. You knew a man once, you never forgot him, and your trails crossed every now and then.

His thoughts were interrupted by Mr. Locks giving a blessing, before the tea.

"Lord Almighty," he said in a strong preacher's voice, "we thank you for delivering us this far, and for meeting such kindly folks on this isolated trail. Give them, and us, safe journey. Amen."

The little knot of humanity echoed the missionary's "Amen" and sipped their tea.

"Do you intend to open a church in Cherry Creek?" Ben asked, by way of conversation.

Mr. Locks smiled and replied, "Perhaps, but we really want to go where we can be closer to the heathen."

"Heathen?"

"The Indians, boy."

Ben felt a chill.

"What do you mean, sir?"

"I feel that our real work is among the Indians, so we might continue down into—what was it, Jed?"

Jed squinted at the other, and said reluctantly, "Ute country."

Ben glanced at Joe. Ute country! One of the most dangerous regions in the West. Utes were no friends of the white man—man of God or not.

"Might be better you stay in Cherry Creek a while," offered Joe. "Them Utes," he glanced at the girl, Martha, "well, they ain't friendly."

"The Lord will protect us," said Mr. Locks, happily. "He always has."

"Nothin' better 'n a Colt," muttered Jed Black.

"What's that?" asked Mr. Locks.

"Oh, nothin'," mumbled Black, then he thought

better of it. "They's a law out here," he said, "that's called pistols and rifles. That there is a law what everybody understands."

"We have weapons, Jed."

"Yeah, but will you use 'em?"

"Of course!"

Mr. Locks turned away to mingle with the others.

"Trouble is," whispered Jed, "he won't. He don't believe in killin' his fellow man."

Joe took over Jed's comments, and Ben drifted toward Martha. As he did so, he paid attention to the others. They were young, excited, and though worn from hundreds of miles of wagon road, still enthusiastic about their mission. They were innocents in the land, an unforgiving land, a land that didn't give a hoot about innocence or good intentions. Look at what had happened to his own family. They had been innocent, too. They harbored no ill will against any man, white or red, and yet . . .

He reached Martha. "I'd like more tea, please," he said, holding out his cup.

She poured, and Ben sipped, studying the girl. She noticed and flushed.

"You shouldn't look at me like that," she admonished.

Ben was surprised. "Why? How am I looking?"

"Well . . . well, like you were . . . interested or something."

"You are pretty, Martha."

"Hush. People will hear. I declare, we hardly know each other."

"Out here, people know each other fast. There's no time to be cute about it."

"I'm not being cute!"

"I know," said Ben gently, his own embarrassment at coming face-to-face with somebody so pretty had vanished. "But we don't have time."

The two were silent for a few moments, pretending to look out over the river. Ben sensed that she was now stealing glances at him, just the reverse of a few minutes before.

"I never met anybody like you," she said suddenly.

"What do you think?"

"Well," her voice dropped, "well, I wish you were with our people, Ben." She glanced at them, as they chatted over their teacups. "They are nice—even noble, I think, but they don't have your experience. I'm afraid, Ben. I've been afraid for a long time."

Ben touched her arm. "Oh, it will be all right," he assured her. "You hear a lot of talk and all, but you'll be all right."

"Do you really think so?"

The blue eyes fastened on him earnestly.

"Yeah, sure I'm sure."

"I still wish you were along. I'd feel safer."

"You got Jed Black. He knows what he's doing. Listen to him."

"I know." Martha covered his hand briefly with her own. "Just the same, I wish you were Jed."

Mr. Locks broke into their conversation with, "Let's go, everybody. It's a long way until night fall—and," he beamed happily, "we'll be that much closer to our destination."

In a matter of minutes, the horses were hitched, and everybody was aboard their wagons. Jed straddled his horse, looked back to make sure there were no stragglers and swung his arm ahead, crying, "Hoooo!" and the procession moved ahead.

Ben watched Martha as long as he could, and he had a bad feeling, as she disappeared. A wild picture flashed through his mind—there was Martha, naked and bloody, and her legs spread-eagled. Vital parts had been slashed out, and black flies circled and buzzed before landing.

He shivered and muttered, "Damn."

Joe glanced at him quizzically. "You kind of liked her, didn't yuh?"

"Who?" Ben was startled by his friend's insight.

"You know danged well who, son."

Ben hesitated only a moment. "Sure, I liked her. She was pretty and nice, and they're going into Ute country, Joe."

Joe nodded.

"So," added Ben, "you can see exactly what's going on in my mind."

"Yup, I can see."

The two were quiet. The great South Platte swished past, and somewhere a thrush piped a plaintive trill. The sun had swung around the trees, and was shining full on them. It was as hot as a blacksmith's forge.

"Let's get out of here," said Ben.

And Joe began to wonder who was the leader in this party of two.

CHAPTER SIX

The two traveled hard for the rest of the day. It seemed necessary to put as much distance as possible behind them, to get some significant mileage into the backtrail. Mileage was a wall that sheltered them from bad thoughts. Mileage was a comforter, a buffer, and the two friends felt better when they camped by another stream.

"They's gonna be a lot of 'em," said Joe over his second cup of coffee.

"Of who?"

"Those kind of people. They comin' into the country now. Lots of 'em. Missionaries, God help them."

"To teach Indians to pray. Maybe they will."

"Like Jed mentioned, I'd rather they had more guns."

But distance wasn't altogether an efficient wall. Ben thought of Martha for a long time, but the wall did help in one way. It created a comfortable illusion. Nothing was going to happen to Mr. Locks and his party. They knew what they were up to, and they did have Jed Black. He was a good man. He'd keep those innocents out of harm's way.

After reasoning his way out of a miserable frame of mind, Ben slept well that night. The next morning, Joe woke him early with a real problem. The mountain man pointed across the rolling plain country to a black knot. The knot was moving, slowly it seemed at that distance, toward them.

"They's Utes," whispered Joe, "an' we better clear out of here."

They were gone in five minutes. They walked the horses rapidly, but didn't run them. It was best to save their energy in case they really had to make a race of it. Joe stopped every so often for a long look back. Ben stared, too, though he wasn't sure of what to look for.

"Anythin' you see movin'," said Joe, "let me know."

They made thirty hard miles that day, but the Utes never appeared again. That night they set up a cold camp.

"We take no chances on fires," said Joe grimly.

They slept on guard, with Joe standing the first watch. Ben's turn came as the moon dipped low in the west. He was nervous, and clutched Joe's .50 caliber Sharps with sweaty hands. What he could see didn't bother him. What he could not see, did.

At dawn, they broke camp, and headed north again. It wouldn't be too long—two, three days, Joe reckoned—before they would leave the Platte, and head into Wyoming Territory. Ben was glad. Somehow, it seemed safer away from the river where all peoples, friends and enemies, met. The river was the great highway of the country, whether a man used a raft, a horse, wagon or feet.

On the third day after leaving the missionary party, they came upon a band of Arapahoes suddenly. Ben and Joe topped a rise, and there they were, teepeed by a creek.

Ben wasn't sure what the Indians were—Arapahoes, Utes, Cheyennes, Comanches, Kiowas, all seemed much alike to him. The Arapahoes he'd killed at the homestead could have been any tribe, until Joe told him which one. Few Indians had passed the Brand place in the two years they'd lived on it. There had been little contact otherwise. Once, traveling to Cherry Creek, the nearest settlement, they'd met a tribe of what people told them were Utes, but all Ben remembered were stolid moon faces, eagle feathers in the hair of the men, blankets draped over bony frames. It was going to take awhile for him to learn the different markings.

But as soon as Joe said 'Rappyhoe, the .44 Dragoon was out of its holster. In a wink of time, Ben turned from boy/man to man—a man with a deep hate. He whipped the .44 out, and cocked the hammer. Joe's gnarled hand grabbed the barrel.

"No, son," he said, "you don't want to do that."

"Let go," snapped Ben.

But Joe's grip tightened.

"Listen," he said, "they's only women and children here. No braves. Something wrong. Take yerself a look."

Ben's gray eyes smouldered, but he saw through the smoke very clearly. Joe was right, there were only women and children. They were ragged and looked half-starved. Their clothes, part white man's, part Indian, hung in shreds, and their horses showed ribs beneath matted hides. There were no firearms in sight.

"What's going on?" Ben wanted to know, but he kept his pistol in sight.

"I'll find out."

Joe advanced, remaining in the saddle of his gelding. He raised his right hand, palm out, pointed at an elderly squaw. She returned his sign with calm eyes, placed her right hand on her left breast, and drew it to the right.

Using a combination of hand-talk and halting spoken Arapahoe, Joe learned the story. In a few minutes he returned to Ben, who remained motionless on Sam. The Dragoon was still clutched in his hand. It was clutched so tightly that his knuckles were white with tension.

"They's all's left of a band of about fifty, way I got it figgered. Soldiers from Laramie surprised 'em, and they fought. 'Rappyhoes is on the Army's git list. Well, they was a big fight, and only the women and kids got away."

"You mean there's no braves here?"

"Nope. You gonna use that?" Joe nodded at the Dragoon.

Ben didn't answer. He sat very still on Sam, and gleaned the small, ragged survivors with hard eyes.

"Put it away, son. Even 'Rappyhoes got grief."

Ben obeyed, but his heart remained stony. Their grief was theirs, not his. Not his, dammit.

He noted some of the younger women looking at

him slyly. Their dark eyes flashed and they bowed their heads and turned aside so that Ben felt uncomfortable. The women seemed in awe of him, afraid, but attracted at the same time. They whispered among themselves.

"What are they saying?" growled Ben.

"They wonder if you are the white eyes who lived in the foothills. The braves who escaped your Dragoon described you. You are Big Medicine."

"Tell them I am," Ben requested. "I am he."

Joe made sign from where he was, and the women drew together. One of them made sign, and Joe, half-grinning, translated for Ben.

"You could have any one of 'em for a bride if'n you wanted, son."

Ben flushed and turned away. He was trembling. He wanted to kill them all. The memory of his family, scalped and dead, burned like prairie fire in his mind.

Joe spoke to the calm, older woman, in sign. She replied rapidly, her face still impassive.

"What was all that about?" Ben demanded.

"They think you are very brave, but Tall Dog wants your hair. His warriors think they will be strong if they count *coup* on you—touch you in battle, wound you, or even kill you."

Joe paused, looking intently at Ben.

"The word is out on your deeds now, son. They know you're after them, especially Tall Dog. The 'Rappyhoes need good medicine right now. Counting *coup* on Iron Heart will make them strong against their enemies."

"Iron Heart?"

"That's the name they done tagged you with." Joe grinned but his own eyes were dead serious. "The braves think you maybe can't be killed. If Tall Dog does, and hangs your scalp in his lodge, he'll be a big man with all the Plains tribes. You got a reputation all acrost the Plains, Ben."

"I'm not proud of that, Joe, considering how it came about."

"No, I guess you wouldn't be. But you got 'er, son. Want 'er or not."

"Let's go."

"Right."

They rode past the camp, and then Ben asked, "Will they starve?"

"No. They will rejoin their tribe in a day or two."

"Too bad," said Ben. "Too damned bad."

Joe, who had smoked the pipe with 'Rappyhoes, had sat in their teepees, and chawed their pemmican, didn't feel quite as bitter as his young friend. He understood Ben's hate, but in his heart he had a wish, and it was that Ben's hatred would not eat him alive. Hate could do that. It could devour a man from the inside, and then puke him up so there was nothing left but pulp. Joe didn't want that happening to Ben. Not to the young man who was becoming a giant, whether he liked it or not, on the Plains.

The two rode until it was nearly dark. Ben didn't trust himself, and wanted as much space between himself and the Arapahoes as possible. His hatred was volcanic and unpredictable, and he didn't trust himself. Would he have sneaked out of camp while Joe slept, and shot the women and children? Ben wasn't sure, so he claimed a lot of miles before nightfall.

Both Joe and he were quiet that evening. They ate their beans and bannock, without Joe's usual chatter about "the good ole days, when they wasn't a hunnert whites in the whole damned country."

"I don't feel right," Joe admitted finally.

"What's wrong?" Ben asked, suddenly tense.

"I just got a feelin' is all."

"Arapahoes?"

"I think we better put that fire out."

Together, they stamped every glowing ember into the ground. Then they quietly moved along the river for half a mile.

"They seen our fire," whispered Joe.

"And can still smell our smoke," agreed Ben.

Joe appraised Ben in the dark. "You're learnin'," he grunted.

"So what do we do now?"

"Wait. Maybe it's all right. You sleep first, then me."

As Ben lay on his blanket, he knew it wasn't all right. He was tight with bad nerves, and there'd been no reason for it. None that he could see, and he was learning something: His body would tell him if something was wrong, even if his eyes didn't see anything amiss. There were other senses, and he had to learn them.

Once again, his hands broke into a sweat. What he could see brought no fear. As he had already learned, it was what he couldn't see that made his hands slippery.

"Scared?" whispered Joe.

"No."

"Don't lie, boy."

"I'm scared as hell."

"Yeah, me too. You almost wish they'd hit, and git it over with."

"Joe?"

"Say it."

"Am I a coward or something for feeling like I do?"

"Nope. It's a fool who ain't scairt when he should be."

Nearby, something snapped. A twig. There was a rustle in the darkness that reminded Ben of bat wings, only this didn't belong to bats.

He sat upright, Dragoon in hand. Joe joined him swiftly, facing in the opposite direction.

Suddenly, a terrible cry split the night air, and a half-naked man fell on Ben with raised tomahawk.

CHAPTER SEVEN

Ben cocked the Dragoon, squeezed the trigger. The motion was smooth, all of a piece, the way he had learned to do it. Jerking the trigger on any weapon was a fault his father frowned on.

"You do that," the elder Brand had admonished, "and you twitch your barrel off target. Always squeeze the trigger, Ben. Press it smoothly in one motion. That way the barrel stays on mark."

The hurtling figure that fell on him now, slashed with a tomahawk. Ben felt his left arm recoil from the blow, but the slug from his thundering Dragoon caught the enemy in the chest. The man slid off sideways, his chest gushing blood.

Even as he fought down the nausea, Ben wondered why he thought of his own actions instead of his attackers. Maybe, he reasoned, that was his protection, what made him so calm in the midst of danger. He was strangely calm now.

Another figure lunged at him in the semidarkness, and Ben plainly saw his face. Arapahoe war paint of bright colors streaked the cheeks. The man was shrieking, and more Arapahoes joined in with a hideous chorus of war cries. Shots threw orange lightning into the night, and Ben heard faint whistles of lead streak past his ears. He cocked his pistol and fired again, and the second man dropped.

Joe, facing the other way, covering Ben's back, let go with his heavy Sharps. The rifle blew away all other sound, like a blast from Gabriel's horn on Judgment Day. Another Arapahoe fell and churned on the dark earth, his death throes triggered by a shredded stomach. Joe didn't carry a pistol, and there was no time for reloading the Sharps. He faced the dimly seen enemy with knife in one hand, tomahawk in the other.

"Come 'n git it, you scamps!" he roared.

Ben had four shots left. He backed up to Joe, and fired steadily, coolly, at the oncoming figures. One crashed into him, throwing both him and Joe to the ground. Joe turned swiftly, his lean waist as supple as that of a snake, and struck his tomahawk into the skull. The sound was crunchy, and squishy at the same time, like a man stepping on stubble grass in wet mud.

Both Ben and Joe jumped to their feet immediately, and Ben continued firing until his Dragoon's hammer fell on an empty chamber. He shoved the pistol in its holster, and waited, his knife and tomahawk ready. His heart was triple-beating. He was short of breath, like a horse who'd just run ten miles, but he grinned with elation. He felt as if he were fulfilling his destiny. Ever since the massacre of his family, his thoughts had been trained on this moment, the moment he killed more Arapahoes.

He smiled into the night, waiting for another charge. It didn't come. He took advantage of the lull, and reloaded the pistol. He poured the powder fast, expertly, rammed the lead balls home. He capped each cylinder, set the hammer at half cock. He regretted not having an extra cylinder that he could slip into the frame already loaded and primed. It was something he'd have to get as soon as he could. A man was foolish to settle for only six shots when he could have twelve. And if he had two extra cylinders, he'd be an army by himself.

He shoved his tomahawk back into his belt, but clutched his knife. His left shoulder was regaining some feeling now—almost too much of it, but he could hold the knife better.

He and Joe crouched to make smaller targets. They waited tensely, sweating, with Joe cursing under his breath, but there was no charging from the Arapahoes. It was impossible to see any distance in the darkness. Yet they both knew that Arapahoes lurked nearby, like scorpions in an empty boot. They could smell them, sense them. Or could they? Ben heard only the sound of his own breathing, but it was magnified, deafening to his ears. After a time, Joe spoke. Ben's heart leaped a foot.

"I think they're gone," ventured Joe, risking a whisper.

"Can't be sure," Ben muttered. He didn't want them to leave. If there were more, he wanted them to come at him again, because he had six pieces of lead for their hearts—or heads, or bellies. It didn't matter to Ben, so long as he killed them.

"Did they run?"

"Indians, they believe in that. They can always fight another day."

"Damn them," growled Ben. "Damn their red asses."

The two fell into silence, listening, straining their ears for alien sounds. They heard the river and they heard an owl send a haunting message across the cottonwood forest, but they heard nothing else. Nothing. Except for the river and the plaintive call of the owl, the silence was punctuated only by the rasps of their twin breaths. The night took on an eerie texture, almost palpable, and Ben shivered. Once again, the unknown oiled his hands with the sheen of sweat.

"Where *are* they?" he questioned, still whispering.

"They's left," decided Joe. "You're too deadly fer 'em, Ben."

"Me?" The boy was surprised.

"You kilt at least six of them devils."

"I think you got a few yourself."

"Yeah, but you're the one, Ben. They was after you. You're Big Medicine now."

"You mean I'm a wanted man?"

"By every 'Rappyhoe warrior alive, and probably by other tribes, too. Iron Heart grows."

Suddenly, Ben noticed something.

"Where's the bodies? They're gone."

"Oh, they took 'em," said Joe matter-of-factly. "They got 'em while we was still fightin'. Indians, they don't leave their dead or wounded."

"Except," Ben reminded his friend, "back at my home."

"Yeah, but that was different. They thought they was fighting a devil."

"Maybe they were," said Ben grimly. After a moment, he asked, "Now what?"

"We move a little ways off this here place."

They crept as silently as possible through the darkness, stopping finally in a grove of cottonwood.

"An' we stay here 'till daybreak," Joe said. "More cover here where the trees is thick. Can't hardly tell a trunk from a man. Just don't make no noise. A man stays still, he's 'most invisible."

"I wish they'd have kept coming," said Ben. "Oh, I wish they had."

In the darkness, Joe looked Ben over carefully. It was too late to bank the fire of hatred now. Ben had become a killer, and would, as time passed, yield to increasing temperatures of vengeance. When Tall Dog was dead, Ben's quest would also die. But until then . . . would hate swallow his young friend? Hate could be a terrible thing.

"I wisht Tall Dog was with 'em," Joe said quietly.

"So do I," agreed Ben fervently.

Each had different reasons. One to save a boy he was growing very close to, the other simply to kill the man responsible for the death of his family. Ben was aware of his hatred for the Arapahoes. He was not aware of its danger to his inner life.

The two spoke no more. Even whispers carried to sharp Indian ears, ears that could hear the *pat pat* of the soft-footed prairie wolf against a high wind.

It seemed to Ben that years passed before dawn raised an eastern eyelid and peeked through. As soon as there was enough light to move without stumbling and causing a racket, the two returned, cautiously, to the battle scene. Ben's Dragoon was cocked and ready. Joe's Sharps was once again lethal with a .50 grain ball of lead in the breech.

There were blood stains on the trampled grass, but that was all. There were no other signs of the fight.

Except for one thing: Their horses were missing.

"The thieving devils took 'em," cried Joe, enraged.

"They got most of our outfit, too," observed Ben.

There was little left. The coffee pot was still sitting not far from the stomped-out fire. It presented an incongruously homey touch, wrapped in gray enamel innocence. Ben shook it, and liquid sloshed. He tilted the lid back, and drank. It was cold and bitter to the taste, but strong, and washed the dryness from his palate. He handed the pot to Joe, who gulped a few jolts.

"Well," said Joe, setting the coffee pot on the ground and wiping his mouth on his sleeve, "at least we don't have no encumbrances. Whatever that means."

"How far to Laramie?" Ben asked.

"Hunnert mile, mebbe hunnert and fifty."

"That's a long ways on foot."

"We could go back to Cherry Creek."

"That's even farther," objected Ben.

Joe smiled, and Ben was reminded of his father's smile. It was one he used, when he caught Ben saying something stupid.

"So we gotta hit fer Laramie," said Joe.

Ben's face reddened under Joe's subtle sarcasm.

"I got a lot to learn, Joe."

The other shook his head.

"Mebbe in some things, but not others, son."

"Like what others?"

"Yer a cool 'un under fire. They ain't many I seen's so cool."

"When you got a reason, it isn't hard, Joe."

"Yeah, well, mebbe." He looked around and shivered involuntarily. "I don't think them rascals'll be back. They made their point, but let's not hesitate to put our feet on the trail, lad."

They set out, horseless and without any gear except the coffee pot. They would have to live off what they shot until they got to Laramie.

"Lucky I still got cash," said Joe. "We can git another outfit."

"Sorry about Sam," said Ben. "You paid good money for him and now he's gone. I liked him, too."

"Pintos is smart. They's one of the best range horses around."

They skirted a bend, and stopped in horror. Sam lay in the trail. His head had been severed and set on his side, neck down, facing the two.

"My God!" Ben muttered.

Joe just stared for long moments before he said, "Iron Heart."

Ben looked at his friend for an interpretation.

"That's you, remember?" prompted Joe. "And that was your horse. That's what they aim to do with you, Ben. That's a warning."

"Those savages," growled Ben, filled with pity for faithful Sam. "Why did they have to do that?"

"To show contempt for anything you might own. Listen, 'Rappyhoes is horse Indians. They know the value of a horse, see? They know they kilt your most

91

valuable thing. They want you next."

"I wish," said Ben, "they'd come at me right now."

Joe, tough as he was, felt a chill. Ben Brand would have killed a thousand Arapahoes right then. Maybe two.

"They were only half-right," said Ben.

"About what?"

"My most valuable possession." He patted his .44 Dragoon. "Sam was a good horse, yes, but my most valuable possession is this pistol. And they haven't got that, Joe. Not yet, they haven't."

Ben walked over to Sam and touched the velvet nose.

"I'll get a dozen Araphoes for this," he swore, "and I'll get another horse that looks just like you, and name him Sam. You are not dead, my friend. No, you are not."

He scratched the severed head between the ears, and then walked on. Joe was in no hurry to catch up. Sometimes a man, or a boy, liked to be alone.

Joe trailed Ben by fifty feet or so, but his Sharps was at the ready. Probably the 'Rappyhoes were gone, but you could never be sure. Iron Heart was Big Medicine, and they could return for another attempt at lifting his hair. Joe's eyes, accustomed to wilderness ways, watched for differences that might spell trouble. An oddly shaped stump, a slight movement in the trees, a bird squeaking in alarm. Those were differences that nature created with help, and it was these, as well as other signs, that Joe looked for.

Ben was saddened by the loss of his pinto, but he didn't grieve. Though he and Sam had been close, they had not shared many days. They'd still been experimenting with each other when Sam was killed. Sam might buck a bit brutally in the morning to see what he could get away with, but Ben stuck to his ribs like glue. Ben might head the horse down an embankment far too steep, and Sam would put the brakes on. He reached bottom at his own pace—and all in one piece.

Ben enjoyed the game. He knew exactly what Sam was doing, and, the way he saw it, the horse was on to him. Getting acquainted. Experimentation. In time they would have complemented each other perfectly, hand and glove. Their minds would have meshed, and there would have been no surprises. Ben missed that relationship. A good horse had been ruthlessly slaughtered, because of himself. That hurt Ben. He aimed to even the score. A dozen Arapahoes or twenty-five of their best horses would lose their lives for what happened to Sam.

Eventually Joe caught up to Ben, and they walked side by side.

"I haven't heard you say anything about your gelding and the mule," Ben remarked. "Don't you miss them? Aren't you mad as hell?"

"Me and the horse has been together for years," replied Joe. "What do you think?"

"And the mule?"

"I aim to get even," swore Joe. "Oh, yes. I won't forget."

They veered north away from the river about sundown. The trail was easy to follow, as it was used often—especially of late by newcomers such as the Locks.

"This go to Laramie?" Ben asked.

"Yep. We are on our way."

For some reason, Ben felt better after leaving the river. It had been a river of strife for him. He had killed many Arapahoes, but his hatred for them had only deepened. He had lost Sam, and he had a badly bruised shoulder where the tomahawk shaft had crashed into it.

Strangely, it had been a river of regret, too. Ever since leaving Martha and the missionaries, Ben had been plagued by a premonition. He shook it off as a reflection of his depressed state of mind, but the premonition returned to bother him. Maybe he should have gone back with them as far as Cherry Creek. Maybe, but there was no use fighting himself now. He hadn't. He was here, and perhaps that was to the good. If the Arapahoes knew that Iron Heart traveled with the Locks group, they would probably have struck them. Yes, he decided, it was best that he and Joe had continued toward Laramie. Still, in spite of such logical reasoning, the matter was not altogether resolved. The premonition returned, and if not so urgent as before, it was, just the same, a bad feeling.

"Glad to get away from the river," he said to Joe.

"Yeah, I know what you mean."

"You feel it, too?"

"A man always feels strange about a place he's kilt somebody."

"I'm going to feel mighty strange about a lot of places, then," responded Ben with grim humor.

"Yeah. I think you will."

Though Ben was not new to hiking, he found the distance from the river to Laramie all he wanted. He and Joe existed on what they could shoot, some rabbits and two antelope. When they sighted the adobe walls that surrounded the fort, Ben heaved a sigh of relief.

"There's old William!" Joe nearly shouted. "By Gar', it's nice to see 'er agin."

"William? I thought you said Laramie."

"Yeah, son, that she is—now, but she used to be Fort William, and I still call 'er that sometimes."

"How come its name is Laramie now?"

"Use your eyes, son. See that river?" Joe pointed.

"Yes."

"That's the Laramie, and t'other, the North Platte, well, they junction here. Only they don't call the place North Platte, they call it Laramie. Enough history?"

Ben nodded. What he wanted now was a bath and clean clothes. He even needed a shave, for red fuzz was showing on his chin. He had never shaved before. He was growing up.

They entered the gates without challenge, and Ben saw a city larger than any since he and his family had left St. Louis. The American Fur Company once owned the town, and their buildings were in evidence everywhere. It was now an Army post, and the military establishment was off to one side. There was a lot to see and do, but—first, that hot bath and a change of clothing—and a shave.

They found a bath and a room upstairs over a saloon. Ben allowed himself a good soak, then he let Joe go buy them both more clothes. And a razor. When he returned, Joe had fresh underlinen, and a straight razor for Ben. He instructed the youth in the careful use of the razor.

"You got to draw down at a slight slant, like this."

Joe shaved as a demonstration, and Ben followed suit—or tried to. He ended up with a skinful of nicks, which caused Joe great merriment.

"Reminds me of when I was your age," Joe chuckled. "Don't mind me."

"Could have done better with my 'hawk," muttered Ben, who was, nevertheless, a bit proud of his first shave. He felt, truly, more like a man than ever.

They stopped at a restaurant, and ordered steaks. The girl who took their order, seemed distant and vague. Her eyes were red-rimmed, and Ben didn't have to be told that she'd been crying.

He hadn't had any experience with girls in his life—the encounter with Martha had been the most prolonged that he could remember. Of course, it was doubtful if he'd forget the blue-eyed blond Martha, even if they had only met and passed. She had that effect on him. He was at ease with her, and he was not at ease now with the waitress. Yet, despite that feeling, he spoke to her.

"You look like you been crying," he said. "Something wrong?"

The girl stared from puffy eyes.

"Oh," she said, "them Locks was so nice. What a pity."

Ben felt his nerves jangle.

"The Locks? Were they the missionaries?"

"Yes, and they was here for a week preachin' and they even had a tent where we could all go. Mrs. Locks she played the organ so nice." The girl wiped her eyes with her thumb. "It was something different,

96

you know?"

A foreboding rolled over Ben like an evil, black cloud.

"What happened to them?"

"Well, ain't you heard?" asked the girl.

"No, for God's sakes, tell us," Ben snapped.

"They was all killed. All of them, every one of them, killed and cut up, I hear."

"The girl Martha, too?"

The waitress looked at him.

"Did you know her?" she asked.

"Answer me," said Ben in a tight voice. "Was she hurt?"

"She was the worst off. They say she was scalped and raped and sliced all up. Some say she was cut up before she died. Her legs was took off at the knees. They say it was Tall Dog."

Ben stood up. He walked stiffly to the door, and, in the street, he was sick. He was terribly sick, and he didn't care who heard him or saw him.

Joe joined him, and put an arm around his shoulder.

"By Gar', son," he said gently. "By Gar'."

"We got to get him, Joe," said Ben. "We got to do it."

CHAPTER EIGHT

Ben began to think that Tall Dog was more than human. More like a ghost.

"He's hittin' every place," said Joe. "Wyomin', Jefferson Territory, down on the Plains, up in the hills."

Everyone had seen him, knew of him, but nobody knew exactly where the warrior chief was. He was like a river at flood, then dropping suddenly to a quiet normal. He was a cyclone striking with ferocity only to dissolve in a hundred harmless breezes. There was no pinning him down to one place, and a pattern that wasn't a pattern evolved.

"We'll never find him," said Joe, "just follerin' along his trail. There ain't any trail."

Ben was frustrated. He wanted only to track Tall Dog, but what Joe said was true. Where was this renegade Arapahoe? He not only fooled professional Indian-watchers like the Army, he fooled the Army's Indian scouts. If anybody could have been able to find Tall Dog, they should have been the ones to do it. Yet, while they knew as much as anyone else, they didn't know any more. Ben talked to several of the Indian scouts they met. Using a combination of signs and trail lingo, he made himself understood. They could give him little. They had no answers.

"If we know," said a wizened little man called Two Feathers, though Ben could see no feathers at all, "we tell Army, huh? They go catch."

Ben raged with a fever that had no warmth. "What you got," said Joe, "can't be measured with no mercury thermometer." With the death of the Locks party, and of Martha in particular, all the horror came back to him—the massacre at home that went on for twenty-four hours, the killing of Sam and the nasty message of the severed head, and Martha naked, without legs, swelling in the sun. What he had, thought his partner, was a cold rage. He was close to the breaking point, Joe thought.

"You got to git aholt of yerself," he said in a kindly but insistent way. "You got to get them things out'n your mind."

"Can you?" Ben demanded bitterly.

"Nope," admitted the mountain man truthfully. "Them things will be forever up here." He touched his head. "But I learnt long ago, if I didn't live with 'em, they'd kill me."

Ben wanted to strike out—go anywhere, just to be going. He hated the stagnation of Laramie. The sitting. The doing nothing.

"Let's head back to my home," he urged. "Maybe he'll go back for a look."

"Nuh. Indians don't like to go back where they lost people in a fight. They think it's bad luck."

"It purely would be," said Ben, "if we were there."

One day Joe came to Ben with a proposition.

"Let's join the scouts," he said. "That way we can be on the move when the Army moves."

"You mean enlist in the Army?" Ben was taken completely by surprise. "We'd have no freedom at all that way."

"We don't have any now, son. We don't know which way to turn, but the Army, it's got feelers out, 'n I reckon it knows more about Tall Dog than it lets on."

"You mean they could maybe get him—while we sat here doing nothing?"

"Since you put it like that, yeah, mebbe so."

Ben was reluctant, but he gave Joe his blessings, and Joe signed up as a scout. The Army was looking for men with experience in the country, and Joe had plenty.

Restless, Ben did some scouting on his own. He made overnight trips into the rough, untrod country, making cold camps, listening to the night sounds. He had purchased another pony, a pinto like the other, courtesy of a loan from Joe. The pony was black and white, not brown and white as Sam had been. Ben didn't mind. Sam the Second, named reduced quickly to just Sam, possessed the same free spirit as the first Sam. He bucked irritably in the morning, slid down embankments cautiously, shied at every stump, turtle, rock, and wooden footbridge, but he ran like hell when Ben put his heels to the animal's flanks. It was going to take awhile for him and the second Sam to know each other, and that suited Ben perfectly. For a few days, he lost himself in his new horse, and was almost happy.

He began his freelance scouting after he had Sam for four days. A great urgency seized Ben, a yearning, a calling almost, to face Tall Dog. He followed the Laramie for miles, and made his cold camps, and listened to the awesome prairie silence. Sometimes, he made a big fire on top of a rise, a fire that could be seen for miles, and once he drew a straggler.

The straggler was a drummer with a great stock of miscellaneous items from matches to combs to clothing. He drove two horses hooked to a wagon with a wooden top—a sort of house on iron wheels.

"That's my home," he explained, while hunkering over Ben's fire in the darkness. "I don't stay in no pay-for rooms. Can't afford it in my business."

Ben asked his question. Did the man hear of Tall Dog along the way?

"Nope—and I come a long way, son, from St. Louis. Never heard of him."

From that, Ben reasoned that Tall Dog kept to the west half of the Plains, with forays into the mountains. Arapahoes were not strangers to the mountains, he knew. They hunted in the mountains and killed innocent humans as well.

Before the drummer left in the morning, Ben asked him if he carried a gun.

"Heaven's no!" was the response. "What would I do with it?"

Ben saw no reason to alarm the man, so he just shrugged and said, "Thought you might do a bit of hunting. Lots of antelope around here."

"You people out here," said the peddler almost scornfully, "how's come you all pack guns? Everywhere I go, I see rifles and pistols."

"We like them," replied Ben grimly, and as the man shook his reins and said goodbye, Ben sent a prayer after him, under his breath. "May God grant safe passage to you, my friend."

A week later word drifted back to Laramie that the drummer had been killed and scalped. His wagon had been ransacked, and the two horses were gone. There was no way to know who had committed the atrocity. It could have been Tall Dog. It could also have been rebellious Cheyennes or a party of Kiowas, who couldn't resist the merchandise. It could also have been white bandits, who were known to prey along the same trail.

Ben blamed it on Tall Dog.

"It's got to be him," he declared to Joe. "Nobody but him has got the nerve and the gall."

"Last I heard, he was way down in southern Jefferson Territory—or like I hear some call it now, Colorady."

"Colorado," prompted Ben.

Joe again brought up a matter that was close to his heart.

"C'mon an' jine up," he urged. "You can search for Tall Dog and git paid for it, too."

"I got some more of my own looking to do," was the stubborn response.

"Where, Ben? Where in hell you going to look? You got to go mebbe five hunnert mile and you won't find him. Listen, son, he knows about you. You think he don't want you, too? But he ain't ready, and you aren't going to find him around here on your two-bit trips."

Ben flushed at the "two-bit trips" part. He was doing the best he could, not knowing the country. On reflection, he realized Joe was right. His Pa told him about that once, when he was just beginning to hunt mountain grouse. He'd only venture a few hundred yards from the house, and one day his Pa had said, half-teasing, and half not, "Ben, you are not going to cross a river on snow shoes."

It took him awhile to figure that one out, then he got the point: You can't do things halfway, and you have to learn what works best.

Joe's arguments, plus the fact that he was broke and living off money borrowed from his friend, finally convinced Ben he'd better do something. He didn't want to work in a store, or cut wood, or become a teamster. He knew he had to be where there was the chance for the most action, and the answer to that was the Army.

He was fifteen, so he lied about his age and made himself eighteen. He was big enough to pass for older. Still, he was inexperienced in scouting. He didn't know the country. A Lt. Noel McCollum questioned him, and Ben immediately disliked the man. He was a spit-and-polish officer, and his attitude plainly told the world that he thought soldiers, and scouts—scouts in particular—were scum.

Then Joe told him that Ben was the famous Iron Heart. The lieutenant looked at the youth before him in disbelief, but a light flickered in the cool eyes.

"If that's the case," he said, "we'll hire you. You can serve as bait." Lt. McCollum laughed nastily. "Tall Dog wants your scalp. We want his." He laughed again. "We sure want him, kid, and you can bring him to us."

When they were alone, Ben said to Joe, "I maybe did the wrong thing signing up, but I'll tell you something. If I get a notion that I can track Tall Dog alone, I'm gone, and to hell with this Army."

Joe nodded. "Fair enough, but stick around long enough to learn something. These here bluecoats has had plenty experience. They can teach you things."

They lodged in the soldiers' barracks, and Ben was appalled by the conditions. The soldiers were issued dirty blankets and uniforms. They ate salt pork and beef, rice, beans, bread, and coffee. They were paid five dollars a month. Sergeants got thirteen and lieutenants, twenty-five.

The life was not easy. When in camp, soldiers didn't loaf. They were continually occupied with some task. If it wasn't adding new buildings to the fort, it might be constructing a fort in a distant locality. With the influx of more whites, tension between the races was mounting, resulting in an increase in military presence. If the soldiers weren't in the construction business, they were cutting firewood, hauling water, making repairs, standing guard. When they weren't working like fools, the bluecoats were drilling. Formations pounded the parade grounds daily, until dust rose in clouds from booted feet.

All of this was a revelation to Ben, who thought the soldier's life must be a romantic one—a life of high adventure, a life where courage was tested daily, and a man had to be a man to endure the dangers. The soldiering life, Ben learned, was far from any of these things.

Punishments were handed out for the slightest infraction: late for duty, reluctance to carry out an order. Even though the offender did his duty by the order. It was the reluctance that suffered punishment, was the crime. A barracks fight could result in a flogging. Hanging a soldier by the wrists for an indeterminate time was considered not a cruel and unusual punishment. Sometimes more serious offenders were treated to a ball and chain, or an iron collar. Meals of bread and water and loss of pay were common punitive measures.

The officers, of whom there were half a dozen at Laramie, did not fraternize with the common soldiers. Soldiers were considered the dregs of humankind, beneath dirt. Except in the field of operations, officers rarely bothered to even speak to them. Ben noticed that the officer class was not much better off, despite the snobbery.

"They drink too much," he observed to Joe.

"Ain't enough fer 'em around here," said Joe. "They go crazy with nothin' much to do."

"Except bully the common soldiers," Ben pointed out.

The officers kept to themselves, a tight little group, some of them West Pointers, others having won their status coming up through the ranks. Promotions were slow, Joe told Ben. It was common for an officer of sixty years of age to still be a captain, and, among the enlisted men, a private might have to sign up several hitches before he gained sergeant stripes.

Ben noticed, too, that the duty rosters were set up according to a racial pecking order. American-born

106

soldiers were given axe work, because they were considered best at it. Irish soldiers were given shovels, and Germans set to pulling weeds, because, in the words of Lt. McCollum, "That was all they were good for."

And the only women allowed to live in camp were officers' wives and laundresses. Laundresses were the wives of corporals or sergeants, and there were few of these at Laramie. As much as Ben disliked Lt. Noel McCollum, there was one thing he did give the man credit for. He had a lovely wife and a beautiful daughter, whom Ben saw from afar.

All in all, it seemed to Ben that a soldier's life in a western barracks was like prison. He wondered why they bothered to stay. Enlisted periods were for five years and up to ten years. How could a man hand over his life to such conditions voluntarily?

He learned something else. The soldiers didn't like him much. They'd heard of "Iron Heart," and as one young private put it to him bluntly, "You're crazy, doin' the things you do."

Ben didn't defend himself. There was in him a reluctance to speak of the tragedies of his life. They were personal, and to speak of them to comparative strangers seemed a betrayal of his dead kin. The people who had been murdered by Arapahoes were dear to him, and their names were not to be slipped off the tongue in casual conversation.

As for the name Iron Heart, he was continually surprised by it. He had done nothing out of the ordinary as far as he was concerned. He had fought when necessary, and had been lucky. He'd won his fights. He was neither brave nor a coward. He was, simply, Ben Brand, a person who was responsible for avenging the deaths of his loved ones. The Indians had dubbed him Iron Heart. It was they who had spread his reputation as a fighter without fear, not he. If the soldiers looked upon him with skepticism, there was little he could do about it.

On patrol, he was generally assigned to the point by the corporal or sergeant, whoever was in charge. It was the most dangerous position. More than one point man had had his hair lifted before he could cry out for help. His body would be found by comrades fifteen minutes later.

Ben never complained. Though he was inexperieced, he rode point, and did his job. His sharp eyes never missed a trick, and saved the patrol from Indian ambush more than once. Sometimes Joe rode with him and taught him tricks of the trade.

"You got to have eyes in the back of your head," he told Ben. "If'n you don't, you'll get an arrow there, or a ball."

Ben never rode with his eyes fixed on a distant place or objective. He rode with his eyes continually roving, watching all horizons, points in between. He also got Joe to teach him more Arapahoe sign and words. Joe, having been in the country when there was peace, or at least, more peace than now, also knew Comanche words and Ben picked these up as well. The sign language was universal, used by most of the Plains tribes, and Joe taught him all that he knew.

"You seem awful curious, son," Joe commented one day. "You aimin' to leave, mebbe?"

"Like I said, Joe," Ben replied honestly, "if I don't

think I'm getting closer to Tall Dog here; I'll go. Yes."

Joe didn't like what he heard. Ben had become more than a friend. The boy was, indeed, like a son to him. He watched with pride as Ben rode point. He noted with a fatherly interest the changes in Ben. He was filling out, even on the Army's substandard grub. He was growing more manly each passing week. He was outwardly calm; he never let his inner rage boil over. He even had a sense of humor.

This subverted quality popped into sight one evening in the barracks. Ben was lying on his bunk, pouring over a copy of a Shakespeare play—the only reading at hand.

Suddenly, he sat up and threw the book at a private two bunks down. The book lit on the man's stomach, and he came up ready to fight.

"What'd you do that fer?" he bellowed. He was the same young soldier who had told Ben he was crazy.

"I am not," said Ben firmly, his gray eyes glinting with amusement.

"You ain't what?" gasped the private.

"Crazy like you said," explained Ben. "A little loony, maybe, but not crazy."

The man stared at Ben for a full count, then broke into laughter.

"All right then, loony."

Those in the barracks who witnessed the scene, joined in the laughter and Joe noticed that the general dislike of Ben eased a bit after that.

On an early fall day rumors hit the fort that Tall Dog was in the vicinity. He'd been seen ten miles up the Laramie.

A patrol was formed at once and set out with Ben and Joe both in the lead, as scouts. The young private who had called Ben crazy, was riding point behind the scouts. The three were a quarter of a mile ahead of the main patrol, and Indian sign was abundant. Shoeless horse tracks scuffed the soft soil everyplace.

"They don't seem to care if anybody sees their sign," remarked Ben.

"I wonder," muttered Joe, "if'n we ain't headin' into ambush. This here trail's like bait . . ."

He was interrupted by a yell from the young soldier behind them. An arrow jutted out of his chest, the shaft still quivering, and he reeled in his saddle, trying to hang on. The shock made the man suddenly sick and he vomited.

Ben and Joe galloped back and caught him, before he toppled to the ground.

A band of Arapahoes, riding wild-eyed horses, galloped into sight, not fifty feet from them.

Without hesitation, Ben charged them, calling to Joe, "Stay with the kid. I'll draw them off."

The suddenness of his attack took the warriors by surprise and, for a moment, victory belonged to Ben. He dashed at them without thought, almost an involuntary act. To see an Arapahoe was to attack him. Though the band was armed with bows and arrows, lances and rifles, Ben charged fearlessly. Even knives and tomahawks bristling in sashes tied around lean, tough waists made little impression.

"Come on, Sam," Ben urged his pinto. "We got work to do."

As he and Sam charged, he fired his pistols alternately. Two Indians fell from their horses and two more yelped in pain.

"I am Iron Heart," Ben cried. "I am he who has killed your brave warriors."

The band, which Ben estimated consisted of about twenty-five braves, heard his words and rode up to fight at a gallop. It was what he had hoped for, because attention was diverted for a moment from Joe and the wounded man. Instead of fleeing, Ben wheeled Sam around, and charged back, firing as he rode. The band split up, screaming insults at him. Lances and arrows flew past, and guns roared, but Ben ignored them. He wheeled again and ran Sam through an opening to the wide prairie beyond.

As he urged Sam to greater speed, he glanced over his shoulder. That was when he realized his mistake. The Arapahoes had closed up and blocked the way back. There was no way he could return to Joe or the patrol.

He reined Sam to a halt, and as he did so, the Indians did the same. Seventy-five paces separated them and Ben waited, pistols cocked for their charge.

None came. The Indians sat their mounts talking among themselves. Ben reloaded his pistols swiftly, a cylinder at a time. He capped each nipple calmly, expecting an immediate assault, but the Arapahoes didn't budge. One thing Ben did note: Tall Dog was not among them. Tall Dog was tall for an Indian. He was also noted for his great strength and two other distinct features. He had a great, hooked nose, and a scar that ran the length of his left cheek. He was also a full war chief, and as such, would have been wearing a great eagle-feathered bonnet. No, Tall Dog was not with these braves.

He now realized fully the implication of Lt. McCollum's remark that young Ben Brand, as Iron Heart, would serve as bait. He would tempt the Arapahoes, especially those with Tall Dog. The braves now gazing at him across a space that might be his eternity, had apparently seen to it that a rumor concerning Tall Dog's presence in the area had reached the fort. They were hoping for a *coup*. They wanted Iron Heart. Iron Heart had, indeed, become the hunted as well as the hunter.

While this flashed through Ben's mind, the Arapahoes made no moves. Instead of charging at him with raised lances, they sent taunts. Some had learned enough English to be vocal.

"Iron Heart, ha! Heart of willows."

"Speak big, deeds small."

There was chanting and singing of an unmistakably sarcastic nature. Ben had learned from Joe that this was an Arapahoe trait. It was almost the same as a *coup* to insult a dangerous enemy, to make fun of him while in battle. Warriors who committed such deeds were lauded as brave among their people. To taunt was, to an extent, a victory in itself.

As Ben listened, he wondered how long this show of contempt would continue. He wondered, too, if Joe and the wounded soldier made it to safety. As the taunts of the braves washed over him, he began to wonder. Would it be possible they were just a little off guard? It sounded to him as if they were bragging to each other, a sort of I-can-insult-him-better-than-you competition was raging.

Sweat beaded up on Ben's forehead. His hands turned slick with sweat. The Indian talk seemed more strident, more shrill. Louder.

Would they be more occupied by their oratory and chanting than with him?

He made up his mind swiftly. He cocked his pistols, checked his knife and tomahawk to see where they were in his belt, and looked to Sam. The horse seemed all right. He wasn't winded, and the racket the Arapahoes were making didn't spook the animal. Ben, in spite of his deadly situation, smiled. He had gotten a fine horse in Sam Two. A fine horse.

There might be another reason the Arapahoes were talking so loudly, he reasoned. And, it made sense. They were also afraid of him!

His jawline hardening, Ben touched his heels to Sam's flanks, and the pinto bolted forward. Ben hunched low in the saddle, began to pick targets. He aimed, squeezed the trigger. One brave toppled, then another. The scene became a melee of horses and men in a whirlwind of free action. Lead balls fried the air over Ben's head. He turned the pony with pressure from his knees, as the Indians did. The braves recovered and closed in on Ben, but he shot two more from their horses before his pistols were empty. He thrust them in their holsters, and drew knife and tomahawk. Something hit him in the rear of the shoulder, but he kept charging, and, weapons slashing, cleared a path through the tangle. Once in the clear, he touched Sam again with his heels and yelled, "Go, Sam! Go! We'll make it easy."

But it wasn't easy. It was a race for life. He wouldn't have made it, but the patrol had heard the shots and were charging at a gallop, forming into a skirmish line. He plowed into their midst and they closed around him like a blue wall. Their Sharps boomed and the Indians fell back. The sergeant, a broad-faced westerner by the name of Clinty, called a halt.

"Don't chase 'em, boys," he ordered. "Might be a hell of a lot more waiting for us."

Joe rode over to Ben. "You're hurt," he bellowed.

"Where?" asked Ben, as yet not fully aware of the arrow sticking out of his back. All he knew was he'd been hit by something.

"Git off," commanded Joe, "and I'll pull it out."

Ben, feeling suddenly faint, slid from his pony, stood on quivering legs, suddenly lightheaded. Joe was on him in seconds, and jerked the arrow out. The pain sent Ben's senses reeling. "Damn it, ouch!" he yelled.

"Well at least it won't grow in you now," grunted Joe. Then he grinned. "*Ouch?* Is that the best ye can do when I pull them barbs out'n you? I'd have burnt the air a bit, I can tell yuh."

Ben reloaded his pistols, spilling black powder with shaky hands, and prepared to fight. He noticed that the young soldier who had taken the arrow in the chest was missing.

"Did you send him back to the fort?" he asked.

"Who?"

"The hurt one."

Joe shook his head. "Count a *coup* for the 'Rappyhoes," he said.

"You mean he didn't make it?"

Joe nodded.

"Well, hell."

"Yeah."

The pair was silent, then Joe asked, "Did you get touched by any of them Indians when you come ridin' through 'em?"

"Yes. I felt something. Fists. Hands. Something iron."

"Sure, you bet they was! They counted *coup* on you, Iron Heart. Even if they didn't kill you, they faced a brave enemy, and that is good medicine for them."

Ben didn't answer. He was feeling dizzy from loss of blood. He wanted to lie down and sleep, but he forced himself to stay alert.

"That was a damned fool thing you did," commented Joe.

"What do you mean?"

"Why ridin' through that bunch of savages the way you did. We all saw it. It was a damned fool thing to do."

"It was all I could do," argued Ben. "They were going to charge me before you got to them, and I'd have been dead. I figured I'd better either get it over, or get through."

"Well, you got through," said Joe proudly.

He had seen Ben, all right. He'd seen him astride Sam plunging into the 'Rappyhoes, who were among the most feared of Plains Indians, like they were so many dolls. He had seen the pistols buck in Ben's hands, and Indians topple, and he'd seen something else. They had not been close, but they were close enough that Joe could read Ben's face. It was dead calm. There wasn't a wrinkle of emotion showing. It was the face of a man intent on killing. The face was too calm, and Joe knew that a great rage burned beneath the smooth exterior. Once again, he wished that the rage would run its course soon. Once again, he hoped that Ben would not become his own victim. That he would not, as he put it to himself earlier, become vomit on the ground.

The soldiers dismounted to rest their mounts, and in so doing, circled around Ben. It seemed to Ben that it was an instinctive maneuver. Sgt. Clinty had given no orders. But they gave Ben a protective circle of deadly marksmanship, and waited silently for whatever might come.

It was then that Ben learned what made soldiers stick it out in the primitive forts, what made them endure the officers' insults and demeaning labor. They were bound together by this. In the field they were different. They moved in comradeship, in complete accord, noncoms and privates alike. Out here, where battle prevailed, and a man lived to the limits of courage, concern for each other was prime. Each man counted here, beyond the regulations and tyranny of fort life. There wasn't a man present, Ben sensed, who would have deserted him now. Each would fight to the death to preserve the life of one no-account scout, *because he was one of them.*

Ben was deeply touched. He was also embarrassed by so much attention, and he didn't like embarrassment.

"I can move," he said to Sgt. Clinty. "If you want to ride after them."

Clinty's features wrinkled in surprise.

"Ride after 'em, lad? Whatever for? Let the bastids go." He grinned roughly. "Yeah, you'd like to git 'em all, I know about that, but," he shook his head, "we had us enough fer now."

"But . . ." Ben began.

To which Clinty raised a hand. "No buts. We go back."

They mounted and started out. Ben, not feeling at all like his normal self, drifted in and out of consciousness, but he did come through long enough to hear Sgt. Clinty swear. And he knew Clinty was swearing because the dead soldier was gone.

"By damn," yelled Clinty, "we had to leave him. We couldn't take fight with a body on our hands. And them thievin' bastids come back and got him. Damn! Damn! Damn!"

The patrol rode back to Fort Laramie in close formation.

Ben felt, for the first time, that he was more than a decoy. That he was a part of these men.

And, somehow, they were a part of him now.

CHAPTER NINE

Ben was on the disabled list because of his wound. He wandered around the fort with his arm in a sling, bored by the lack of activity.

During one of his rambles, he ran into Melanie McCollum. He was rounding a corner of the officer's mess, when he saw her. She was returning from town after a shopping trip, and her arms were full of packages. The encounter was so sudden, Ben bumped into her. The packages tumbled from her arms, rolled in every direction.

Embarrassed, Ben mumbled as he helped the girl recover her parcels.

"I'm an ox," he muttered.

"Really?"

There was amusement in the girl's smile.

"I'd have thought you were a human being." She surveyed him closely. "Yes. You have two legs, two arms, and a nose. You are not only human, but an Army scout, as well."

Ben grinned back, and his embarrassment

dwindled. Here was a girl he could like.

"How'd you know I was a scout?" he asked. "Besides having two legs and all that."

"Don't you know that Scout Brand, better known as Iron Heart, is famous? Everybody knows about you."

Ben didn't know he was famous. He hadn't given the matter any thought. He liked listening to the girl though. He liked her looks. He liked everything about her without knowing exactly why.

"Do you know who I am?" she asked.

"Yes. You're old Scowl—I mean Lieutenant McCollum's daughter, Melanie."

"Scowl?" The girl laughed, and Ben liked the sound. "Is that what they call Daddy?"

"Sorry," Ben apologized, "I mean, they call him that and all. It just slipped out unexpected."

"Oh, that's all right. Don't you know I know? Daddy's always been that way. He is the same at home, too, you know. Nothing ever satisfies him."

"Some people are like that I guess."

Ben wanted to change the subject. He didn't care for Noel McCollum, and time with this girl was too rare to spend on him.

"Do you know," he asked, "we are probably the youngest people in the fort?"

"I know." Melanie nodded sadly. "It certainly is tiresome. All they—the officers—can talk about is fighting Indians and promotions. And all they do, socially, is drink."

Ben agreed that fort life was dull. He offered to help her home with her packages.

"I can manage," said Melanie. "You don't want to

120

take chances with your wound. But," she added, "why not walk along with me?"

Ben happily accepted the invitation.

As they walked toward officer's row, Melanie asked, "Does it hurt?"

"Does what hurt?"

"Why your wound, of course."

"No. Not now."

Melanie scowled. "Those Indians!" she exclaimed. "Haven't they anything better to do?"

"I don't think so."

She cast him a glance, but was silent. Ben noted that she was pretty, but in a different way than Martha had been. Melanie was the opposite, dark-haired and dark-eyed. Her lower lip was full and moist, and cupped under her upper lip to form a kind of pout. Ben thought about kissing her and his face turned red as a bee sting.

Melanie saw the blush and whispered, "Why are you turning red, soldier boy?"

"I'm not a soldier," said Ben, not knowing just what else to say.

"All right, then," Melanie teased, "why are you blushing, famous scout?"

"No reason," stammered Ben. "Must be the heat."

"Yes," was the knowing response. "I know what you mean. I've felt it a time or two myself."

Ben remained tongue-tied for the rest of the way to her quarters. Lt. Noel McCollum was not a high ranking officer, but compared to the soldiers' quarters, his house was a palace. A sign, posted on the wall near the door gave his rank and name.

"Come on in," invited Melanie.

"Oh, I don't know about that," said Ben reluctantly. "Your father wouldn't want one of us commoners to dirty his floor."

"I'll handle my father," said the girl. "Come, I want you to meet my mother."

"Mrs. McCollum?"

"I only have one mother, Scout Brand."

Ben still hesitated, so Melanie took him by the arm, while juggling her packages, and led him into the house.

He was startled by the cleanliness of the front room. Ben had become so accustomed to the enlisted men's quarters, he'd forgotten what clean was. The place reminded him of the home he'd burned the previous spring. Not that that had been so grand as this, but his mother kept it clean. She insisted on it, and the house sparkled, even during the muddy times of spring and fall. Ben knew he'd like Mrs. McCollum before he met her.

She bustled in from the kitchen, a comely woman, weathered some, from life on the Plains.

"Mama," said Melanie, "this is the famous scout, Iron Heart."

"Well," said her mother, "we finally meet you."

"I'm glad," said Ben, realizing at once it had been an idiotic response, and turning red again. "I mean I'm glad to meet you, Mrs. McCollum."

Both women laughed at his discomfort, but Mrs. McCollum put him at ease by inviting him into the kitchen for coffee and fresh baked bread.

He gobbled the bread hungrily, the first such he'd tasted in a long time. As he finished the first piece, he noted the two women staring and once again, Ben blushed. He'd behaved like a pig, and he knew it.

"I don't seem to be doing so well with my manners," he apologized. "Pretty soon I won't have any embarrassment left."

"Oh, I wouldn't say that," commented Mrs. McCollum in a motherly way. "You seem like a nice boy—ah, man," she said, a puzzled look on her face.

Before her sat a boy of what—sixteen years, perhaps? And yet, one wouldn't call him a boy. There was a maturity in the gray eyes that belied sixteen. It spoke of thirty—no, it spoke of agelessness. And the body that went with those eyes, what of it? It was a sixteen-year-old body, with its lanky arms and developing legs—but was it? There was a maturity in the body, too, that gave lie to the years. It was a body that had killed, a body that had fought, had drawn blood from an enemy, for Mrs. McCollum had also heard of Ben's fighting ability. Was it the physical frame of a sixteen-year-old she was seeing, or, like the eyes, was it also ageless? It might gain more weight, with the passage of time, and even, more strength, but Ben Brand was a full-grown man right now, in every sense of the word. She glanced at her daughter quickly, and knew her daughter felt the same.

Ben spent an enjoyable hour in the presence of two women whom he knew liked him. He wished that Mrs. McCollum would find an excuse to frequent some other part of the house, but she stayed close to them, a watchful chaperone. He liked Mrs. McCollum, but he was dazzled by Melanie. Her laughter was catching, and she seemed utterly delighted that she'd found a companion who spoke the same language she did—the language of youth. For in spite of Ben's maturity, he had a youthful heart, and he understood Melanie McCollum.

It seemed to him, he could have remained in the kitchen—in the McCollum household, for that matter, forever, but the head of the house, Lt. McCollum returned.

He greeted Ben with a sharp, "What's this?"

"I invited him for coffee and fresh bread, dear," said his wife.

McCollum glared. "You should have asked me first, Winona," he said coldly.

"I reckon I better be going," Ben said. "Thanks, ma'am, for the 'freshments."

Melanie accompanied him to the door.

"Don't let Daddy scare you off," she said. "His bark is worse than his bite."

Ben nodded, and started to leave.

"Will we see each other again?" Melanie asked. "I mean, to talk and things."

Ben nodded quickly. There was hope in the girl's voice, hope that was almost a promise.

"Of course," he answered, "but I don't know about here. Your father doesn't want me around, Melanie, and you know it."

"Maybe not." The pouty lips thrust out prettily. "I do, though."

"Well, I'd like to see you again, and you know that, too."

The girl nodded, her dark eyes revealing more wisdom and insight than a young lady her age was supposed to have.

"Please come back," she whispered.

"When?"

"Daddy is always gone until three in the afternoon. You can come anytime before then. I—we, Mama and me, will be happy to see you."

"All right."

He pressed the girl's hand and left for his own quarters. Actually, as a member of the scouting branch of the fort's contingent, he was allowed more freedom than regular soldiers. His duty was to make reconnaissance, to travel ahead of the troops and, as a scout, he often worked alone. His judgment was trusted by military leaders, the officers and noncoms. Having such responsibility placed him in a sort of limbo land. He was neither officer nor enlisted man, but a being apart. He was subject to the same disciplines if the offense were serious, but he was not bothered with the daily drill and routine labor. Lt. McCollum and the other officers generally left him to his own devices while at the fort, though in the field their word was law. As a scout, he could come and go as he wished, but he'd better never miss a patrol that he'd been assigned to take out.

He therefore had no reason to fear Lt. McCollum, but McCollum's dislike of him put Ben on guard. He had no wish to tangle with Melanie's father. First, he wanted to keep on the good side of him because he was the father of a girl he was fond of and, second, as an officer, McCollum could make life miserable for him. Perhaps McCollum wouldn't put him to cutting wood, as happened to other American men, but he could send him to another fort. Kearny was three hundred miles east, for example, and that would end any relationship with Melanie.

It became Ben's habit to visit the McCollum

household when he was sure the lieutenant was gone. Lt. Scowl. Ben could never remember when he'd seen the man smile. The men didn't like him. They felt he had no business being on the frontier. He was a desk officer, better suited to quartermaster work back in Washington. He went by the book, because he had no natural aptitude for fighting wild Indians, as he called them. As far as the troops were concerned, McCollum was a danger to them. They obeyed, because they were trained to obey. They often marched in ignorance of their goals, and if McCollum gave a wrong order, they wouldn't know it until it was too late.

The relationship between Ben and Melanie ripened. Ben realized a developing closeness was inevitable. The loneliness of fort life, the eagerness on both their parts for some kind of excitement, cut a path through the veneer of "do's and don't's" laid down by the gentility of their upbringing. Ben fell in love with Melanie and he knew she felt the same by the misty look of longing in her dark eyes. He also knew that his feelings for the girl were strongly physical and, again, he saw the response in the girl's eyes. They kissed when they could; when Mrs. McCollum was absent for a few moments, they kissed passionately. They were like secret drinkers, who swallowed as much liquor as possible in a hidden place, but dared not linger too long and become suspect. They kissed, and Ben might allow a hand to rest on a breast, before Mrs. McCollum returned.

"I want more," Melanie whispered urgently during one of their furtive love scenes. "More!"

"So do I," agreed Ben, "but we have neither the

time nor the place."

"We'll find it," decided Melanie. "We must."

"Yes," agreed Ben breathlessly.

Mrs. McCollum liked Ben. If she knew anything was happening between her daughter and him, Ben never caught a hint of it.

"You're a bright young man," she told him. "You read well, speak well, and act like a gentleman. I should think that if you continued your education back East, you'd amount to something."

Ben didn't refute the lady who unknowingly had insulted him. He had amounted to something already. He was Iron Heart, Indian killer, a legend of sorts. In this part of the world he was feared. People wanted him dead. He was hunted, and he was a hunter, and the quarry he hunted was a human being.

Amount to something? Ben smiled to himself at that caprice, but he agreed with Winona, as she insisted he call her.

"Yes, ma'am," he said, "perhaps one day I'll travel East and take up education seriously."

"Oh, you must, Ben!" cried his hostess with eagerness. "It is so important."

If Ben wondered why it was so important, he said nothing. The importance in his life was not education, but a killer named Tall Dog. Until that business was settled, nothing else really mattered.

He realized that sooner or later, he and Melanie would be found out. The law of averages were against their romance continuing to flourish in secret. Fort Laramie was too small for that. For that matter, all of Laramie was too small, and one day while he was kissing Melanie behind the McCollum house, the lieutenant himself burst upon them.

"By God!" McCollum cried furiously. "I thought so! My God, my daughter with a lowlife like you!"

He swung at Ben, and Ben sidestepped the blow easily.

"Daddy," shrieked Melanie, "stop!"

Ben backed away, knowing the danger of striking an officer. McCollum stalked him, his eyes smoldering with distaste and anger.

"Stop, damn you," McCollum ordered, but Ben continued his backstepping.

The frustrated lieutenant snatched his pistol from a shiny holster, and holding it by the barrel, leaped on Ben. He brought the butt down hard, striking Ben on his wounded side. Though the bandage had been removed and the wound healed, it was still sensitive. Pain shot through Ben's shoulder and back, like fingers of hot lightning.

For a moment, anger joined Ben's pain and he acted instinctively. In one movement, he grabbed McCollum's gun and wrenched it from the man's hand. In the next, he threw the gun aside and encircled the officer's neck with his arm. He placed a knee in the center of the blue coat and pressed, forcing McCollum to the ground. Ben, until that moment, never knew the extent of his strength. In battle, he had never come to grips with the enemy, but let his pistols do the fighting. Even as McCollum was collapsing helplessly, Ben made note of his own power. It would, he knew, come in handy before his quest was over.

Once McCollum was on the ground, Ben placed a

booted foot on the officer's chest and pinned the man.

"Never do that to me," he said in a voice loaded with fury. "I won't stand for it and you aren't man enough to dish it out, anyway."

He allowed McCollum to get up. The lieutenant brushed his trousers free of dust, his eyes never leaving Ben's.

"I'll get you for this," he said. "You're a dirty killer, as far as I'm concerned, and no hero. You'll pay, believe me. And stay away from my daughter, you scum!"

He turned and marched off stiffly, as if trying to salvage what was left of his wounded pride.

Melanie stood there, transfixed. She seemed to Ben like a small girl again, not the passionate woman he'd embraced.

She glanced up at him, then at her father, and with screwed-up face wet with tears, she stamped her foot and cried at Ben, "Now you've spoiled everything."

Then she ran to catch up with her father.

As Ben turned to leave, he found he had an audience. Watching from a distance were Sgt. Clinty and a dozen troopers. Joe was approaching.

"By Gar'," Joe said, "how'd that come about?"

"That bastard. Come on. Let's get out of here."

The gawking troopers grinned at the two scouts as they passed.

"About time that ass got his," said one, looking straight at Ben, "but, brother, you are in for a devil of a time now."

Ben scowled.

Joe had to grab his arm to keep the boy from taking on the trooper.

"You better haul in that temper quick, son," said his friend. "You already got yourself up a creek without a paddle. You're just liable to get put in irons."

"Shut up," said Ben.

But he knew Joe was right.

Maybe Melanie was right about him, too.

CHAPTER TEN

In the days that followed his fight with Lt. McCollum, Ben caught sight of Melanie only from a distance. If she saw him, she gave a quick, furtive wave, but made no effort to join him. Ben reasoned she was under orders from her father to see Ben Brand no more. However, her coy, sidelong glances told him that she was still interested.

In examining his own feelings toward the girl, Ben was confused. He didn't know anything about girls. Martha, though he'd felt her death deeply, had still been only an acquaintance. There had been no physical bond between them. There hadn't been time for that. But Melanie aroused him. The confusion he felt now was genuine when he asked the question—what was love? Did he feel love for Melanie? Or was it simply lust? He had no way of knowing for sure the difference between love and lust. At sixteen, Ben had never known a woman. Was he curious about the "final act," as he'd heard it called, or was he really in love?

Early one evening, he was jolted from his intro-spection.

"We go out tomorrow," Sgt. Clinty announced, "so get ready."

"Where we goin'?" Joe asked.

"There are a bunch of Sioux raisin' hell along the Oregon Trail. They're young braves and I heard there were Cheyennes and 'Rappyhoes with 'em. They already burned a dozen wagons and killed all the people, took scalps."

"I ain't heard of no reason for somethin' like that," mused Joe.

"Do they have to have a reason, Winter Bear?" Clinty used the Indian name for Joe. Joe's beard was turning silver and white, the color of snow.

"Nuh, but the reason is they's too many whites," grunted Joe. "Indians is losing hunting ground to whites. Whites been comin' in by the thousands."

Joe was bitter. He'd smoked a pipe with many of the tribes not so many years ago when things were better—when whites were more a curiosity than a threat.

"Yeah, well, whatever," said the sergeant, "we got our orders. Them Indians just can't run around killin' folks."

The barracks came alive with excitement. The men welcomed action outside the fort, dangerous as it was. It afforded a relief from the routine of the daily grind. Anything was better than cutting wood, hauling water or monotonous close-order drill. Even the risk of death.

Ben cleaned his Dragoon and Navy Colt that evening. They were already spotless, but he cleaned them anyway. He now had added a Sharps rifle to his arsenal. It was a carbine, of .52 caliber, thirty-seven and one-half inches long, carrying Edward Maynard's markings as patentee. It had the long swiveling-ring bar on the left side. It was a breechloader and Ben admired it. It was too heavy, but the rifle had a redeeming feature: the fifty-grain bullet carried a long distance, much farther than his Colt's. If an Arapahoe escaped his pistols, the Sharps would bring him down.

In the turmoil of the evening, Ben forgot about his love or lust or whatever it was, and listened to soldier tales of former encounters with the enemy. He shared rum with them, which Clinty had procured.

It was powerful stuff.

"Gar'," spat Joe on taking a swig, "that poison'll take the black paint off'n a cannon."

Ben was not a drinker. His family had frowned on drinking, save for the occasional bottle of celebration wine, and the boy never learned. He didn't like the taste of the rum either, but after the first few swigs, it didn't seem so bad. He found he felt quite jolly and joined in the singing and general good feeling. At one time during the evening, he found himself wearing a blanket, Indian style, and talking sign language with a soldier, who pretended he was a white.

"But you are white," Ben pointed out.

"So I am," mused the other. "All right, I'll be a green. Now jabber at me in that lingo you got. I like to see your fingers fly," added the soldier, "they look like white birds flapping."

It got pretty hazy after that, and then pretty sick.

Ben found himself holding his head and groaning, with Joe casting a sympathetic, but amused, eye on him.

"Yuh sure took on a tankful," observed Joe. "What you tryin' to do? Shame them soldier boys? Hell, lad, they can drink a lake and keep bangin' the table for more."

In the morning, at reveille, he fell out of his bunk still sick. The smell of food in the mess made him even sicker, and he went to the outhouse and retched. "Good God, help me," he moaned. "What have I got, the influenza?"

When he sprang that diagnosis on Joe, the mountaineer almost collapsed with laughter.

"The influenza? My land, boy, wherever did you come up with that?"

"Well, I got a terrible headache, and I keep throwing up. . . ."

"Son, you have just got yourself a Platte-sized hangover. The way you was swillin' that stuff down last night, it's a wonder you ain't got a hole burned clean through your innards."

So that was it. Ben tried a sickly grin.

"Iron Heart," he muttered, "mushroom stomach."

They fell in at 0700 hours, official Army time. An entire company was to go on the hunt, they learned. Ben, Joe and three Shoshone Indians were to scout. The man who would lead them was none other than Lt. Noel McCollum, old Scowl himself.

"There should be a captain heading a company, shouldn't there?" whispered Ben. He didn't like the idea of following McCollum anyplace.

Joe nodded, but said, "They can do as they please.

Mebbe the other brass is got other assignments. Or mebbe," he added deadpan, "they drank too much 'who hit John' last night and just simply can't make it."

The oldtimer's words were no comfort at all. Ben's head still throbbed like a snakebite.

Orders were given to head out and the troopers fell in behind McCollum, including the five scouts. Ben was astride Sam, and prayed for even country. Every jolt of the hoofs sent splinters of pain into his skull. If he ever drank that stuff again, he would shoot himself afterwards, rather than undergo such torture.

Once the company was beyond the fort a few miles, Lt. McCollum halted the column. He summoned the scouts.

"You Shoshones go that way," he pointed southeast. "Spread out. You, Cardwell," he said to Joe, "you go that way," and he waved a gauntleted hand to the northeast.

His slitted eyes landed on Ben, and Ben swore he saw red flash in them.

"You," he said vindictively, "will take the trail down the middle."

Joe gasped. "But, Lieutenant, them Indians is waitin' for anybody comes along that trail."

"If the boy is afraid," said McCollum loudly, "I'll assign another scout to that duty. Brand can bring up the rear."

Ben edged Sam around so he could meet McCollum squarely.

"You put me on tail," he said almost pleasantly, "and I'll break your neck."

Half the column heard the insult, and stiffened.

Had a soldier dared utter such words, he'd have been returned to the fort under guard.

But McCollum only grinned. "You and me," he said softly, "have a lot to settle."

"Yes, sir," agreed Ben, still as pleasant as sunshine. "I hope we can reconcile our differences."

Lt. McCollum carried a quirt. It was loaded to its tip with double ought buckshot, a nasty weapon. His veneer shattered under an explosion of anger. He whipped the quirt across Ben's face. A great ugly welt rose like a stitched scar on the tender skin. Ben didn't touch it. He didn't flinch. He smiled, but his words were so cold that Joe winced.

"I'll be heading up the trail now, Lieutenant," Ben said quietly. He swung his pony, galloped away.

"You report to me every hour," shouted McCollum after him, his anger out of control. "All of you scouts do that, hear? You don't toe the mark, I'll have you flogged until your skin peels off."

Ben hightailed it down the rutted trail. When he dipped into a deep gully, he took out a kerchief, and gently dabbed his face. The cloth was bloodstained.

Ben seldom swore hard language. That, too, was a reflection of his upbringing. His Pa swore rarely, and even then, it was confined to a "damn," or "hell." But Ben knew what swearing was. He'd heard enough since joining the Army to fill a book. He also was aware of the relief a good bout of swearing could bring to the soul, and he cut loose.

"That son of a bitch," he cried to the empty land. "That dirty son of a bitch!" he repeated with great emphasis. And then he dropped into the lower and grimier oaths with great heat, until his soul felt better, even if his face did not.

He reached over and patted Sam's neck.

"You close your ears when I use that language," he ordered. "It is not fit for a good, clean pony like you to hear. Understand?"

Sam twitched his ears.

"Good."

Despite his rage, Ben's eyes stayed keen, alert. He might swear great curses, he might dab at his face and soothe his humiliation, but he never once forgot who he was and why he was there. He was a scout. As such, he was responsible for lives. His ears, eyes and training all focused on one objective: to sight the enemy, before the enemy sighted him.

He had heard McCollum's insane scream about reporting on the hour. He carried no watch, and usually relied on the sun. If it lit the sky, it was day. If it sank below the horizon, night would follow. Hours could only be guessed at by its track across the vault of the heavens.

For the more demanding requirements of time, Ben had developed a method that was nearly infallible. Some inner sense wound the watch, and a gut instinct ticked off the hours. It had started on the ranch, and became finely tuned after he joined the Army as a scout. He often tested himself when riding with Joe, who did carry a watch. After hours on the trail, Ben would guess the time, and Joe checked him on his watch. Ben was rarely more than ten minutes off.

"That's pretty good," Joe admitted, pleased. "But it ain't surprisin'. They's men I know could do better."

Joe himself was fairly adept at telling time from the inside, but not as good as Ben.

Ben walked Sam carefully along the trail. It had been a busy place lately. Some kind of religious organization called the Mormons were using it, though it was said they were staking out their own trail somewhere south of the Platte. Prospectors were appearing on the scene, following a rumor of gold in California, and then there were settlers. The new Republic of Texas was wide open for homesteading, and, as far as Ben knew, so was the entire West. Families were moving in, innocent people, who hadn't the least idea of the hardships they would endure—the isolation and loneliness, attacks by hostile Indians, and illness. Ben's own family had been one of the innocents, and he knew what happened to them.

With the increase of white traffic, an increase in Indian rebellion followed. More and more whites had been killed, and the federal government back in Washington was sending more troops to fight the Indians. It was a vicious circle. More whites, more Indian hostility, more protecting bluecoats, and the circle grew by the month.

When Ben's inner clock told him it was time to return to the column, he went back. McCollum, riding at the lead, greeted him coldly.

"Well, Scout Brand?"

"Nothing, sir."

The lieutenant's eyes were dark with distaste and rancor, but he held on to his control.

"Very well. Move out."

"Lieutenant?"

"Yes?" The voice did not invite further conversation.

"I think an hour is too short, sir. We can't get far enough ahead for a good look if we have to report back in an hour."

"I couldn't care less what you feel about it, Brand. You have your orders."

McCollum flicked his loaded quirt just a bit. It twitched like a rattler stirring in the sun. Ben's hand dropped to his Navy Colt, and the snake stopped twitching.

"You'd like to kill me, wouldn't you, Brand?" hissed the officer.

"No, sir," replied Ben coolly, and wheeled Sam back up the trail.

He had lied. He would have loved to have killed Lt. Noel McCollum, and if that whip had landed on him again, he didn't doubt that the Navy would have done what it was meant to do—shoot.

At noon, Ben chewed on hardtack and jerky, washed it down with water from his canteen. The water was warm and tepid, but wet. The jerky was tough, the biscuits as hard as rock.

Sam, tied to a willow in a hollow, grazed quietly below Ben's perch on a boulder, high above the trail. As he swallowed the last of the hardtack, two sights grabbed his attention.

One was the dust of three wagons coming along the trail. They were a mile away, and oxen-drawn. The other movement was a shimmer of sun on horseflesh. It came from a position half a mile in front of the wagons, and Ben's suspicions were instantly alerted.

139

Leaving Sam tethered, he advanced swiftly, keeping well off the trail. He circled back and then in, forming an arc which brought him up on the offside of the place where he'd seen the horse, or the piece of it. He crept to a ridge and peered over, using a clump of grass as a shield for his face.

His heart leaped in a savage thrill. In a great hollow, completely hidden from the wagons, was the war party. There were at least a hundred Sioux, Cheyennes, and Arapahoes present, all young braves. The Arapahoes wore black paint over most of their faces, giving them an especially hideous appearance. Ben's trigger finger itched as anger welled up inside. For a brief, hot moment, he thought of standing up and firing on them. With his single-shot Sharps and the two pistols, he had thirteen rounds he could count on. That would mean thirteen dead or seriously wounded Indians, mainly Arapahoess. He didn't feel the personal animosity toward the others that he did the latter, and he decided he would not shoot at them except in self-defense. His fight was with the Arapahoes only.

He pulled his Navy Colt from its holster and aimed at a black-faced man, who seemed to be the leader of the Arapahoe war party. He picked a spot in the center of the man's forehead, and cocked the hammer. He aimed for a long time, until the target changed his position, but Ben never squeezed the trigger, for reason had returned. To do so would invite disaster. He would almost certainly be killed, and there would be many of the war party left to carry on. Nothing would be gained except another notch for personal vengeance. It wasn't enough, considering all that would be lost.

Ben slipped the pistol back into its holster and crept away. He had wasted much time. The wagons would be drawing close now and he'd have to hurry to prevent a massacre.

Sam was waiting, ears pricked, and Ben climbed aboard. The creaking leather sounded loud in his ears. He made it back to the troopers in fifteen minutes, riding hard. He dashed to Lt. McCollum in a swirl of dust, reining Sam to a skidding halt.

"The party is two miles up the trail, sir," he cried.

McCollum eyed him coolly.

"I know," he replied. "We are about ready."

For the first time, Ben noticed Joe, who was eyeing him with anger. Why, wondered Ben, would Joe be mad at him.

"Scout Cardwell brought word," said McCollum. He turned to Sgt. Clinty. "Troops ready, Sergeant?"

"Ready and waiting, sir," was the obviously impatient reply.

McCollum glanced at the man. "I had to be sure," he said crisply.

"Yes, sir," replied Clinty. "I was certain you did, sir."

Ben was aware that under the polite phrasing of Clinty, there was contempt.

"Should we move 'em out now, sir?" inquired the sergeant.

McCollum hesitated, looked around at the horizons as if he expected some kind of word from God, and nodded.

"Let's go," he said, "at a canter."

The column moved forward at the almost leisurely pace.

"Sir," cried Ben, "those Indians will be on the wagons in minutes. We should hurry."

"And give our position away?" countered McCollum scornfully.

"We should get on, sir," Joe said, backing Ben's request. "There ain't much time."

He'd no sooner uttered his words, than shots were heard in the distance.

"They're attacking the wagons," cried Sgt. Clinty. "We'd better move out, Lieutenant."

"All right, then," was the querulous reply, "sound the bugle for a charge. Form a skirmish line."

The bugler blasted the air through his instrument and the company raced ahead. They thundered down the trail and off it, in a fanned-out charge toward the shots.

Ben and his pinto, Sam, were passed by soldiers who knew the full necessity of speed. They'd all seen Indian killings before. None wanted to see them again, but none doubted that they would—and soon.

Lt. McCollum led the rest, and Ben had to admit the officer was no coward. He might be a fool, but he had guts. In a matter of minutes they closed with the surprised war party. The wagons had been overturned, but life could be seen, as men fired their weapons at the circling Indians. Several figures lay still on the ground, and these included the skirted bodies of two women. A few minutes later, and all would have perished.

Ben picked his targets. He used his Dragoon and .44 Navy, saving the Sharps for long-range. He sought out the black-faced Arapahoes and shot them from their ponies. They fought back, and once Ben heard the cry in English, "Iron Heart!" Every Arapahoe raced toward him. Powerful medicine sat on the bare back of a black and white pinto. Every Arapahoe wanted him. They wanted his horse if they couldn't get him, and the lead flew like hornets on all sides of him.

One by one, cocking his pistols carefully, aiming and squeezing the trigger, Ben picked off his enemy. The arrows, lances, and lead balls flew past both him and Sam. The two seemed to lead a charmed life. The noise of the battle was straight out of hell, as wounded men shrieked and the war cries from both Indians and whites gouged the clear air. Wounded horses whinnied in pain, and riderless mounts, both Indian and trooper, galloped aimlessly.

There was hand-to-hand combat near the wagons, for the Indians were trying to carry off women and children as prisoners. Soldiers engaged the would-be captors, in fierce, to-the-death struggles, in which not only Indians were killed or wounded.

Lt. McCollum had ridden beyond the wagons, and failed to give himself protective fire. When Ben noticed him first, McCollum was alone, and a dozen Indians were riding toward him. The officer was completely cut off, but he fought, firing his pistol until it was empty. Then he drew his sword and slashed empty air in a futile attempt to ward off the attack. It was a desperate measure, meant to hold tomahawks and knives at bay, though the effort gave no protection against bullets.

Ben didn't hesitate. With reloaded pistols he

charged toward McCollum, weapons roaring in his hands. He was a fury unleashed by the devil, a force of destruction akin to a tornado. He and Sam crashed into the Arapahoes, Cheyennes and Sioux, all crowding McCollum. Ben was forced to fire at all half-naked bodies, no matter the tribe.

His aim was deadly, and three Arapahoes toppled from their mounts, along with two Cheyennes. The others whirled to face this power of destruction that had descended upon them and, once again, Ben heard the words, "Iron Heart!" Indians rushed him, touched him, tried to club him, but he fought back with such venom and viciousness that no warrior could break through. When his pistols were empty Ben jerked his knife and tomahawk free of his belt and lashed out. He kept Sam stamping and thrusting against enemy ponies, keeping them off balance.

The battle lasted only moments before the Indians raced off. McCollum, bloody and dazed, stared at Ben. Ben grabbed the officer's horse by the reins and galloped back to the main body of troops. The fighting was over for the time being, and the Indians were in full retreat.

"Shall we pursue, sir?" Sgt. Clinty asked McCollum.

"Widen the perimeters, sergeant, but don't pursue."

The soldiers fanned out to form a protective circle, then held to that line. Half a dozen Arapahoe braves lingered atop a rise a quarter of a mile away.

"Iron Heart!" shouted one.

Ben raised his hand.

The six warriors dipped their lances in salute, and

then dashed off. Too late, Ben remembered his Sharps tucked in its scabbard by his leg. He shrugged. There would come another time, of that he was certain. He would be ready. He was ready now.

And Tall Dog had not been among the attackers— he was still alive.

CHAPTER ELEVEN

The three wagons belonged to settlers. The survivors included four men, three women, and five children. They were stunned by what had happened, stood there dazed as the soldiers tried to give them comfort.

"They struck us like a flood," exclaimed a black-bearded man. "We traveled clean from St. Louis with no Injun trouble, and now this."

His eyes wavered as they took in the destruction.

"My wife," he muttered, "she was one of the first to die. Lolly. Why, hell, she'd have taken 'em into her home and give 'em tea. And the grisly bastards shot her like a dog."

Ben hovered in the distance, close enough to hear the man, but far enough away so he didn't have to see the murdered woman. He remembered his own mother too well, and his sister, his aunt, and Martha.

"Well," he heard the bearded man declare bitterly, "they'll pay for it. Every redskin I see from now on better come to me on his hands and knees."

147

And so another length in the circle was stitched. This group, what was left of them, would carry the war to the Indians. Henceforward, they would be the implacable enemies of all red men.

"And it's your fault," came the voice of Scout Joe Cardwell.

He rode to Ben's side and stopped, his face still carrying the anger it did before the fight.

"Why is it my fault?" Ben questioned.

"I saw you spyin' on them warhoops," was the acid response. "I saw you sightin' your pistol. What in hell was the matter with you, anyways?"

"There was nothing wrong with me," Ben shot back, yielding to anger of his own. Joe had never talked to him like that before. "I was just weighing the odds is all."

"Listen," said the man known to Indians as Winter Bear, "you ain't out here to take care of your own personal quarrel, boy. You're here to protect people like on that train, and you didn't do 'er."

"I rode like hell to get McCollum," Ben defended.

"Too late. You waited too long." Joe's face softened. "For that matter, so did I."

"Oh?"

"I was waitin' for you to start shootin'."

"And if I had?"

"I was goin' to join you." Joe's voice grew hostile again. "But it's your fault because the delay cost lives which could have been saved."

Ben pulled Sam away. He didn't want to hear any more. Joe's words rang true. He'd let personal vengeance stand in the way of his responsibility.

He galloped back to Joe, who was watching the

dead and wounded getting care. It was a sad business. Three bluecoats had been killed, and ten wounded seriously. They would all return in wagons that had been part of the column.

"What about McCollum?" Ben asked. "He was sure dragging his feet."

"That's inexperience," was the rejoinder, "and being a damned fool. But if you'd got back when you should, even McCollum's fiddlin' around wouldn't have been so bad."

"So you're trying to blame the whole thing on me?"

Joe was silent a moment, as though figuring it out.

"Nuh," he said at length, "I won't put it all on you. Them Indians rode up to meet them wagons, and mebbe we wouldn't have got there in time. Mebbe."

"Are we having a fight, Joe?"

"Mebbe." Joe met Ben's eyes squarely. "Look, you're like a son to me, and I want you to do right, Ben. I don't want you to get eat up by your hate. By Gar', I don't want that."

"Is that happening, Joe?"

"I dunno. Mebbe. All's I got to say is be careful of it."

The two were silent a moment. In the meantime, Lt. McCollum and the noncommissioned officers, with Sgt. Clinty directing, were trying to make sense out of chaos. McCollum stayed away from Ben. He preoccupied himself with details that could have just as well been left to the noncoms.

"He's avoidin' you," observed Joe.

"That's all right with me."

"But you saved his worthless hide," Joe pointed out. "We all saw it. Boy, you ain't scared of nothin', are you?" Joe's voice was touched with pride.

"I'd have done the same for a pig," said Ben, and the two smiled at each other. Ben liked that, and he hoped it meant a healing in the rift. He didn't want Joe's anger. The silver-bearded mountain man had become important in his life. Joe had been his main support since his family perished. Joe had been his teacher, his—yes, his father. He wanted no quarrel with this pioneer, this man of men. Yet, Ben had a sad feeling in his heart. Instinctively he felt that, perhaps, Joe was drawing away a little. He hoped not. Time would tell.

McCollum rode up to him. The man's face was as impassive as stone.

"Thanks," he said, "but I'd have made it all right without your help."

Then he galloped off to head up the return column.

"Jackass," muttered Joe. "His scalp would have dangled from some warrior's lodgepole tonight, except for you."

Ben shrugged. "It doesn't matter. I got some Arapahoes. That matters."

"Yeah," muttered Joe, "and that scares me."

"Why should it?"

"Hate, boy. Hate, she's gettin' to you. You kill them people like you was shootin' knots out'n a board. No feelin' in you at all."

"Should there be? Should I feel anything for the people who killed my family?" Ben found his anger rising again. Why shouldn't he hate them? Why was

150

Joe taking their side in this?

"If'n you don't understand, then I allow we shouldn't talk any more about it," was the decisive reply.

"Good enough," cried Ben. He touched Sam with his heels. Sam raced to join McCollum at the head of the troopers.

"You ride at the rear," McCollum snapped to Ben. "Since you're so good with those," he nodded at Ben's pistols, "you can hold off a surprise."

There would be no surprises. Ben knew it, and so did the lieutenant. The war party had had enough. There was no telling how many dead they suffered, because they had managed to cart them off, but many had died. Many more had been wounded and fight had been bled out of the whole band. They would return to their respective tribes. Perhaps they would form again some day, but for now, it was over.

Ben retreated to the rear of the column. On the way, he was greeted by the soldiers with cheers and grins.

"Hey, Iron Heart," said one, "you can patrol with me any time."

Their attitude had changed from what it had been during Ben's first months as a scout. He was a hero to the men. He was respected, and Ben was proud of that. To be respected by such fighting men as these was a high honor. Yet, the sadness in his heart persisted. His friend Joe rode at the head of the column with the lieutenant. Joe might not have considered that a privilege, but what bothered Ben was that his friend never looked back. He never looked back once.

In Fort Laramie, the routine was quickly reestablished and Ben grew restless. He made an effort to see Melanie, and finally succeeded. He met her once again, as he had on their first meeting, as she was returning from a shopping tour at the sutler's store.

He was startled to see how pretty she was. Her dark eyes flashed as she tossed her long, dark hair.

"I hear you are a hero," she said by way of greeting.

"We are all heroes," replied Ben, trying to tease. There was something edgy about this girl he loved, or lusted for.

"Not according to my father," said Melanie firmly. "He talks about it at home all the time. He hated being saved by a low-down, dirty scout like Ben Brand!"

Ben listened to her words in amazement. He couldn't have cared less what McCollum thought, but what about his daughter?

"I don't know what to think," she responded in reply to his question. Her pretty lips pouted. "Honestly, Ben, it's all your fault this has happened."

"I don't understand you," returned Ben, puzzled.

"If you hadn't humiliated my father in front of his men, he wouldn't have broken us up."

"I'm sorry that happened, Melanie."

The girl watched him, from under dark lashes. She shifted her packages from one arm to the other and suddenly blushed.

Ben caught it and knew, instinctively, what to do. He leaned over and kissed the pouty red lips.

The effect was electrifying. He could feel a tingling clear to his toes. He swept her into his arms in a giant hug, feeling her woman's body up against his. Her packages tumbled from her arms. He'd never kissed a woman like that before, but inexperience didn't keep him from savoring every sensual moment. He had no doubt in his mind that what he was feeling was pure lust, and that the same went for the lovely, passionate girl clinging to him.

"Mmmmmm," she murmured. "I've been waiting a long time for this."

"Me, too," Ben whispered huskily. "Me, too."

Into this dreamlike moment, there came a rasp. It took a moment for Ben to realize that the rasp belonged to Lt. McCollum.

"Get away from my daughter, you scum!" he said tightly.

He grabbed Ben by the shoulder and spun him around. Then he hit Ben full in the face. The quirt marks of a few days before were still tender, and McCollum placed his blow well. Ben's senses spun, but he managed to hold his body erect.

In a rage, he jerked his knife from his belt, and squared off. His pistols were in the barracks.

"Ben!" shrieked Melanie. "What are you doing?" She stared at the knife in horror.

Ben came out of his red haze and quickly returned the knife to its place.

"Sorry, Melanie," he said. "I just forgot."

"You could have killed my father," cried Melanie. "While I watched."

McCollum grinned in triumph.

"I told you he was dirt, my girl. Now let's go home. We'll say no more about this, except," he turned a hard eye on Ben, "keep away from Melanie, or I'll kill you."

Ben ignored the remark and looked at Melanie, who had only moments before been a woman, not the "girl" that McCollum addressed.

She answered the question in his eyes with, "Oh, you! I don't know. I just don't know what to think."

With that she burst into tears and ran off, leaving her father behind.

"I'll tell her what to think," said McCollum. "Keep away," he warned. "I meant what I said."

Two days later, Melanie and her mother caught a stage bound for St. Louis. Word reached Ben via gossip, that they would not return. Life at the fort was too hard on them.

Ben had to hand it to Lt. Noel McCollum. He'd won. He missed Melanie. She had been exciting, and he now believed that there was love in his feelings for her. Physical attraction was in their relationship, he admitted, but Melanie had more to offer. She was young, but with maturity she would be a woman a man could hold to him with pride. However, she was also impetuous, and that trait could be an enemy. Lt. McCollum would not always be present to guard against it.

Her departure added to Ben's sadness, which he was able to diagnose as more a sense of loss. He had lost some of Joe's respect. He had lost Melanie and, for him, Fort Laramie had lost all its attraction. He had also lost Tall Dog. The Arapahoe chief had disappeared, except for rumors. He had been seen high in the Rockies; he had been seen near Kearny; he had been seen in Ute country to the southwest; he had been seen on the Rio Grande!

The fact was, nobody knew just where Tall Dog was. It was probable that he'd gone into winter camp. Where that was could be anywhere on the Great Plains, or in the mountains. Arapahoes were at home in both kinds of territory.

A week after Melanie left, Ben walked into town with Joe.

"Joe," he blurted, "I'm leaving Laramie."

Winter Bear nodded. "I ain't surprised," he said, "but hell, was she worth it?"

"You mean Melanie?"

"Yup, unless you got another one tucked away."

"No, I haven't Joe, and it isn't only Melanie."

"Well, what then? McCollum gettin' tough to work for, mebbe?"

"He hasn't been exactly a joy."

"Nuh." Joe grinned. "Old Scowl never will be."

"But it isn't him altogether, either."

"Oh? Well what, then?"

"Joe." Ben searched for words, slightly embarrassed by such talk. "Well, I note we haven't been exactly chums lately."

Joe didn't hedge.

"Yeah, I guess you're right," he said. "I don't know what to say about that, Ben."

"You think I'm wrong, killing the way I do."

"Cold-blooded, like?"

"Yes, if that's how you want to put it."

"It is. I see you in battle and, Ben, I shudder. You got a great hate and I can understand why, but you got to let up. It's already drove a wedge between us."

"I have to get Tall Dog, Joe."

"I can understand that."

155

"And every Arapahoe I see, until I get him, is Tall Dog to me. Don't you understand that?"

"Sure, but," the mountain man shrugged, "but . . ."

He stopped. Words for the deeper emotions were not in his vocabulary. How could he tell this boy he loved like a son that he'd seen others turn into killers, and they never stopped. How could he tell this boy that he loved him like his own, and that he had visions of the boy hanging from the end of a rope? For murder. How could he tell Ben Brand, Iron Heart, he grieved about this? Men didn't talk about such things. There were no words for them. So, Joe Cardwell shrugged. He had no words.

"It's time for me to be moving along," said Ben. "Tall Dog has fell off the earth, and I have to find him."

"Then if'n that's what you must do, do it," replied Joe, "and I got to say, I wish you well, son. Mebbe, as you say, we ain't seemed that close lately, but, well . . . you know what I mean. I wish you the best."

Ben resigned the next day. McCollum received his resignation with the following words: "I'm glad to see you go. You've caused enough trouble for me around here, and I'll tell you something else."

"What, sir?" asked Ben with what he hoped was infuriating politeness.

"You keep away from Tall Dog. Oh, I know what you're after. We all do. The whole country does, but I'm telling you here and now, the Army does the Indian hunting, not civilians. If you kill Tall Dog, I'll see that you're hanged for it."

"Right, sir," replied Ben coolly.

He spun on his heel and went to the paymaster's office. After drawing the pittance the government owed him, he returned to the barracks and rolled up his blankets.

The soldiers were sorry to see him leave.

"It's late in the fall, Ben," said one. "You'll freeze your ass off." He glanced contemptuously around the place. "It ain't much here, but you won't freeze."

But Ben left. Joe accompanied him to the edge of town.

"I'm sorry, lad, for yuh," said the mountain man, "but you have to go, I guess."

"Why are you sorry?" asked Ben.

"Because you ain't never going to know what peace is like until you get Tall Dog, and that might be a long time."

"Not if I go where he is," Ben said.

He stuck out his hand and Joe grasped it. They held thus for a moment, then Ben turned Sam and rode out of town.

Joe watched, his heart heavy. He was going to miss Ben. They'd been companions for a long time, been through a lot and now he was gone. He wondered if they'd ever meet again, and if they did, under what circumstances.

As Joe returned to the barracks, a few snow flakes drifted to the ground. Cold.

This had, indeed, been a cold day.

CHAPTER TWELVE

Ben rode south, shivering as the winds blew down on him from high, snow-capped peaks somewhere in the distance. An advance warning? He wondered. Winter would stiffen the Great Plains soon. It would also impartially stiffen the bones of any who failed to dress properly. Though Ben was well mounted, and armed better than most, his clothing was thin. It was Army issue, and he'd worn the same uniform practically every day since joining.

Had he thought about it, he would have asked the quartermaster to issue him winter clothing before quitting.

But, he had not. Once he made up his mind to leave, leaving was what was on his mind. Not clothes. For a wild instant, Ben thought about returning to Laramie. Maybe he could get Joe to draw some clothing for him. Or he could buy some things at the store. Before the fleeting wish could harden into a decision though, Ben tossed it out of his mind. He didn't want to see Joe again. Not yet, and certainly not to beg for clothes. The stores might have what he needed, but, well, he'd left Laramie and the place was already becoming a chapter in his past. It was a part in the book of his life that he had no wish to read again. Not now.

He urged Sam on. Winter had not arrived yet. It was making its war dance in the distant high mountains and Ben heard the chanting wind, but he wouldn't freeze for awhile.

His one goal in life was to reach Tall Dog. Tall Dog had become his obsession. There was no meaning in his life except that the man responsible for killing his family still lived. The weather, no matter what it might be, hot as the devil's pitchfork or cold as a glacier, hardly counted. The death of Tall Dog counted. Not the weather, not his clothing, not even his falling-out with his treasured friend, Joe. Tall Dog, damn him, was his prime goal in life. To kill him, to deprive him of life. To spill his blood and empty his lungs of all breath for all time to come. That was his purpose. That was what drove him on, like a madness, like a demonic wind roaring in his ears.

Yet, Ben was a practical person. At least that is what he had always believed of himself. If Tall Dog could not be found through the intelligence of the white eyes, he would do well to join the brown. It would be wise to move in with the Indians, live with them, learn their ways, follow them on buffalo trails, see through their eyes, and seeing, perhaps find Tall Dog.

The Indians he chose to dwell with would have to

160

be enemies of the Arapahoe, just as he was. They had to be aggressive, and willing to fight. He had learned, through Fort Laramie talk, that Indians did not war with the whites only. They fought among themselves. They battled over territorial boundaries, hunting grounds; captured slaves, and stole horses from each other. Some tribes sold the slaves in Mexico for horses and blankets. The Amerindian, the native American, was not a peaceful man. He fought for vengeance and, also, simply for the sheer joy of battle. Counting *coup* was a way of life for the awesome Comanches, most powerful of the Plains Indians. Some tribes hated each other and that automatically meant periodic clashes. The Comanches detested the Apaches; the Utes and Kiowas threw the word "friend," out of their mutual greetings; the Cheyennes liked to see Osage scalps dangling from their lodgepoles.

Ben also knew that Indian enmity was an unknown quantity. It could not be counted on. Allegiances changed yearly. If the Comanches raided the Cheyennes for horses, the Cheyennes might call on Osage warriors to combat the menace. If the Utes failed in the hunt for winter meat, they might barter with Kiowas. Enemies became allies in the face of necessity, though that did not mean they would be brothers forever. Expediency plotted the curve of war and peace.

Ben knew what he wanted of the tribe he joined. The people must be fearless, owe no allegiances, and hate Arapahoes. It was a big order, a picky order, and yet there was such a band. They were the Tonkawas, a small tribe named after their chief. They now resided in a southern part of Jefferson Territory, having left Texas, their original home. They were renegades who decided their own fate and were not well received among other Plains Indians. One of the reasons for this was their number, total population about three hundred and fifty. Their wealth was not such that attracted war parties. The Tonkawa didn't want war because their numbers were so low that they were afraid of eventual extinction. They kept a shadowed profile—save for their Arapahoe hatred.

Another reason the Tonkawas were not welcome among the lodges of the other tribes on the Plains was their suspected cannibalism. It was rumored that nothing pleased them more than a haunch of Cheyenne. It didn't matter that some Indian nations practiced incest, others polygamy—the eating of human flesh was taboo.

Ben had heard the talk. The Great Plains was, in a sense, a small community of people. Though separated by vast prairies, one tribe knew what another was doing, knew its customs, and the whites learned by both first-hand experience and trail gossip. Many southwest tribes had practiced cannibalism at one time. It was a custom inherited from ancient Mexican peoples and the Aztecs of a bygone era. Even the northwest Indians who lived along the Pacific Ocean's bountiful rim were known to roast choice portions of a slain enemy. There was no intratribal cannibalism. Victims of war provided the ingredients for which there was a ceremonial overtone.

Ben didn't like that part of the Tonkawa lore he had picked up. The practice of one human eating another chilled him. Yet there was nothing new about it, and Indians were not the only participants. He'd heard of whites, trapped by snow and out of food, resorting to cannibalism. When people were starving, civilization's thin veneer dissolved. When survival depended upon human flesh, the instinct to survive won the wars of custom and conscience.

In spite of what he thought or how he felt, Ben wanted to live with the Tonkawas. His purpose was to find Tall Dog. Tonkawas hated Arapahoes. They could lead him to Tall Dog, if any Indians could.

His intentions resolved, he set out to find them. The southern portion of Jefferson Territory was no small valley. It was big country and Ben had no idea where to look first. He met occasional friendly Indians, with whom he exchanged sign, and he always asked about the Tonkawas. His questions were met with stares. Either he hadn't made his sign clear, or the question was deliberately ignored.

Finding the Tonkawa camp was not going to be easy, but there were ways. One was to send them signals that he, too, was an Arapahoe enemy. If he could not find them, perhaps they would find him. Such a small band could use even a one-man increase.

Ben sought out Arapahoes.

He rode into their country and followed the same antelope and buffalo herds that they did. He looked for loners, scouts, small hunting parties, and then stalked them. He learned much from them, from his first fight.

Three braves ran relays on the antelope. Ben marveled at their horsemanship, their cunning. They were young, he figured, not older than he. The grass was high, the antelope swift, and Ben saw the pattern. One brave started the antelope herd running, and when one of the animals broke away he chased it until the next Arapahoe rode up to relieve him. Then, the third took over at a point where the second brave reined up, his pony pushed to its limit.

The first man waited, and Ben rode up on him.

"I am Iron Heart," he signed, and charged. The two fought with knife and 'hawk. Ben knocked the brave from his pony, leaped down and drove at him with a savagery that made the warrior back up.

Ben came in low, drove his knife into the youth's liver. The brave shuddered and died.

Ben took his scalp and threw it contemptuously on the dead brave's chest.

Then, he waited for the others.

He invaded their territory and fought them. He fought them singly or in small bands. He killed many, took many scalps and, always, he cried, "I am Iron Heart. See me! I am the white man who put your warriors to shame in the mountains. I am he who seeks the justice of vengeance."

How much of this was understood, he wasn't sure. But he knew they understood the words "Iron Heart," and he knew they understood his victory boasts.

He struck and then disappeared, knowing large bands would be looking for him. He became a ghost figure riding the Plains, appearing as if by magic wherever there were only a few Arapahoes. And when the fight was over, he sent survivors fleeing with the ringing words, "I am Iron Heart. I will kill Tall Dog one day."

And after a battle, whether with one warrior or half a dozen, he scalped the slain and laid their scalps on the bodies. This was the height of arrogance, for it signified he found no glory in an Arapahoe scalp. It was as worthless as the life that grew it.

The legend of Iron Heart spread across the Plains. His great hatred for the Arapahoes was known to all, but Ben never sought the fame that came to him. He was looking for the Tonkawa. He was looking for Tall Dog. For him life was simple. Far to the north, Lt. Noel McCollum heard of a white man who rampaged among the Arapahoe and he knew who it was. He had warned Brand. He could now hang him. McCollum smiled. Some time he would capture the fellow, and see him dangle at the end of a rope. It would be one of the few satisfactory moments in his life.

Joe Cardwell, Winter Bear, also heard of Ben's daring and ruthlessness. If he'd have known how to pray, he would have done so, but he did not. All he could do for Ben was wish him safety and hope the boy's fire would not consume him. He, too, was worried about their split and he thought about it often, but he never regretted his words to Ben Brand. Because of Ben and Joe, for Joe included himself, people had lost their lives. Responsibility without substance had led to tragedy. Joe couldn't bring himself to blame McCollum's foot-dragging, though it did contribute, no doubt. The blame must, finally, rest with Ben. He hoped the boy had learned. Young ones were apt to make mistakes. He wished Ben well.

Winter, poised over the Plains like an upland cougar, pounced at last. Ben closed his eyes one night on a clear sky. The stars were silvery diamonds on black velvet. When he flicked his eyes open in the morning, the world was white. A wet, sticky snow was falling, the season's first. It wouldn't last because the ground was not frozen yet, but it was an earnest warning.

Ben shook the snow from his blankets and built a fire. Sam, tied to a bush several yards away with enough rope to graze, gazed at him reproachfully.

"There's enough feed for you, if that's why you keep giving me those looks," said Ben defensively. He examined the dried grass clumps. The wet snow had fallen thickly and several inches lay on the ground.

"But," he admitted, "give it two, three more weeks, my friend, and you'll have to dig some. We got to find those Tonkawas. They are probably camped where winter graze is good. Maybe down by the Arkansas."

He hung a pail of snow water over the flames and boiled some coffee. He mixed some flour and water and strung a length of dough around a stick. Then he baked it slowly while he hunkered next to the fire, turning the stick to bake his bread evenly. He was not the best camp cook in the west. He was not even the most mediocre. He didn't like cooking but did so because he had to eat. Sam could have bunch grass. No preparation whatsoever. All Sam had to do was wrap his lips around a chosen sheaf and flip the stuff into his mouth.

"Sam," declared Ben, "you sure have an easy . . ."

He broke off. Sam's ears were perked and he was staring at a point over Ben's shoulder. Suddenly, the horse whickered, and Ben sprang to his feet. An arrow sang past the spot where he'd squatted moments before.

The arrow was followed by three Arapahoes. They were mounted and bore down on him, yelling in triumph. One stopped and fitted another arrow to his bow. He shot rapidly, a snap shot, the equivalent of firing a pistol from the hip. The archer was good, for the arrow struck Ben in his chest. In spite of himself, he felt the world slipping away. He fell to his knees, firing both the Dragoon and the .44 Navy Colt. The heavy pistols bucked in his hands and just before his world swam away over a dark horizon, he saw one of his attackers crumple.

Then the white, wet earth claimed him. He toppled forward on the arrow thinking that was the end of him.

When he regained consciousness, he was immediately aware of his situation. Hushed voices drifted to his ears. Odd. Arapahoes should be chanting victory songs over downing Iron Heart. He lay perfectly still, listening. The words spoken were not those of the Arapahoe tongue. He dared a look, opening his eyes a squint. He did not recognize the tribe. They were Plains Indians. That was all he knew.

A pain stabbed his chest and he groaned involuntarily.

The Indians hovered over him in an instant. They smiled. Their dark eyes were concerned, their weathered faces reflected kind intentions.

"Iron Heart?" asked one.

Ben nodded. The pain in his chest was ghastly. He coughed and blood spilled from his lips. He spat and cleansed his mouth.

He had one question.

"Arapahoe?"

He asked, using English for the spoken word, but universal signs to back it up.

The Indian who had spoken gave a grunt and pointed.

Three bodies lay sprawled twenty or thirty feet from the fire. The Indian held up one finger and nodded to Ben. Then he held up two fingers and made a circle in the air, encompassing himself and the others. From that, Ben knew they'd saved his life. What he didn't know was how they guessed he was Iron Heart. After all, there were many whites in the country, loners like himself. Why hadn't they killed him? His weapons and horse were valuable booty. Nobody would have known Tonkawas had murdered a white man. The blame could be placed on any of half a dozen tribes.

He tried sitting up again. Coughed more blood and noticed the gaping hole in his chest. The sight of it, raw and bloody, made him giddy and he nearly fainted. Strong hands eased him gently back to the ground and he lay still awhile, gathering strength. One thing was certain: He was among friends.

One brought him coffee. He drank it gratefully, for he was burning up and any liquid, even hot coffee, soothed his parched mouth.

One of the Indians pointed to Ben's chest and jerked his hand back. It was he who had pulled the arrow free. Ben nodded thanks.

The question persisted: How did they know he was Iron Heart?

He began the complicated procedure of finding out. Using a combination of signs, English, Arapahoe, and Comanche, which he'd learned from Joe, Ben finally made his question clear.

Ben counted six warriors. When they understood what he was asking, they laughed softly in unison, a sound of reeds brushed by the wind. One pointed at Sam, and Ben got the point at once. Sam, the black and white pinto, was the horse Iron Heart rode. Sam was as well known as he.

"Nicely done," he muttered to the horse. "You probably saved my life, Sam boy."

The pain came again and with it more coughing, more blood. The fever mounted, and in spite of the chill weather, Ben broke into a sweat. He felt hot liquid on his chest. Boiling water, he thought. Somebody was washing his wound. He felt Sam under him, and a rawhide rope tied him in place.

He had no idea how far they traveled. He drifted in and out of consciousness, babbled in delirium. The world grew large, then small many times, as his fever attacked, then receded. At all times, he knew he was being gently treated. His wound was bathed regularly, and his bodily functions attended to with the help of gnarled, but impersonal, hands.

After several days of travel—Ben was never sure of the number—they arrived at a village. A river, now frozen, snaked past and Ben guessed it was the Arkansas. The entire population turned out to greet them and it seemed to be a joyous occasion. Men, women, and children whooped and smiled at Ben and he saw people sign the name Iron Heart often.

A powerful man strode through the crowd and gave the welcome sign to Ben. Ben, still weak, returned the courtesy. He swayed on Sam and was quickly helped to the ground. He was taken to the powerful man's teepee and placed on a bed of buffalo hides and blankets. Somebody brought him water, which he drank eagerly. Food was placed beside him but he wasn't hungry.

His host nodded at that, but sighed, "You well?"

Ben returned the nod. He was well, but sleepy, and his eyelids kept drooping on him.

"I am Tonkawa," said the powerful man, "chief of this people."

"I've been looking for you," Ben replied, using his polyglot language.

"And we, you," was the reply. The chief seemed pleased. "My braves search for you many moons, but you are like spirit. You melt into the sky like warm mists from hot springs. You strike Arapahoe, kill them and are gone. But," he touched Ben's arm, "we find you. You will be one of us now. You want that?"

Ben signed yes, that it was good what Chief

Tonkawa said. Yes. Then he slipped into a deep sleep. The buffalo robes, soft as feathers to him after weeks of blankets and bare ground, wrapped him in a cocoon of comfort and security.

Even in his half-dazed state, Ben knew he was home at last.

CHAPTER THIRTEEN

Ben's wound was more ragged than deep.

The Tonkawa tribe thought the white warrior was protected by the Great Spirit.

Ben did not tell them any different.

He examined the torn flesh to see why the Arapahoe arrow hadn't taken his life. The head had been deflected by a large button on his Army jacket. The flint carried into his chest, glanced again, this time off his breast bone. By a miracle the shaft had sunk a couple of inches into the cavity between his lungs, missing them. Though he coughed up quantities of blood, the wound had not been mortal.

Through herbal medicines and continual care, Ben's wound began to heal.

"You will have mark," signed Tonkawa, who had made Ben his special responsibility.

Ben assumed the chief meant a scar. He didn't mind. In fact, he took pride in it. He now had two, both the product of Arapahoe arrows, one in his back, one in front. They were proof that he had stood against his enemy. They were, to him, medals proving combat and honor.

Tonkawa, the chief, was intrigued by this white boy/man who had fought the detested Arapahoe single-handedly. Had, indeed, gone looking for them. He sat by Ben's couch of buffalo hides for hours, saying nothing, speaking if Ben wished to speak.

Ben was confined for nearly a month, except for trips to the place of personal business once or twice a day. In that time, he made it a point to learn as much of the Tonkawa language as possible. It would be important later on.

He found that the six braves who had saved his life had been present through no accident. They'd seen the yellow of his fire and had approached cautiously on foot. It wasn't until they saw the black and white pinto Sam, that they began to understand who this lone man was. At about the time they made that discovery, the Arapahoes had struck. In time, the fight would become Tonkawa legend, recorded in that year's winter count.

"My braves look for you many moons," said Tonkawa. "There were this many parties looking for you." The chief held up three fingers. "We want you. We know what you are saying when you kill Arapahoe and boast 'I am Iron Heart.' Across the winds we heard you cry and we search for you."

"I am glad that the winds were my friend," said Ben, "or my scalp would now be dried in some Arapahoe teepee."

"When," he asked one day, "do we ride again?"

Tonkawa's face was so deeply lined it was difficult

to read any expression in it, but Ben saw amusement in the chief's eyes.

"We won't seek Arapahoe until our horses can eat the fresh grass," he said. "They would starve if we left now. Also," a gnarled hand touched Ben's chest lightly, "I think you had better be still yet awhile."

Ben understood. Tonkawa was not a hasty man. He had survived a nomadic life because he thought things out. If the young white eyes was impatient, if he wanted Arapahoe scalps, that was good—but he would have to wait for the proper time. The time was not now.

Ben chafed, but he understood. He knew, also, that his wound was slow in healing and he was not ready to travel yet, but his impatience was difficult to contain. He wanted Tall Dog. He had said nothing of his personal wish. It was a goal he kept to himself. An obsession so consuming as this would lose power with talk. Already too many knew of it. Joe did, and also McCollum. There were too many who knew his secret already. Too much talk of these things was like an arrow shot too far. The target would shrug the arrow off like an insect.

Still, the questions would come. They were inevitable.

One Finger, so called because the index finger on his left hand was missing, asked the question.

"Why do you hate Arapahoe?"

"Because they killed my family," replied Ben. "They murdered my family without a chance."

"You have vowed revenge?"

"I have. And I have kept my word."

"Ahhhh," agreed One Finger, "it is known."

If the Tonkawas suspected any further motives, they made no hints, asked no more questions.

It was his turn to ask questions.

"Why are you here? I have heard you were first in Rio Grande country."

Chief Tonkawa answered him. He was not an old man, though no longer young. Ben judged him to be about the same age as Joe Cardwell, nudging fifty, perhaps.

"We do not hate whites as many Indians do. We became Army scouts in Texas for the Rangers. Other Indians don't like us for what we do. We are traitors, they say."

Tonkawa snorted derisively.

"Traitors? Ha! We are not big tribe. Other Indians they trip to wipe us out. They want our horses, our weapons, our women. So we get whites on our side. It is better they are for us than against us. We are safe— or that is what we think."

The chief shook his head.

"Then Texas quit fighting. They join what you whites call a Union, many tribes all bound together. They do not need us any more, and we are turned loose. It is like the lamb facing twenty knives."

"So you left that part of the country?"

"We leave, yes, but not before we fight many fight and lose many warriors." He drew himself up proudly. "We are not afraid."

"No," said Ben quickly. "I know you have strong hearts—courage."

"But we are small tribe. We cannot survive for long when so many are against us. Arapahoe, they are the worst. They kill our warriors, take our women, burn

176

our villages, so we must leave. We are here now. It is a good place."

"But you still fight Arapahoe."

"Whenever we can," was the heated response, "for as long as the heart beats in the last brave, we will fight them."

Among those who cared for Ben was a girl named Blue Flower. Her hands were cool when he was fevered, her voice soothing when he woke in the night trembling from nightmarish dreams. She was his day-to-day nurse. When he was still too weak to walk to the place of personal business, it was Blue Flower who cared for him. She showed no embarrassment, but Ben was bothered about it. He was highly thankful when he could walk and went to the place in the company of men.

The girl was the daughter of a warrior, Strong Arm, who had been in the party that rescued Ben. He was a respected man in the tribe and was often made war chief when raiding parties were conducted against the Arapahoe. He visited Ben often.

As Ben grew stronger and was able to ride Sam again, Strong Arm accompanied him several times. There was always one brave with him, sometimes two, and Ben realized this was because, as Iron Heart, he was Big Medicine. His feats were known throughout the land and his being with the Tonkawa sent a signal to the other tribes. Beware! We have the man of many lives in our midst and he is a friend. His presence would help keep raiding Arapahoe away and, on the other hand, his being there would draw them, too. It was a paradox and Ben decided not to dwell on it. He would take life one day at a time.

Ben eventually moved out of Tonkawa's teepee and into one of his own. It was provided by Tonkawa himself, an honor. Strong Arm and One Finger gave Ben buffalo robes and utensils so that he had comforts as good as any the Great Plains could provide.

There was one thing wrong with his life and One Finger brought it up.

"You have no woman," the Indian said on one of their rides together.

"No," agreed Ben.

"You must have a woman."

"Why?"

"Because you have no family here. A man without a woman is no good. Who will cook your food? Make your clothes? Comfort you in bed?" One Finger shook his head in dissatisfaction. "No, you must have a wife."

Ben was startled. A wife? Not since Melanie had he thought of marriage, or even of lust. His life had been too full of fighting and recovering from his wound. But a lull had come into his life. There was no fighting. His wound was healing. Spring was a long way off yet, when Arapahoe hunting would fill his time again. He was a bachelor in a tribe where such a status was considered a lack of responsibility. Marriage meant children, and children would build up the tribe's strength once again. Every man and woman had a duty to the survival of the Tonkawa as a band.

"But I am not one of you," Ben objected. "And I have no horses."

"You belong to Tonkawa Indians," said One

Finger, "and we will give you horses."

What One Finger was saying was that Ben had been adopted into the tribe. He was also saying that he would be given five horses for his own from the tribe's stock. Ben would send the horses to a girl's family as a gift, and the gift would be an offer of marriage.

Ben thought. Had he not sought the Tonkawas in hopes of spending a safe and warm winter? Had he not wanted new clothing? Had he not wanted Tonkawa knowledge about Tall Dog? Though he had not himself spoken of the Arapahoe chief, the Tonkawa had a good idea where the main body of Arapahoe were. Tall Dog would be with them. And had not Tonkawas saved his life?

For all of this, Ben felt he owed them something. He would marry. He did, in fact, look forward to it. He had felt a lack in his life. He had wandered much since his family had been killed and he missed the reality of a home hearth, the stability. But what girl should he choose? There were a dozen maidens in the village, any of whom he could have. One Finger solved his dilemma.

"You are blind?" he asked.

"What do you mean?" Ben was puzzled.

"Blue Flower. She of the gentle hands, she who helped you in personal matters when you were weak, she the daughter of Strong Arm. You think she has no feelings, eh?"

"No," replied Ben. "I am not blind, but I thought she was taken."

"You will get your five horses now. Come."

Ben accompanied One Finger to Tonkawa's

teepee. The two men talked so rapidly in their native tongue, Ben found it difficult to follow. He did glean this much from their rapid-fire talk: He was to be given the horses, he would take them to Blue Flower's lodge. If she accepted them, it meant she would marry him.

The horses were fine, long-legged, deep-chested ponies, descendants of Spanish stock. In Tonkawa eyes, they were prize animals, built for endurance and speed.

He left the horses in front of the lodge, as directed. Then returned to his own teepee to wait for Blue Flower's decision. According to his inner clock, half an hour passed. The palms of his hands were sweating, for this was an unknown. He never realized he could be so nervous in a nonbattle situation, but it seemed that romancing was not so simple as it appeared.

When an hour by the gut clock had passed, Strong Arm stood before Ben's teepee. He had five different horses with him.

"Blue Flower accepts your offer," said Strong Arm formally. "She sends you these in return." He smiled. "We will have a wedding feast tomorrow."

"You mean I've been accepted?" asked Ben, astonished by the simplicity of the ceremony.

"When hearts mingle, need there be long words?" Strong Arm replied.

No, thought Ben, there needn't be. Yet, he couldn't help thinking what a difference there was in marrying Blue Flower compared to Melanie. Had Melanie's father approved, there would have been a six-month's engagement period, then a three-month period before the wedding. There would have been weeks and weeks of preparation—a minister to be found, wedding dress and uniforms to be tailored, a feast to be planned, best man and best woman to be chosen. Ben would have chosen Joe to be his best man.

Here, on the Great Plains, marriage was taken in all seriousness, but matters moved much more swiftly. The feast was a bounty of buffalo, deer, and antelope meat, both roasted and stewed. There was quail and jackrabbit and snake, which was considered a delicacy. The snakes had been found hibernating in caves and killed for the occasion. Wild peas and prairie turnips were fed into the stew. Dried corn, beans, and squash rounded out the meal, and Ben was curious. Where had the Tonkawas obtained the domestic vegetables? In trade with other Indians, who grew them?

After the feast, Ben and Blue Flower retired to his teepee. She had already brought her wardrobe, cooking utensils, and blankets. Once inside, they were allowed their own world, allowed to be by themselves.

Ben found the moment exceedingly awkward. What to do? He knew what passion was. He had found it with Melanie. But he had known her and had not been bashful. Though he had just married Blue Flower, she was still a stranger to him. Though she had nursed him in intimate moments, he felt no closeness to her and the memory only fueled his shyness.

"It will be all right," said Blue Flower.

"What will?" Ben almost shouted.

"You and I together," said the girl.

She sat next to him and placed her hand on his. It was a simple gesture, but so gentle, so loving, so assured, that Ben's awkwardness dissolved like frost at the edge of fire. This dark woman of the prairie was offering herself to him. She was not acquainted with false coyness. She had no meaningless sophistication, no arch preamble. She was his wife. She wanted him and she made it known to him.

All at once Ben warmed to the girl by his side. He was seized with a great, quiet joy as he kissed her on the lips. She gazed into his eyes with an expression of such devotion, that Ben knew he would, on that night, complete his voyage into manhood. He had fought, he had killed, he had been foolish and irresponsible. He had known what lust was and he knew the power of hatred. All of these things were adult, but he was not yet a man. He was only part of a man, for he had not known the love of a woman.

Until now.

And now—the time had come.

CHAPTER FOURTEEN

Ben rode with the Tonkawas when they hunted buffalo. His Sharps brought meat to the band and they praised his marksmanship.

"Rifle shoot far, kill much," said Strong Arm in admiration.

Ben let the braves shoot the Sharps. It was something one learned to do because it held a heavy charge of powder. He loaded the rifle with ninety to a hundred grains of FFFg black powder for big game. Several braves sprawled on their backs after pulling the trigger. The rifle carried a potent kick. The Tonkawas owned guns, old muzzle-loading percussion and flintlock weapons, into which they could measure their own amounts of powder. None banged their shoulders like the Sharps.

"You got to keep it tight against your shoulders," Ben instructed. "A loose rifle butt is like the hind heel of your horse."

During those next two years, Ben changed considerably. He became, in effect, an Indian. He dressed as they did, ate as they, spoke in their tongue. He learned to use the bow and hunted more often with this weapon than with his rifle. He saved his ammunition for Arapahoe hunting.

There were many scrapes with Arapahoe braves, usually on hunting forays. Whenever Ben saw Arapahoes, he fought with them. If he was alone, he charged into them, pistols smoking. If he was with the Tonkawa, he held his counsel and a senior brave plotted the course of attack.

And whenever he fought, Ben cried, "I am Iron Heart! Tell your people."

In the second year, Tonkawa decided to move the band westward to the foot of the mountains.

"There is good water there," he told his council, "and sweet grass for the horses."

It was also rumored that Tall Dog was not far off. Tales of his exploits came to the Tonkawa camp. Tall Dog had massacred a family of whites in the mountains; he had attacked a wagon train; he had fought with soldiers. Ben wondered if they were Laramie soldiers, and if Joe had been with them.

Joe would no doubt know where his former partner was, and that he'd become an Indian. Although the Tonkawa were friendly with whites, it wasn't always true in reverse. Bluecoats, under inexperienced officers, struck at any Indians. They shot first and asked questions afterward. Should that happen, would Iron Heart fight the soldiers?

"It is difficult to kill one's own kind," said Tonkawa during a council meeting, "but we have asked the question among ourselves, Iron Heart, and ask you. Would you shoot at soldiers?"

Could he, Ben asked himself, fire at Joe? Would Joe fire on him?

He was now a Tonkawa brave. Because of his fearless attacks on the Arapahoe, he had lately been named chief of hunting parties. The next step would be war chief. To be a war chief, he owed allegiance to the Tonkawas. It was a responsibility—his mind flashed to Joe's anger, when, in Joe's lights, Ben had failed his responsibility prior to the three-wagon fight. Ben had delayed letting the troops know, because of his personal vendetta, and had cost lives. If he were made war chief, and they faced the whites, could he refuse to return fire? No. He would have to accept the responsibility. He would have to give the order to shoot.

"I would shoot," he said to Tonkawa, and the others nodded. Iron Heart's word was his law. He would live by it.

It was here that Ben resorted to subterfuge. He didn't want a confrontation with any troops, so he told Tonkawa something that might—or might not—have been the truth.

"If we fight white eyes," he said, "and we lose, we will be sent to a reservation. It will be like prison."

"We will win," said Tonkawa.

Ben shook his head.

"You know different," he replied. "Some of your braves scout for the bluecoats now. They bring stories of how many soldiers there are." Ben shook his head. "The Tonkawa is a proud warrior with great courage, but one man cannot stand against as many as there are stars in the sky."

It was an exaggeration, but Ben wanted to make

his point clear.

"Tonkawa does not like reservations," said Tonkawa, spitting.

"Then we must be careful," argued Ben, and the chief nodded.

Ben knew that his own arguments would have meant little had it not been for the backing of the Army scouts. And there was Tonkawa's intelligence to be reckoned with as well.

"It was not always like this," the chief told Ben one evening, when they smoked the pipe in Tonkawa's teepee. "Once the whites and Indians lived together in peace."

Ben remembered Joe, and the mountain man's words about that. He, too, had known shining times.

"But in recent snows," said the chief, "many whites have come." The Tonkawa leader frowned. "Too many, like rain from the sky. People, they come and build houses and live in them. People who know of a great God in the sky, they come. Many and most go far into Ute country. Other whites look for yellow dust. With the new grasses after winter, more come, more and more, and they shoot buffalo. I don't know how many they kill, but we must now hunt for them. Not so long ago, buffalo come to us. The Great Spirit sent them to us."

One Finger and Strong Arm were present during this talk. They agreed with their chief.

"Once, long ago, some Indian tribes do not belong here. Cheyenne come from across the big rivers. Yes, and Cherokee and Choctaw. White Father send them to Indian Territory. Dakota come down from Dakota land then trouble begins for all."

Tonkawa took a long pull on his pipe and let clouds of smoke drift toward the teepee's smoke hole, before he continued. Each man had his own pipe, for this was not an official ceremony and ritual was not necessary.

"Buffalo were what we all ate. Buffalo supplied us with robes and lodges, without buffalo we were poor, but the buffalo were disappearing. If too many are killed here, they will move to safer place. We must follow. If safer place is in Arapahoe hunting ground, they will fight us. It is the same all over. Now whites come, and they kill buffalo. Buffalo move, and we move, and Indians fight for survival."

For the first time, Ben began to see the Indian's side of what was a battle to stay alive. He began to understand why the whites were intruders to the Indians, interlopers that could endanger their livelihood. Among themselves, the whites were settlers, prospectors, traders, and trappers, but to the Indians transplanted by Presidential decree twenty or so years before, the whites proved an intolerable addition. As many buffalo as there were, there were simply not enough. So there was war and hatred and massacres.

"The Arapahoe," said One Finger, "are called the Blue Cloud People by some, because they seek peace." His eyes grew hot. "But they follow us, want our buffalo, our women, and they make war. They," he glanced swiftly at Ben, "kill your own people. That," he finished with great irony, "is not peaceful."

"I want to kill Tall Dog," said Ben suddenly. It seemed the time to talk of the matter.

Tonkawa nodded. "Yes. We know that."

Ben was not surprised. He should have known. The people he lived with were not ignorant savages. They were, in their own land, highly cultivated. Their customs went back hundreds of years. They also knew about vengeance and how it must be won. If Arapahoes had massacred his family, their chief must somehow pay. Tall Dog was chief. The Tonkawas knew he must be the one Ben really sought.

"I have waited long enough," said Ben. "It is time for me to act."

"You do not ask us to go with you?" asked Tonkawa.

"I have no wish to put your braves in the way of enemy weapons. This is my private matter."

Tonkawa shook his head. "No," he said. "you are one of us now. If you fight, we fight. We will make up a war party."

"But . . ." Ben began, but Tonkawa raised his hand for silence.

"Don't you think, Iron Heart, that we, the others of us in your tribe, need to fight with the Arapahoe, too? We are tired of their war. We will end it."

And so it was decided. A war party of sixty braves, led by Tonkawa, Strong Arm, and One Finger, would search for Tall Dog's band. It would be a decisive battle, winner take all.

Scouts were sent out and returned with exciting news. Tall Dog had murdered a white family on the South Platte. Soldiers were looking for him and Tall Dog was on the run.

"Who are the soldiers?" Ben asked.

"One who leads is called Scowl. One who scouts is

called Winter Bear."

Ben's heart bumped. There was going to be a head-on collision between the Tonkawa and bluecoats. He could feel it in his bones. They were both after the same quarry and their trails would cross. Would he pull his Dragoon on Joe Cardwell?

Yet, he could no longer wait for his meeting with Tall Dog. Nearly three years had passed since his family was killed. In the meantime, Tall Dog had killed many more, and was still at it. The hatred in Ben had not lessened. When he killed an Arapahoe he scalped his victim with a savagery that pulled grunts from even the most experienced Tonkawa brave. They approved. Here was a man who knew how to kill. None of the Arapahoe who fell to his pistols lived to tell of it. If they were still alive when Ben dashed to their sides for his trophy, he split their skulls with one powerful chop of his tomahawk. He delighted in their death struggles and laughed at the Reaper's involuntary dance.

It was fall again. Late fall, and Ben noted the timing. It was said that Tall Dog was taking his people into the mountains. Deep snow would make it impossible to track him down. He would be safe for another winter. In the spring, he would melt away with the snow and the hunt would go on for perhaps another year.

"We do not know the mountains well," said Tonkawa at an official council. "If Tall Dog goes far, we will lose him."

"I think I know where he is going," said Ben. "I think I can beat the bluecoats to him."

"How do you know this, Iron Heart?"

189

"He is in the mountains above the place where I lived, where my family died. It is the place where my family's blood flowed into a little stream above the plain where the big river runs."

Tonkawa nodded.

"Mmmmmm." He looked at the others in council. "It is good."

There was no dissent.

"I realize now," said Ben softly, so that all present must lean forward to hear, "that Tall Dog's country is in the mountains. That is why he disappears like a ghost. He makes a village in the high mountains for the winter and cannot be found."

The others nodded. "It is so."

The mountains where Tall Dog was thought to be were many sleeps away. Ben put it at two to three weeks of travel, at a steady pace.

"And if we run into Arapahoe hunting parties," Tonkawa said, "none can escape to bring the news to Tall Dog."

There was preparation for the journey. Good horses must be chosen, for the trail would be arduous. Pemmican was crammed in elkhide pouches, but the warriors would live mainly off the land as they traveled. Bows and arrows and lances would be the weapons, to save powder and ball, and to eliminate noise.

"Sound like rifle," said Strong Arm, "carry far in cold, thin fall air."

Dances were held and the entire tribe joined in. Even the women, who were not allowed to join the men, danced on the sidelines. This was an important event. Much depended on the outcome. If Tall Dog could be defeated, the Tonkawa would live in peace, at least for awhile. Tonkawa hunting grounds would not be invaded, wives and children would be safe. There were other Arapahoe bands, but they were far to the south, and would not be a threat. Tall Dog was their enemy. He who had left his own nation to become a leader of his own band, was considered a renegade by both Arapahoe chiefs and the military. With Tall Dog out of the way, Tonkawas would need to fear nothing.

"Yet," said Tonkawa himself, "we need to fear all, for we are a small tribe. One big battle could be the end of us as a people."

This tendency to forecast and to be forewarned, was one of the qualities that made Tonkawa a good chief. He left nothing to chance, never relaxed his guard.

During his own preparations for the trip of his life, Ben noted that Blue Flower was unusually quiet.

"Why is my woman so still?" he asked, teasing. "Her tongue is frozen to the bottom of her mouth. What must I do to thaw it?"

"Do not go on this journey," came the unexpected reply.

Ben was stopped dead in his teasing.

"But I must go," he said. "It is what I have lived for."

"You have lived to kill Tall Dog?"

"Yes."

"You have not lived or me, for us, for our lodge together?"

So that was it.

Ben was quick to reply. "I have lived the life of a

man with you, Blue Flower. You have made me a whole man, not just part of one. This lodge, it is my home. You, you are my family. You fill my heart, and I leave with my heart on the ground."

"But must you go?"

"Would you have me stay here, while others fight my fight?"

Blue Flower shook her head but, like a flower in the fall, she drooped.

Ben took her to him. He heard her heart thumping under her buckskin dress. His own heart matched hers, and the two allowed the rhythm to continue unaltered by outside sounds for several moments.

"We are good together," Blue Flower murmured.

"Yes."

"If you go, our hearts will no longer touch."

"What do you mean?"

"If you kill Tall Dog, then it will be over. You will have fulfilled your destiny. Like the sun, your hate has heated your body, but when Tall Dog is gone, the sun will set and shadows grow. You will forget Blue Flower. You will no longer need to be Indian."

Except in grief, Plains women wept little. Their lives were fashioned after a pattern of hard living. Plains women were accustomed to extreme cold, to marrow-sucking heat, to hunger, to the pain of childbirth, to constant uprooting as they searched for food. Bad as these conditions were, they were part of a pattern of long standing, and the women accepted what life offered. If a man died, though, whether of sickness or enemy tomahawk, he could not be replaced. His passing left a gap never to be filled, and this was cause for grief.

As Blue Flower gazed at Ben, tears filled the brown eyes.

"What's this?" questioned Ben. "I am not dead, woman." He kissed her. "Why do you weep?"

"No," murmured Blue Flower, "you are not dead. You might not die in the days to come, but you are dead to me."

"I will return," swore Ben. "You are life for me."

He kissed her again, and it became quiet in the teepee of Iron Heart.

Later, in his deepest thoughts, he wondered at Blue Flower's words. After Tall Dog's death, and Ben was sure the Arapahoe chief would die, how would Iron Heart feel? Did Blue Flower speak a truth? Would his destiny be finished here?

And Ben admitted in the soul of his mind, that Blue Flower could well be prophetic.

In killing Tall Dog, would he not also kill Iron Heart as well?

CHAPTER FIFTEEN

The war party left the next day.

Ben twisted around on Sam to see Blue Flower. He waved and the wave was returned, but there was no happiness on his wife's face. Other women called to their braves and made promises of a great feast on their return, but Blue Flower's lips were silent.

"Young women," said Tonkawa, who had observed, "sometimes do not understand war."

"Perhaps that is it," agreed Ben, though he knew why sadness lay in Blue Flower's heart.

He turned resolutely away, to ride silently by Tonkawa's side.

Ben Brand, known always to the Tonkawas as Iron Heart, had earned his position by the chief's side. He was a fierce warrior and had proved his bravery in many skirmishes with the Arapahoe. He was a good hunter, skilled with both the bow and lance. He had learned the Tonkawa tongue well, a fact that pleased the people. After two years, it was said only half-jokingly, that Iron Heart was more Indian than the most resolute Tonkawa.

For this journey, for this trail to destiny, Iron Heart had been made a war chief. The way he rode, back straight, eyes ahead, but always watchful, the way he spoke, direct and to the point, stirred excitement in the breasts of those who followed. They knew this was not going to be an ordinary raid. Iron Heart was not after a few scalps, Tonkawa was not after just booty. Big Medicine was in the making. They knew, with so many braves in the party, that something great was about to happen, and Iron Heart was leading them to it. That was good. They would follow the young chief where he led them, for he was trusted.

One thing that galled Ben was the necessity for hiding whenever Arapahoes were sighted. It had become his habit, almost by now his instinct, to rush into Arapahoes on sight, but if he did so on this journey, word would get back to Tall Dog. That would not do. Ben wanted to surprise his enemy. He wanted him face to face. He would not use his Dragoon or his Navy Colt on Tall Dog. His Sharps would remain in its elkhide scabbard. He would challenge Tall Dog, man to man, knife against knife, tomahawk against tomahawk. It was the only way he could fight Tall Dog. He had to *feel* this man's body against his. He had to test the muscles of the other, the strength, the fighting drive, and he had to overcome them all. A bullet would not do for Tall Dog, and Ben made sure that every brave knew it.

"Tall Dog is mine," he told them after their first day's journey. "Let no man take him, unless I am dead."

It was understood.

They traveled northwest for a week, until they reached the Platte, then they turned north. If Ben was right, Tall Dog would be a day's journey beyond his former home. He would be in the high mountains, near a pass. He would probably be near the forks of the St. Vrains rivers. There were elk in that country, and deer, and sometimes sheep. It was good hunting, and Tall Dog would camp there.

Scouts sent ahead by Tonkawa, returned with news.

"Arapahoe are near town of Cherry Creek now."

"Good," said Ben.

"Also, bluecoats come down from the north. Scowl leads."

That wasn't so good. It could work out against his wishes, if the soldiers reached Tall Dog first. Damn McCollum. For that matter, damn Joe, the Winter Bear, for it was he who guided the troopers through the mysteries of the mountains. That ass McCollum couldn't find his way to the mess hall without a lifeline. And Joe was probably guessing where Tall Dog would camp. He would aim for that place, and he would not miss.

Tonkawa sent the scouts out again. They watched not only for Arapahoe and bluecoats now, but any Indian. Nobody must know that a party of Tonkawa was in the region, for it was known throughout the Plains that Iron Heart was the enemy of Tall Dog. Should the Tonkawas be seen, Tall Dog would hear of it.

Reaching a ford, the war party crossed the Platte above Cherry Creek. That night they made a cold camp and Ben could see the lights of Cherry Creek shimmering in the distance. It was a sad sight for him, bringing memories of a terrible day three years before. He gripped his tomahawk and chanted to himself. He shut his eyes against Cherry Creek, but he could not shut his mind to the fires of memory. He thought of his own family, and of Martha and the Locks family, and of the drummer, and when the sun rose, Ben had not slept. The sky was bloodred, and so were his thoughts.

They rode into the hills now, following a course by landmark. Ben knew the hills they traveled now and steered by them. To the left of a high chimney, to the right of a jutting rock. Through a valley of pine so narrow it was a perfect V. Ben had been through these hills with his father on the several occasions they visited Cherry Creek.

They passed the latitude that would have taken them to Ben's old home. He was tempted to detour for a look. He wanted to see if the grave remained untouched, but there was no time for it. Tall Dog would be close to his winter camp now. He would also have his own scouts on reconnaissance, and if they sighted the Tonkawa band, they might run. They could, also, stand and fight, but Ben wanted to take no chances. The sooner he caught up the better.

Iron Heart was now in full charge of the war party. Tonkawa gave him this honor because of the young white warrior's knowledge of the country. The Tonkawa were Plains Indians, and had little to do with mountains.

On the second night after leaving the lights of Cherry Creek, a scout brought news. Scowl's column was also deep in the moutains, and was trying to reach the pass. Once there, Ben knew, McCollum would take a careful look. Joe Cardwell would know where to search. He would find Tall Dog's camp and report it to Scowl, good old Lt. Noel McCollum, and McCollum would rush into battle.

Ben shivered. To be beaten out of his just reward by a fool, after three years, would be an irony he could never forget. He must get to Tall Dog first. He knew shortcuts. He would take them.

That night a messenger from the Tonkawa village hundreds of miles away, arrived. He went directly to Iron Heart.

"My news is for you," he said.

Ben was alarmed. "Blue Flower," he exclaimed, "is she all right?"

"Oh, yes," was the happy reply. "She will have your child in the spring."

So, Blue Flower was pregnant. He, Iron Heart, was to become a father. Ben grinned widely, because the news pleased him. Under Tonkawa law, he could return. He could leave the war party, for it was voluntary, even insofar as he was concerned. He could return to Blue Flower. Tonkawas believed the father of the child should live, and Iron Heart was facing death.

"You will go back?" asked Strong Arm.

"We will find Tall Dog," said Tonkawa, "and bring his scalp to you."

"It is for you to say," One Finger put in.

But for Ben there was nothing to say. He hadn't come this far, hadn't waited three years to get Tall Dog, only to turn back now. The reason for leaving was important, and every brave would understand, but he was not going back.

"I cannot leave now," he said firmly, "and you all understand why."

There was a murmur of assent, and Ben nodded. "It is settled then."

The messenger was given food, an hour's rest, then sent back to the village.

Iron Heart had a message of his own.

"Tell Blue Flower I hope she has a girl child who looks just like her."

It was a cryptic message and caused Tonkawa to glance at Ben, but nothing was said.

The band rested for the night and snow began to fall. By dawn, heavy clouds cowled the mountains. They would be laying their chilling eggs before long, for a storm was brewing. By tomorrow, the war party could be in snow too deep for horses, or for men on foot. Ben would have to find Tall Dog that day.

By midmorning, Ben knew he was close to Tall Dog's camp. There was the faint tang of wood smoke in the air. It couldn't be seen, but the scent was easily picked up by nostrils that could smell buffalo half a mile away.

Though the fires could have belonged to McCollum's troopers, Ben doubted that. Scouts brought word that the soldiers had reached the pass. Oddly, the bluecoats had stopped to make coffee, when they should have been marching on Tall Dog. Even so, smoke from their fires was three hours away, too far for even experienced Tonkawa senses to detect.

Ben's heart pounded, his pulse raced. It would not be long before he and Tall Dog stood face to face.

Shortly before noon, two scouts brought in the body of an Arapahoe. He had been killed not far from the Tonkawa party.

Ben ordered the man scalped. Then the dead man's genitals were sliced off and hung around his neck. The body was tied to the horse it had been riding half an hour before, and the horse was sent galloping. Ben thought of following the animal, but reasoned that the critter would not return to the Arapahoe camp directly. After the manner of his kind, he would meander, and Ben didn't want to waste the energy of his warriors in such a chase.

He then did a strange thing. He sliced a piece of a tree and carved it into a heart. Then he thrust a sliver of iron pyrite into the center of the heart. He hung this from a branch, where it could be plainly seen.

"That will tell Tall Dog we are here," he said to Tonkawa.

The chief nodded. "Maybe he knows already. He has many scouts."

Ben agreed, but grinned, and the grin was not pretty. It was tempered with the stored-up hate of three years, and became a knife slit in his face.

"I want him to know, for sure, who is with the Tonkawa."

Again the chief nodded. He understood. To unnerve the enemy was like having five more arrows in the quiver.

Joe Cardwell led McCollum's troops through the pass. The going was hard, and progress was slow. Snow was falling, making visibility poor, and Joe had to test his ground thoroughly before proceeding. The pass was no wagon road. Few ever used it. A stranger would have thought this irregular cut through the granite mountains a haphazard trail ending in a blind canyon. A stranger would have scorned the pass, but Winter Bear knew where he was going, and kept the column moving forward steadily, if slowly.

He knew that Tonkawas were in the area. Pawnee Army scouts had brought that information. They also said there was a war chief with the party who had light eyes. This could only mean that he was half-breed or white, and Joe had his suspicions. He would be Ben Brand, called Iron Heart by the Plains Indians, and he would be after Tall Dog. Though two years had passed since he and Ben had spoken— two years since their unhappy parting—he still thought of the youth as a close friend, a relative, a son. He had heard of Iron Heart's deeds. He had heard of the white youth's skill as a warrior, and of his rise in the Tonkawa band. All of this was part of the gossip of the Great Plains.

Joe was also concerned because McCollum, now a captain, knew about Ben also, and this seemed to fuel Scowl's hatred. Ben Brand had humiliated him before his men. He had never forgotten. Further, he had been saved from scalping by the youth, and McCollum hated Ben for that, too. McCollum's incompetence had flared like gunflash on that occasion, and all had seen. And there was one more thing. Melanie. She was fickle, yes, but to have chosen somebody who was actually an enemy was an insult the captain carried deep in his heart.

Two years before, he had ordered Brand to leave Tall Dog to the Army. If the onetime scout killed the Indian chief, he, McCollum, would see to it that Ben hanged for murder. McCollum hoped with all his heart that the murder would take place. He would like nothing better than to see Iron Heart swing from the end of a hangman's rope.

McCollum knew from scouting reports that the Tonkawa were closer to Tall Dog than he was. Ben Brand would arrive first. He would kill the Arapahoe chief—or get killed trying. McCollum would be satisfied with either eventuality.

Joe knew what was going through McCollum's mind. He could read the captain like he could read the mountains. For this reason, he tried to hurry the troopers along. He had to reach Tall Dog first. The troopers had to take the renegade Indian and save Ben from a hanging. But McCollum delayed. He insisted they pause for coffee, he insisted they try a branch of the pass that led nowhere, he insisted they pause often to "reconnoiter," a word that irritated Joe. If you were "gonna have a look," you were "gonna have a look." What in hell was "reconnoiter?"

The snows flew at them, borne by the building wind, as the line of soldiers worked through the pass.

Dark clouds settled lower in the sky, ominous, threatening.

Joe felt time running out.

McCollum was moving too slowly, and the scout knew it was deliberate.

If the snow picked up, tracks would disappear in seconds. There was a chance that Tall Dog would get away.

Worse, there was the chance that Ben would get to him first, and kill the Arapahoe chief as he had vowed.

And if that happened, Ben would hang.

CHAPTER SIXTEEN

Tall Dog saw that the scout he had sent out was dead, and had been tied to his horse. He had been scalped and his genitals hung from his neck. Tall Dog stared at the man, one of his best warriors, with a sense of doom peculiar to him. The Tonkawa were closer than he thought.

A shiver of apprehension rippled through the camp. Death among the Arapahoes had never occurred in this high place before. They had always been safe where no men but themselves ventured. Suddenly, death came riding into camp on a horse. Even the sturdiest brave felt the Medicine.

Tall Dog knew what they must do.

There were a number of small caves near camp. It was one of the reasons the place was chosen every year. The caves were too small to hold them all, but Tall Dog sent the women and children into hiding there. After that, he placed his warriors strategically.

Another scout returned. He held the heart that Ben had carved.

Tall Dog examined it curiously.

"It is from him," said one of the chiefs.

"Iron Heart?"

"It has to be him."

"They have as many men as we," said the scout. "They are on foot."

"Will they be here soon?"

"Soon. Before the snow falls this much more," said the scout, and opened his fingers a pinch. "And the bluecoats will come at this time." The scout opened his fingers a little more.

Tall Dog nodded, showing no emotion.

"Where are our enemies?" he asked.

"The bluecoats over there," the scout pointed in the direction of the pass. "The Tonkawa," the scout hesitated, then fanned out the fingers on both hands, "coming fast."

Tall Dog knew then that they were trapped. He hadn't thought the soldiers would come this far, but they were closing in. He knew the Tonkawas, being Plains Indians, wouldn't have ventured into the mountains. Not now when the snow fell, for they didn't like the mountains, but they had a leader who knew the mountains well.

"Iron Heart leads?" he asked, knowing the answer.

The scout nodded.

"Who," asked Tall Dog, "leads the bluecoats?"

"Scowl and Winter Bear."

Tall Dog felt a rage building in his heart. He had fought often, had killed much, and expected to be killed one day. But to be outsmarted by two white men, even such a one as the legendary Iron Heart, made his heart fall to the ground.

"We will fight to the death," he cried. "I will stake myself out. No man here will flee. This is where we live. This is our home. Let no man desert."

He had a brave drive a stake into the ground deeply. It was driven in so far that even a strong Arapahoe horse would have trouble pulling it out.

Then Tall Dog tied himself to the stake. He tied a rawhide rope around his ankle and the other to the stake, so that he had about ten feet of free movement, a ten-foot circle. He could not go beyond that, he could not retreat nor charge. The enemy must come to him.

"Let Iron Heart fight me, if he will," shouted Tall Dog for all to hear, and take courage from his action. "I wait . . ."

Iron Heart knew that he was near the Arapahoe camp. Scouts told him that the bluecoats were also near.

"Damn that Joe Cardwell," growled Ben, but he was for some reason pleased, too. Perhaps, he thought, it was the pleasure that comes from knowing a favored teacher has done well. It was also knowing that the teacher was about to place himself in jeopardy for a friend. Joe was after Tall Dog, the killer of the Brand family. Joe and he had parted under strained circumstances, but their friendship ran deep. It transcended such differences. Joe might never speak to him again, if he chose, but he would defend Ben Brand. And he would avenge him and his, as well.

"We are not far from the Arapahoe camp," said

207

One Finger.

There comes a time just before battle, when the tension on both sides reaches a breaking point. Tonkawa, the experienced chief, knew this. Iron Heart, young and not fully tested, did not.

"I think," said Tonkawa quietly, "that the birds sing."

"What do you mean?" Ben asked, surprised. "There are no birds. They have flown south for the winter."

"True, these birds cannot be heard, but do you know why they sing?"

"Because they are talking to one another."

"Yes," said Tonkawa, "and they talk of war. Birds sing to warn others to stay away. There are tightened stomachs, and nerves that twang like bowstrings. Our warriors are like that, as, indeed, are warriors of the Arapahoe."

Ben got the point. His braves were feeling tensions of their own. To a degree that was good. Beyond that point, the tension could be demoralizing—what he had hoped for in the Arapahoe camp. But if that demoralization occurred among his own warriors, that was not good.

It was time to act.

He gave the signal, and the band moved forward. With unerring sense of direction, the Tonkawas reached the perimeters of the enemy camp. It was quiet. There was a muscular man, naked to the waist, tied to a stake at the edge of the compound. He wore no bonnet, but several eagle feathers were woven into two lengths of braided hair. He was well armed, and he kept turning in a slow circle. Looking for us, thought Ben.

"That is Tall Dog?" he whispered to Tonkawa.

The chief flicked his eyelids in agreement.

"It is quiet," said Ben. "Where are the women and children?"

"Hidden in the caves beyond their camp."

"And the braves?"

"They wait in ambush."

Iron Heart raised his arm in a prearranged signal. He dropped it, and shots rang out, arrows flew. Tall Dog was not hit, though he was an open target. He belonged only to Iron Heart.

Tonkawas charged the camp, and were driven back by the weapons of concealed Arapahoes. The Tonkawas regrouped, and charged again. This time they broke through the front line of the enemy. There was fierce fighting on both sides. Hand-to-hand combat swirled over the freezing, snow-covered ground. Tomahawks flew, lances streaked, and gunpowder burned. Again the Tonkawas were driven back.

The Arapahoe band of Tall Dog might have been a killer band, serving under a murderous chief, but they were not cowards. They were skilled fighters. When the Tonkawa retreated the second time, the Arapahoes charged. The air was shrill with their war cries, as they closed on Ben's forces.

Ben stood at the head, facing the brunt of the charge. His pistols blazed, and he fought in true Iron Heart fashion. He was cool, and his shots were well placed. The enemy fell, but as the hammers clicked on empty chambers, Ben had no time to reload. He grappled hand-to-hand as the Tonkawas rallied and drove the opposition back into their camp once more.

Reloading his pistols quickly, Ben ran into camp for the first time. Tall Dog was firing his pistols, and One Finger stumbled. He fell, a hole in his chest.

Ben aimed his pistol at Tall Dog's head, and his finger tightened on the trigger. Years of hate were focused on his front sight, years of frustration urged his finger to finish its job. Before him was the man who had killed his beloved family. It was true, Crooked Nose had led the party that committed the deed, but he was acting under Tall Dog's orders.

All Ben had to do was squeeze the trigger of his Dragoon and vengeance would be his. But he lowered the weapon. There was something unsatisfactory about it. Tall Dog would be getting off too easy. He would never have known the man who was his undoing, and Ben wanted him to know.

As the shrieks and sounds of battle raged, Ben stepped forward. He walked toward Tall Dog. An Arapahoe brave ran at him, and Ben fired. The man dropped. Another Arapahoe tried the same thing, and Ben dropped him in his tracks.

He stopped twenty feet from Tall Dog, whose back was to him. The chief fired a brace of pistols. He seemed enveloped in white smoke.

"Tall Dog," Ben called above the roar of battle. "I am here."

The chief whirled. He instantly cocked his pistols, and aimed them at Ben. For a few seconds the two eyed each other, men from different worlds, but bound by a common hate for each other.

Ben made no move to cock his own weapons. He shoved them in his holsters instead.

"Will you shoot me now?" he called, using as much Arapahoe as he knew, and making sign for the rest.

Tall Dog straightened. "You are him—Iron Heart?"

"Yes."

"Why do you not fire your weapons at me? You could have lifted my hair by now. See?" He swung his tied ankle up. "I cannot run. I will live, or die, right here."

"You deserve to die. You killed my family who never fired a shot at you. I have come for vengeance, which is rightfully mine."

Tall Dog threw his weapons on the ground. He drew a knife and tomahawk from a sash at his waist.

"This, then," he said, "is what you want?"

"Yes."

"Come, then."

Ben drew his own knife and tomahawk and closed in. The two faced each other warily, weapons at the ready. Ben knew he had a tough adversary, because of the difference in their skills with the weapons they held.

But what he lacked in skill, Ben made up for in rage. At last he had the man who changed his life so tragically. Before him was the killer of innumerable white families. This was the savage who had had Martha sliced into pieces. He was the one who killed the drummer. And what surprised Ben was that this murderer, this beast who tortured his victims, who let his warriors defile the belongings of survivors with their stinking bladder water, looked like any man. He was muscular, he had a facial scar, but he had only two feet, two legs, and one body .The most feared chief on the Plains was, after all, just an ordinary man.

Ben thrust with his knife. Tall Dog dodged easily and counterwhipped with his tomahawk. Ben saw the blow coming and jumped out of range.

"You fly like a grasshopper," sneered Tall Dog. He beckoned with his knife. "Come. I will kill you quickly. You will feel no pain."

Ben lunged in again. He was swift, and his knife drew first blood, a nick in Tall Dog's upper arm.

"Who," he said with a grin, "will kill who?"

They spoke, and they understood each other clearly, but neither was skilled in the other's tongue. Pidgin English, Arapahoe, Tonkawa, and sign language were used, but there was more. Each knew what was in the other's mind. Each had taken a measure of the other's hate and rage, and they met on this common ground. There was no need for talk, but speak they did, and the gaps were filled with mutual understanding. Death provided the words they did not have, and their communication was as smooth as if they were brothers.

Ben was only vaguely aware of the battle that continued to swirl around them. He heard shouts, saw men fall, both Arapahoe and Tonkawa, but his life was centered on the man he fought. No other life mattered now. The universe was comprised of himself and Tall Dog—and their mutually interested observer: Death.

He lunged again, trying to close with Tall Dog. He was thrown quickly to the ground. Tall Dog's tomahawk, a weapon with a flared head, and fancy cover of buffalo hair slipped securely over the handle, crashed down. Ben rolled, and the tomahawk bit into the snow-covered earth. He sprang to his feet, and gave a backward slash with his own tomahawk. The blade caught Tall Dog on the shoulder, and drew blood. Before he could leap back to safety, his enemy's 'hawk found his upper arm, and left a nasty gash. Ben hardly noticed.

Tall Dog crouched, his eyes triumphant.

"You bleed, Iron Heart," he said. "From what I know, you never bleed, for no weapon has touched you."

Ben said nothing, conserving his breath.

Tall Dog leaped, thrusting his knife viciously. The blade barely missed Ben's throat, as he swung his tomahawk instinctively. The blade struck Tall Dog's skull a glancing blow. Tall Dog staggered, but recovered quickly, blood streaming down his face.

He seemed a bit unsteady, but Ben wasn't sure whether that might be a ruse, so he kept his distance.

Tall Dog grinned. "I cannot fool you, eh?"

Both men lunged at each other.

The two bodies crashed together, and Ben knew this was the instant he had been waiting for. He had wanted to feel his enemy, to get the measure of him physically, to know what form of a man it was who killed innocent people. He wanted flesh on flesh, heart against heart, hate against hate. He wanted to kill the man who killed his people with a blow he delivered personally. He wanted to feel the man quiver under the hand that delivered the lethal strike. It was the only way in which he could satisfy the blood lust that had driven him for three years. The man must die under his hand.

He withstood Tall Dog's rush, which had been meant to crash him to the ground. He locked with Tall Dog, and pushed back. He whipped a leg around the back of Tall Dog's calf, and the man toppled over backward. Ben fell on him, and without hesitation, plunged his knife deep into the Arapahoe's breast.

Tall Dog stiffened. He arched his back, lifting Ben, and for a moment hung there. Then he settled back to earth. A strange smile curled his lips, and he whispered, "It is well that I have been killed by Iron Heart."

The Arapahoe shuddered, and lay still. His eyes remained open, frosted over with the mist of death.

It was over. Tall Dog would never again kill anybody. His legend might ride the Plains, his memory might linger in the minds of those who fought that day, but Tall Dog was dead. He had become both dust and spirit.

Ben leaned over and took his enemy's scalp, aware of a sudden silence. He glanced around. Both Tonkawa and Arapahoes were watching. The fighting had ceased.

"It is over," said Iron Heart. "Will we continue to fight?"

"To the caves," cried Tonkawa, "the women and children are there."

"Where are the Arapahoe braves?" Ben asked.

"Some have fled," said Strong Arm, "others are

214

our prisoners, many are dead." He grinned. "We have many scalps."

"Then," declared Ben, "we have done enough." He hung the scalp of Tall Dog from his belt. This one he would keep.

There were fine women among the Arapahoe. They would be sold into slavery to Mexicans for a good price. The Arapahoe braves could be sold, too, or kept, and their muscles would be used in heavy work.

The scalping went quickly. A scout came in from the north.

"Bluecoats come. Winter Bear and Scowl. Many rifles. Many ponies."

"I think you should go now, Tonkawa," said Brand.

The chief looked Ben in the eye. "You do not come, too?"

"I must see an old friend first."

Tonkawa nodded. He turned to his braves and pointed toward the plains. Without a word the Tonkawas left, and Ben rode toward the pass.

Snow dusted him until he was almost pure white. His ears still rang with the sounds of battle, but the blood lust was gone.

He had avenged his family at last.

There was an emptiness in him, but a fullness, too. But he could not yet put a name to it.

CHAPTER SEVENTEEN

Captain McCollum rode at the head of the column with Joe Cardwell, Winter Bear. When they were within a hundred yards, McCollum raised his hand, and the column stopped.

"Who are you?" Joe demanded.

He raised his rifle and cocked the hammer.

"Speak, damn it, or I'll blow a hole in those dirty buckskins you could light a fire in."

"Why, Joe," said Ben mildly, "you wouldn't do that to a friend, would you?"

The mountain man's jaw dropped.

"Jesamighty!" he exclaimed. "It can't be . . ."

"It is, though."

"Well, by Gar'!"

Joe urged his horse ahead and in moments he was wringing Ben's hand.

"By Gar', son, I never thought to see you again! You been with the Tonks I hear."

"They are my friends, yes," said Ben. "And I hear you've become a famous name in this part of the world."

"What, Winter Bear?" Joe spat. "That's what the Indians call me, I guess. But I'm Joe Cardwell to ever'body else."

McCollum brought his horse alongside.

"What's going on here . . ." he began, then recognized Ben.

It was obvious his dislike for Ben hadn't lessened. Captain McCollum's eyes widened.

"You beat us to the Arapahoes. You fought them. You killed Tall Dog?"

Ben did not reply.

The captain's face flushed with anger.

"I told you I'd have you hanged if you killed Tall Dog," he snapped, "and I meant it." He smiled maliciously.

"Guess you would," said Ben casually, "but you're not going to do it."

McCollum's hand dropped to his holster. "Why not?"

"Because you have no proof."

"What's that scalp hanging from your belt?"

"Oh, this? I found it back there."

"We know there was a fight."

"That's your opinion, McCollum, but who was fighting?"

For a second the captain nearly lost control. His hand tightened around the butt of his pistol and his eyes flamed. Ben tensed. He waited. He looked beyond McCollum briefly. Sgt. Clinty was near the head of the column. Clinty shook his head almost imperceptibly. Ben looked at Joe. Cardwell took in a deep breath.

Ben spoke.

"Don't draw, McCollum. It would only complicate matters. You have nothing on me. I say, let it rest."

His words must have reached McCollum, because the man slowly let his hand drop. He heaved a great sigh, then, without a word, rejoined the troops.

Ben heard him say, "Let's go, Sergeant Clinty. I want to see what the shooting was about."

The soldiers rode past. Clinty gave Ben a grin and nod. Ben knew most of the others, too, and they acknowledged him with everything from snappy salutes to remarks about his long hair. Then they were gone, and he and Joe were alone.

"That there's Tall Dog's scalp a-danglin' from your belt, Ben. Did you get it all out of your craw?"

"I had enough of killing, Joe."

Joe smiled. He had heard what he wanted to hear.

"Tell me," said Ben, "how is Melanie?"

"I'll tell you how she is," said Joe with a great laugh. "She married a blacksmith in St. Louis. McCollum about pissed his pants."

"A *blacksmith?*"

"She were a strong-minded woman, Ben. Yes, indeed. She knew what she wanted."

"No use being cruel, Joe."

"Ain't there?"

Ben grinned. "No, there ain't."

"Are you comin' with us?" Joe asked.

"No."

"Will you go back to the Tonkawa, then?"

"I don't know. I don't like whites much, Joe, and I get along with the Tonkawa pretty well. The trouble is Tonkawa days are about over." He thought about that a moment, and added, "But, then, maybe mine are, too."

"They's talk of Jefferson Territory becoming a state. They's goin' to be a lot of changes next few years."

"The whites really going to take over?"

"Yeah. Somethin' like that."

"Then there will be a big war between Indians and whites."

"Yeah. Mebbe so, Ben."

The two were silent a moment, then Joe said, "I got to catch up to McCollum." He snorted. "Even with the smoke to follow, he could get lost."

Ben didn't detain him. The two shook hands and went their separate ways.

Joe called back once. "Whichever way you decide to go, I'm your friend, Iron Heart."

"And I," Ben called back, "am yours."

The snow was falling in large flakes, covering tracks quickly. Tonkawa sat his horse some distance away. He was on a high rise, overlooking the pass, and he had been watching Joe and Ben. He watched Joe ride off to catch up to the soldiers. Then he saw Ben go after him. Snow obscured Tonkawa's vision, so he came down from the rise and followed the dimming tracks.

Ben's followed the troopers' for aways, then veered off as the rider made a wide circle.

Tonkawa followed the tracks at a distance, and when they reached the flat country, he noted they turned south. He studied them for a moment, and then turned south himself, following them. His band waited in a stand of trees by the big river. Iron Heart sat his pony, waiting, his head held high, proud. He held up his hand in greeting. Tonkawa signed that his heart now soared like a hawk. He knew it would be good riding away from this winter country. The snow would cover their tracks, even if the bluecoats decided to come after them. Winter Bear, despite his skills, could not find tracks that were not there.

Iron Heart rode beside him and Tonkawa knew the tribe's medicine was strong. Did he not kill the Arapahoe's most feared warrior? Was he not the man of Blue Flower, who was heavy with his child?

Truly, nothing on earth could harm the Tonkawa now.

Iron Heart was their magic.

That night over a foot of snow fell on the plains, and the world was very quiet.

THE NEWEST ADVENTURES AND ESCAPADES OF BOLT
by Cort Martin

Outside, the weather is ~~cold~~ Harlequin Presents, we've got the books to warm the temperature inside, too!

Don't miss the final story in Sharon Kendrick's fabulous THE DESERT PRINCES trilogy—*The Desert King's Virgin Bride*—where Sheikh Malik seduces an innocent Englishwoman. And what happens when a divorced couple discover their desire for each other hasn't faded? Read *The Pregnancy Affair* by Anne Mather to find out!

Our gorgeous billionaires will get your hearts racing.... Emma Darcy brings you a sizzling slice of Sydney life with *The Billionaire's Scandalous Marriage,* when Damien Wynter is determined that Charlotte be his bride—*and* the mother of his child! In Lindsay Armstrong's *The Australian's Housekeeper Bride*, a wealthy businessman needs a wife—and he chooses his housekeeper! In Carole Mortimer's *Wife by Contract, Mistress by Demand,* brooding billionaire Rufus uses a marriage of convenience to bed Gabriella.

For all of you who love our Greek tycoons, you won't be disappointed this month! In *Aristides' Convenient Wife* by Jacqueline Baird, Leon Aristides thinks Helen an experienced woman—until their wedding night. Chantelle Shaw's *The Greek Boss's Bride* tells the story of a P.A. who has a dark secret and is in love with her handsome boss. And for those who love some Italian passion, Susan Stephens's *In the Venetian's Bed* brings you Luca Barbaro, a sexy and ruthless Venetian, whom Nell just can't resist.

QUEENS *of* R♥MANCE

The world's favorite romance writers
New and original novels you'll treasure forever from
internationally bestselling Presents authors:

Helen Bianchin

Emma Darcy

Lynne Graham

Penny Jordan

Miranda Lee

Sandra Marton

Anne Mather

Lucy Monroe

Michelle Reid

Cathy Williams

Anne Mather

THE PREGNANCY AFFAIR

QUEENS *of* R♥MANCE

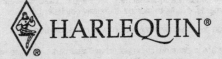

HARLEQUIN®

TORONTO • NEW YORK • LONDON
AMSTERDAM • PARIS • SYDNEY • HAMBURG
STOCKHOLM • ATHENS • TOKYO • MILAN • MADRID
PRAGUE • WARSAW • BUDAPEST • AUCKLAND

ISBN-13: 978-0-373-12629-3
ISBN-10:   0-373-12629-8

THE PREGNANCY AFFAIR

First North American Publication 2007.

All about the author...
Anne Mather

I've always wanted to write—which is not to say I've always wanted to be a professional writer. For years I wrote only for my own pleasure and it wasn't until my husband suggested that I ought to send one of my stories to a publisher that we put several publishers' names into a hat and pulled one out. The rest, as they say, is history. And now, more than 150 books later, I'm literally— excuse the pun—staggered by what happened.

I had written all through my childhood and into my teens—the stories changing from children's adventures to torrid gypsy passions. My mother used to gather these up from time to time, when my bedroom became too untidy, and dispose of them! The trouble was I never used to finish any of the stories, and *Caroline,* my first published book, was the first book I'd actually completed. I was newly married then, and my daughter was just a baby, and it was quite a job juggling my household chores and scribbling away in exercise books every chance I got. Not very professional, as you can see, but that's the way it was.

I now have two grown-up children, a son and daughter, and two adorable grandchildren, Abigail and Ben. My e-mail address is mystic-am@msn.com and I'd be happy to hear from any of my readers.

CHAPTER ONE

THE sign informing passengers to *Fasten Seat Belts* flashed on above Olivia's head and she automatically reached to check that her belt was in place.

'We'll be landing at Newcastle International Airport in fifteen minutes,' the saccharine-sweet voice of the flight attendant announced smoothly. 'Please ensure that all your hand luggage is put away in the overhead lockers and that your tray tables are securely stowed.'

The aircraft dipped to begin its approach to the airport and Olivia's stomach lurched in protest. But it wasn't the amount of coffee she'd consumed that morning that was giving her such a sickly feeling. It was the knowledge that she was returning to Bridgeford after so many years that was tying her stomach in knots.

The landing was swift and uneventful. The airport was busy and the plane taxied efficiently to its unloading bay as passengers and crew alike began gathering their belongings together. There was little chit-chat. This was primarily a business flight, most of the passengers either on or returning from business trips, with only a handful of holiday-makers to make up the numbers.

Olivia's trip was neither business nor pleasure, she thought, and she wasn't at all sure she was doing the right thing by coming here. She doubted her father would want to see her, whatever reassurances her sister had given her, and there'd be no sympathetic shoulder for someone who'd messed up her life, not just once, but twice.

Still, it was too late to have second thoughts now. The plane had come to a complete standstill, the door was open, and her fellow passengers were all jostling to be first to alight. Eventually, of course, she had to get up and follow them. She should have worn flats, she thought as her ridiculously high heels caught in the metal of the stairway. But pride was a stubborn companion and Olivia was determined not to appear as desperate as she felt.

A short walk across the tarmac and she was in the terminal buildings, offering her passport for inspection and lining up to collect her suitcase from the carousel. She'd only brought one suitcase, leaving the rest of her belongings in storage in London. Because that was where she was going to find herself an apartment, she told herself firmly. This trip to Bridgeford was just to prove to herself—and her family—that she wasn't afraid to come back.

Her suitcase was one of the first to appear and Olivia pulled a wry face as she hauled it off the carousel. OK, she thought, it was time to face the music. Linda, her sister, had said she would come to meet her. Which was a relief. She was likely to be the least-judgemental of the family.

Beyond the doors, a crowd of people was waiting to greet the passengers, many of them carrying name boards to identify themselves. One thing, Olivia thought drily, there was no way she wouldn't recognise Linda. Whether Linda would recognise her was another thing altogether.

And then she stopped dead in her tracks, the suitcase she was towing behind her running on into the backs of her legs. But she hardly noticed the bump or the momentary discomfort it gave her. She was staring at the man who was standing at the back of the crowd of people, and, although she couldn't believe it, it seemed he was waiting for her.

She glanced quickly behind her, half convinced he wasn't looking at her at all but at some other person who'd followed her through the doors. But there was no one immediately behind her, no one else to coincide with his line of vision.

And then, to confirm her disbelief, he moved towards her, pushing his way through the waiting mob to fetch up by her side. 'Hi,' he said, taking the handle of the suitcase from her unresisting hand. 'D'you have a good journey?'

Olivia stared at him blankly. 'What are you doing here?' she asked, aware that it probably wasn't the politest thing to say in the circumstances, but she couldn't help it. If she'd been anxious on the plane, she was a hundred times more nervous now. Her heart was pounding, the blood rushing through her veins like wildfire. What the hell was Joel Armstrong doing here? She'd have expected him to avoid her like the plague. 'Wh-where's Linda?'

If he noticed the stammer, he gave no sign of it. 'At home,' he replied evenly, and because he started walking away from her, she was obliged to follow him. 'Your father's having a bad day,' he continued. 'She thought it would be wiser not to leave him alone.'

Olivia blinked. She could have said all her father ever had were bad days in her estimation, but she didn't. She was too busy trying to keep up with his long strides. Trying to ally herself, too, to the man who was walking beside her. Fifteen years ago, he'd been little more than a boy. Now he was a man.

And what a man, she thought, permitting herself a covert look in his direction. He'd always been tall, but now he'd filled out, the shoulders of the leather jacket he was wearing owing nothing to padding she was sure. A lean jawline showed just the trace of a five o'clock shadow, while his unruly dark hair was shorter than she remembered, exposing the handsome shape of his skull.

Not that handsome described him exactly. His youthful good looks had given way to a harsher profile altogether. Fans of lighter skin flared from the corners of his cool grey eyes, while deeper ridges framed the narrow-lipped beauty of his mouth.

God, he was attractive, Olivia thought, feeling a pang of awareness she'd never expected to feel again. It hardly seemed possible that they'd once been married. Had she really allowed a sense of pride to rule her reason? Would things have been different if she'd chosen to stay and fight?

She stumbled as they stepped out into the watery sunshine of an April day. It had been cool in London, but it was amazingly mild here. As Joel turned at her muffled exclamation, she regretted the urge she'd had to dress up for the journey. She'd wanted Linda to envy her her trim figure and designer clothes. She'd even chosen the shortest skirt in her wardrobe to show off the slender length of her legs. As for how much it had cost to have the ash-blonde highlights in her honey-brown hair renewed… She must have been crazy to think anyone would care.

'You OK?' Joel asked now and she nodded automatically.

'I'm fine,' she said quickly. 'Where are you parked?'

'Not far away,' he responded, slowing his pace a little. 'Be grateful it's not raining. It was earlier.'

Olivia pulled a face, but she refused to answer him. Dammit, here they were, meeting one another after fifteen years, and all he could talk about was the weather. Why was she feeling so tongue-tied suddenly, when he was obviously quite at ease with her?

Whatever had happened to him in the last fifteen years had definitely changed him. And for the better, she mused. He'd left school at eighteen and, despite getting excellent results, he'd gone to work for her father. He'd wanted to marry her and they'd done so as soon as she was eighteen. Everyone had expected it would last, even Joel. Or at least she'd thought that was what he'd believed. Looking at him now, she was beginning to wonder if that was just another of her many mistakes.

'So—how are you?' she managed at last, relieved when they turned between the aisles of parked cars. Surely it wouldn't be much further. 'It's been a long time.'

'Hasn't it just?' he agreed, a faintly mocking twist to his mouth as he looked at her and Olivia knew damn well he'd never looked at her like that before. It was as if she amused him. 'You seem OK,' he added. 'I guess living in the States agrees with you.'

It didn't, actually, Olivia was tempted to respond, but that had had more to do with the man she'd been living with than with the country itself.

Joel stopped behind a huge four-wheel-drive and juggled his keys out of his pocket. Flipping open the rear door, he stowed Olivia's suitcase in the back and then went round and opened the passenger door.

Olivia was still admiring the vehicle, its mud-splattered wing in no way detracting from its sleek appearance. Was this Joel's or her father's? she wondered uncertainly. Whosoever it was, things at the farm must definitely be looking up.

'Nice car,' she said, and wished he wasn't watching her get in. The seat was high and her skirt rode up to her bottom as she levered herself onto it. And she was fairly sure Joel was suppressing another of those mocking smiles.

'I like it,' he said, without expression. He walked around the bonnet and climbed in beside her, the high seat offering no obstacle to his long legs. 'All set?'

'As I'll ever be,' said Olivia tartly, not seeing why he should have it all his own way. Then, as his hands gripped the wheel, she noticed the wedding ring on his third finger. Not the ring she'd given him, she realised, but a much more expensive band altogether. Her stomach tightened unpleasantly. 'Are you married?'

It was an impertinent question and she knew as soon as she'd voiced it that it was nothing to do with her. But dammit, he had been her husband first. Didn't she have a right to know if he'd replaced her?

'Do you care?' he countered now and, despite her determination not to let him see how she was feeling, Olivia felt the hot colour stain her cheeks.

'I—not particularly,' she muttered, turning her attention to a plane that was just coming in to land. 'This airport's busier than I remember.'

'Things change,' said Joel, reversing out of the space

and turning in the direction of the exit. 'And I'm divorced. For the second time,' he appended drily. 'I guess neither of us has had any luck in that direction.'

'What do you mean?'

Olivia's eyes were drawn to him now, and he gave her a sardonic look. 'Linda told me your second marriage broke up,' he said. 'Isn't that why you're back in England?'

Olivia expelled a resentful breath. Linda, she thought irritably. She might have known her sister wouldn't keep something like that to herself. 'I've come back to England because my work's here,' she retorted shortly. 'I don't know enough about the US housing market to get a comparable job in New York.'

'Ah.' Joel allowed the distinction, but Olivia still felt as if he didn't believe her. 'So you're going to do what? Join an agency in Newcastle?'

'London, probably,' she responded swiftly, hating the need she felt to justify herself in his eyes. Why did she care what he thought of her? If Linda hadn't seen fit to ask him to meet her, they might never have had this conversation.

Joel used the ticket he'd bought earlier to let them out of the car park, and then turned north towards Ponteland and Belsay. The sky had cleared and it was that shade of blue that seemed almost transparent. The trees were already greening with spring growth and here and there late daffodils bloomed along the hedgerows. Olivia had forgotten how beautiful the countryside could be. Living first in London and then New York, she'd become so much a city animal.

'Um—how is my father?' she asked at last, realising she was to blame for the uneasy silence that lay between them.

She tried to adopt a humorous tone. 'Still as irascible as ever, I suppose.'

'He has good days and bad days, as I'm sure Linda's told you,' answered Joel, permitting her a rueful grin. 'But since the stroke—'

'The stroke?' Olivia didn't let him finish. 'What stroke? Linda said nothing about a stroke.'

Joel blew out a breath. 'Didn't she?' His tone was flat. 'Well, maybe I shouldn't have either. I dare say the old man doesn't want it broadcasting to all and sundry.'

'Hey, I'm not "all and sundry"!' exclaimed Olivia, her efforts at conciliation forgotten at his words. 'I'm his daughter. Don't you think I have a right to know?'

Joel's thick dark brows arched indifferently. 'I suppose that depends on the kind of relationship you two have had over the years,' he remarked mildly. 'How long is it since you've seen him?'

Olivia huffed. 'You know exactly how long it is. I wasn't exactly encouraged to come back after—after we split up.'

Joel regarded her for a brief compelling moment. 'Is that supposed to be an excuse?'

'No.' Olivia felt herself colouring again. 'It's the reason why I haven't seen him. I have phoned, and written letters. I've never had a reply.'

Joel moved his shoulders in a rueful gesture. 'I didn't know that.'

'No?' Olivia wasn't sure whether she believed him. 'Well, why would you? I dare say you hoped you'd never set eyes on me again.'

Joel shook his head. 'You're wrong, Liv. I got over what you did years ago. I moved on. I got married. I had a son.

I realised we were too young when we got married. Neither of us knew what we really wanted out of life.'

Olivia had to force herself not to turn and stare at him now. He had a son! Of all the things he might have said, she realised that was the least expected. And the most painful, she acknowledged as the bile caused by too many cups of black coffee rose sickly in the back of her throat.

She had to say something, she thought, aware that she was taking too long to make a rejoinder. And, dammit, why should she care if he had a child? It wasn't as if she was the maternal type. But, all the same, it hurt. It hurt deep inside her. Like a wound that had been partially healed that was suddenly as raw and painful as the day she'd lost their son.

'Well—good,' she said at last, hoping he couldn't hear the thickness of her voice. 'But, even so, I wish Linda had warned me.'

'I imagine she was afraid that if you knew the truth you might change your mind about coming,' observed Joel shrewdly. 'Ben Foley isn't the best of patients. Without Dempsey's help, the farm would have gone down the drain long ago.'

Olivia was surprised. 'Martin?' she said curiously, speaking of her sister's husband. 'Does he work at the farm as well as at the garden centre?'

'They let the garden centre go,' replied Joel, accelerating past a tractor. 'They live at the farm now. It seemed the most sensible solution in the circumstances.'

Olivia was totally confused. When she'd gone away, Joel had virtually been running the farm for her father, and it had been understood that he'd take over when Ben Foley retired. That was one of the reasons why her father had been so angry with her when their marriage broke up. He'd depended on Joel. A lot. She caught her breath suddenly. Surely he hadn't punished Joel because she'd walked out?

They turned a bend in the road and suddenly it was possible to glimpse the sea in the distance. Redes Bay gleamed in the early-afternoon sun, shimmering like a mirage in the desert. Bridgeford was just a mile from the sea as the crow flies. A little further than that on the twisting roads that honeycombed the area.

'You must be hungry,' Joel said, glancing her way again, and Olivia managed a faint smile. But the truth was she felt too knotted up inside to care about an empty stomach. Though there was no doubt she'd probably feel better if the amount of coffee she'd consumed wasn't sloshing about inside her.

'I expect Linda will have a meal ready for you,' he continued. 'She still makes the best steak and kidney pie in the neighbourhood.'

'Does she?' Olivia felt even queasier at the thought of all those calories. In recent years she'd become accustomed to eating sparingly, always watching her weight for any fluctuation, living on tuna fish and what her sister would call rabbit-food. The idea of sitting down to a lunch of steak and kidney pie horrified her. Even empty, as she was, she knew she'd never get it down.

'It looks as if you could use a few extra pounds,' remarked Joel, slowing at yet another crossroads, and Olivia wondered at his perception. It was as if he'd known exactly what she was thinking.

'Oh, does it?' she said, her incredulity giving way to resentment. 'I suppose you prefer women with more flesh on their bones.'

Joel chuckled. He actually chuckled, and Olivia was furious. 'You could say that,' he agreed, and she badly wanted to slap him. She knew she was looking good—by New York standards, at least—and it was mortifying to have him *laugh* at her.

'And I suppose your second wife was everything I'm not,' she flung at him angrily, uncaring at that moment how peevish she sounded. 'Well, where I come from women care about their appearance. We don't all want to be milch cows!'

Joel sobered. 'No, I think you proved that when you got rid of our baby,' he retorted harshly, and she realised that for the first time she'd caught him on the raw. His jaw clamped shut for a few moments, as if suppressing another outburst, but when he spoke again he had himself in control. 'Forget it. I shouldn't have said anything.'

Olivia swallowed, remembering she'd promised herself she wouldn't say anything if she saw Joel either. But she couldn't stop herself. 'For the record,' she said unsteadily, 'I didn't *get rid* of our baby. At the risk of repeating myself, I had a miscarriage. Believe it or not, these things happen!'

Joel's tanned fingers tightened on the wheel and she saw his knuckles whiten at the pressure he was putting on them. 'Whatever,' he said flatly, but she knew he didn't believe her now any more than he'd believed her before. 'We'll be there in a few minutes. I'll drop you off and then I've got to get back to college.'

Olivia blinked. 'To college?' she echoed blankly.

'In Newcastle,' he agreed, without elaborating.

'You're at college?' she persisted, staring at him incredulously.

'I work at the university,' he corrected her drily. 'I gather Linda didn't tell you that either.'

Olivia's jaw dropped. 'No.'

In actual fact, Linda hadn't mentioned Joel at all. That was why she'd been so surprised to see him at the airport. She'd assumed she'd have to meet him sooner or later at the farm and that Linda was being tactful by putting off the evil day.

'Have I shocked you?'

Joel had relaxed again and Olivia knew she had to say something or run the risk of appearing envious. She'd never gone to university, although she had eventually taken an economics degree at evening classes.

Not that she'd ever needed it. By the time she'd graduated, she'd already been working in a large London estate agency. Her aptitude for the job, and the fact that she got on so well with the clients, had accelerated her climb up the corporate ladder. At age twenty-six, she'd already been earning a high five-figure salary, with added perks like her one-bedroom apartment in Bloomsbury.

Of course, she reflected, she'd given it all up when Bruce Garvey asked her to marry him. Despite her success at work, her life had seemed empty, and she'd found she missed her friends and family and the life she'd had in Bridgeford. She'd even missed Joel, though she'd been sure she'd never forgive him for walking out on her.

'I expect your parents were pleased when you left the farm,' she said at last, hoping she didn't sound as bitter as she felt. She moistened her lips. 'I'm sorry. I assumed you were still working there.'

Joel shook his head. 'I couldn't stay after—well, after what happened.'

Olivia's eyes went wide. 'You mean, my father asked you to leave?'

'Hell, no.' Joel gave her a satirical look. 'Not everything revolves around you, you know. I did what I should have done years ago. I took my qualifications and got myself a degree in IT at Leeds University.'

Olivia blinked. 'IT?'

'Information technology,' he said patiently. 'Computers, for want of a better word.'

Olivia pressed her shoulders back into the soft leather of the seat. 'I see.' She paused. 'I'm glad things have worked out so well for you.'

'Oh, yeah.' Joel was sardonic now. 'Two failed marriages and a child that might or might not have been aborted. Life's been peachy, Liv. So how has it been for you?'

CHAPTER TWO

FORTUNATELY, Olivia was saved the need of answering him. They'd reached Bridgeford and the Lexus splashed through the ford at the edge of the village before accelerating up the slope to the village green. She could pretend she hadn't heard him, pretend she hadn't been knocked off balance by the callousness of his words. Struggling with emotions she didn't even want to acknowledge, she looked instead at the Georgian homes and the handful of cottages that circled the village green. As a shiver of remembered agony slid down her spine, the beauty of her surroundings was a blessed panacea.

The village, at least, didn't seem to have changed much, she thought gratefully, although she could see the roofs of some new houses just visible beyond the trees in the churchyard. There were daffodils blooming here, too, and the almond blossom was just beginning to appear.

'Do your parents still live in the village?' she asked a little stiffly, feeling obliged to say something. The Armstrongs had never approved of Joel's relationship with her, and even after they were married Olivia had been left in no doubt that Mrs Armstrong didn't consider her good enough for her son.

'My father's retired now,' replied Joel amiably enough. Mr Armstrong was an accountant and had used to work for a firm in Chevingham, a small town some ten miles south of Bridgeford. 'They still own the house in Blades Lane,' he added, 'but they've recently bought a place in Spain. They spend a lot of time there in the winter months. They're in El Fuente at present, actually.'

Which explained a lot, thought Olivia cynically. She wondered if Joel would have been so willing to come and meet her if he'd had to explain himself to his parents first.

They passed the house Joel's parents owned on their way to the farm. Rose Cottage was set a few yards back from the road, screened by a tangle of wild roses that blossomed profusely in the season.

It reminded Olivia irresistibly of when she and Joel were teenagers. How many times had she come running down from the farm to find him waiting for her at his gate? They'd both attended the comprehensive school in Chevingham and the school bus used to pick them up at the end of Blades Lane.

Of course, Joel had been a year older, and once they'd got to school there'd been no opportunity to be together. Was that why their relationship had progressed so swiftly? she wondered. Had the excitement of forbidden fruit coloured that youthful infatuation?

'Does everything look the same?' Joel asked abruptly, and Olivia was grateful for the reprieve. She'd been in danger of remembering things that were best forgotten. As Joel said, they'd both moved on.

'Pretty much,' she said after a moment, forcing herself to take an interest in her surroundings. They were turning between white-painted gateposts now, crossing a cattle-grid that caused the vehicle's wheels to vibrate, and then accelerating up the drive to the farmhouse itself.

When the Lexus stopped, Olivia knew the journey was over. However, she felt—and she really wasn't feeling very good—she had to get out of the car and face whatever was to come. It would have been nice, she thought, if her father had invited her here. But it was Linda who'd suggested this visit. Linda, who'd told her so little of what to expect.

'You OK?'

She realised that Joel was looking at her now, probably wondering why she hadn't opened her door. And, dammit, she so didn't want to show him how she was feeling. Joel, with his new career and his precious son.

So, 'Why wouldn't I be?' she answered, with assumed lightness. She gathered her handbag into her arms and reached for the door handle. 'Thanks for the ride, Joel. It's been—illuminating.'

Now, why had she said that? she chided herself impatiently, as Joel's eyes narrowed on her face. 'Why do I get the feeling that you're mad at me?' he countered, but before Olivia could say anything else, Linda came out of the house.

At once, Olivia fumbled with the door catch, as eager to get away from Joel as she was to greet her sister. But she was all thumbs and, without asking her permission, Joel leant past her and thrust the door open for her, the hard strength of his forearm pressing briefly against her breasts.

She scrambled out then, dropping down from the high seat, almost ricking her ankle in her haste to get away from him. Steadying herself against the wing, she mentally squared her shoulders before starting a little uncertainly across the forecourt.

'Hi, Linda,' she said, in what she hoped was a confident tone. 'It's good to see you.'

Her sister shook her head and Olivia was surprised to see tears in her eyes. 'Oh, Livvy, it's good to see you, too,' she exclaimed eagerly and, opening her arms, she gathered the other girl into a welcoming hug.

Olivia was shocked. She hadn't expected such a warm greeting. Linda had never been a touchy-feely kind of person and when they were younger any contact between them had always been initiated by Olivia herself.

But evidently the years had mellowed her, and when she drew back she regarded Olivia with what appeared to be genuine affection. 'I'm so pleased you decided to come,' she said. 'This is still your home, you know.'

Olivia was trying to absorb this when Linda's eyes moved beyond her to where Joel was standing beside the Lexus. 'Thanks, Joel,' she added. 'We owe you, big time.' She paused. 'You'll come in and see Dad, won't you?'

'Not right now,' said Joel, opening the back of the car and hauling out Olivia's suitcase. 'I've got a tutorial at four o'clock, I'm afraid.'

A tutorial!

So he was a lecturer, no less. If Olivia was surprised, Linda clearly wasn't, going to take charge of Olivia's luggage without further argument. 'Well, come back soon,' she said, as he climbed back into the vehicle. 'Just because Livvy's here, you don't have to be a stranger.'

'Yeah, right.'

If Joel's response was less enthusiastic, Linda didn't

seem to notice it, and, with an inclination of his head towards Olivia, he reversed the car across the yard. Still cringing from the childish name her sister had always called her, Olivia was motionless, and it wasn't until he'd driven away that she realised she hadn't even waved goodbye.

Pulling herself together, she went to rescue her suitcase from her sister. 'I can take that,' she said, but Linda wouldn't let it go.

'In those heels?' she asked, with just a trace of the animosity that had blighted Olivia's childhood after their mother died. 'No, I can manage. Come along. I've warned Dad to expect you.'

'You didn't warn me that he'd had a stroke,' ventured Olivia as she climbed the shallow steps after her, and Linda's back stiffened in what might have been resentment.

'I thought it was wiser,' she said as they entered the square hall of the farmhouse. She set the suitcase down at the foot of the stairs and then went on, 'You know how sensitive he's always been about his health. And if he'd thought you were only coming here because he was ill…'

'I suppose.' Olivia shrugged, half understanding her reasoning. 'So how is he? Joel said very little.'

'Oh, he's improving every day,' Linda assured her. 'But you'll soon see for yourself.' She paused. 'You, on the other hand, look half-starved. I suppose you're on one of those fancy diets.'

Olivia caught her breath. 'I'm fine,' she said, wishing she dared say that obviously Linda didn't worry about her weight.

'Oh, well, you know best, I dare say,' remarked Linda carelessly. 'Come on. We'll go and see Dad before I show you your room. His bed's in the old morning room. It saves him having to climb the stairs. I hope you don't mind, but I've given you Mum's old sewing room. Jayne and Andrew have our old rooms and Martin and I are sleeping in the main bedroom at present.'

Olivia nodded. She didn't much care where she slept. She had the feeling she wouldn't be staying very long. But she had forgotten about her niece and nephew, who'd been little more than babies when she'd left Bridgeford. Jayne must be eighteen now, with Andrew a year younger. Jayne was the same age as she'd been when she'd married Joel, she reflected incredulously.

'So are the children in school?' she asked as Linda led the way across the hall, and her sister turned to give her an old-fashioned look.

'You've got to be kidding!' she exclaimed. 'Jayne works at a dress shop in Chevingham. She's doing really well, actually. And Andy's probably gone into Alnwick with his father. Martin said he needed to pick up a new rotor arm for the tractor.'

Olivia couldn't hide her surprise. 'I see.'

'I suppose you think we should have encouraged them to continue their education as you did,' went on Linda, a note of aggression in her voice now. 'Well, it didn't do you much good, did it? For all Dad scraped and saved to let you stay on at school, you just upped and married Joel Armstrong as soon as you were eighteen.'

Olivia was taken aback. She hadn't known her father had had to scrape and save to let her stay on to take her A levels.

All the same...

'In any case, we don't have a lot of money to throw around, Livvy,' Linda continued. 'What with losing the cattle to foot-and-mouth, it's been a struggle, I can tell you. We got some compensation from the government, but it's never enough. That's why Martin's trying to persuade Dad to diversify—'

She broke off abruptly at that point and Olivia couldn't decide whether Linda thought she'd said too much or because they were nearing her father's door and she didn't want him to hear what she was saying. Whatever, she lifted a finger to her lips before she turned the handle, putting her head around the door before advancing cheerfully into the room.

'Dad,' Olivia heard her say in a sing-song voice as she followed her in. 'You're awake. That's good.' She glanced behind her. 'Livvy's here.'

Her father made some kind of gruff response, but Olivia could barely hear it. However, when she managed to circle her sister's bulk to see the man who was lying in an armchair by the windows, a rug covering his bony knees, she thought she could understand why. The stroke had evidently left one side of Ben Foley's face paralysed and his hair was completely grey. When he spoke he did so with apparent difficulty.

'Hi, Dad,' she said, very conscious of Linda's eyes watching her. She struggled to hide the shock she felt as she went closer and bent down to kiss his lined cheek. Then she forced a smile. 'It's been a long time.'

Ben Foley grunted. 'Whose fault is that?' he got out thickly, and she was relieved that she could understand him.

'Mine, I guess,' she said, although she doubted he would have welcomed her back any sooner. When she'd lost the baby her father, like Joel, hadn't believed her explanation. And, when he'd heard she and Joel were splitting up, he'd told her to find somewhere else to live.

She wondered now if he'd have felt the same if he'd known Joel was going to leave the farm. They'd been sharing the house with her father and, although it wasn't the best arrangement, it had been all they could afford at that time. Joel had already moved out of the house, but she guessed her father had hoped he'd come back after her departure. Perhaps he had, but not for long. It must have been a bitter pill for Ben Foley to swallow.

Trying to put the past behind her, she went on, 'Well, I'm here now, Dad. So how are you feeling?'

'How do I look?' demanded her father, with a little of his old irascibility, and Linda bustled forward to lay a conciliatory hand on his shoulder.

'Livvy's only showing concern for your welfare,' she said soothingly, but Olivia couldn't help wishing she'd leave them alone. 'Now, do you want some tea? I'll make us all a cup while Livvy settles in.'

Ben Foley scowled. 'I thought she'd come to see me,' he muttered, giving his younger daughter a look from beneath a drooping eyelid.

'I have,' began Olivia, but once again Linda intervened.

'You'll have plenty of time to talk to Livvy later,' she said firmly, tucking the rug more securely about him. 'Come along,' she added to her sister. 'I'll show you where you're going to sleep.'

Joel slept badly and was up before seven the next morning, making himself a pot of coffee in the sleek modern kitchen of his house.

The house was large, but graceful, situated in a village just half a dozen miles from Bridgeford, where his ex-wife still lived. He'd bought it, ironically enough, after he and Louise had broken up. With four bedrooms and three bathrooms, it was really too big for his needs, but it meant Sean could come and stay whenever he liked.

He came fairly often, for weekends and holidays. Joel and Louise had had a fairly amicable divorce, both admitting they'd made a mistake in rushing into marriage. Louise had married again, and, although Joel wasn't overly fond of her new partner, he had been forced to concede that Sean should make his permanent home with them.

Still wearing nothing but the cotton boxers he'd slept in, Joel moved to the kitchen window, staring out over the large garden that happily he employed a gardener to keep in order. An expanse of lawn, where he and Sean played football, stretched away to a hedge of conifers, and beyond the hedge there were fields where sheep and their newborn lambs grazed.

It was all very peaceful, but Joel felt anything but untroubled at the present time. The smooth tenor of his life had been disturbed, and no matter how often he told himself that Olivia's return meant nothing to him, he couldn't quite make himself believe it.

Seeing her again had definitely unsettled him. When he'd agreed to go and meet her, he'd anticipated coming away with a certain smug satisfaction that he'd done the right thing all those years ago. What he'd expected, he realised, was that the image he'd kept of her all this time would have been flawed by age and experience. But it wasn't true. Instead, she was just as lovely, just as sexy, as he remembered.

Which annoyed the hell out of him. Dammit, just

because she'd taken care of her appearance didn't change the woman she was inside. The most beautiful creatures in the world could be deadly. Even so…

He scowled, rubbing his free hand over his jaw that was already rough with stubble. Then, swallowing a mouthful of his coffee, he turned away from the window and started towards the door. He needed a shave and a shower, not necessarily in that order. He'd probably feel better if he could look at himself without immediately noticing the bags beneath his eyes.

He'd made it as far as the stairs when the doorbell rang. He glanced at his wrist, realised he wasn't wearing his watch, and cursed under his breath. What the hell time was it? Not later than seven-thirty, surely. It had to be the mail, but he wasn't expecting any parcels as far as he knew.

He set his cup down on the second stair and trudged back to the door. The wooden floor was cold beneath his bare feet and he wished he'd stopped to put on a robe. But who knew he was going to have to face a visitor? he thought irritably. Particularly this morning, when he was feeling so bloody grumpy to begin with.

The door was solid oak so he couldn't see who it was until he'd released the deadlock and swung it open. Then his eyes widened and he stared disbelievingly at the child who was standing outside.

'Sean!' he exclaimed blankly. But then, noticing that the boy was shivering, Joel hurriedly stepped back and invited him in. He closed the door as Sean moved inside, dropping a backpack he'd been carrying on the floor. His brows drew together. 'How the hell did you get here?'

Sean shrugged. He was tall for his age, lean and wiry,

with Joel's dark hair and colouring and his mother's blue eyes. He was approaching his eleventh birthday, and in recent months Joel had noticed he'd developed an increasingly stubborn attitude.

'I caught the bus,' he said at last, moving into the kitchen. 'Got any cola?'

Joel paused in the doorway, watching as his son took a can of cola out of the fridge and flipped the tab. 'There are no buses this early in the day,' he said, as Sean swallowed thirstily. 'Does your mother know you're here?'

'She will soon,' said Sean, removing the can from his lips and glancing about him. 'Can I have something to eat?'

Joel sucked in a breath. 'What does that mean, exactly? *She will soon.*' He repeated what his son had said. 'Come on, you might as well tell me.'

Sean shrugged. 'I've left home,' he said, opening the fridge door again and pulling out a pack of bacon. 'Can I make myself a sandwich? I'm really hungry.'

Joel stared at him. 'Hold it,' he said. 'Before we go any further, I want you to explain how you got here and why your mother doesn't know yet. Then I'll ring her and put her mind at rest.'

'I shouldn't bother.'

Sean was fiddling with the plastic wrapper of the bacon but before he could go any further his father stepped forward and snatched it out of his hands. 'Answers, Sean,' he said. 'Then we can talk about breakfast. Why are you shivering? For God's sake, have you been out all night?'

'No.' Sean was indignant, but Joel didn't believe him.

'So where have you been?' he demanded.

'I can walk, you know.' Sean hunched his shoulders. And

then, seeing his father's expression, 'All right, I spent the night in the barn up the road.' He grimaced as Joel showed his horror. 'It wasn't so bad. There was some straw in the loft and a horse blanket. It smelled a bit, but it wasn't bad.'

Joel stared at him. 'So how come your mother doesn't know yet?'

'How'd you think? She and the hulk went out last night and they don't usually check on me when they come in.'

'Don't call Stewart "the hulk",' said Joel, though he had to admit Louise's second husband did have a beer belly. 'And what are you saying? That they went out and left you in the house on your own?'

'Hey, I'm old enough,' protested Sean, eyeing the bacon enviously. 'Look, couldn't we just have something to eat before you phone Mum?'

Joel hesitated, then he tossed the bacon back to him. 'I'll ring your mother,' he said resignedly. 'Don't set the place on fire.'

'Thanks, Dad.' Sean grinned now. 'D'you want some, too?'

His father shook his head. 'I'm going to take a shower after I've made that call. If you're cold, just adjust the thermostat on the Aga. You know how, don't you?'

Receiving his son's assurance that he did indeed know how to adjust the stove which heated the entire house, Joel went across the hall to the stairs again and rescued his coffee. As expected, it was cool now, but he intended to ring Louise before doing anything else. And from his bedroom. He had no intention of allowing Sean to listen in.

His ex-wife answered the phone with a note of irritation in her voice. 'Yes?' she said, and Joel guessed she'd probably had a late night. For the first time, he resented the fact that she and Stewart had custody of Sean. What kind of role models was he being faced with every day?

'It's me,' he said abruptly. 'Do you know where Sean is?'

'Still in bed, I expect.' Louise didn't sound worried. 'I've banged on his door and told him he won't have time for any breakfast, but does he listen? No way. Anyway, if you want to speak to him, Joel, you'll have to wait until tonight.'

The temptation to say 'OK' and ring off was appealing, but the last thing Joel needed was for Stewart Barlow to accuse him of kidnapping his son. 'He's not in bed, he's here,' he said, without preamble. 'As you'd know, Louise, if you'd bothered to check on him last night.'

Louise was briefly silenced. She wasn't used to Joel criticising her and he guessed she was wondering how to respond. 'Are you saying he's been with you since yesterday evening?' she demanded, after a moment. 'Don't you think you should have taken the trouble to let me know before this?'

'How do you know I didn't ring last night?' asked Joel flatly.

Another silence. Then, 'So he has been with you all night? Oh, Joel—'

'No.' Joel interrupted her. 'I was only making the point that you weren't there, even if I had phoned.' He sighed. 'I thought children had to be at least thirteen before being left alone.'

Louise sighed. 'We weren't out for long—'

'Even so…'

'What's he been telling you?' She sounded suspicious now. 'He can be a little monkey, you know.'

'I know.' Joel was reluctant, but he had to be honest. 'As a matter of fact, he only arrived on my doorstep a few minutes ago.'

'So where did he spend the night?' She sounded worried now.

'He says in a neighbour's barn.'

'My God!' Louise was horrified. Then she hesitated. 'So why didn't he come to you last night?'

'I'm afraid I was out, too,' said Joel unwillingly. 'I had a meeting at the college. I didn't get back until late.'

'So you weren't part of the welcome-home committee for Olivia Foley?' teased Louise, not without a touch of jealousy. 'I expect you've heard she's come back to see her father.'

Joel quelled his impatience. He had no desire to discuss Olivia's return with his ex-wife. 'If I'd known Sean was likely to turn up, I'd have been here,' he retorted shortly. 'And I don't think you should have left him alone in the house.'

'I don't, usually.' Louise was defensive. 'But Stewart wanted to go out and I didn't think there was any harm in it. We were only down the road, for goodness' sake! If he'd needed anything, he had the pub's number.'

'Whatever.' Joel wasn't prepared to discuss it over the phone. 'Look, I haven't had time to talk to him yet. I need to find out why he decided to do a bunk. Give me the rest of the day, can you? I'll give you a ring tonight.'

'But what about school?'

'He can take a day off, can't he? It wouldn't be the first time, I'm sure.'

'What do you mean?'

'Nothing.' Joel backed off. 'Come on, Louise. Give the kid a break.'

Louise was obviously not happy about the situation, but she decided not to be awkward. Perhaps she was afraid Joel might report her to the authorities. The custody order could be changed in his favour if he chose to complain.

'Well, OK,' she said at last. 'But I think you should bring him home tonight.'

'We'll see.'

Joel didn't argue, but he didn't promise anything either. He still had to find out why Sean had chosen to run away.

Fortunately, he only had one tutorial this morning and he could take his son to the university with him. Sean could play on the computer in his office while he was in the lecture hall.

His coffee was cold now, and, putting it aside, he studied his reflection in the mirror above the bathroom basin. He didn't look good, he thought ruefully. He looked as if it were him, and not Louise, who'd had a heavy night.

He wondered now why he'd married her in the first place. It wasn't on the rebound. Well, not precisely, anyway. After Olivia left, he'd wasted no time before applying for a place at university, and the next four years had passed with the minimum amount of pain.

It wasn't until he'd returned to Bridgeford that the whole sorry mess of his marriage to Olivia had come back to haunt him. Had he thought that marrying someone else and having a child would make him happy? It hadn't, although the son they'd had meant everything to him. And he was determined to ensure that Sean didn't suffer because of his mistakes.

CHAPTER THREE

OLIVIA was in her room, sorting through the clothes she'd brought with her and wondering whether a trip to the nearest town for reinforcements was needed, when Jayne knocked at the door.

Since her arrival a few days ago, her niece had become a frequent visitor, always making some excuse for disturbing her, finding reasons to stop and chat. Olivia guessed the girl·found the fact that her aunt had lived in New York for several years fascinating, and her obvious admiration was reassuring in the face of her brother-in-law's hostility.

Not that Olivia had seen that much of Martin Dempsey, thank goodness! Apart from the evening meal, which they all shared, he spent much of his time outdoors.

'Hi,' Jayne said now, coming into the room at her aunt's summons and casting an envious eye over the clothes spread out on the bed. The girl was tall and slim, much like Olivia herself, but her hair was russet-coloured, like her father's, and her features were almost completely his. 'Oh, my, what are you doing?' She fingered the ruched sleeve of an ivory tulle shirt. 'You have such beautiful clothes.'

'Thanks. I think.' Olivia pulled a wry face. 'I was just

wondering if I ought to buy myself some jeans and a couple of T-shirts. I didn't bring a lot of clothes with me and those I have brought don't seem appropriate somehow.'

'Who says?'

Jayne spoke indignantly, but Olivia could tell she wasn't really interested. And Olivia knew better than to say the girl's father resented her being here. Martin apparently didn't like women who showed any independence, and her clothes seemed to be an added source of aggravation.

Jayne perched herself on the end of the bed and regarded her aunt consideringly. 'Can I ask you something?'

'You can ask.' Olivia was half amused.

'Well, were you really married to Joel Armstrong?' she ventured, and Olivia was taken aback.

'Yes,' she said at last, warily. 'Why do you want to know?'

'Oh…' Jayne looked a little embarrassed now. 'I just wondered. I mean, Mum said you were and I believed her. But since I've got to know you, you don't seem the type to—well, play around.'

'Play around?' Olivia caught her breath. Was that what they'd told her?

'Yeah, you know. There was another man, wasn't there? Or so Mum says.'

'There was no other man.' Olivia spoke tersely. 'We were just—not compatible. It didn't work out. That's all.'

'Really?' Jayne stared at her. 'Cos, like, he's really hot, don't you think? Or no, I suppose you don't. But he drives that really powerful SUV, and I think he's, like, totally the man!'

Olivia was stunned. Did Linda know her daughter thought of Joel in this way? Obviously she didn't share her confidences, and the last thing Olivia needed was one of his groupies on her own doorstep.

'I think I ought to finish sorting these things,' she said at length, not wanting to offend the girl, but not wanting to continue this conversation either. For heaven's sake, Joel was old enough to be Jayne's father.

'Oh—yes.' The girl got up from the bed now and pressed her fingers to her mouth. 'I've just remembered. Grandad wants to see you.' She pulled a face. 'He said to say he'd like you to come down.'

Olivia didn't know whether to be glad of the invitation or sorry. She'd been looking forward to finishing this task and then taking a bath. She'd discovered it wasn't wise to expect to have the bathroom to herself in the mornings. Someone was always hammering on the door, asking how long she was going to be.

'OK,' she said now, and, seeing Jayne admiring a silk camisole, she picked it up and tossed it across the bed. Perhaps it would take her mind off other things, she thought hopefully. 'It's yours,' she told her when Jayne looked up at her with disbelieving eyes. 'If you'd like it.'

'Would I?' Jayne was evidently delighted, cradling the scrap of lace to her chest. 'Thanks so much, Aunt Livvy,' she added gratefully. 'I've never worn anything as sexy as this.'

Olivia managed a faint smile at her pleasure, and, passing the girl, she opened the door and allowed her to precede her from the room. But she hoped it wouldn't prove another black mark against her. With a bit of luck, Martin Dempsey might never find out.

Downstairs, she bypassed the dining room, where Linda and Martin were still sitting. She could hear their voices, though not what they were saying, and instead she made her way along the hall to her father's room. She'd visited him several times in the last few days, but this was the first time she'd been on her own. Usually, either Linda or Jayne was with her, ostensibly to ensure that the old man didn't upset her.

Tonight, however, Jayne had scurried off to her room. Probably to try on the new camisole. Which meant Olivia entered her father's room without an escort, feeling almost conspiratorial in consequence.

He wasn't in his chair tonight, he was in the bed across the room, and, closing the door behind her, Olivia crossed the floor. 'Hello,' she said, when she saw his eyes were open. 'How are you tonight?'

'Better for seeing you,' he muttered, and, although his words were slurred, they were perfectly audible. 'I see you managed to shake off your watchdog.' He lifted his good arm and gestured for her to take the chair nearest to him. 'Come and sit down where I can see you.'

Olivia didn't know if he was joking about her having a watchdog, but she acknowledged that Linda and Martin did want to know where she was every minute of the day. 'Thanks,' she said, deciding not to take him up on it. 'I must admit, I've wondered how you felt about me coming back.'

Her father frowned. 'Because of what happened with young Armstrong?' he demanded.

'Well, yes.'

He nodded. 'That was all a long time ago.'

'You never answered any of my letters,' she reminded him painfully. 'According to Linda, you rarely mentioned my name.'

'Yes, well, we all make mistakes, Liv. Mine was in not seeing you were too headstrong to take any advice from me.'

Olivia sighed. 'If it's any consolation, I haven't exactly made a success of my life.'

'No?' Her father's lids twitched in surprise. 'I heard you were doing well in London. Of course, then you upped and went off to America with that man, Garvey. I gather that marriage wasn't happy either.'

Olivia bent her head. For a moment she'd been tempted to say that her marriage to Joel Armstrong *had* been happy. Until she'd discovered she was pregnant, that was, and panic had set in.

She could remember well how she'd felt at that time. It wasn't how she'd have felt now, but that was irrelevant. Then, all she could think was that they were both too young to have a baby, that they couldn't afford another mouth to feed. She'd wanted Joel's baby, of course she had. She'd spent hours—*days*—trying to find a way out of their dilemma that wouldn't entail her losing the child. Like any other would-be mother, she'd fantasised about what it would look like, whether it would take after him. But the problems had seemed insurmountable at first. After all, they could barely support themselves.

But her father wouldn't want to hear that. He and Joel had been on the same side and she had no intention of trying to change his mind now. So instead, she said, 'I should never have married Bruce. I made the mistake of thinking that because he said he loved me, I'd have everything I'd ever wanted.'

'Was he wealthy?'

Olivia shrugged. 'I suppose so.'

'Was that really why you married him?'

'No.' Olivia shook her head. 'Believe it or not, I was lonely. I needed someone who'd care about me. He was smart and good-looking and it seemed like a good idea at the time.'

'You were lonely?' Her father picked up on that. 'So why didn't you come home?'

'I didn't think I'd be welcome,' she confessed honestly. 'And—well, I assumed Joel would still be here.'

'He left. A couple of weeks after you went to London.'

'Yes, I know that now. But not then.'

'Linda kept in touch with you, didn't she?'

'Yes.' But her reports were decidedly selective, Olivia thought, though she didn't say so. 'Anyway, it's all in the past, as you say.'

'So tell me about this man you married. Bruce Garvey. What went wrong? Did he treat you badly?'

'No.' Olivia sighed. 'It's a long story, Dad.'

Her father made an impatient gesture. 'Well, I'm not going anywhere, as you can see.'

'Why not?' Olivia used his words to try and change the subject. 'Don't you have a wheelchair? Don't you ever go outside?'

'I don't want a wheelchair,' retorted the old man grumpily. 'Bloody things. They're for invalids. I'm not an invalid. I'm just—stuck here, that's all.'

'In other words, you are an invalid,' said Olivia, without trying to be tactful. She knew her father of old. He could be totally stubborn, even at the risk of cutting off his nose to spite his face.

'And d'you think I want everyone to know that?' he snapped shortly. 'It's all right for you, coming here and telling me what to do. I don't want anyone to see I can hardly stand, let alone walk!'

'I should think everyone knows that already,' replied Olivia practically. 'This is a small village, Dad. People know you. People care what happens to you.'

'Yes, well, I don't need their pity,' said her father, mopping at the trail of saliva that trickled from the paralysed side of his mouth. 'Nor yours, either,' he muttered. 'If that's all you've got to say to me, you can go.'

Olivia sighed. 'All right, all right. We won't talk about it.' She smoothed her palms over the knees of her trousers. 'I didn't come here to upset you.' She paused. 'Actually Jayne said you wanted to see me.'

'Hmmph.' The old man relaxed again. 'Well, why wouldn't I want to see my daughter? You're a sight for sore eyes, and that's a fact.'

Olivia smiled. 'Thank you.'

'Don't thank me. You were always the beauty of the family. And the brains, more's the pity!'

'Dad!'

'Well, you must know Linda and Martin are running the show around here while I'm—while I can't.' Olivia nodded, and he went on, 'So what do you think of their bright idea?'

Olivia frowned, not at all sure she ought to ask it, but doing so anyway. 'What bright idea?'

The door opening behind them and Linda bursting into the room drowned out any reply the old man might have made. 'Dad!' she exclaimed crossly. 'And Olivia. I thought you were in your room.' She turned back to her father. 'You know you're supposed to be resting. Anything you have to say to Olivia can wait until tomorrow, I'm sure.'

* * *

Olivia was up early the next morning. She'd had enough of being confined to the farm and she intended to catch the bus into Newcastle and spend the day doing some shopping. She also intended to find an agency and hire a car, though she kept that part of her plans to herself.

'Couldn't you get what you want in Chevingham?' Linda exclaimed, when she heard what her sister intended to do. 'Andy could give you a lift in the Land Rover. That would save you having to take the bus.'

'Thanks, but I prefer to go into Newcastle,' said Olivia politely, still feeling some resentment towards Linda for the way she'd behaved the night before. She'd acted as if Olivia had had no right to go and sit with her father. Not without clearing it with her first.

And, of course, any chance of further private conversation with him had been over. Although he'd protested, Linda had been adamant that he'd had enough visitors for one day. Olivia had only had time to squeeze his hand and tell him she'd see him later, before her sister had bustled her out of the room.

It was strange being back in the city after so many years had passed. It seemed so different, so modern, the alterations that had only been in the planning stage when she left now making the centre of town a vibrant, exciting place to visit.

She found a café and, after ordering an Americano, she took a seat in the window overlooking a shopping mall. It was a relief to be away from the farm and drinking a decent cup of coffee again. The instant brand Linda favoured was so bitter in comparison.

Revitalised, she left the café and spent some time exploring the shops. There were certainly plenty to choose from and, despite what Jayne had said, Olivia bought jeans and a couple of T-shirts, as well as a pair of combat boots to wear around the farm. The boots looked incongruous with the suede jacket and matching fringed skirt she'd worn to come to town, and she was laughing with the assistant when she looked through the shop window—straight into Joel Armstrong's eyes.

She couldn't help it. Her eyes widened and her breath caught somewhere in the back of her throat, so that when the assistant spoke again she found it very hard to answer her.

'Um—yes. Yes, I'll take them,' she said, knowing the girl was looking at her strangely. 'Thanks,' she added, quickly slipping her feet into the high-heeled pumps she'd taken off to try the boots on.

She was at the counter, paying for the boots with her credit card, when she became aware that Joel had entered the shop. It wasn't that he'd spoken to her or done anything to announce his presence; it was just a premonition she had that it was him.

It was madness but she could feel him near her, sensed the pressure of the air had changed since he came in. She wanted to turn and look at him, to ensure herself that she wasn't mistaken. God, she was going to be so disappointed if she was wrong.

But she wasn't wrong. When her purchase was completed and she could justifiably collect the bag containing her boots and turn around, he was there waiting for her. 'Hi,' he said as she crossed the shop towards him, and once again her stomach started its crazy plunge.

He looked so good, she thought helplessly. Even in a worn corded jacket with leather patches at the elbows, he looked big and dark and disturbingly familiar. His jeans hugged his legs, worn in places she knew she shouldn't be looking. And, goodness, she shouldn't be so glad to see him.

'Hi,' she answered in return, uncertain what to do next. 'Are you looking for shoes, too?'

'Do I look as if I need to?' he countered humorously as they stepped outside, drawing her eyes to the scuffed deck shoes he was wearing. 'No. You know I'm not.' His eyes skimmed her face. 'Are you on your own?'

Olivia nodded. 'Are you?'

'Until half-past two, when I've got to see one of my students,' he agreed, his warm breath fanning her cheek. 'Have you had lunch?'

Olivia swallowed. 'No.'

'So—d'you want to get a sandwich with me?'

There was nothing Olivia would have liked more, but she knew getting involved with Joel again was dangerous. She'd been sure she was so over him. Now she had goose-bumps just because he'd invited her to lunch.

'Well—I was going to see about renting a car,' she said lamely, and knew immediately from his expression that he wasn't fooled by her excuse.

'In other words, you'd rather not,' he said, lifting one shoulder dismissively. 'OK.' He paused. 'Some other time, perhaps.'

'No, wait!' As he would have turned away, she caught his sleeve and stopped him. 'I—I can see about renting a car after lunch. And I've got to eat. So—why not with you? If the offer's still good.'

Joel regarded her consideringly, wondering if he wouldn't be wiser to just call it a day. He still wasn't sure why he'd asked her, why he wanted to prolong what could only be an awkward interlude in his day.

'I get the feeling you're just humouring me,' he said, and her hand dropped quickly from his arm.

'I'm not.' Olivia's tongue circled her dry lips. 'I just didn't think it through, that's all.' She paused, and then added huskily, 'I didn't want you to feel—obliged to ask me.'

'Why would I feel that?'

He wasn't making it easy for her, and Olivia wondered now if he had had second thoughts. 'You know what I mean,' she said defensively.

Joel shook his head. 'I assume you mean because of what we once had.' His eyes darkened. He wouldn't let her humble him. 'Liv, I've told you already, I'm long past caring what you did or didn't do.'

Olivia wanted to scream. It wasn't fair, she thought. She'd done nothing wrong. Did he think she had no feelings at all?

But Joel wasn't finished. 'If you can't see I was only being civil,' he declared tersely, 'then perhaps we should just go our separate ways.'

Well, that was certainly telling her, he thought, refusing to back down. But, seeing the flush of colour that swept into her cheeks at his words, he couldn't help wondering why he felt this need to punish her. She'd inadvertently saved him from himself, hadn't she? He'd never have been satisfied with working at the farm permanently. And how could he have been able to afford four years at college if he'd had a wife and child to support?

'If that's what you want,' she said now, and in spite of himself, Joel couldn't let her go.

'It's not what I want,' he said between clenched teeth.

'For God's sake, I asked you, didn't I? I just never thought such a simple request would result in this inquisition.'

Olivia sighed. 'I'm sorry.'

So was Joel. But not for the same reason.

'So—where would you like to go?' she asked, and Joel jammed his balled fists into his pockets. *Bed*, he thought savagely, an insane image of Olivia spread-eagled on his sheets, her silky hair draped across his pillow, suddenly front and centre in his mind. 'It's very busy,' she went on. 'Do you think you'll have time?'

Another opportunity, but Joel didn't take it. 'How about buying a sandwich and eating it outdoors?' he suggested. 'Lots of people do that.'

'OK.'

She was annoyingly cooperative and as they walked to the nearby sandwich bar Joel reminded himself that he'd engineered this meeting, not her. He'd be far more convincing if he behaved pleasantly. Allowing her to bug him, to make him angry, would only convince her he wasn't as indifferent to her as he claimed.

CHAPTER FOUR

HOWEVER, the nearby park was buzzing with young people. As well as there being nowhere to sit, Joel realised he had no desire to share the space with his own students.

He should have thought of that, he told himself irritably, turning his back on the open area with a feeling of frustration. Where now? he asked himself. And could only come up with one solution.

'Look, how do you feel about coming back to my office?' he suggested, and saw the way her eyes widened at his words.

'Your office?'

'My room at the university,' he explained abruptly. 'It's just a short walk from here.'

'All right.'

After a moment's pause, Olivia agreed, keeping any doubts she might have had about the advisability of doing such a thing to herself. After all, Joel couldn't have made his feelings any plainer. If she was suffering any pangs of memory they were hers alone.

The City University was one of the smaller places of learning. Concentrating mainly on computer technology, it attracted students from all over the country as well as some from further afield. It had an unparalleled reputation and Joel never stopped feeling amazed that he'd been accepted onto its faculty. There was even a certain amount of satisfaction in taking Olivia there, even if he'd never intended to do so.

His room was on the second floor, overlooking the central courtyard. Below his windows, a quadrangle of grass was surrounded by a cloistered walkway where both lecturers and students could walk even on the wettest days.

Predictably, Olivia walked straight across to the windows, looking out with such concentration that Joel wondered if she was estimating her chances should she have to make her escape that way.

'Nice,' she said at last, turning and resting her hips on the broad sill, and he didn't know whether she was referring to the view or to the generous proportions of his room.

'I'm glad you like it.' Joel unloaded the carrier containing the sandwiches and two bottles of mineral water onto his desk. 'I have to admit, it took some getting used to.'

'What?' She left the window and came over to the desk. 'This room—or your appointment?'

'Both, I guess,' he said, with a wry smile. 'I was lucky.'

'Oh, I doubt that.' Deciding she might as well try and relax, Olivia flopped down into the leather chair behind his desk and swung it round in a full circle as a child might do. 'I'm sure you're very good at your job.'

'Gee, thanks.' Joel was sardonic. 'Your approval means a lot to me.'

Olivia pursed her lips. 'Don't be sarcastic!' she retorted,

and then, sensing he was laughing at her, she pulled a face. 'Anyway, what do you do?'

'Try to instil my love of technology into my students,' he replied, tearing open the sandwich wrappers.

'Is that all?'

Joel's brow ascended. 'Isn't it enough?' And when she continued to look at him, he said, 'Actually, I'm studying for a doctorate myself.'

'So you write, too?'

'Some.' Joel pushed the sandwiches towards her. 'Help yourself.'

Olivia reached for a bottle of water instead, unscrewing the cap and raising it to her lips. She was thirsty, she realised, or perhaps it was just being alone here with Joel that was making her mouth feel so dry.

'Tell me what you've written,' she said, watching as he pulled a sandwich out of its container and took a bite. She was trying to divert herself from noticing how strong and white his teeth looked against the undoubtedly sensual curve of his mouth. 'Could I have seen it?'

'Not unless you're into artificial intelligence,' responded Joel, swallowing rapidly. He studied his sandwich for a moment before continuing, 'I have had a couple of articles published in *Nerds Monthly*.'

Olivia stared at him 'You're making that up!' she exclaimed. 'I'm sure there's no such magazine.'

'Isn't there?'

He was evidently enjoying her confusion and she pulled a face. 'Joel—'

'OK, OK.' He finished his sandwich and reached for his own bottle of water. Then, before taking a drink, he added, 'They were in *Hot Key*, actually,' mentioning the name of an international computer publication that even Olivia had heard of.

'Fantastic,' she said applaudingly. 'Do you have copies?'

'I guess so.'

Joel was telling himself not to be seduced by her obvious admiration, but he couldn't help feeling impatient at his deliberate choice of verb. Dammit, they were talking, that was all. So why was he enjoying the sight of her sitting in his chair so damn much?

'Here?' she asked, looking about her.

'No, not here,' he replied flatly. 'At home.'

'Your home?' Olivia cradled her water bottle between her palms and regarded him curiously. 'Where do you live? In town?'

'Now, why would you want to know that?' Joel asked the question and then wished he hadn't. He was making too much of it. Before she could respond, he went on swiftly, 'I have a house in Millford. I bought it after Louise and I were divorced.'

'Louise?' Olivia said the name slowly. 'That would be your second wife?'

'Well, I haven't had a third. Yet.'

'Yet?' She picked up on that, as he'd known she would. 'Do you have someone in mind?'

'And if I had, do you think I'd tell you?' he countered smoothly. 'Eat your sandwich. It's getting warm.'

Olivia ignored his instruction, her tongue appearing briefly at the corner of her mouth. 'So—did you meet Louise at university?'

Joel sighed, wishing he'd never mentioned his ex-wife.

'I met her again when I went back to Bridgeford,' he said resignedly. 'After I'd got my degree.'

Olivia's jaw dropped. 'You don't mean to tell me you married Louise—*Webster*!'

'Why not?' Joel was defensive now. 'We always liked one another.'

'She liked you,' said Olivia with sudden vehemence. 'My God! Louise Webster. You used to say she was boring as hell!'

'I used to say a lot of things,' retorted Joel, pushing his other sandwich aside with a feeling of revulsion. 'And perhaps *boring* was what I wanted. I hadn't had a lot of success with anything else.'

Olivia glared at him for a few moments, her lips pursed mutinously, and then she pushed herself up from his chair and started towards the door. 'I knew I shouldn't have come here,' she said, and now Joel could hear a faint tremor in her voice. 'Thanks for the water. I find I'm not very hungry, after all.'

'Liv!' Despite the warning voice inside him that was telling him to let her go, Joel found himself taking the couple of strides necessary to put himself between her and the door. He leaned back against it. 'I'm sorry. I shouldn't have said that.'

'No, you shouldn't.'

Olivia halted uncertainly, her heart tripping over itself in its efforts to keep up with her hammering pulse. It wasn't just what he'd said that was making her heart race and causing the blood to rush madly through her veins. It was the painful realisation that she was jealous: jealous of his ex-wife, jealous of the child they'd had together, jealous of the success he'd made of his life once she was out of it.

'Look, why don't you go and sit down again and eat your sandwich?' he suggested gently, and something inside Olivia snapped.

'I'm not one of your bloody students,' she exploded, charging towards him with every intention of forcing him out of her way. 'You go and sit down. I'm leaving.'

Joel didn't move, however. He just lounged there against the door, lean and indolent, one ankle crossed over the other, apparently indifferent to her futile display. And, unless she wanted to grab his arm and try to drag him bodily away from the door, she had to stand there, feeling like an idiot, waiting for him to make the next move.

'What do you want me to say, Liv?' he asked suddenly, his voice lower, deeper, disturbingly sensual. He put out his hand, his lips twisting when she flinched, and plucked a silvery hair from the shoulder of her jacket. 'You and I know one another too well to indulge in this kind of lunacy. Does the fact that Louise and I got together annoy you? Is that why you're behaving like a spoiled brat?'

'You wish!'

But Olivia was panicking now. When he'd reached out, she'd been half afraid he was going to touch her cheek. And, conversely, now that he hadn't, she felt cheated. She'd wanted him to touch her, she wanted to feel those strong fingers stroking her heated flesh.

Oh, God!

'Just get out of my way, Joel,' she said, controlling the quiver in her voice with an effort.

'What if I don't want to?' he countered, and the breath she was taking caught somewhere in the back of her throat.

'Now who's being childish?' she panted. 'Be careful,

Joel, I'll begin to think you're the one who's got a problem. Why should I care who you chose to marry? I just hope you made her happier than you made me.'

Joel moved then. His hand grabbed her wrist, twisted it viciously behind her, forced her towards him whether she wanted it or not. 'Take that back,' he snarled, but Olivia was too stunned to do anything but gaze up at him with wide, startled eyes. 'Go on,' he persisted. 'Do it, or I'll break your bloody arm.'

Olivia blinked, and just like that the realisation that it was Joel who was holding her, Joel who was crushing her breasts against the rough lapels of his jacket, took all her fear away.

'You wouldn't do that, Joel,' she said, with amazing confidence in the circumstances. And although there was a heart-stopping moment when she thought she was wrong, finally, with a muffled oath, he thrust her away from him.

'No, I wouldn't,' he said hoarsely, stepping away from the door. 'I have more self-respect than that. Now—get out of here!'

Olivia hesitated. She knew that was what she should do. But she also knew that in some strange way the tables had been turned. Seeing the grim look on Joel's face as he waited for her to open the door, she sensed that, for all his harsh words, he wanted her out of there now just as much as she'd wanted to go a few minutes earlier.

But why?

It was an intriguing puzzle.

Was it only because he was angry with her for questioning his masculinity? Or had touching her disturbed him as much as it had disturbed her?

'What are you waiting for?'

He would have reached past her and jerked the door open then, but now Olivia put herself in his way. 'Joel,' she said huskily, moving towards him and grasping his forearms. 'We can't leave it like this.'

'Why not?'

He would have shaken himself free of her, but she was insistent, holding on to his arms, feeling the muscles bunch hard beneath her fingers. 'I thought we were friends, Joel,' she murmured, her thumb caressing the sleeve of his jacket. 'I'm not your enemy, you know.'

'This isn't going to work, Liv,' he warned, but she just gazed up at him with innocent green eyes.

'What isn't going to work?' she queried softly, and he growled deep in his throat.

'This,' he said savagely, gripping the back of her neck, pushing the silky shoulder-length hair aside, his fingers digging into her flesh. 'I should have known I couldn't trust you.'

Olivia opened her mouth to deny his claim, but the words were never spoken. With a muffled oath, Joel fastened his lips to hers, silencing anything but the moan of pleasure she couldn't quite restrain.

The kiss was deep and erotic, the sexual thrust of his tongue igniting all the raw, primitive emotions she'd suppressed for so long. She wanted him with an urgency that defied rhyme or reason, sinking into him completely, hazed by desire.

Without her hardly being aware of it, her arms were around his neck and he was moving her back against the door behind her, leaning into her sensually, his hands burning her hips. She only realised he'd rucked her skirt above her knees and parted her legs with his thigh when she felt the cool air upon her skin.

His mouth ate at hers, bruised the soft flesh, left her weak and trembling beneath the weight of his body as he leant against her. She could feel every part of him, feel every bone and angle. And every unguarded muscle, so that when the pressure against her stomach became unmistakable, she put down a hand and caressed his length through the taut fabric of his jeans.

She heard him say an oath thickly, and then he was tipping her jacket off her shoulders, tearing open her blouse so he could press open-mouthed kisses between her breasts. His palms pressed against the taut nipples swelling against her half-bra, his fingers rough against her soft skin.

He groaned and she felt an answering pain deep in her belly. There was a pulse throbbing between her legs and she knew she was already wet. When his hand dropped lower, cradled her thigh, before moving round to probe beneath the thin silk of her thong, she let out a moan of protest. But she didn't try to stop him. She honestly didn't think she had the strength.

'Dear God, Joel,' she whispered unsteadily, wondering if he intended to take her there against the door of his office. It was possible. She was certainly making it easy for him. Like some cheap tart, an inner voice taunted, and suddenly she felt sick. Had she really sunk that low?

Thankfully, it wasn't a question she had to answer. Whether Joel would have unzipped his jeans and pushed himself into her hot, wet heat became a moot point when someone knocked at the door.

They both froze, and Joel at least was reminded of a

similar occasion when they were both still at school. Then, they'd arranged to meet in her father's loft and, like now, things had rapidly got out of hand. Until Ben Foley had come into the barn…

Predictably, it wasn't something he wanted to remember at this moment. Dammit, he thought, he'd sworn Olivia would never get under his skin again. And now here he was, caught like some guilty schoolboy, the only difference being he was still wearing his trousers.

Olivia was the first to recover. Scrambling out from under him, she scooped her jacket off the floor and put it on. Dragging the two sides together over her unbuttoned blouse, she reached for her bag.

'Aren't you going to answer it?' she hissed, checking that her skirt didn't look too creased. It did, of course, and she was sure anyone with half an eye would know what they'd been doing. But there was nothing she could do about it. She was fairly sure she hadn't a scrap of make-up left on her face.

Joel extended his arms and pushed himself away from the door with an effort. He'd sagged against the panels when she'd moved, reluctant to display the treacherous evidence of his need. God, he realised, feeling dazed, it was half-past two already. It would be Cheryl Brooks, ready and eager to discuss the finer points of binary calculus.

He was so screwed, he thought dully, or rather he wasn't. He flexed his shoulders and straightened, turning to regard Olivia through narrowed eyes. He should be grateful for the interruption, so why was he feeling so frustrated? But heaven help him, he could feel Olivia's essence on his fingers, was still breathing the potent scent of her arousal into his lungs.

She was getting agitated. He could see it. She arched her

brows, nodding pointedly towards the door, showing him in every way she could without speaking again that he should see who it was. Joel felt his lips twitch in spite of himself. Would she still be as eager when she saw Cheryl was his visitor?

'OK, OK,' he mouthed, running slightly unsteady fingers through his hair, checking there were no tell-tale signs to betray him. Then, turning, he reached for the handle. Without further ado, he opened the door.

Olivia tensed. She couldn't help it. Whoever it was, she had no desire to stay and be introduced. She wanted out of there, immediately. Her senses had cooled now and she was appalled at the way she'd behaved.

The girl waiting outside only looked to be about eighteen, but she was probably older. It hadn't occurred to Olivia before now that Joel would have female students as well as male and the knowledge disturbed her. The girl had long blonde hair, worn over one shoulder, her tight jeans and cropped top accentuating her youthful appearance.

'Hi, Joel,' she said, proving their relationship was fairly familiar. Then she saw Olivia and the smile she'd been wearing faded.

'Cheryl,' Joel said feebly, aware that he wasn't quite up to this. He glanced at his watch. 'You're early.'

'Just five minutes,' Cheryl protested, and Olivia could tell she wasn't suited either. She'd probably been looking forward to a cosy tête-à-tête with her professor, and now Olivia had spoiled the mood.

'Yeah, right.' Joel glanced briefly at Olivia and then back at his visitor. 'Well, why don't you come in? Um—Mrs Garvey was just leaving.'

CHAPTER FIVE

THE next couple of days passed without incident and, waking up one morning, Olivia realised it was almost a week since she'd arrived at Blades Farm. How long was she going to stay? she wondered. She had planned for this to be just a flying visit. But somehow now she was in no hurry to get back to London and Linda hadn't mentioned anything about when she was going to leave.

There had been a little animosity when she'd arrived back from Newcastle driving a small Renault from the rental agency. But it had soon blown over and Olivia was finding the sense of freedom having her own transport gave her well worth any unpleasantness from her brother-in-law. Besides, it enabled her to get out and see something of the area she'd grown up in, and she had every intention of persuading her father to join her. Eventually.

The car had even helped to put her encounter with Joel to the back of her mind. She hadn't forgotten what had happened. How could she? And sometimes, particularly at night, she'd wake up and find her breasts tingling and a moist place between her legs.

But she'd get over it. The pangs of frustration she was

feeling were just her body reminding her that she was still a young woman with a young woman's sexual needs. During her marriage to Bruce she'd had to stifle those needs, and it was unfortunate that it had been Joel who'd aroused them again.

But any attractive man would have done, she assured herself fiercely, flinging back the duvet and swinging her legs over the side of the bed. It was her misfortune that she'd let Joel get close enough to stir emotions she'd kept in check for the better part of six years.

And remembering how their encounter had ended, she felt again the surge of resentment that had filled her when he'd dismissed her. OK, she'd been planning to leave—desperate to get out of there, actually—but had he had to make her feel as if she'd been just another drain on his precious time?

She breathed deeply, refusing to let thoughts of Joel ruin her day. She'd seen him, they'd talked, and now she didn't care if she didn't see him again. Let him make eyes at his adoring students. The female ones, of course.

For once the bathroom was empty, and, aware that there were no guarantees that that state of affairs would continue, Olivia quickly washed and cleaned her teeth. Promising herself a more thorough inspection later, she returned to her room and dressed in jeans and a T-shirt, her only concession to style the scarlet chiffon scarf she knotted about her neck.

Downstairs, she found her sister in the kitchen, loading the dishwasher, the crumbs and dirty dishes from breakfast still littering the table.

'Let me do that,' said Olivia at once, but Linda merely shook her head.

'Don't be silly,' she said, her glance saying that, even in the stone-washed jeans and cotton T-shirt, Olivia looked over-dressed. 'There's coffee on the stove. Help yourself.'

'Has Dad had his breakfast?' asked Olivia, doing as Linda had suggested. She took a sip of the coffee and stifled a grimace. 'I'll go and see how he is, shall I?'

'He's resting,' said Linda, as she said every morning. So far, Olivia had been unable to repeat the occasion when she and her father had had a chance to talk alone together. 'D'you want some toast?'

'I'll get it.'

Olivia refused to let her sister wait on her, and, taking the cut loaf out of the stone barrel, she extracted a slice and popped it in the toaster. Then, tucking the tips of her fingers into the back pockets of her jeans, she added, 'Haven't you ever thought of getting Dad a wheelchair?'

It was the first time she'd mentioned it to Linda, hoping against hope that she'd have another chance to speak to her father about it. But beggars couldn't be choosers and she was determined to get him out of the house.

Linda stared at her now. 'A wheelchair!' she echoed disparagingly. 'You can't think Dad would ever use a wheelchair!'

'Why not?'

'You know why not.' Linda returned to her task. 'He's far too independent.'

'He's not very independent, stuck in that room all the time,' retorted Olivia steadily. 'It would do him good to get some fresh air.'

Linda shook her head. 'I suppose that's why you insisted on hiring that car, is it?'

'No—'

'You didn't think we might have tried to get him out in the Land Rover or his old Saab?'

Olivia could feel herself weakening, but she stood her ground. 'And have you?'

Now it was Linda's turn to look defensive. 'What would be the point? I've told you, Dad will go out when he can do so under his own steam and not before.'

'And when will that be?'

'Who knows?' Linda's voice had sharpened. 'Nurse Franklin comes in every week to help him with his physical therapy. Perhaps you ought to ask her. Though I have to tell you, you're wasting your time.'

Olivia heard the bread pop out of the toaster and was grateful for the opportunity to have something else to do. Buttering the slice with a knife she found on the table, she helped herself to a smear of marmalade before taking a bite.

'Anyway, I wanted to talk to you,' said Linda with a distinct change of tone. She closed the dishwasher and switched it on. 'Martin's gone into Chevingham, but he'll be back about half-past ten. Maybe we could all have coffee together?'

Olivia kept her eyes fixed on the slice of toast she was holding, wondering what had brought this on. In the week since her arrival, she and Martin had barely said more than a dozen words to one another. She couldn't imagine him wanting to sit down and share morning coffee with someone he evidently despised.

Unless...

She recalled suddenly the silk camisole she'd given to Jayne. Had they found out about that? And if so was she to bear the brunt of their joint displeasure? Had Linda decided she needed her husband's support on this occasion?

'Um—well, I was thinking of going out,' she murmured awkwardly, even though what she'd really been hoping to do was spend a little more time with her father. With or without Linda's chaperonage.

'I see.' Linda stood at the other side of the scrubbed pine table, regarding her coldly. 'Oh, well, don't let us stop you. Not if you'd prefer to go out.'

Olivia sighed. Perversely now, she felt ashamed. They were trying to be friendly, and she was throwing their kindness back in their faces.

'No,' she declared firmly. 'I can go out any time. What do you want to talk about, anyway? I hope I haven't done anything wrong.'

'Heavens, no.' Linda was all smiles now. 'It's just—well, you've been here a week now and you've got some idea of the way the farm works. Martin and I have come up with an idea that we'd like to put to you. But I'd rather wait until he's here to explain it to you himself.'

In spite of her misgivings, Olivia was intrigued. Was this anything to do with what her father had started to tell her when Linda had burst in on them the other evening? He had definitely mentioned some idea his daughter and son-in-law had had. Was she to find out what it was from an entirely unexpected source?

The time between her agreeing to listen to what they had to say and Martin's return dragged. Having checked that her father was indeed sleeping and therefore unable to be disturbed, Olivia decided to go for a walk. She had over an hour before the half-past-ten deadline, and it was a pleasant morning. Collecting her boots and a jacket from upstairs, she let herself out of the front door and walked briskly away from the house.

She had no particular direction in mind. Just a need to escape Linda's overpowering presence. Despite being a pushover where her husband was concerned, Linda certainly liked to throw her weight around with the other members of the household.

Avoiding the immediate environs of the house for fear Linda would see her, Olivia skirted the trees that screened the paddock and made her way across the stockyard to the barn. There were chickens running loose here and even a couple of geese that hissed alarmingly. But Olivia wasn't troubled. It was amazing how the memories of childhood came flooding back.

She could see her nephew in the distance. Andy was up on a ladder, apparently painting one of the cottages that housed the families of the men who worked on the farm. Which was odd, she reflected, frowning. The tenants usually looked after the cottages themselves.

Perhaps he wasn't painting, she thought, dodging into the barn so he wouldn't think she was spying on him. He could just be repairing the guttering. Or cleaning the windows—but that wasn't likely either.

The barn was familiar. Although she would have preferred not to think about it, this was where she and Joel had used to meet after school. There'd been a loft, fragrant with the heat of the sun on the hay her father had stored there. It had been their own private hideaway—though she guessed now that her father had known exactly what was going on.

The ladder leading up into the loft was still there and,

after assuring herself that she was alone, Olivia couldn't resist climbing it. For old times' sake, she told herself firmly. To see if anything had changed.

However, as she started up, she heard a rustle in the straw and she stiffened instinctively. Rats? she wondered uneasily. Or just a bird that had taken up residence in the roof. She sighed. Was she really going to let anything, bird or animal, frighten her away? Whatever it was, it would be far more frightened of her.

She continued up, listening hard for any other sound, but she heard nothing. All the same, when she stuck her head above the hatch, she knew a moment's apprehension. She'd seen enough horror films to be able to imagine the worst.

But all appeared to be as it should be and she started down again. Only to come to an abrupt halt when she heard something scrape across the floor above her head. That was no bird, she thought. No rat, either. Her fingers tightened on the rungs of the ladder. She ought to go and report what she'd heard to Andy or one of the other men.

But, come to think of it, she hadn't seen any other men about the farm. Of course, she hadn't spent much time on the farm since she'd come back, so perhaps that wasn't so surprising. And calling Andy seemed like such a feeble thing to do. Who could be up there? Wouldn't they have tackled her sooner if they'd intended her any harm?

It was nerve-racking but, steeling herself, she started up again. 'Hello there,' she called, giving whoever it was plenty of warning if they wanted to escape. She seemed to remember there was a gantry at the other side of the loft where the hay had been loaded. It was at least an eight-foot jump to the ground, but if the intruder was desperate…

Once again she reached the hatch, but this time she climbed up into the loft. It had occurred to her that it might be kids. What an ideal place to bunk off school.

Olivia looked about her. 'I know there's somebody here,' she said, trying to see beyond the tumbled bales of hay into the shadowy corners of the loft. 'If you don't come out, I'll—I'll—' she had a spurt of inspiration '—I'll go and fetch one of the geese to find you.'

Not that that was remotely likely, she acknowledged. Although she wasn't afraid to cross the yard, she doubted she'd have the guts to pick up one of the geese. But, hopefully, a kid might not know that. Particularly one who wasn't familiar with birds or animals.

There was no movement, however, and Olivia sighed. 'OK,' she said. 'If that's what you want.' She pretended to take hold of the ladder. 'I'll be back—'

'No, wait!'

The voice was definitely that of a child's, she thought with some relief. It had occurred to her that some vagrant might have spent the night in the barn. But, as she watched, a boy detached himself from the pile of sacks where he'd been hiding. A tall boy, but not much more than eleven years old, she thought.

He stood beside the sacks for a moment, his face in shadow, only his eyes reflecting the light. Blue eyes, Olivia saw; resigned yet mutinous. As if he'd been expecting someone to come looking for him, but that didn't mean he had to like it.

'Hi,' said Olivia after a moment. 'You do realise you're trespassing, don't you?'

'How do you know?' he demanded, and she realised she

didn't. Could he possibly belong to one of the families who lived on the farm?

'What's your name?' she asked, but this time he didn't answer her. 'You don't live on the farm, do you? You might as well tell me. I'm going to find out anyhow.'

The boy's chin jutted. 'No, I don't live on the farm,' he admitted at last. 'I wish I did. Anything would be better than living with my mum and the hulk!'

Olivia gasped. 'Don't call your father the hulk!'

'He's not my father,' retorted the boy at once, and Olivia felt a glimmer of understanding. Obviously his parents were separated, and he wasn't happy with the arrangement.

'All the same,' she said, trying to think of something positive to say, 'I expect they'll be worried about you. Shouldn't you be in school?'

The boy shrugged, which she assumed was a yes, and leaned down to grab the handle of a backpack lying on the floor. As he did so, a ray of sunlight streaming through a crack in the wall illuminated his thin features, and Olivia felt her heart turn over.

'What's your name?' she asked again, though she was fairly sure she knew his surname. Goodness! She moistened her dry lips. He had to be Joel's son. And it all fit, she realised. Him, living with his mother; his parents separated—*divorced*! The only thing Joel hadn't told her was that Louise had married again.

'Sean,' the boy muttered now, completing his identity. 'What's yours?'

'Olivia. Olivia—Foley.' She used the name deliberately, guessing he would know who owned the farm.

He regarded her defiantly. 'Are you going to tell Mum where I am?'

Olivia sighed. 'I've got to. I can't leave you here. How long have you been up here anyway? What time did you leave for school?'

'I didn't,' said Sean, low-voiced, and Olivia stared at him in disbelief.

'Oh, no!' she exclaimed. 'Don't tell me you've been up here all night?'

Once again, Sean didn't answer her, and she was left to fill the gaps herself. His mother must be desperate by this time. Losing a child was every parent's nightmare.

'I must tell your mother you're safe,' she said gently. 'What's her name?' Not Armstrong, obviously. 'Where do you live?'

'I'd rather you told Dad,' said Sean miserably, and once again Olivia's heart flipped a beat.

'Why?' she ventured, aware that it wasn't really anything to do with her, but assuring herself she was only trying to make sense of his answer.

'Cos he didn't believe me last time,' the boy declared obliquely. 'I told him I didn't want to live with Mum and—and Stewart.'

'Stewart?' Olivia was fishing, and Sean took the bait.

'Stewart Barlow,' he said without thinking, instantly supplying the one name she didn't have.

Olivia absorbed this without saying anything, aware that Sean was regarding her with hopeful eyes. 'Will you speak to my dad?' he asked, twisting the strap of his backpack round his thin wrist. 'Honestly, he won't be mad at you if you don't tell Mum first.'

Olivia tucked her thumbs into the back pockets of her jeans. 'So what's your dad's name?' she asked, realising she wasn't supposed to know who he was.

'It's Armstrong,' said Sean much more cheerfully. 'Joel Armstrong. He's a teacher,' he added, as if that carried more weight.

A quiver of apprehension ran down Olivia's spine and she shivered. She could hardly believe she was standing here, talking to Joel's son, trying to decide what was best for the boy. She was fairly sure Joel wouldn't like the idea of her being involved in his private affairs. But, in spite of that, she couldn't deny a tremor of excitement at the power Sean had inadvertently given her.

'Where do you live, Sean?' she asked again, and the boy's eyes narrowed.

'You're not going to tell my mum, are you?' he blurted. 'Oh, please, I don't want to live with them any more.'

'Why not?' Olivia frowned. 'They don't—well, they don't hurt you, do they?'

'No.' Sean was sulky. 'I just don't like my stepfather, that's all.'

Olivia considered. Bearing in mind her own feelings about Martin Dempsey, she could sympathise. But Sean was too young to make that kind of decision for himself. 'Why don't you live with your father, then?' she asked. 'You like him, don't you?'

'Oh, yes!' Sean's face lit up. Then he hunched his shoulders as reality kicked in. 'But he works at the university in Newcastle. Besides, Mum said I needed two parents, not just one.'

'I see.' Olivia was beginning to understand the situation.

'But Stewart's not my parent!' exclaimed Sean, his expression darkening with frustration. He broke off and looked at her, waiting for her to say something. 'Please, don't tell my mum.'

'Tell me where you live and I'll think about it,' replied Olivia cautiously, and Sean expelled a heavy sigh.

'Twenty-six Church Close,' he muttered unwillingly. 'But she won't be there. She'll be at work.'

Olivia doubted Louise would be at work if she knew her son was missing. In the same situation, Olivia knew she'd have been doing everything in her power to find out where he'd gone. 'Church Close?' she said. 'Is that in Bridgeford?'

Sean nodded. 'It's one of the new houses behind the church.'

'Ah.'

'It's a horrible place. I don't like it,' he added vehemently. 'My dad's house is much nicer. And it's bigger, too.'

'Is it?' Olivia accepted his assessment, but she couldn't help thinking it was the people who occupied the houses, not the houses themselves, that were determining his opinion. 'OK,' she said at last, deciding she owed Louise no favours. 'I'll ring your father.' But when his face cleared, she went on warningly, 'Be prepared. He probably knows all about the fact that you're missing by now.'

CHAPTER SIX

JOEL was in the library at the university, doing some research for a paper he was writing, when his mobile phone trilled.

Immediately, half the eyes in the room turned in his direction and he made an open-handed gesture of apology as he reached to turn the phone off. Whoever it was would have to wait until he finished what he was doing, he thought impatiently. Certainly none of his colleagues would think of disturbing him here.

But he couldn't help noticing the number being displayed as he flipped the mobile open. It was unfamiliar to him and conversely that troubled him. He was remembering what had happened a few days ago, and, although he had no reason to suspect this call had anything to do with his son, he gritted his teeth and pressed the button to connect the call.

'Yeah,' he muttered, barely audibly, though the pained looks he was receiving proved he wasn't fooling anybody. Stifling an oath, he gathered his papers together and thrust them one-handed into his case, quitting the room with ill grace.

'Joel?'

Bloody hell, it was Olivia. Joel thought he'd have recognised her voice even in his sleep, but that didn't make him feel any the less aggressive at having to take her call.

'What do you want, Liv?' he demanded, and even to his own ears he sounded belligerent. He half expected her to make some biting comment and ring off.

But she didn't. With creditable coolness, she said, 'There's someone here who wants to speak to you, Joel,' and a moment later a timid voice said,

'It's me, Dad,' and he knew he hadn't been wrong in anticipating trouble.

'Sean!' he exclaimed. 'Hell's bells, why aren't you in school?'

'Because I'm not,' said Sean defensively. 'Can I come and see you?'

Joel sagged back against the wall outside the library, dropping his book bag at his feet, raking impatient fingers through his hair. 'Sean, I'm at the university. I've got a lecture in—' he consulted his watch '—in exactly forty-five minutes. I don't have time to see you now.'

Sean made no response to this but Joel heard a muffled exchange going on in the background. And as he listened, he realised something that he should have questioned right away. Sean was talking to *Olivia*! How had *that* happened?

'Sean,' he said sharply, resenting the fact that he couldn't hear what they were saying. 'Sean, where are you?'

There was another pause, while frustration welled up inside him, and then Olivia spoke again. 'I'd have thought you'd have had the grace to abandon your lectures while your son was missing,' she said accusingly, and Joel felt as if the ground had just opened up beneath his feet.

'What did you say?' he asked harshly, but he already knew what she meant.

'Sean didn't go home last night,' said Olivia flatly. 'Don't pretend you don't know.'

'I don't. Or rather I didn't!' exclaimed Joel, trying desperately to get a handle on the situation. 'What do you mean, he didn't go home? How do you know? Did Louise tell you?'

'Louise, no.' Olivia sounded impatient. 'I haven't spoken to Louise. Sean told me. And he insisted on me calling you first.'

'Damn!' Joel pushed himself away from the wall, unable to control his agitation. 'So how long has he been with you?'

'Well, not all night, obviously,' retorted Olivia crisply. She paused. 'I—found him in the barn about an hour ago.'

'The barn?'

'Yes, the barn. In the loft, actually. I suppose that was why no one knew he was there.'

Joel groaned. Unwillingly the memory of their meetings, their lovemaking, in the loft came back to haunt him again. But evidently Olivia had no such sensibilities.

'He apparently spent the night there,' she continued evenly. 'What I can't understand is how you didn't know he was missing.'

Joel could have told her. It was obvious that when—*if*—Louise had discovered her son's disappearance, she'd immediately assumed that once again he'd sought refuge with his father. But he hadn't, and Joel's blood ran cold at the thought of what could have happened to the boy.

'Did he tell you this is the second time he's run away in less than a week?' he asked, though it was hardly an explanation.

'No.' There was another brief silence while Olivia absorbed this. Then, 'Are you saying he came to the university to find you?' and Joel blew out a weary breath.

'To my house in Millford, actually,' he said tersely. 'Now do you see why I might not have been told what was going on?'

'I'm beginning to,' she answered. And then, in an entirely different tone, 'What do you want me to do? Take him home?'

Joel heard Sean's vehement protests that she'd promised he could see his father and made an immediate decision. 'Do you think you could bring him to Millford?' he asked, aware he was going to have to get someone to cover his lecture. 'I know it's an imposition, but I could meet you there in—say, forty minutes?'

Another pause, shorter this time, before Olivia said, 'I could do that.' She took a breath. 'OK. Sean can give me directions. We'll see you in about three-quarters of an hour.'

Although she knew Linda wouldn't be very pleased that her plans were being disrupted, Olivia didn't tell her what was going on. She guessed if Linda found out that Joel's son had spent the night in the barn, she would insist on informing his mother. And while that was possibly the most sensible thing to do, if Louise was worried about her son, why hadn't she been going from door to door, asking if anyone had seen him?

Fortunately, Martin hadn't come back yet so Olivia was able to collect her keys and unlock the rental car without incident. All the same, after reversing up to the barn and telling Sean to jump in the back and keep his head down, she felt absurdly guilty. This wasn't her problem and she was all kinds of a fool for getting involved.

It was still too early when they arrived at Joel's house, but Olivia was happy to be away from Bridgeford. She knew no one in Millford; hoped no one would recognise her. And, besides, it gave her a little more time to talk to Sean.

Joel's house overlooked the village green; an elegant Georgian structure, it had windows on either side of an oak door, with a distinctive fanlight above. What had once been a coach-house now served as a garage, Sean told her. He obviously liked being her guide and proudly showed her round to the back.

There was a football lying on the lawn and Sean immediately dropped his backpack onto the patio and started kicking the ball around. 'Can you play football?' he asked, seeing her watching him, and Olivia shook her head.

'You've got to be kidding,' she said, laughing. 'I've got two left feet.'

'What does that mean? Two left feet?' Sean looked puzzled.

'It means I'm no good at sports,' explained Olivia wryly. 'I go running instead. That doesn't need any skill at all.'

Sean started heading the ball. 'Where do you run? Around the farm?'

'No.' Olivia realised she hadn't had any exercise since she'd arrived in Bridgeford. 'I used to live in New York. I did all my running there.'

Sean stopped what he was doing and stared at her. 'New York,' he echoed. 'That's in America, isn't it?'

'Yes. Have you been there?'

'Not to New York,' said Sean seriously. 'But Dad took me to Disneyworld last year. That's in Florida,' he added, in case she didn't understand, and Olivia made an admiring face.

'Cool,' she said. 'And did you enjoy it?'

'Oh, yeah.' Sean picked up the ball, cradling it in his arms. 'It was great.' He grimaced. 'Stewart doesn't like holidays. Not unless he can play golf all the time.'

Olivia bit her lip, not wanting to get into family politics. 'Do you play golf?' she asked instead, hoping to divert him. 'My—my ex-husband was very keen.'

'You were married?' Sean gazed at her. 'Was that when you lived in America?'

'I—Yes.' She glanced about her. 'Do you come here a lot?'

It was the wrong thing to say. She knew that as soon as Sean's lips turned down. 'Hardly at all,' he muttered gloomily. 'Just some weekends, that's all.'

'That sounds like quite a lot to me,' said Olivia cheerfully. 'So what do you and your dad do? Go to football matches, that sort of thing?'

'Sometimes,' admitted Sean, still looking dejected. 'Do you think he'll be long?'

Realising Joel's arrival was playing on the boy's mind, too, Olivia endeavoured to distract him. 'Tell me about when you went to Florida. Did you see any alligators?'

Sean brightened at once. 'Oh, yeah,' he said. 'When we stayed in Miami, we went on a trip into the Everglades. We went on one of those hover-boats. It was really exciting.'

'You mean an airboat,' said Olivia, nodding. 'Mmm, I've been on one of those, too. They go really fast, don't they?'

'They're awesome,' said Sean, with boyish enthusiasm. 'Dad says we can go back some time and do it again.'

'Hey, well, that's something to look forward to,' said Olivia, hoping to sustain the mood, but Sean hunched his shoulders now.

'Holidays aren't very long,' he muttered. 'I want to live with my dad. Not just see him now and then.'

Olivia sighed. 'I'm sure you love your mother, too,' she said. 'How would she feel if you lived with your father?'

'She wouldn't care,' said Sean sulkily. 'So long as she's got Stewart and—and—'

'And who?'

'Nobody.' Sean scowled. 'Do you think I should go and look for Dad's car?'

Olivia frowned, but she couldn't think of any reason why not, and, nodding, she let him go. But she sensed he had something on his mind, something more than just his eagerness to be with his father. Could his stepfather have anything to do with it? She didn't want to think so, but there was something he wasn't telling her. Perhaps he'd tell his father. After all, she told herself again, it wasn't her problem.

Following Sean round to the front of the property, she was just in time to see Joel's Lexus pull to a halt at the gate. He thrust open his door and got out and, despite everything, her heart quickened and her mouth went dry.

He was so attractive, she though painfully. Even now, in khaki cargo pants and a cream chambray shirt, the neck open to reveal the brown column of his throat, he looked dark and disturbingly male. Despite the worried expression marring his deeply tanned features, he was strikingly familiar. Big and strong, coiled strength and brooding grey eyes. Heavens, no wonder she'd behaved so outrageously in his office at the university. Just looking at him now, she felt her palms dampen and her body begin to heat.

Sean hesitated a moment and then ran back around the

house and Olivia wondered if he thought his father's grim expression was solely directed at him. She didn't kid herself. Her involvement hadn't gone unnoticed. Joel might be grateful to her for bringing the boy here, but he was probably resenting every moment of it.

If Joel wondered why his son should have run away, he didn't show it, and Olivia shifted a little nervously as he slammed the car door and strode through the wrought-iron gate that footed the garden path. But she refused to scurry away like a scared rabbit. She found she cared too much about Sean to do that.

Joel's eyes found hers and she steeled herself to face his censure. But all he said was, 'Thanks for bringing him here, Liv. God knows what he might have done if you hadn't found him when you did.'

Olivia managed a careless shrug. 'What do you think he'd have done?' she asked, stepping out of his way.

'Found his way here. I hope,' said Joel fervently. 'As he did a few days ago.' He shook his head, looking along the path his son had taken. 'Crazy kid! What the hell am I going to do about him?'

Olivia took an unsteady breath. 'He wants to be with you,' she said, aware as she did so that she knew exactly how Sean felt. Being with Joel again was reminding her of how it had been when they were together. Despite what he'd done to her, she still had feelings for this man.

'And how am I supposed to handle that?' Joel pushed agitated fingers through his hair. 'Dammit, I agreed that he should live with Louise and Stewart. I thought their situation was a more normal one for an impressionable child.'

'Stewart's not his father,' said Olivia, unable to ignore

his anxiety. She paused. 'How old was Sean when you—well, when you and your wife split up?'

'Six,' said Joel tersely. 'But the marriage hadn't worked for ages. Louise and I were already living separate lives.'

'Stewart,' said Olivia, understanding, and when Joel nodded in assent she badly wanted to put her arms around him and comfort him.

But that was too much, even for her. Swallowing, she pushed a hand into the front pocket of her jeans and pulled out her keys. 'Well, I'll leave you to it,' she said, with enforced lightness. 'Don't be too hard on him. He's a good kid.'

'I'm glad you think so.' Disturbingly, Joel's voice had thickened and she found she couldn't look away from his searching gaze. 'He should have been our son, Liv,' he muttered fiercely. 'Yours—and mine.'

Olivia felt a quiver of awareness sweep over her. The intimacy of the moment, his nearness and the bone-deep remembrance of all they'd shared—and lost—was turning her legs to jelly. For a moment she couldn't move, frozen by the force of words that tore her composure to shreds. The desire to reach out to him was almost overwhelming, but then, as if regretting his own weakness—or had she only imagined it?—Joel inclined his head.

'Thanks again for looking after him,' he said stiffly. 'I appreciate it.'

'You're not going!'

Unnoticed, Sean had ventured back along the path, probably wondering what was taking so long, Olivia reflected tensely. He had the football in his arms again, clutched to his thin chest like a talisman, his blue eyes round and filled with concern.

'Mrs Garvey's got to get back,' said Joel at once, going towards him. As he passed her, Olivia's nostrils were assailed by the mingled scents of soap and man, but her response was arrested by the indignant expression on Sean's face.

'You said your name was Olivia Foley!' he exclaimed, proving he hadn't forgotten their conversation. 'You said you lived at the farm.'

Olivia didn't remember saying that, but she understood his confusion. 'My name is Foley,' she told him. 'It used to be Garvey, but I changed back to my old name last year.'

'When you got a divorce,' said Sean, turning triumphantly to his father. 'You see. I knew I was right.'

'Well, it's good to be right about something,' remarked Joel drily, still angry with himself for confronting Olivia. 'So—let's go indoors and you can tell me why you ran away. Again.'

'Can she come, too?'

Evidently Sean had decided he needed some support, but all Olivia wanted to do was get away. 'I can't, Sean,' she said, hating having to disappoint him. 'You talk to your father; I'm sure he'll understand how you feel.'

She was forced to look at Joel then, willing him to re-inforce what she was saying, but conversely, Joel didn't im-mediately respond. He could see Sean had taken a liking to Olivia and, while that ought not to please him, the temp-tation to have a woman's angle had to outweigh his own feelings towards her.

'You can stay if you like,' he said offhandedly, half hoping she'd turn him down. At least, if she did, Sean couldn't blame him for her decision. God, he thought incredulously, was he really pandering to the boy after the way he'd behaved?

'Oh, well, I—'

'Please!' Sean came forward now and touched her sleeve. 'I want to show you my room.'

Olivia shook her head, but it wasn't an indication of what she was thinking. 'I'm sure your father would rather have you to himself,' she said, glancing at Joel's taut face for a moment. 'Wouldn't you?'

Joel's jaw tightened. 'Stay and have coffee at least,' he said carelessly, but Olivia knew he was deliberately forcing her to make the decision.

'O—K,' she said, unable to resist smiling into Sean's relieved face. 'Now, you're not going to take that football into the house, are you?'

CHAPTER SEVEN

JOEL had no real idea how he felt as he fished his keys out of his pocket and opened the door to his home.

Despite the fact that he hadn't lived like a monk in the years since his second divorce, he'd never brought a woman to his house before. And the fact that it was Olivia made it all the more unsettling. He didn't want her here; didn't want the certain knowledge that after she'd gone, he'd still feel her presence. But it was too late now.

Beyond the heavy door, a square entrance hall gave access to the main rooms of the house. A polished parquet floor was spread with a couple of colourful rugs he'd picked up on a trip to India, and a carved oak chest sat at the foot of a curved staircase.

Joel closed the door and Olivia concentrated on her surroundings. That way, she hoped, she wouldn't reflect on the fact that apart from Sean they were alone here.

And it was easy to admire the high-ceilinged rooms she glimpsed as Joel led the way to the kitchen. Without the obvious financial restrictions they'd had when they were married, he'd proved he had excellent taste. The mix of ancient and modern, of different textures and subtle colours, was exactly what the old house had needed.

'I'm hungry,' said Sean at once, opening the fridge with the familiarity of long use and looking inside. 'Can I have some cheese, Dad?'

'I suppose so.' Joel had gone immediately to fill the filter with coffee, but now he glanced over his shoulder with a resigned expression. 'Don't they feed you at Church Close?'

Sean's face darkened. 'Yes,' he muttered sulkily. 'But I haven't had any breakfast.'

'And whose fault is that?' retorted his father at once and Olivia closed her eyes for a moment, knowing that was exactly the wrong attitude to take with his son.

'Mine, I suppose,' blurted Sean, and she was sure there were tears in his eyes when he dropped the unopened cheese onto the counter and charged out of the room. They heard his footsteps thundering up the stairs and then the distinctive thud of a slamming door.

Joel hunched his shoulders and turned from what he was doing to rest his hips against the fitted unit. Then, looking absurdly like his son, he exclaimed, 'Now what did I say?'

'You know what you said,' Olivia told him evenly. 'Be a bit more understanding, can't you? He's very —fragile right now.'

Joel snorted. 'And you'd know this, how? Or have you a growing family I know nothing about?'

Olivia propped her shoulder against the door frame, but she didn't say anything in response to this provocation, and after a moment Joel muttered an apology.

'I just don't know what's wrong with him,' he sighed wearily. 'I mean, he's never been exactly happy living with

Louise and Stewart, but until recently he didn't have a lot of complaints. God knows, it's not what I want for him either, but I don't have an alternative.'

Olivia frowned. 'Why couldn't you and Louise share custody, at least until Sean's old enough to make an informed decision? Surely there's someone who could look after him when you're not here? Your mother, for instance.'

'Yeah, right.' Joel was sardonic. 'Like she's going to give up her freedom to look after a precocious ten-year-old.' He shook his head. 'And why should she? It's not her problem.'

'Sean's no one's problem,' said Olivia firmly. 'He's just a growing boy who wants to spend more time with his father. And—well, I think it might be a good idea to give him a break, if you can arrange it. If he's run away twice in one week, you have to see it as a cry for help.'

Joel's gaze sharpened. 'Has he told you something I should know?'

'No.' Olivia wrapped defensive arms about her midriff. 'It's just a feeling I have, that's all.' She paused. 'Couldn't he stay for a few days? Given enough time, he might tell you what's troubling him.'

Joel scowled. 'So you do think something's troubling him?'

Olivia sighed. 'At the risk of sounding like his social worker, I think he has—issues.'

'What issues?' Joel was perplexed.

'If I knew that, we wouldn't be having this conversation.' Olivia frowned. 'You know what it's like. When you're a child, problems assume a lot more importance than when you're older.' She paused. 'Can't you remember what you were like at his age?'

Joel looked up at her through lashes that were long and thick and dark as pitch. 'My memory doesn't kick in until the day you started at the comprehensive,' he told her roughly. 'You were waiting for the school bus when I got there and I thought—'

But he broke off at the point, pushing himself up and away from the unit, turning back to switch on the coffee machine. 'This won't take long,' he said, despising his sudden weakness. 'Then I'd better go and make my peace with Sean.'

'Would you like me to speak to him?' Olivia didn't know why she was prolonging this, but she knew it wasn't wholly for Sean's sake.

Joel shrugged, glancing at her over his shoulder. 'If you think you can talk some sense into him,' he said tersely, aware that Olivia gave him an impatient look before walking out of the room.

They were down again in a little over ten minutes. Sean still looked uneasy, but at least he wasn't sulking. 'Sorry, Dad,' he mumbled as they entered the kitchen, and then, with a quick look at Olivia, he came and gave Joel a hug.

Joel met Olivia's eyes over the boy's head, but he couldn't read anything from her expression. And, after returning the hug with interest, he turned his attention to the boy. 'That's OK, son,' he said, nodding towards the table. 'Sit down. I've made you a toasted cheese sandwich.'

'Cool,' said Sean at once, pulling out a chair and giving Olivia a grateful grin. It was obvious he was seeking her approval, and Joel wondered why it didn't annoy him that she seemed to have such a good rapport with his son.

'Coffee,' he offered, holding out a mug of the steaming beverage. Olivia took the cup and tasted it approvingly.

'Um, that's good,' she said, smiling at him now. 'You always made—that is, *I* always enjoy a good cup of coffee.'

She'd almost betrayed their previous relationship, she realised, wondering if Joel was aware of it. It wasn't that she wanted to hide it from Sean, but right now she felt he had enough to contend with.

'Let's go into the sitting room,' Joel said now. He smiled at his son. 'Finish your sandwich first, right?'

'OK, Dad.'

Sean seemed quite content to do as he was told for the moment, but Joel guessed that as soon as his stomach was full he'd begin to have second thoughts.

Which was why he wanted to have a quick word with Olivia before his son joined them. But to his surprise, she apologised as soon as they were out of earshot of Sean. 'I'm sorry,' she said. 'I mean, I don't mind if you tell him.' She paused. 'But perhaps he doesn't need to hear it right this minute.'

Joel's brows drew together. 'Am I missing something here? What doesn't he need to hear right this minute?'

'That we were married,' she said awkwardly, aware that their time alone was limited. Then, when he continued to regard her uncomprehendingly, 'Well, obviously you didn't notice the slip I almost made. I'm sorry I mentioned it.'

She subsided huffily onto a soft leather sofa, one of two that flanked an open grate set in a delicate marble surround. Taking another sip of coffee, she cradled the mug between her palms, feeling frustrated. Was she the only one who was aware of the anomalies here? He was asking his first wife for advice about the child he'd had with his second, and she was worrying because she'd almost said the wrong thing. Unbelievable!

To her surprise—and a certain amount of apprehension—Joel came and sat beside her. The powerful muscles of his thigh depressed the cushion nearest to her. And, when he leaned forward to set his coffee mug on a glass-topped occasional table in front of the sofa, the hem of his shirt separated from his trousers.

Dear lord!

She sat back abruptly, directing her eyes anywhere but at that tantalising wedge of brown skin. Yet, she couldn't deny, there was something incredibly vulnerable about it. It proved how agitated he'd been when he'd got into his car at the university. He hadn't even stopped to grab a jacket before making the twelve-mile drive to Millford.

Her eyes darted irresistibly in his direction again. Evidently, he still tanned as easily as he had used to when they were together. An image of them skinny-dipping in Redes Bay when they were teenagers was as vivid now as it was unwelcome.

But he ensured she couldn't ignore him for long, whatever her feelings. Turning towards her, he unsettled her still more by laying one arm along the back of the sofa behind her. 'Now, tell me what you mean,' he said as her eyes fastened on the cluster of hairs just visible in the open V of his shirt. 'Don't you want Sean to know about us?'

'There is no "us",' she told him stiffly, in no state to have this conversation.

'I know that.' His voice rasped. 'But there used to be.'

Now, why had he said that? Joel asked himself irritably.

Just because he was sitting so close to her, because he could smell the indefinable perfume of her skin, he'd spoken recklessly. But it wouldn't do. Dammit, she'd always been able to drive him crazy when he was near her. Right now, all his heat-hazed brain could think about was that scene in his office and how much he wanted to touch her again.

But it wasn't going to happen!

Then she spoke, her voice low and a little unsteady, and the intimacy of their situation swept over him again. 'It's up to you—whether you want to tell him or not. I just didn't want to say the wrong thing.'

'As opposed to doing the wrong thing,' he muttered, unable to pull his eyes away from the rounded swell of her breasts. She was wearing a black T-shirt today and tight jeans that emphasised the slender curves below her waist. And a scarlet chiffon scarf, like a flag of defiance. He would have liked to wind that scarf around his hand and use it to drag her provocative body into his arms. 'Yeah, I see what you mean.'

'Are you saying I've done the wrong thing by coming here?' she asked, her words distracting him, and Joel closed his eyes for a moment against the pull of an attraction he'd been sure he'd conquered long ago.

'No, I have,' he said at last, opening his eyes again and scowling at her. 'By inviting you into my house.'

Her lips parted. 'Well, I'm sorry—' she began indignantly, but he didn't let her finish. Before he could control the impulse, he'd reached out and brushed his knuckles over the visible peaks of her breasts. He was almost sure she wasn't wearing a bra, and the notion drove all sane thoughts out of his head.

'Joel!'

She scrambled backwards, but he was too quick for her, his hand reaching for the arm of the sofa, keeping her in her seat. 'Now do you see what I mean?' he demanded, gazing down at her with oddly possessive eyes. He used his free hand to trace a tantalising path from her breast to the button at her waist. 'I'm wondering if we had sex together if it might help me to get you out of my skull. What do you think?'

'In your dreams!' Olivia sucked in a trembling breath, horrified by her own reaction to his outrageous suggestion. Oh, yeah, her libido applauded. Go for it, girl! Let's get it on. But what she forced herself to say was, 'Let me get up, Joel. I'll get out of here and solve your problem.'

Joel shook his head. 'You think it's that easy?'

Olivia didn't think it was easy at all. Her heart was pounding, her pulse was erratic, and her body felt as if it was on fire. If she wasn't careful, he was going to realise her dilemma, and that made her edgy. 'I have no desire to have sex with you, Joel,' she insisted, and then recoiled with a gasp when his nail scraped down her zip.

For a breath-stealing moment she thought he'd opened it, and she knew her panties were already wet. Heavens, she thought with relief, discovering she'd been mistaken, if he'd slipped his hand inside her jeans he'd have soon found out what a liar she was.

But he wasn't finished with her. 'Sure?' he asked, lowering himself until his chest was just touching hers. The clean male smell she'd noticed earlier rose from his opened shirt, and she could tell from the stubble on his jawline that he hadn't shaved since the night before.

She couldn't deny the moan that rose into her throat as he deliberately pressed closer. His chin scraped her cheek and he used both hands to pull her T-shirt out of her jeans. Then warm palms spread against her midriff, his thumbs brushing the undersides of her breasts with wilful intent.

'In my dreams, hmm?' he taunted her softly, and this time she wasn't mistaken about the invasion of his hand. 'Oh, baby,' he muttered thickly as his fingers found her secret, and then his mouth sought hers and the room began to spin dizzily about her.

The sound of footsteps crossing the parquet floor was instantly sobering. 'Damn,' muttered Joel savagely, hauling himself away from her, and by the time the boy appeared in the doorway his father was standing by the window, apparently watching the lambs in the distant field.

Olivia didn't want to get up. Her legs felt like jelly and every nerve in her body felt as raw as an open wound. But she had to prove—to herself as well as Joel—that she was no pushover. Pushing her T-shirt down and herself up, she turned to smile at the boy.

'Feeling better?' she asked with assumed brightness and Sean made a face.

'That depends,' he muttered, his eyes moving to his father. 'What have you two been talking about?'

'Not that it's any business of yours,' said Joel irritably, and Sean hung his head.

But the truth was, Joel was feeling both thwarted and guilty. Dammit, his son was more important than the unwanted hunger Olivia inspired in him. Yet he only had to look at her to feel again the mindless need of total fascination.

How many more times was he going to let her make a fool of him? OK, she hadn't exactly invited him to make love to her, but she hadn't tried very hard to stop him either. Aching with frustration, he struggled to remember what was important here.

'I'll—talk to your mother,' he told the boy flatly, and then wished he hadn't made it sound like a done deal when Sean flung himself into his arms.

'Thanks, Dad!' he exclaimed fervently. 'I knew Olivia would help you see it my way.'

'Olivia?'

Joel scowled, and Olivia hastily tried to put him straight. 'I just said I was sure you'd put things right with his mother,' she mumbled awkwardly, and Joel gave her a suspicious look.

But when he spoke to his son, he didn't question it. 'I'm not promising anything, Sean,' he said, peeling the boy's arms from around him and holding him by his shoulders. 'But I've got to tell her where you are, anyway, and I'm sure she'll agree to let you spend the night here at least.'

She'd better, Joel added silently, meeting Olivia's eyes again, letting her see his frustration. When would Louise have asked him about their son's whereabouts? he wondered angrily. Did she even care?

Then, realising Olivia would interpret his expression differently, he continued, 'You approve?'

Olivia lifted her shoulders but, before she could make any response, Sean intervened. 'Just tonight?' he asked plaintively, and she realised he did tend to push his luck with his father.

'Look, I've got to be going,' she said, hoping to prevent another confrontation. 'Nice to meet you, Sean.'

Sean's face dropped, and he swung away from Joel to stare at her. 'But we'll see you again, won't we?' he protested. And then, to his father, 'Olivia's staying with her father, too,' almost as if their situations were comparable.

'I know.' Joel nodded. 'Say goodbye, Sean. And thank Mrs—'

'Olivia,' put in his son at once. 'She said I could call her Olivia.'

'OK.' Joel forced a tight smile. 'Thank—her for taking the trouble to bring you here.' Then, gritting his teeth, 'We both appreciate it.'

'Do you?'

Olivia's lips twisted and Joel's stomach tightened in spite of all his efforts to ignore what had happened. Dammit, was having an affair with her the only way he was going to get her out of his mind?

'You better believe it,' he responded now, but even to his own ears he sounded rattled. 'Sean?'

'Oh, yeah. Thanks, Olivia.' His son had no such hang-ups. 'But I can come and see you at the farm, can't I?'

'Sean!'

'Of course you can,' she responded, her eyes challenging Joel to contradict her. 'See you—both—later.'

CHAPTER EIGHT

OLIVIA drove back to Bridgeford, her head buzzing. What had happened to all her brave predictions of not getting involved with her ex-husband? Here she was, befriending his son, letting Joel back into her life and her emotions.

And why?

In Sean's case, it was easy. She liked him, she liked him a lot. All her thwarted maternal instincts came to the fore when she saw how unhappy he was.

With Joel, however, it was anything but easy to understand. Hadn't he hurt her enough? Was she so desperate for a man that she was prepared to go to any lengths to satisfy her sexual needs? If so, she was pathetic!

But that wasn't the whole story. In truth, she'd forgotten how vulnerable she'd always been where Joel was concerned. Hadn't that day at his office taught her anything? She should have remembered that in the old days he'd only had to look at her in a certain way and she'd be begging him to make love to her.

She'd only been fourteen when she'd become aware that Joel was interested in her. Oh, she'd noticed how attractive he was. All her friends had thought he was totally hot! Ironic, really, that Jayne had used the same adjective. But it had been such a thrill when he'd first asked her out.

Naturally, her sister had warned her against getting involved with a boy who was older than she was. At fourteen, sixteen had seemed like a great age. But she hadn't been willing to listen to anyone's advice. She'd assured Linda she knew what she was doing. The physical attraction that had initially brought them together had deepened into love, and she'd believed that nothing and no one would ever split her and Joel up.

Until she'd succeeded in doing it herself...

Martin's car was in the yard when she got back to the farm, and she took a guilty glance at her watch. It was a quarter-past eleven, three-quarters of an hour later than she'd intended. But surely, when she explained the circumstances, they'd understand.

However, when she entered the kitchen, only Linda was sitting at the table, glancing through some coloured brochures spread out in front of her.

'Hi,' said Olivia awkwardly. 'Sorry I'm late.'

Linda looked up. 'Where have you been?'

'To Millford.' Olivia realised some further explanation was needed, and added, 'Joel's son needed a lift.'

'Joel's son?' Linda frowned. 'You mean Sean?'

'Mmm.' Olivia moved to the stove to help herself to some coffee, not wanting Linda to study her too closely. 'Where's Martin?'

'He's gone to help Andy clear out one of the cottages.' Linda got up from her chair. 'How did you meet Sean Armstrong? I didn't know you knew him. Shouldn't he have been in school?'

'I expect so.' Olivia looked down into her cup of coffee, refusing to meet her sister's accusing gaze. She told herself she wouldn't be intimidated into revealing things that were really none of Linda's business. 'What did you want to talk to me about?'

Linda was taken aback. 'Oh, well, Martin's not here at the moment—'

'I'm sure you don't need Martin to hold your hand,' said Olivia, her taste buds protesting at the bitter taste of the coffee. 'Come on, Linda. Do you want me to leave?'

'Heavens, no!' Linda sounded horrified. 'You're welcome to stay here as long as you like.'

'So?'

Linda sighed, and then she bent and picked up one of the brochures she'd been looking at when Olivia came in and handed it over. 'What do you think of that?'

Olivia put down her coffee and looked at the glossy publication. It had been issued by the local tourist board and contained a list of holiday accommodation in the area. It dealt primarily with farms offering bed and breakfast and others that had cottages to rent.

'Well?' There was a trace of excitement in Linda's voice now. 'Could Martin and I handle something like that?'

Olivia blinked. 'Offer bed and breakfast, you mean?'

'No!' Linda clicked her tongue. 'We don't have enough room here to offer bed and breakfast. No, I meant the cottages. We want to modernise the ones we have and offer them as holiday rentals. What do you think?'

Olivia looked at the brochure again, trying to concentrate. 'But aren't the cottages occupied?'

'Not any more,' said Linda at once. 'I told you about the

sheep and cattle being destroyed. There was no point in paying men we didn't need and couldn't afford.'

'You asked them to leave?'

Linda was dismissive. 'Some of them left of their own accord. They got jobs elsewhere.'

'And the rest?'

'I believe they were offered council accommodation.' She sighed. 'It wasn't our problem. Livvy. We all have to do what's necessary to make a living.'

Olivia shook her head. She doubted she could have been so ruthless. Or her father either. Had this had anything to do with his illness? It must have been a blow when he lost everything.

Now she said, 'If you think renovating the cottages is viable, go for it.' She hesitated. 'What does Dad say?'

'Oh, you know Dad.' Linda was impatient. 'In any case, he's not running the farm now, Martin is. And once Dad sees how successful we are, he'll come round. It's not as if he's ever going to be able to run the place himself again.'

Olivia shrugged. 'Well, it's really nothing to do with me, is it? I mean, I don't live here.'

Linda bit her lip. 'No,' she conceded. 'But—well, we do need your help.'

'My help?'

'Yes.' Linda hesitated. 'Look, I won't beat about the bush, we need—financial assistance. We can't go to the bank because they won't lend Martin any money while the farm still belongs to Dad. And you know what he's like about going into debt.'

Olivia stared at her. 'So Dad's opposed to this venture, then?'

'Need you ask? He's never forgiven us for giving the men notice. He's not practical, Livvy. Whatever he thinks, we can't live on fresh air.'

Olivia nodded. Actually, she sympathised with their predicament. She might not like Martin, but she'd never accuse him of being lazy. And the leisure industry was booming.

'It sounds—feasible,' she said at last. 'I'm sure you'll have no trouble attracting visitors to this area. But—' She pulled a face. 'I can't help you, Linda. I wish I could, but I don't have any money. Just enough for a deposit on an apartment, if I'm lucky.'

Linda looked stunned. 'You're not serious.'

'I'm afraid I am.'

'But you told Dad that Bruce was a wealthy man.'

'He was.' And then before Linda could interrupt her again, she went on, 'I left Bruce, Linda. He didn't want me to and consequently there was no generous settlement when we divorced. Besides, I didn't want any of his money. I wanted a clean break. That's partly why I came back to England.'

'But what about your own money? You'd been earning a good salary. What happened to that?'

Olivia was tempted to say it was none of her sister's business, but she didn't want to fall out with her, so she answered truthfully, 'Lawyers' fees are expensive, Linda. And although I earned a healthy salary when I was in London, I'm afraid I never saw the need to save in those days.'

'So why did you leave Bruce? Was there someone else?'

'Not as far as I was concerned, no.'

'But if you're saying he was the guilty party,' Linda said, 'you were entitled to half his assets, weren't you?'

Olivia didn't want to get into the reasons for the break-up or relate how impossible it would have been for her to prove that Bruce was seeing someone else. 'I just wanted out of the relationship,' she said quietly. 'I'm sorry, Linda. I wish I could help you, but I can't.'

'Yes, well, being sorry isn't going to pay for the renovations. Those cottages have needed updating for years.'

Olivia sat down in the chair opposite. 'If there was anything I could do—'

'There is.' As if the idea had just occurred to her, Linda stared at her through narrowed eyes. 'You could talk to Dad, persuade him that this is the only way to keep the farm.'

'Oh, I don't know…'

'Why not? You said you wanted to help, and he'll listen to you. You're the prodigal daughter. If you say you're in favour, he might be prepared to consider getting a loan.'

As luck would have it, Andy came in at that moment and Olivia was able to make her escape without answering her. She knew it was only a temporary release, that sooner or later she would have to come to a decision. But for now, she was grateful for the chance to be on her own.

But, in the days that followed, it seemed that Martin had persuaded his wife to give her sister some breathing space. The plan wasn't mentioned again and Olivia was able to pretend she didn't have the sword of Damocles hanging over her head. Instead she pursued her efforts to get her father to use a wheelchair, seducing him with promises of taking him out in her car, away from the prying eyes of Bridgeford.

Nurse Franklin agreed with her and, whether she thought that leaving them alone together would achieve her own ends or not, Linda put her considerable weight behind it, too. So much so that Ben Foley said he was heartily weary of being put upon. But then he delighted them all by agreeing to give the wheelchair a chance.

Consequently, a week later, Olivia and Linda helped the old man out of the wheelchair and into the front seat of the Renault. It had been arranged that Olivia would drive him down to the coast and Linda had prepared a flask of coffee for them to take with them. She was evidently doing her best to sweeten the atmosphere and Olivia had been so pleased with her father's progress that she hadn't thought of leaving for days.

Olivia drove to Redes Bay, driving down the precarious cliff road and parking on the dunes above the beach. The place seemed deserted; the children were all in school and it was too early in the season for holidaymakers to brave the cool north-east wind that was blowing off the sea. Across the road from the beach, the small pub was doing better business, but no one was taking advantage of the outdoor tables today.

However, inside the car it was snug and cosy. And the view was magnificent: a stretch of almost deserted sand with the white-capped waves stretching as far as the eye could see. Ben Foley heaved a sigh and then turned his head to look at his daughter. 'Thanks for this,' he said sheepishly. 'I've been an old fool, haven't I?'

'Just stubborn,' said Olivia gently. 'No change there, then. Now, do you want a cup of Linda's coffee? Or would you rather have a beer?'

Her father gaped. 'A beer,' he said fervently. 'It's six months since I had a beer.'

'You're probably not supposed to have alcohol,' said

Olivia doubtfully, half wishing she hadn't mentioned it. 'But one beer won't do any harm, will it?'

Her father agreed, and, leaving him sitting in the car, she walked across the road to the pub. She was wearing jeans and a warm woollen jersey but she was still cold. She really would have to toughen up, she thought, if she was going to make her home in this area.

Now, where had that come from?

She'd been thinking about it for some time, she realised. Having got to know her father again, she was loath to go back to London and only get the chance to see him a couple of times a year. If she got a job with an estate agency in Newcastle, she could buy herself an apartment there. That way, she'd be able to visit the farm as often as she could.

There was a big four-wheel-drive vehicle parked in front of the pub. It looked like Joel's Lexus, she thought uneasily, but when she stepped into the bar there was no sign of him. And, after all, she told herself as she ordered her father a beer and herself a diet cola, there must be other cars like his in the area. When the weather was bad, a four-wheel-drive vehicle was invaluable.

After paying for the drinks she stepped outside again, shivering as a gust of wind blew her hair across her face. Scooping it back, she hurried across the road to where she'd left the Renault, and then stopped short when she saw the man beside her car.

It was Joel.

So what's new? she thought irritably. Although it was over a week since she'd seen him, she couldn't deny she'd thought about him. A lot. And Sean, she defended herself, noticing that her father didn't seem to have any objections to the visitor. His door was open and Joel was standing with one arm draped across the roof of the vehicle and one foot propped on the sill.

Joel straightened at her approach, though she observed the smile he'd been giving her father was distinctly thinner when it was directed at her. In tight jeans and a black T-shirt, a leather jacket left open, he didn't seem to feel the cold. 'Liv,' he said, and she didn't know whether to get into the car or stand and face him. 'Linda said I'd find you here.'

Olivia frowned. 'You went to the farm?'

'No.' Joel spoke levelly. 'I tried your mobile—'

'How did you know my number?'

Olivia spoke impulsively, but Joel merely said, 'My phone records all calls.' He paused. 'Anyway, as you probably know, I could only get voicemail. That was when I called the farm.'

'Oh.' Olivia remembered rather guiltily that she'd turned her phone off. But she'd reasoned that no one was likely to call her here. 'So you spoke to Linda?'

'Right.' Joel was patient. 'She said you'd taken your father to the coast, so I guessed you'd come here.'

'Did you?' Olivia's lips twisted.

'Yes.' His grey eyes were penetrating. 'I knew it was a favourite haunt of yours.'

'Of yours, too, if I remember correctly,' she replied tartly. Then, as his eyes darkened, 'Why did you want to speak to me?'

Joel sighed. 'I've got a problem.'

'What kind of a problem?'

'Why don't the two of you go for a walk along the beach and he can tell you?' suggested her father, mopping

his mouth. 'I'll just sit here and enjoy my beer in peace.'
He held out his good hand. 'Joel, will you just unscrew the
cap for me?'

Olivia was forced to hand the bottle to Joel and she
watched somewhat resentfully as he opened it and put it
into Ben Foley's hand. There was a gentleness about him
as he dealt with her father that she hated to acknowledge.
But it was there just the same: an understanding of the old
man's dignity that she couldn't ignore.

'I don't have a coat,' she said now, wrapping her arms
about herself.

'Here, you wear this,' said Joel, taking off his leather
jacket. 'I've got a duffel in the boot.'

'No, it's all right,' she began, but he'd already shed the
coat and wrapped its folds around her.

'Just give me a second,' he said, and sprinted off across
the road to where the Lexus was parked.

'I didn't say the wrong thing, did I?' her father asked
anxiously and Olivia was obliged to reassure him.

'No—'

'I mean, he picked you up from the airport, didn't he?
And Linda tells me you gave his son a lift to Millford the
other day.'

'It's OK, Dad.' Olivia forced a smile. 'Now, are you sure
you'll be all right on your own?'

'I'm not a baby, Liv,' he said, the unparalysed side of
his face twisting in resignation. 'Besides, it'll be good for
the two of you to catch up.'

To catch up!

Olivia gritted her teeth and thrust her arms into the
sleeves of the soft leather jacket. As if she and Joel needed

to catch up. It would be truer to say they knew too much about one another as it was.

Even so, she couldn't deny the jacket protected her from the wind. It was redolent with his distinctive maleness, still warm from the heat of his body, and she wrapped it closely about her. And refused to accept that her rising temperature was caused by anything more than the quality of the leather.

Joel came loping back wearing a hooded duffel. Once again the coat was unfastened, but his hands in the pockets kept the two sides together. 'All set?' he asked, with a quick smile for her father.

'As I'll ever be,' said Olivia ungraciously, but he had to understand this was at his instigation not hers. She'd half expected him to avoid the farm so long as she was around.

They left the car and walked down the path that led through the dunes and onto the beach. The wind was considerably stronger here, and Olivia sucked in a breath as it tried to drag the jacket sides away. 'Let me,' said Joel, and, brushing her hands away, he swiftly attached the zip and pulled it up to her chin. 'Now put your hands in the pockets,' he instructed. 'That should work.'

Olivia did as he said because her fingers were already tingling with the cold. And it was true, now that the jacket was fastened, it had no chance to billow in the wind.

'Thanks,' she said offhandedly, and Joel cast her an ironic look.

'Yeah, right,' he said, and then cursed as the soft sand spilled into his loafers. Emptying them out, he walked barefoot onto the firmer sand.

Admiring his fortitude, Olivia hurried after him, grateful

that her own boots prevented the sand from invading her feet. Not that Joel appeared to notice that the firmer sand was damp and chilly. With his gaze fixed on the horizon, he seemed indifferent to his surroundings. And to her.

'You wanted to talk to me?' she prompted, not happy at being ignored when he'd come here expressly to find her. She glanced up at his unsmiling face. 'How's Sean?'

Joel's jaw compressed. 'Do you care?'

Olivia caught her breath. 'You know I do.'

'Do I?'

Olivia sighed. 'Is this going to be another pointless argument? Of course I care about Sean.' She paused, her eyes widening. 'Don't tell me he's run away again.'

'No.' Joel blew out a breath. 'As a matter of fact, Louise and I have come to an agreement. She's letting Sean stay with me for the next two weeks.'

'That's great!'

Olivia was genuinely pleased for him, but Joel's expression didn't change. 'It's not great as it goes,' he told her flatly. 'I told her I'd be available, but now I won't.'

Olivia frowned. 'Why not?'

'Because the tutor who was going to cover my absence has broken his hip.' Joel grimaced. 'Hell, I feel sorry for the guy, but it couldn't have happened at a worse time as far as I'm concerned.'

Olivia's brows ascended. 'So—what now?'

Joel bent his head, aware that when she'd left his house in Millford a week ago he'd determined that, whatever Sean said, they weren't going to be seeing Olivia again. Yet here he was, telling her his troubles, hoping, he acknowledged ruefully, that she'd be able to help him out. Again.

'When are you leaving?' he asked suddenly, and Olivia pulled a hand out of the pocket of the jacket and pressed it to her throat.

'Well, that's pointed enough,' she remarked, despising herself for feeling hurt by it. 'What's it to you? You're not going to tell me you'll miss me. That would be totally out of character.'

'Can't you stop trying to score points, Liv?' Joel sounded weary. 'I only asked when you were leaving because I was hoping you might be agreeable to working for me for a couple of weeks.'

'Working for you?' Olivia stared at him. Then comprehension dawned. 'You want me to look after Sean?'

'Yeah.' Joel bent and picked up a pebble and sent it skittering across the waves. 'I know it's presumptuous and you're probably going to blow me out, but I do think you're the only person I could ask.'

Olivia shook her head. 'And what would I have to do?'

'Not a lot.' Joel looked at her. 'Just take him to school in the mornings and pick him up again at half-past three. Then stay with him until I get home. He can wait and have his supper with me. I can't give you my actual schedule. It can change from day to day. But unless I have any evening tutorials, most days I'm home about six.'

Olivia's breathing quickened. 'And while Sean's at school?'

'Your time's your own, of course.'

'I'd sleep at the farm.'

Joel looked away. 'Of course.'

Olivia considered. 'Well—OK. I'll do it.' She paused. 'But I don't need any payment. I'll do it for Sean.'

Joel exhaled heavily. 'I don't need charity, Liv.'

'Nor do I,' Olivia retorted shortly. She glanced back along the beach to where she'd left the car. 'If that's settled, I presume we can go back.'

CHAPTER NINE

ON MONDAY morning Olivia was up at half-past six.

Hurrying into the bathroom, she washed her face and cleaned her teeth, and then, because it felt chilly, she dressed in warm woollen trousers and a purple sweater. She didn't bother with much make-up, just a trace of eyeliner, mascara and a smear of lip gloss. Then, with her leather coat over her arm, she went downstairs.

Linda wasn't about, but someone—Martin, possibly—had made a pot of tea and left toast crumbs all over the drainer. Olivia wasn't hungry, but she poured herself a cup of lukewarm tea and drank it on the move.

She still had to tell the rest of the family what she was doing, and as she swept the crumbs away and washed both her cup and Martin's she hoped they would approve.

Her father knew, naturally. She hadn't been able to hide what Joel had wanted from him, and he'd looked at her a little oddly when he heard that she and Joel were planning to share responsibility for the boy.

'Are you sure about this, Liv?' he'd asked as they drove back to the farm. 'I mean, giving the kid a lift is one thing. Committing yourself to two weeks of driving back and forth to Millford, just so Sean can spend a few days with his father, does seem quite a chore.'

'You can't say two weeks on the one hand and then imply it's only for a few days on the other,' Olivia had pointed out evenly. And then, because she'd known her father was only thinking of her, 'Well—I couldn't refuse, could I?'

'Why not?' Ben Foley had been indignant. 'OK, you and Joel have got history. No one can deny that. But he got over you soon enough and married the Webster girl. What does she think about you looking after her son?'

'I doubt if she knows.' Olivia had been terse, stung by her father's assessment of Joel's behaviour. Was that what he'd done? she'd wondered. It had been galling to think that that was what everyone in Bridgeford thought.

Thankfully, the old man hadn't questioned how well she knew Sean. He'd probably assumed the boy had accompanied Joel when he'd picked her up at the airport. But Linda had still to be told and she could only hope it wouldn't become a bone of contention, before she told her what she was doing.

Joel had said Sean had to leave for school at a quarter-past eight, but Olivia realised it was only a quarter-to when she reached Millford. She was far too early and, not wanting to look too eager, she parked some distance from the house and got out of the car.

Millford was smaller than Bridgeford, but just as picturesque. Pulling her coat out of the back of the car, she put it on and strolled across to the church.

Evidently there'd been an early-morning service and the vicar was standing at the door, saying goodbye to the few stalwarts who'd braved the uncertain weather. Olivia halted by the lych-gate, feeling an odd sense of familiarity when she looked at the man. But that was silly, she thought impatiently. She'd never been to this church before.

She was about to turn away when he hailed her. 'Liv! Olivia,' he called, striding towards her. 'My goodness, it is you. What are you doing in Millford?'

Olivia watched the man as he approached, realising why he'd seemed so familiar. Despite the fact that his angular frame was disguised by the flapping folds of his surplice and he'd lost most of his hair, she recognised him at once.

'Brian!' she exclaimed. 'My Go—I mean, Brian Webster!' She paused. 'You're a vicar!'

'For my sins,' he said drily. 'And Olivia Foley.' He said her name again. 'I heard you were in the States.'

'I was.' Olivia shook her head. 'And I thought you were in the army.'

'For almost eight years.' He nodded. 'I thought it was what I wanted to do, but after Kosovo—' He blew out a harsh breath. 'I knew I had to get out.'

'But a vicar!' Olivia could see that he was still emotionally disturbed by his memories and tried to lighten the mood. 'Who'd have thought it? Brian Webster! Mrs Sawyer's personal nemesis. I don't think she ever got over you putting that frog in her desk.'

Brian laughed. 'Innocent times,' he said ruefully. 'Today it would probably be a tarantula or something equally terrifying.'

Olivia smiled. 'So how long have you been—living here?'

'How long have I been a vicar, do you mean?' He turned briefly to acknowledge one of his parishioners. 'About five years, give or take. How about you? Are you staying with your dad?'

'At present,' said Olivia, remembering that time was passing and she really ought to go. But with that thought came another: Brian Webster was Louise's cousin. If Joel hadn't informed his ex-wife of the arrangements he'd made, she was soon going to find out.

'So what are you doing in Millford?' Brian frowned, detecting she was uncomfortable with that question. 'Don't tell me you're looking for Joel Armstrong! I thought that was all over between you two long ago.'

'It was. It *is*.' Olivia glanced away across the green to where Joel's house was situated. 'I—well, his son's staying with him at the moment and I've promised to give Sean a lift to school.'

Brian regarded her curiously. 'You?' he said blankly. 'Why can't Joel take him himself?'

'Because I said I'd do it,' replied Olivia, not wanting to discuss Joel's schedule or her own. 'And I'd better get going. They're expecting me.'

Brian stepped back, spreading his arms dramatically. 'Well, don't let me hold you up,' he said, though she sensed he didn't approve. 'Perhaps I'll see you again—when you're visiting Millford,' he added pointedly. 'Give Joel my best, won't you? Tell him it's too long since he graced the doors of my church.'

'I will.'

Olivia smiled as she turned away, but she doubted Joel would appreciate the sentiment. He and Brian had never liked one another, due in no small part to the fact that Brian had been in her year at school. They had just been friends, but Brian had loved to rub Joel's nose in it, exaggerating their closeness and chiding him about baby-snatching when Olivia and Joel got together.

She was tempted to leave the car where it was, but that would have looked foolish, so she slipped behind the wheel and drove the few yards to Joel's house. However, as she shifted into neutral, Joel came out of the door and down the path, and she knew at once that he'd seen her talking to the other man.

'At last,' he said harshly, pulling her door open. 'I was beginning to wonder if you'd forgotten why you were here.'

'And good morning to you, too,' retorted Olivia, swinging her legs out of the car and getting to her feet. 'It's only five-past eight, Joel. I've got plenty of time.'

She met his brooding gaze with a defiance she was far from feeling, but for once Joel was the first to look away. 'OK,' he said. 'Perhaps that was unjustified. But before I go, I want to give you some—some information.'

'Don't you mean instructions?' Olivia taunted. 'Come on, Joel. I have looked after kids before. One of Bruce's business colleagues had twins and they didn't come to any harm when their parents left them with me.'

Joel sighed, allowing her to precede him into the house. 'If I've offended you, I'm sorry,' he said heavily, and she actually thought he meant it. 'But this situation is new to me, and I don't want anything to go wrong.'

'Like Louise finding out?' suggested Olivia, waiting for him to close the door and then following him across the hall and into the kitchen. 'Well, I'm sorry about that, but you should have warned me that Brian Webster was the vicar of All Saints Church.'

Joel grimaced. 'The vicar of All Saints,' he echoed. 'Why does that make me want to laugh?'

'You did see us, then?'

'Oh, yeah.' Joel heaved a sigh. 'I wasn't spying on you,' he added. 'I was in Sean's bedroom, trying to persuade him to get dressed, and I happened to look out of the window.' He shook his head. 'Brian Webster, preaching the good word to the people. After the things he said to me when you and I split up.'

Olivia wanted to ask him what Brian had said, but something else Joel had mentioned was more important. 'You were trying to persuade Sean to get dressed?' she asked, confused. 'Don't he and I have to leave in about ten minutes?'

'You do.' Joel was resigned. 'Oh, don't worry, he's had his breakfast. But he's decided that, as you're coming, he doesn't want to go to school.'

Olivia stared at him. 'But doesn't he know I'll be picking him up from school this afternoon?'

'Well, that won't be necessary today, actually,' said Joel apologetically. 'I'm free from two-thirty, so I can pick him up myself.'

Ridiculously, Olivia was disappointed. But what had she expected? That Joel would want her in his house any more often than was absolutely necessary? 'I see,' she said, trying not to let her feelings show. 'Well, you've got my number if you need it.'

'Yeah, right.'

Joel regarded her through narrowed eyes for a moment and now she was forced to look away. 'Was that all you wanted to tell me?' she asked, much too aware of how easily he could get under her skin. 'As you're picking him up—'

'These are for you,' Joel interrupted her, holding out a bunch of keys. 'You might as well have them. You'll need them tomorrow afternoon, anyway.'

Olivia's lips parted. 'These are for the house?'

'What else?'

'But—are you sure you want me to have them?' She moistened her lips nervously. 'I mean, you said—'

'I know what I said,' Joel told her harshly, not at all sure he was doing the right thing. But it was too late now. 'The situation's changed,' he added. 'And I won't be here when you are, will I?'

'Won't you?'

Not if I have any sense, thought Joel grimly, but he said, 'I'll go and give Sean a shout.'

However, before he reached the door, they both heard the boy's feet running down the stairs. Sean paused in the doorway, gazing at both of them with anxious eyes. 'I've changed my mind,' he said unnecessarily, though his shirt was buttoned unevenly and his tie was skewed. 'You're not sending Olivia away, are you?'

'Why would I do that?' Joel was impatient. What did Olivia have that caused both him and his son to make fools of themselves over her? 'Come here, kid. Let me put that tie straight.'

Sean beamed at Olivia as he did so. 'You're taking me to school,' he said, and she nodded. 'Cool!'

When Olivia got back to the farm, Martin and Andy were sitting at the kitchen table, tucking into bacon, eggs and sausages. She knew they sometimes came back for a proper breakfast, so she wasn't surprised. But when Linda turned from the stove, there was something less pleasant about her expression.

'Where've you been?' she asked, and, although Olivia resented her tone, she had the feeling her sister already knew.

'Um—Sean's staying with Joel at the moment and he needed someone to take him to school, so I—'

'Volunteered,' broke in Linda scornfully. 'Honestly, Livvy, I'd have thought you had more sense.'

'I didn't volunteer.' Olivia flushed in spite of herself. 'Joel asked me to do it. Didn't Dad explain?'

'Dad?' Her sister looked puzzled. 'Dad knew?'

Now Olivia looked doubtful. 'Well, yes, I thought—oh, was it Brian Webster?'

'Louise rang,' said Linda, scowling. 'One of the other mothers saw you delivering Sean to school and called her. She wants to speak to you about it. I told her I'd get you to give her a ring as soon as you got back.'

'Did you?' Olivia objected to Linda making any promises on her behalf. 'Well, don't worry. I'll go and see her. I want to know what kind of mother doesn't know— or care—if her son's missing.'

Linda blinked. 'Sean's not missing.'

'He was.' Immediately regretting the impulse to put Linda on the defensive, Olivia was forced to explain how she'd found Sean in the barn. 'And it wasn't the first time,' she declared defiantly. 'He doesn't want to live with his mother. He wants to live with Joel.'

Linda grimaced. 'I see.' She paused. 'And I suppose Joel can't look after the kid on his own.'

'No.'

'He could employ someone,' Linda said thoughtfully. 'Other people do.'

'Perhaps you should offer to look after the boy on a permanent basis,' suggested Martin surprisingly. 'I'm sure he'd be willing to pay you the going rate.'

'Oh, I don't think so...'

Olivia shook her head, but she had to admit it wasn't totally off the wall. After all, Joel had offered to pay her. But she was a trained estate agent, not a nanny.

'You should give it some thought,' Linda put in, after exchanging a glance with her husband. 'That way you wouldn't have to leave Bridgeford. I know you're worried about Dad and you'd like to stick around.'

Olivia was taken aback. 'Well, I had thought of getting a job in Newcastle,' she confessed, and Linda nodded eagerly.

'That's a great idea,' she agreed. 'Then you wouldn't need to buy an apartment. You could stay here with us.'

Olivia was getting the sense that she was missing something here. 'But—wouldn't that be an imposition?' she asked warily.

'Heck, no.' It was Martin who spoke now, wiping his mouth with the back of his hand. 'This is as much your home as ours. If you can put up with us.'

Olivia didn't know what to say. 'Well—thanks,' she said at last. 'I do appreciate it. But if I get a job in Newcastle, I'll buy an apartment there.' She took a breath. 'I'm sure you'll agree that one bathroom isn't enough for five of you, let alone six.'

'Dad can't get upstairs,' pointed out Linda at once.

'And we're thinking of dividing the main bedroom so

Linda and I can have an *en suite* shower room,' Martin added swiftly. 'Anyway, at least think about it, Livvy. We are your family. And I know Ben would be delighted if you stayed.'

Which was probably true, Olivia conceded, accepting a cup of tea from Linda but refusing anything else. She felt a little hollow inside, but she wasn't hungry. All of a sudden she had a family again, and she wished she didn't feel as if none of them was being quite sincere.

Church Close was, as Sean had said, a road of new mock-Tudor houses. Driving into the road later that morning, Olivia hoped she was doing the right thing. She had no idea if Joel would approve of what she was going to say to Louise really. But she had to put the woman straight about hers and Joel's relationship. The last thing she needed was more gossip about her and her ex-husband.

Belatedly, it occurred to her that Louise might not be at home now. Sean had said his mother had a job, and it was certainly true that most of the houses in the road looked unoccupied. There was a car parked on the drive of one house, but, although Olivia's spirits lifted, it was the house next door to the Barlows. Still, she was here now. It was worth taking a chance.

It was as she was locking the car that she looked up and saw Louise watching her. She was standing at the bedroom window, staring down at her visitor, as if she didn't quite believe her eyes.

Olivia didn't attempt a smile, but merely nodded before walking up the open-plan drive to the house. And, by the time she reached the door, Louise had it open, her expression mirroring the obvious agitation she was feeling.

'Well,' she said tersely. 'You've got a nerve!'

Olivia blew out a breath. 'May I come in, or do you want to discuss Sean out here?'

Louise's lips tightened. 'You'd better come in,' she said, albeit unwillingly. 'I just hope nobody recognises your car.'

'It's a rental,' said Olivia flatly, following the other woman across a narrow hall and into a pleasant sitting room. Then, noticing how pale Louise was looking, she added, 'I'm sorry if I've upset you, but Joel should have told you what he was going to do.'

'Yes, he should.' Louise nodded to a chair. 'You'd better sit down and tell me why he isn't looking after Sean himself.'

Olivia sighed. 'The tutor who was going to cover his lectures has broken his hip.'

'So why didn't he tell me he couldn't have Sean and been done with it?'

'You'll have to ask him that.' Olivia hesitated. 'I assume because he didn't want to disappoint the boy.'

'And I dare say he was glad of any excuse to ask you to help him out,' said Louise scathingly. 'If it wasn't so embarrassing, it would be pitiful!'

'Actually, it wasn't like that,' said Olivia, taking the seat she'd been offered and crossing her legs as if she was completely at her ease. 'Did he tell you I found Sean after he'd spent the night in our barn?'

Louise sagged a little, and then sank onto the sofa opposite. 'It was you who found him!' she exclaimed. 'No, I didn't know that. Joel just said someone had found him and Sean had insisted on being taken to Millford.'

'Well, it was me.' But Olivia was feeling concerned now. Louise did look incredibly white and exhausted. 'I— we—he did insist on speaking to his father. And I have to admit, I was pretty peeved that you apparently hadn't even noticed he was missing.'

Louise nodded. 'I suppose it did look bad,' she admitted in a much less confrontational tone. 'But he had run away just a few days before, and I've been feeling so—well, so sickly, I suppose I didn't give it the significance it deserved.'

Olivia frowned. 'You've been ill?'

'No.' Louise flushed. 'Just a bit under the weather, that's all.'

'And you assumed Sean had gone to Joel's again?'

'Yes.' Louise pushed weary hands through her tumbled dark hair and Olivia saw with some concern that she was sweating. 'I suppose you think I'm a bad mother. But Sean's not an easy kid to deal with. Not when he and Stewart don't get on.'

Olivia shook her head. 'It's nothing to do with me, Louise.'

'So you're not going to spread the fact that I neglect my child around the village?'

'No.' Olivia was horrified. 'I came here because I didn't want you to get the wrong impression about Joel and me. He was in a bind and I was—available.' *Oh, God!* 'There's no hidden agenda,' she added hurriedly. 'I'm not trying to cause trouble between you two.'

Louise regarded her curiously. 'You and Joel aren't getting back together, then?'

'Heavens, no!' Olivia was very definite about that.

But even as she said the words, she wondered at the pang of regret that stirred deep in her stomach. Was it possible to want a man you didn't like? She had to believe it was, or face the alternative. That these feelings she couldn't seem to control weren't going to go away.

'I wondered,' Louise was saying now, and Olivia found it very hard to remember their conversation. The other woman pulled a wry face. 'It took him a long time to get over you, you know.'

'Oh, I don't think—'

'It's true.' Louise had evidently decided to be generous now that her own position wasn't threatened. 'I've thought, since the divorce, that he only married me because he wanted to prove to himself—and all the gossips in the village—that he'd moved on; made a success of his life.'

Olivia shook her head. 'Well, thanks for that, but Joel isn't the reason I came here. You probably know, my dad had a stroke and I wanted to come home to see him.' If that wasn't quite the way it had happened, it served the purpose. 'I am thinking of staying on for a while, but just so I can be with the family.'

'All the same—'

'Louise, really, I'd rather you didn't say anything about Joel and me to anyone. You may not know it, but I only came back to England because my second marriage didn't work out either.' She paused, and then, realising she had to say something dramatic to wipe that smug look off Louise's face, she added, 'Bruce and I were together for much longer than Joel and me.'

Louise's eyes widened. 'So you're divorced again?'

'Afraid so.' Olivia got to her feet, trying to sound philosophic. 'Anyway, I'm glad we've had this talk, Louise. I think we understand one another now.'

CHAPTER TEN

OLIVIA parked her car above the dunes and turned off the engine. It was a beautiful evening. It had been an incredibly mild day for early May and, now that the sun was sinking in the west, the sky above Redes Bay was streaked in shades of red and orange and purple.

Reaching into the glove compartment, Olivia pulled out a scrunchie and tugged her hair into a high pony-tail. Then, thrusting open her door, she got out of the car.

She was dressed in just a khaki tank-top and running shorts, and, after checking that her trainers were safely tied, she tucked the car keys into her pocket and set off.

It was weeks since she'd run any distance. When she'd first returned to England she'd contented herself with exercising at the local gym, but there was nothing like running in the fresh air. And today, particularly, she'd needed to get out of the house.

It wasn't that either Linda or Martin had said anything to upset her. On the contrary, during the past week or so, since she'd been ferrying Sean about, they'd been very supportive. In Martin's case, amazingly so, but she still felt as if sooner or later the axe was going to fall.

She had talked to her father about Linda and Martin's ambitions for the farm. It was he who'd brought the subject up and she'd had to admit that she thought it had some merit. But Ben Foley was opposed to letting strangers have free use of his land, even if he could offer no other solution to the problem.

Nevertheless, Olivia enjoyed the time she spent with the old man. Unlike the rushed awkward encounters she had with Joel, she and her father had long conversations about everything under the sun. She'd even told him about Bruce and why he hadn't wanted her to leave him. And discovered that the pain of that betrayal no longer had the strength to hurt her.

Her relationship with her first husband did not progress so easily, however. Not that she saw a lot of Joel really. He was there to say goodbye to his son in the mornings. And on those occasions when she was obliged to stay with Sean until his father got home in the evenings, she'd usually got her coat on before he'd got out of the car. Their exchanges were brief and always subjective. They spoke of Sean, of any conversations she'd had with Sean's teachers, and little else.

On the other hand, she and Joel's son had become much closer. Indeed, she was dreading the time when he would have to go back to his mother. It was almost two weeks now, but talk of his return hadn't been mentioned yet, and Olivia was hoping that Joel would be granted a stay of execution.

Tonight she hadn't been needed, however. Sean had gained permission from his father to spend the night at his best friend's house. They were having a sleepover, Sean had told Olivia that morning, full of excitement at the thought of the midnight feast they were planning. She wouldn't be needed in the morning either, because the other boy's mother would take them both to school.

Now Olivia stopped at the edge of the dunes, doing some warm-up exercises before stepping down onto the sand. She intended to run along the shoreline where the sand was damp and firm. Then she might call in the pub for a cool drink before heading back.

Drawing one knee up to her chin and then the other, she felt a rising sense of anticipation. Running had always given her a feeling of freedom, of the confidence she could have in her own muscles, her own strength.

And then she saw him. He was doing what she had planned to do, running along the shoreline, pounding the sand in a steady pace, long strides stretching long, powerful legs.

Joel!

Olivia blew out an impatient breath. Wouldn't you know it? she asked herself. Two minds with but a single thought. Why hadn't she considered that he might take advantage of his freedom? Redes Bay had always been a favoured spot for both of them.

She would have turned away then, but he'd seen her. There was a moment when he faltered, when she was sure he would simply acknowledge her with a lift of his hand perhaps and go on. Contrarily, he didn't do either of those things. He stopped for a moment, and then jogged towards her. What now? she wondered uneasily. She hoped she didn't think she was following him.

For all that, she couldn't help watching him as he drew nearer. A grey tank-top clung damply to the contours of his chest and his arms bulged with muscle. Tight-fitting cycling shorts did nothing to hide his maleness, and with sweat beading his forehead he looked big and impressively virile.

'D'you want to join me?' he asked, surprising her. He was closer now, but remained on the damp sand, jogging on the spot, not allowing his body to cool down.

'I—well, if you don't mind,' said Olivia, stepping over the soft sand and testing the damp sand for its firmness. 'Do you often run here?'

'Why? So you can avoid it in future?' Joel asked drily, realising he had probably made a mistake by inviting her company. But the beach was free to all, for goodness' sake, and he'd sensed that if he hadn't spoken she'd have abandoned her run.

'No.'

Olivia's response was defensive, and, breaking away from him, she jogged away along the beach. She took it slowly at first, only increasing her pace when she felt the muscles in her legs loosen and the adrenalin started flowing through her body.

Joel let her go, let her get some distance ahead of him, knowing that in a few loping strides he'd overtake her. As he watched her, however, he felt his body tighten. In the skin-tight tank-top and running shorts, she was every man's wet dream come true and heaven knew he wasn't immune to her appeal.

She was so sexy, that was the problem. Long, slim arms and legs; hips that swelled into the provocative curve of her bottom. She might not have been aware that her breasts had puckered when he'd challenged her, but he was. Distinctly upturned, they'd pushed delicately against the cloth of her vest.

Hell!

He saw her glance back over her shoulder then and guessed she was wondering if he'd changed his mind about them running together. He should, he acknowledged grimly. But although his brain might protest his reckless-ness, his flesh was shamefully weak.

Picking up his pace, he went after her and seconds later he came alongside her. She was running smoothly now, taking long, ground-covering strides, her breasts bobbing rhythmically beneath the tank-top.

They ran in silence for a while, but then Joel saw the line of dampness appearing in the small of her back. 'Don't overdo it,' he warned, feeling obliged to remind her that, unless he was mistaken, she hadn't done any running since she'd come to Bridgeford.

'I'm OK.' Olivia spoke breathily. 'It's a beautiful evening, isn't it?'

'Beautiful,' agreed Joel, dragging his eyes away from her and looking towards the horizon. 'On evenings like these, it feels as if it's going to stay light forever.'

'I know what you mean.' Olivia was relieved that he seemed prepared to meet her halfway. 'At this time of year, you don't want to go to bed.'

Joel couldn't help himself. 'I suppose that depends who you're going to bed with,' he remarked wryly, and Olivia gave him an impatient look.

'You had to say that, didn't you?'

Joel arched mocking brows. 'Well, you asked for it.'

Olivia shook her head. 'Must you bring sexual innuendo into everything? Is that what comes of mixing with amorous adolescents like that girl I saw at your office?'

Joel stifled a laugh. 'Oh, Liv, have you any idea how prudish you sound?' He turned, running backward so he could see her face. 'For your information, Cheryl Brooks is twenty-four. She's already a graduate and working towards her second degree.'

'Bully for her.' Olivia resented the ease with which he was keeping up with her. 'In any case, she's too young for you.'

Joel gasped. 'Did I say she wasn't?'

'No, but as you were talking about taking women to bed—'

'I wasn't talking about any such thing.' Joel was indignant. 'You brought it up, Liv. Not me.'

'Whatever.'

Olivia could feel her legs beginning to tire. She'd passed the pain barrier some minutes ago, but now it was becoming a distinct effort to keep putting one foot in front of the other. However, she wasn't going to let Joel get the better of her in this as well as everything else, and, making an especial effort, she quickened her pace until she was actually pulling away from him.

The pain was excruciating, her knees burning as if they were on fire. But there was such satisfaction in besting him that she could actually numb her mind to the agony in her legs.

It didn't last. As soon as he realised what she was doing, Joel quickened his own pace and within seconds he'd caught up with her.

'Crazy woman!' he exclaimed, one look at her contorted face enough to tell him that she was in danger of doing some permanent damage to herself. He put a restraining hand on her arm, feeling the trembling muscles, the sweat that was streaming out of her. 'For heaven's sake, Liv, you're going to kill yourself!'

Olivia sagged. She couldn't help it. Even the warning touch of his hand was too much, and, stumbling, she fell to her knees on the sand.

'Liv, are you all right?'

Instantly abandoning any thought of continuing his own run, Joel came down on his haunches beside her, one hand on the back of her neck, the other gripping her upper arm, supporting her when she would have sunk onto the sand. Despite his own exertions his hands were cool and firm, and, unable to help herself, Olivia slumped against him.

'For pity's sake!'

Joel swore to himself, looking about him as if assistance was going to materialise by magic. But there was no one else on the beach. And they were some distance from where they'd left their cars. Part of the beauty of Redes Bay was its absence of human habitation. Apart from the pub, that was, but that was some distance away, too.

'I'll—I'll be all right in a minute.'

Olivia spoke faintly, still struggling to regulate her breathing. Her lungs burned and it was incredibly difficult to take the gulping breaths she knew she needed to recover. She was beginning to feel cold, too, the breeze off the North Sea picking up as night drew in.

She shivered and Joel felt it. Dammit, she was going to develop hypothermia if he didn't get her warm soon. There was no way she was going to be able to walk back to her car in her present condition. He was going to have to leave her here and go and get help on his own.

He hesitated a moment, aware that his tank-top was rank with his own sweat, but then he pulled it over his head and wrapped it about her shoulders like a shawl. 'Stay there,' he said, and when she tried to protest he held the top tighter about her. 'I won't be long,' he promised grimly. 'Please, Liv. Just stay here until I get back.'

'But—you'll get cold,' she protested, and he managed an ironic grin.

'I don't think so,' he said, getting to his feet in a swift, lithe movement. 'Baby, just looking at you burns me up. Now, be good. I won't be long.'

Olivia had managed to get to her feet and was taking several tentative steps across the sand when she saw the Lexus barrelling towards her. For the first time in her life, she appreciated the advantages of having a four-wheel-drive vehicle. Its huge tyres ate up the beach as if it was the smoothest highway, only the spray of sand behind showing its passing.

Joel braked beside her and sprang out. He'd evidently found a T-shirt to cover his bare chest that Olivia had admired so briefly and in his hands he carried a sheepskin jacket that he quickly exchanged for the ratty tank-top. Feeling the comfort of the jacket envelop her, Olivia began to feel warmth radiating inside her, the spasmodic shivers that had racked her fading swiftly with its heat.

'Come on.'

Not giving her a chance to object, Joel swung her up in his arms and carried her to the Lexus. Swinging open the passenger-side door, he lifted her into the seat, pausing long enough to secure the safely belt before circling the bonnet and getting in beside her.

'Better?' he asked, looking sideways at her, and she nodded her head.

'Much.' She moistened her lips. 'Thanks.'

Joel didn't make any response. He just held her gaze for a few moments longer and then, thrusting the Lexus into drive, he did a U-turn and drove back to where the vehicle had carved a path across the dunes.

However, when they were safely on the coast road again, he didn't take her back to where she'd left her car. Instead, he turned up the cliff road, negotiating the precipitous bends with admirable speed.

Olivia looked at him then, and, feeling her eyes on him, he said, 'You're not fit to drive yourself home right now. Your body's had a shock. You need to chill out before you get back behind the wheel of a car.'

'Perhaps so.' Olivia blew out a breath. 'But I am feeling much better now.'

'That's good.' Joel was approving. 'But you don't realise how exhausted you are. What you need is a long, hot shower and a cool glass of wine. That's my recommendation anyway.'

Olivia's lips tightened. 'Yeah, right,' she said drily, wondering what Linda would say if she used all the hot water. 'I'll—think about it.'

'We'll do better than that,' said Joel blandly, and, blinking, Olivia realised something that she should have noticed minutes ago. She was so used to driving to Millford these days that she hadn't questioned the route they were taking. But now comprehension dawned.

'This isn't the way to Bridgeford!' she exclaimed, her tongue adhering to the roof of her mouth. 'Joel, I can't go to your house.'

'Why not?' Joel was complacent. 'You spend a couple of hours there most days. You must be quite familiar with it by this time.'

Olivia shook her head. 'That's different.'

'I know. Sean's there. And he provides a chaperon. But that doesn't mean we need one, does it?'

Doesn't it? For a moment, Olivia thought she'd said the words out loud, but Joel hadn't responded so she knew she'd only been thinking them. But, dear God, going to Joel's house late in the evening, using his shower! Wasn't that just asking for trouble?

Joel parked the car at his gate and without waiting for his assistance Olivia thrust open her door. But her legs felt like jelly when she climbed down from the seat and she couldn't decide whether it was exhaustion or anticipation.

'Here, let me help you,' he said, but Olivia lifted a warning hand to keep him at arm's length.

'I can manage,' she said, with more confidence than she was feeling. But she could just imagine the Reverend Webster's reaction if he saw Joel carrying her into his house.

Joel opened the door and, unwillingly, Olivia stumbled up the path and into the house. It was all familiar, yet strangely unreal. For the first time since that afternoon in his office, they were alone together.

Joel closed the door with his foot and looked at her. Then, when Olivia evaded his gaze, he dropped the tank-top he'd been carrying onto the floor and walked across to the stairs. 'Can you make it?' he asked, indicating the climb, and Olivia took a deep breath.

'If you think that what we're doing is wise,' she said at

last, trudging across the floor. 'What if Louise finds out? Aren't you worried that she might use it against you?'

Joel rested one hand on the newel post at the foot of the staircase. 'The way I heard it, you apparently put her in her place. And why should she care what I do? It's not as if Sean's a witness to my depravity.' He regarded her impatiently. 'Come on, Liv. You're wasting time and I'm getting cold.'

'Oh—sorry.' Olivia made a helpless gesture, indicating that he should go first. Although she'd been upstairs before and had a pretty good idea where Joel's bedroom was, she had no intention of letting him know that. 'Go ahead.'

Despite her determination not to show any weakness, it was an effort going up the stairs. By the time she reached the landing, she was panting again and she had to acknowledge how out of condition she was. But to her relief Joel chose not to call her on it, and, walking across the gallery, he opened the door into one of the spare rooms.

'You can use the bathroom in here,' he said, his voice cool and objective. 'Take as long as you like. You'll find plenty of towels on the rack.'

'Thanks.'

Olivia moved past him into the bedroom, admiring the gold satin counterpane on the colonial-style bed. There were gold and green patterned curtains at the windows and a carved *armoire* where one could store clothes. The carpet underfoot was a cream shag pile, its softness evident even through her shoes.

She turned to say how much she liked his style of decoration, but Joel was gone. He'd closed the door silently and left her, and she beat back a sudden surge of disappointment. This was what she wanted, wasn't it? she asked herself: their relationship to remain on civil terms. She felt tonight had proved that friendship was out of the question. She was much too aware of the pitfalls she faced when she tried to be sociable with him.

The bathroom was delightful. A claw-footed tub flanked a glass-walled shower cubicle, with twin basins matching the low-level lavatory. A rack of towels occupied the wall beside the shower and Olivia didn't hesitate before stripping off her tank-top and shorts and stepping into the cubicle.

Unlike at the farm, it was a power shower, and, feeling the hot spray massaging her shoulders, pummelling her hips, shedding its heat all over her body, she felt her exhaustion easing into a healthy tiredness. It was so good to feel thoroughly warm again, inside as well as out, and, finding a tube of shampoo on a ribbed shelf inside the cubicle, she decided to wash her hair as well.

She left the shower with real regret. It had been so wonderful to wash herself without the ever-present prospect of being disturbed hanging over her head. And, although it was satisfying to feel clean again, she was sorry it was over.

She dried herself rapidly. There was no lock on the bathroom door and, though she doubted that Joel would intrude on her here, she was intensely aware of her nakedness.

That was why, when there was a knock at the bathroom door, there was a rather ungainly scramble to get the towel wrapped securely about her before she spoke.

CHAPTER ELEVEN

'YES?' she called, her voice sounding absurdly weak and thready. What could he possibly want?

'I've left a robe on the bed,' Joel responded equably. 'If you'd like to put it on and bring your running clothes downstairs, I'll put them in the washer with mine.'

'Oh.' Olivia swallowed, thinking hard. But, although she knew that accepting his offer would inevitably delay her departure, the idea of wearing dirty clothes when she felt so deliciously clean swung it for her. 'OK,' she agreed. 'I'll do that. Thanks again.'

'No problem.'

She waited until she heard the outer door close behind him before venturing a peek into the adjoining room. Sure enough, a white towelling bathrobe was lying on the bed, along with a pair of chunky white athletic socks she could wear instead of her trainers.

Giving her hair one last rub with the towel, Olivia combed it with her fingers before sliding her arms into the sleeves of the bathrobe. It was much too big. Joel's, she guessed, though she chose not to dwell on that. Fastening the belt tightly about her waist, she pulled on the socks, also too big, and collected her dirty clothes.

Even if she hadn't known the way to the kitchen, the delicious smell of food would have guided her. Someone, Joel obviously, was preparing his evening meal, and the mingled scents of frying meat and sautéed vegetables drifted up the stairs.

Her feet making no sound in the chunky socks, Olivia padded downstairs and across the hall. Joel was standing at the Aga, stir-frying the food in a rather professional-looking wok. Like her, he'd evidently had a shower, because there were droplets of water sparkling on his dark hair and trickling down into his collar at the back.

Her mouth drying at the sight of him in faded jeans, unbuttoned at the waist, and a short-sleeved shirt that was open down his chest, Olivia knew she had to say something before he caught her watching him. 'I didn't know you could cook,' she said, recalling her own early disasters in that direction. She crossed the tiled floor and peered over his shoulder. 'It certainly smells good.'

Joel started. He'd not been aware of her approach, and his eyes darkened at the picture she made in his robe and socks. Judging by the bundle of clothes in her arms, he was fairly sure she had nothing on under the terry-towelling, and the sudden urge to find out was hardly a surprise in his present mood.

'It's just steak and vegetables,' he said, his voice harsher than it should have been. 'Are you hungry?'

Olivia took a backward step away from him. She was realising that this was hardly keeping her distance, as she'd planned to do when she was upstairs. 'Oh—don't worry about me,' she mumbled awkwardly. 'I—er—I'll just wait until the clothes are dry and then I'll go.' She indicated the bundle in her arms. 'Shall I put these in the washer? It's in the utility room, isn't it?'

'Don't you know?'

Joel growled his answer, but he wasn't feeling particularly charitable right now. Earlier on, going into his spare bedroom, knowing she was naked in the next room, had left him with a hard-on he could do without. But, dammit, his body ached with the need to bury itself in her, the memory of how it used to be between them never totally fading away.

'I suppose I do,' she replied a little stiffly now, moving past him to the outer door. 'I assume you've put yours in already.'

'Yeah.'

Jake gave the stir-fry a vicious shake, unable to prevent his eyes from following her slim form. She'd been right, he thought irritably. This had not been the wisest move he'd ever made.

He heard her close the washer and then the unmistakable sound of running water as she turned the machine on. She came back into the kitchen, carefully averting her eyes as she shut the utility-room door, and his temper erupted. This was crazy, he thought angrily. They were acting as if they were strangers. Intimate strangers, perhaps, but with an atmosphere between them you could cut with a knife.

Taking the pan off the heat, he spun round to face her. 'What is it with you?' he asked savagely. 'I practically save you from pneumonia. I bring you here, to my house, give you free use of my bathroom, offer to wash your clothes and give you half my supper, and what do you do? You say, thanks, but no thanks. I'd rather sit on my own in the other room than share a meal with you!'

'That's not true!' But Olivia's face burned with embarrassment even so. 'I am grateful, truly I am.'

'Well, you have a bloody funny way of showing it.' He raked his nails across his chest where a triangle of dark hair grew between his pectoral muscles and arrowed down to his navel and beyond. 'What did I ever do to make you hate me, Liv?'

Olivia's eyes widened. 'I don't hate you, Joel.'

'What, then?' he demanded, something darker than frustration in his eyes. 'Come on, Liv, tell me what it is you want from me. Because God knows, I'm running out of ideas.'

Olivia shook her head. 'I don't know what you mean.'

'Sure you do.' He was relentless. 'We've tried hostile and neutral. And yes, there have been times when I've stepped over the line. But tonight, I was really trying to be civil. To show you another side to my nature, one you don't seem to believe is there.'

Olivia drew a breath. 'Well, I'm sorry—'

'Yeah, you should be.'

'But you weren't exactly jolly when I came downstairs.'

'You startled me.'

'Did I?' Olivia didn't know where this was going, but she refused to let him walk all over her. 'Or were you in a black mood because you regretted bringing me here? Come on, Joel. Be honest. You made it plain enough before that you didn't want me in your house.'

'Before.' Joel latched on to the word. 'That's the pivotal difference. As you've probably been in the house as much

as I have the past couple of weeks, it would be freaking crazy to try and bar you from the place now.'

'Ah, but you weren't there when I was, and vice versa,' retorted Olivia at once. 'This isn't the same.'

Joel watched her balefully. She had no idea how he was feeling, he thought, or she wouldn't be standing there, trading put-downs with him. Without make-up of any kind, she was even more desirable than she'd been earlier, her cheeks flushed a becoming shade of pink, her green eyes sparkling with what she thought was a victory.

'You could be right,' he said at last, and although his words were innocent enough, she seemed to sense that he meant something different by it.

'You—you're agreeing with me?' she asked warily and Joel spread his hands.

'That being here alone with you is different from being with Sean? Hey, you'll get no argument from me.'

Olivia gnawed on her lower lip. 'Well—good.'

'No, this is much more interesting,' he said, lowering his arms and shoving his thumbs into his dipping waistband. 'Much more interesting, believe me.'

Olivia swallowed. He saw the jerky movement in her throat, saw the way she gathered a handful of the terry-towelling between her breasts. 'Joel,' she said nervously, her eyes flickering to the opening *V* of his jeans. 'Joel, I thought we understood one another.'

'What's to understand?' He looked at her from beneath lowered lids. 'I think we know one another well enough by now.'

She caught her breath. 'Joel,' she said again, but it was more of a plea now. 'Joel, we can't do this.'

'Can't do what?' He placed one bare foot in front of the other. 'What did I say?'

Olivia backed up a pace. 'You didn't have to say it,' she protested, and once again Joel spread his arms.

'I'm not a mind-reader, Liv,' he said, but this time when he lowered his hands he allowed one finger to hook the belt of the bathrobe. 'Perhaps you'd better lay it out for me.'

Olivia shook her head, aware that she'd have to loosen the belt to escape him. 'I think you know exactly what you're doing.'

'No.' Joel was very definite about that. 'No, you know, I don't. But, damn, I'm beginning not to care.'

'Joel—'

Her voice was plaintive, and Joel's mouth took on a sensual curve. 'Yeah,' he said, using the belt to pull her towards him. 'Yeah, say my name, Liv. Say it like you mean it, 'cos I know you do.'

Olivia tried to hang back, but it was a losing battle and she knew it. When he bent his head and covered her lips with his, she couldn't prevent herself from sinking into him. Joel's lips—Joel's tongue—her world suddenly seemed bounded by the sensual invasion of his kiss, and when he parted the robe and found her breasts her nipples thrust eagerly against his palms.

'Oh, baby,' he groaned, pushing his hips towards her, and, feeling the rough fabric of his jeans against her bare legs, she realised the bathrobe was now completely open. 'I knew you were naked,' he added hoarsely, looking down at her. His teeth nuzzled her ear. 'Do you wonder why I can't fasten my jeans?'

'It's not something I've thought about,' protested Olivia,

not altogether truthfully, and Joel regarded her with smouldering eyes.

'No?'

Olivia quivered. 'Why don't you tell me?' she found herself saying, her voice as unsteady as his. His words had been unbearably sexy and she wanted to prolong the moment. 'Do I—do I turn you on?'

'Why don't you find out for yourself?' he breathed, taking one of her hands and letting her feel the hard ridge that was threatening his zip. 'Do you have any idea how long it is since I was in danger of losing it completely?'

Olivia's tongue circled her lips almost consideringly. Then, averting her eyes, she deliberately loosened his zip so she could slip her hand inside his jeans. He wasn't wearing underwear and when her fingers closed around his thick shaft he bucked violently against her.

'Hell, baby, take it easy,' he groaned, drawing back from her and restoring himself to some semblance of dignity. 'D'you want me to come in your hands?'

'I wouldn't mind.' Olivia realised this had gone too far now for her to pretend. Lifting her hands, she cupped his face, not even thinking about her nakedness. 'But I'd rather you were inside me.' She nudged him provocatively. 'What about you?'

'God!' Joel stared down at her. 'Need you ask?'

'Good.' Without a shred of shame, Olivia tipped the robe off her shoulders, letting it fall in a soft heap about their feet. 'Is this better?'

Joel moved his head a little dazedly. But then the realisation that they were standing in a room that was lit by fluorescent tubes that ran beneath the wall units caused him to utter a muffled curse.

'Not here.' He gripped her waist and lifted her so that she was able to wind her legs about his hips. His voice thickened. 'Let's go upstairs.'

He crossed the hall and climbed the stairs without any visible effort on his part. On the landing, he made straight for his own bedroom. He could have taken her into either of the two spare rooms, but he didn't. He wanted her in his arms in his bed, and, as if she knew how he was feeling, Olivia spread herself invitingly as soon as he laid her on the slub silk coverlet.

'Why don't you lose the socks?' he suggested as he sloughed his shirt and kicked off his jeans and she turned onto her side and lifted first one leg and then the other, making the removal of the socks a deliberate provocation. Her breasts rested full and luscious against the coverlet, the curve of her hips as sleek and smooth as the rest of her.

'You weren't kidding,' she mocked him softly, admiring his erection. 'I do turn you on, don't I?'

'Baby, I've had a hard-on since I saw you doing those sexy moves on the beach,' he told her huskily. He knelt on the bed, rolling her onto her back so he could move over her. Supporting himself on his hands so he didn't crush her, he bent and bit one swollen nipple. 'Did you think I hadn't seen you? Or was it all for my benefit?'

Olivia's lips parted, half in protest, half in delicious pain. 'I was stretching, Joel.'

'And the rest.' Joel transferred his attentions to her other breast and sucked hungrily. 'You knew exactly what you were doing.'

'Yes. I was warming up,' she insisted, catching her

breath at the sudden heat between her legs. 'I didn't even see you at first.'

'Well, I saw you,' said Joel, moving lower to circle her navel with his tongue. 'I couldn't take my eyes off you.'

Olivia quivered, her nails digging into the coverlet at either side of her. 'I'd never have guessed.'

'Liar!'

'No, I mean it.' She took an uneven breath. 'Does that mean you liked what you saw?'

Joel's eyes flicked briefly to her face. 'What do you think?'

Olivia tried to reach for him then, but he evaded her hands, moving lower to part the soft brown curls at the apex of her legs. He watched her as he touched her there, his fingers discovering how wet she was before he bent and replaced them with his lips.

'Joel—'

She shifted feverishly, but Joel wouldn't let her get away. 'You taste incredible,' he said thickly. 'Shall I make you come? You want to. I can tell.'

'I want you,' whispered Olivia helplessly, and he lifted his head and met her tormented gaze.

'I think you do,' he said, his tongue making one last intimate invasion before he moved over her again. 'I want you, too, baby.' He lowered his body onto hers. 'Hmm, that feels so good.'

Olivia clutched his shoulders, winding her fingers into his hair, shifting restlessly beneath him. She parted her legs, trying to show him she was ready, but his sex continued to throb silkily against her thigh.

Joel understood how she was feeling. His body was aching with needs only she could satisfy. His mouth found hers, his breathing hoarse and unsteady. If things were moving too fast, he couldn't control them any longer, and, lifting her legs until her feet were flat against the cover, he pushed his hard length into her slick sheath.

He heard the moan she gave as he entered her, but it wasn't a moan of protest. Her legs were already lifting, winding around him, urging him so deeply inside her that he was sure he touched the vulnerability of her womb.

Then his own needs took over. As he moved, she tightened around him, showing him more clearly than in words how close to the edge she was. Her breasts were crushed against his chest as she arched her body against him, the sensual dance of their mating growing more and more intense.

Olivia's senses were spinning out of control, yet some coherent part of her brain knew that this was Joel she was with, Joel who was inside her; Joel, whose thrusting hips were causing her to experience the kind of wild abandon she hadn't known since the last time they were together.

Sweat was slicking their bodies, and Joel's mouth ravaged hers, his tongue plunging over and over in imitation of his lovemaking. And she clung to him as if she'd never let him go again, as if he was the only safe place in this furious storm of emotion.

When she felt her excitement was in danger of exploding, she tried to control it. She didn't want this to end, didn't want to lose the spiralling delight that Joel was giving her. But it was too hard to hold it back, too tantalising to be restrained by her trembling efforts. Like a fountain, it rose inside her, enveloping her in its heat and sensuality. And, when the peak was reached, she fell through mindless caverns into heavenly space…

Joel felt the racking tremors as they swept over her, knew the moment she climaxed and he was drenched in the heat of her release. It was all he needed to tip him over the edge and his body convulsed almost simultaneously. He spilled his seed helplessly, his limbs shaking long after he was spent. And knew if this was a mistake, it was a doozy. There was no way he could explain this to himself.

CHAPTER TWELVE

HE MUST have fallen asleep because Joel opened his eyes to find soft fingers stroking back his hair from his forehead, trailing down his roughening cheek to his chin. The same fingers continued on over his throat and the muscled contours of his upper chest to where his flat nipples received similar attention.

He didn't know if Olivia knew he was awake or not, but what she was doing was so pleasurable that he didn't want her to stop. He could feel himself hardening from the state of semi-arousal he'd awakened in, and wondered if she knew his jutting sex meant he was fully aware of her ministrations.

Whatever, she didn't look at him, concentrating instead on caressing the hair that grew low on his stomach. Fine and dark, it couldn't compare to the curly thatch that surrounded his erection, and he sucked in a breath when she bent her head and took his length into her mouth.

His blood pressure erupted. He'd thought he was totally spent but one touch of those tempting lips, of that sensuous tongue, and he was as hard as a ramrod. He clenched his fists when he felt her soft breasts swing against his thighs, and stifled a groan when she parted his legs so she could cup him in her hand.

'Oh, Liv,' he muttered then, the sucking motion of her mouth creating an explosive heat he wasn't sure he could contain. The temptation was to let her have her way with him, to pump whatever strength was left inside him into the liquid fire of her mouth.

He was shuddering with the effort of resisting this when she lifted her head and gave him a teasing look. 'Did I do something wrong?' she asked, continuing to caress him. And, when he would have grabbed her shoulders and rolled her over onto her back, she swiftly straddled him.

'My turn,' she said, deliberately lowering herself so that her wet heat burned his thighs. 'Is this what you want?'

'You know what I want,' muttered Joel hoarsely, his hands gripping her knees almost painfully. 'Liv—for pity's sake! Put me out of my misery.'

Olivia smiled then, and Joel was struck by how beautiful she was, more beautiful now than he had ever seen her. 'Oh, all right,' she said with assumed resignation. 'If I must.'

'You—must,' said Joel grimly, and with a toss of her head she lifted herself until the very tip of his shaft was brushing her core.

'Like this?' she asked, unable to deny the breath of satisfaction that issued from her as she impaled herself upon him. 'Yes?'

'Yes,' said Joel, thrusting his head back into the pillow. 'Yes, yes, yes.'

She rode him with a sensual expertise that had him reaching for her breasts, dragging her head down and savaging her mouth with his. And although once again

Olivia would have liked to prolong their pleasure, her body was too finely attuned to his. When he began to buck beneath her, the white-hot heat of her own desires swiftly swept her away.

However, when she sank onto his chest, Joel rolled her over onto her back, and she experienced another orgasm before he allowed himself to share her climax. Totally exhausted, she found she couldn't keep her eyes open, and the last thing she remembered was Joel's heavy weight slumping beside her.

She awakened feeling amazingly refreshed. She didn't know how long she'd been unconscious, but, although it was completely dark beyond the uncurtained windows, she felt as if she'd slept for hours.

She stirred and immediately the lamp was lit next to the bed. And now she saw that Joel was sitting beside her, a glass of white wine in his hand.

'Hey,' he said, leaning over to kiss her, and the hair on his chest tickled her bare breasts. It made her instantly conscious of her nakedness, though someone, Joel apparently, had removed the coverlet and covered her to the waist with a linen sheet.

'Hey,' she answered, responding to his kiss, but then almost immediately drawing away. 'What time is it?'

'About one.'

Joel spoke carelessly, but Olivia was horrified. 'One o'clock?' she echoed. 'In the morning?'

'Well, it looks like the middle of the night,' agreed Joel mildly. 'Here.' He reached for a second glass from the bedside cabinet. 'Have some Chardonnay.'

Olivia ignored the glass. 'I must have slept for hours.'

'A couple of hours,' he conceded, returning the second glass to the cabinet. 'Chill, baby. Linda knows where you are.'

Olivia's jaw dropped. 'She does?'

'Yeah.' Joel took a sip of his wine before continuing. 'I phoned her and explained you'd fallen asleep.' His mouth tilted. 'Of course, I didn't tell her where you'd fallen asleep exactly. I let her think we'd been having a drink after our run and you'd flaked out.'

'Well, thank you.' But Olivia didn't sound grateful. 'My God, Joel, what's my father going to think?'

Joel regarded her steadily. 'If I know Ben, he'll have guessed precisely what we've been doing. He may have had a stroke, Liv, but he's not a fool.'

'I know that.' Olivia levered herself up against the pillows, and then, seeing where his eyes were riveted, she hauled the sheet up to her chin. 'I've got to get back. I can't stay here. No one's going to believe I slept on your sofa all night.'

Joel's eyes darkened. 'Does it matter what anyone thinks?'

'Of course it matters.' Olivia looked anxiously about her. 'You may not care what anyone in Bridgeford thinks of you, but I've got to live there.'

Joel sighed and put his glass aside. 'Stop stressing,' he said, one hand sliding sensuously up her arm to her shoulder. 'Can't we talk about this in the morning?' He nuzzled her shoulder with his lips. 'There's so much I want to say to you.'

Olivia shook her head. 'You don't understand—'

'No, *you* don't understand,' said Joel huskily. 'Do you think you can share what we just shared and walk away?'

His hand curved along her cheek, turning her face towards him. 'I want you, Liv. Not just for one night, but for the rest of my life!'

Olivia sagged back against the pillow. 'You don't mean that.'

'I do.' His lips brushed the corner of her mouth as his hand slid familiarly beneath the sheet she was clutching to her with desperate hands. 'Oh, baby,' he breathed, cupping her breast. 'You must know I never stopped loving you.'

'Joel—'

'No, listen to me,' he persisted urgently. 'Louise knew I didn't love her. Not in the way I'd loved you, anyway. But by the time I'd discovered my mistake, she was expecting my baby. And however much I might regret my second marriage, I'll never regret having my son.'

Olivia moistened her lips. 'I can understand that.'

'Can you?' Joel's hand had found its way between her thighs and she gave a helpless little moan. 'Oh, God, Liv, you don't know how much I wished he was ours. When I first held him in my arms, I wanted him to be our son.'

'Oh, Joel…' Olivia could feel tears burning at the backs of her eyes. It had been such an emotional few hours and hearing him say how he'd felt when Sean was born really tore her apart. 'Thank you for saying that.'

'Don't thank me,' he muttered hoarsely, his mouth seeking hers. 'It's the truth.' He bit her lower lip. 'And maybe you were right to do what you did all those years ago. We were too young—'

'Wait!' Olivia's hand against his chest obviously surprised him, but it gave her the chance to scramble off the bed. Snatching up the silk coverlet, she wrapped it protectively about her. 'What are you saying, Joel? That after everything—everything that's happened, you still think I aborted our child?'

'Liv—'

But his persuasive tone cut no ice with her. 'Answer me, damn you,' she demanded. 'Do you still believe I murdered our baby?'

Joel slumped back against the pillows, resting one wrist across his forehead. 'Don't be melodramatic, Liv,' he said wearily. 'I didn't bring it up to hurt you. I wanted you to know that I've forgiven you—'

'Big of you!'

'—and that as far as I'm concerned that part of our lives is over and forgotten.'

'I haven't forgotten,' said Olivia bitterly. 'How could I forget something that almost destroyed me? *You* almost destroyed me, Joel. You left me, just when I needed you most.'

Joel's hand fell away and he regarded her through heavy-lidded eyes. 'And how do you think I felt when I discovered you'd run away to London rather than face me?'

'I had faced you, Joel.' Olivia was indignant. 'I didn't leave you, Joel. It was you who walked out.'

Joel pushed himself into a sitting position. 'And didn't it occur to you that I might need a little time to get over it?'

'So you went running home to Mummy and Daddy and I bet they didn't advise you to—how would they put it?— give me a second chance.'

'They were as shocked as I was,' retorted Joel, his temper rising. 'They'd thought they were going to be grandparents. How do you think they felt?'

'Well, they never liked me.'

'They thought we were too young to get married, that's all.'

'Then they should have been pleased that we'd split up.'

'Liv—' Once again, Joel tried to appeal to her. Swinging his legs out of bed, he got to his feet. 'We were too young. I accept that now. Can't you just meet me halfway?'

'No!' Olivia stared at him through suddenly tear-wet eyes. 'Joel, I've told you this before, but I'll tell you again. When I found out I was pregnant, I was frightened. Not of having the baby, but of what it might mean to us. You were twenty years old. OK, you were working at the farm, but I knew that wouldn't satisfy you forever. I needed to get a job, a decent job, if only to support you. How was I going to be able to do that with a baby we couldn't possibly afford?'

'Liv—' he tried again, but she wasn't finished.

'I didn't want to lose you,' she said painfully. 'I'd seen how Linda and Martin had had to struggle when they got married. It nearly drove them apart. It wasn't until Martin got that job at the garden centre that they could afford a home of their own.'

'They managed,' said Joel flatly.

'Well, I didn't want that for us. I didn't want us having to live at the farm for years and years. I wanted us to be independent, too. To have a home of our own.'

'So you decided to abort our baby.'

'No!' Olivia was desperate now. 'All right, I did make an appointment at the clinic in Chevingham. I've never denied that. But when I got there I cancelled the appointment. When it came to the point, I couldn't destroy something we'd made together. In love.'

Joel reached for his jeans and started pulling them on.

'I'll take you home,' he said flatly. 'Your clothes should be dry by now. I put them in the dryer when I got the wine.'

Olivia's shoulders sagged. 'You won't listen to reason, will you?'

'Oh, please.' Joel regarded her with scorn in his eyes. 'Your story is that you changed your mind and left the clinic without having the abortion—'

'Yes.'

'And that you had a miscarriage when you got home?'

'You know it is.'

'Bull,' said Joel succinctly. 'You didn't cancel the appointment; you went through with it. And then, when you got home, you cooked up this story about having a miscarriage while there was nobody in the house but you.'

'No!'

'Yes, Olivia. How do you think I found out about the abortion in the first place?' His face contorted. 'You must have thought you were so safe: patient's confidentiality and all that rubbish. You never thought that someone else might care enough to tell me I was being taken for a fool. I've never felt so shattered as I did that day, believe me.'

'But who—?'

'D'you think I'm going to tell you?' Joel shook his head. 'I'll get your clothes,' he said, making for the door. 'And by the way, Sean's going home tomorrow—or rather today. I was going to phone you and thank you for what you've done for him. But it looks like we're all out of explanations, doesn't it?'

CHAPTER THIRTEEN

THANKFULLY, Olivia had a key and when Joel dropped her off she could let herself into the house without waking anyone. But, as she started across the hall to the stairs, she thought she heard someone calling her name. It could only be her father, she thought, making a detour to his room. Pushing the door ajar, she put her head round it, and found Ben Foley propped up on his pillows, as wide awake as if it were the middle of the day.

'Dad!' she exclaimed, pausing a moment to check there was no suspicion of wetness on her cheeks. She sniffed, and moved further into the room. 'What are you doing? You're supposed to be asleep.'

'I sleep a good part of the day,' retorted the old man drily. 'What about you? I thought you were spending the night at Joel's.'

'Linda told you that, I suppose,' Olivia said tightly. 'No. I fell asleep, that's all. When I woke up, he brought me home.'

'So why did he have to bring you home? Where's your car?'

'I left it at the beach.' Olivia made a careless gesture. 'I'd overdone it—running, I mean—and Joel drove me back.'

'To his house.'

'Yes, to his house.'

'Is that why you're looking so tearful now?'

Olivia gasped, rubbing furiously at her eyes. 'I'm not looking tearful.'

'You've been crying,' declared her father steadily. 'You needn't bother to deny it. When a woman's eyes and nose are red, it's a dead giveaway.'

Olivia sniffed again. 'Well, all right. I've been crying. It's not a sin, is it?'

'No.' Ben Foley shook his head. 'But I'd like to know what young Armstrong's done to upset you.'

'Young Armstrong!' Olivia tried to force a laugh. 'Dad, Joel's thirty-five, not nineteen.'

'I'm aware of that.' Her father frowned. 'What's happened? Did you sleep with him?'

'Dad!'

'Don't look at me like that, Livvy. I may be old and crippled, but I'm not numb from the neck down.' He sighed. 'If that man's hurt you, I want to hear about it. He may be thirty-five, but he's not too old to feel the sharp edge of my tongue!'

'Oh, Dad!'

'Well, did you?'

To her dismay, Olivia could feel the tears running down her cheeks again and she fumbled for one of the tissues from the box on the table beside her father's bed. 'I don't want to talk about it, Dad,' she said, scrubbing her eyes again. 'It's late. I ought to get to bed myself.'

'So you did sleep with him,' remarked the old man resignedly. 'I knew you would. Sooner or later. But obviously it didn't work out.'

'Dad!'

'Stop saying "Dad" as if I was a juvenile. You forget, Livvy. I was both mother and father to you for years after Elizabeth died. All right, it's been some time since we spent any time together, but I haven't forgotten one small thing about you. You'll always be my baby, Livvy. The little girl I had such high hopes for.'

Olivia gripped his hand lying on the duvet beside her. 'Linda told me you had to scrape and save to keep me at school until I was eighteen,' she said. 'Is that true?'

'Linda had no right telling you any such thing. I was happy to do what I could. And I'm proud of the way you've turned out, although you may not believe me. You're a good woman, Livvy. Caring and generous and too honest for your own good.'

'What do you mean?' Olivia frowned.

'I mean, all those years ago, telling Joel you'd arranged to have an abortion. If you hadn't told him that, no one would have been any the wiser. Miscarriages happen all the time. Your mother lost a baby just after we got married. Then we had Linda, without any bother at all.'

Olivia stared at him. 'I didn't know that.'

'Why should you? It's not something most people brag about. Your mother was very upset, but we got over it. Things happen!'

Olivia felt a smile tugging at her lips. 'Thanks, Dad,' she said. 'You've made me feel so much better.' She sniffed again. 'Is there anything I can do for you before I go?'

'Yes.' Ben Foley's brows drew together. 'You can tell

Linda I've decided to ask the bank for a loan.' He paused. 'Talking to you, being with you, has made me see there's more to life than lying here, waiting for the devil to come and get me. Martin's right. I'm never going to be able to run this place again. Why should I stand in their way? I've got better things to do.'

Olivia caught her breath. 'Like what?'

'Like getting out of this bed, for one thing,' declared her father grimly. 'I'm going to get myself one of those electric wheelchairs, so I can get about by myself. Having that beer the other day reminded me of how long it's been since I had a drink in The Bay Horse. Who knows, maybe some of my old pals won't have forgotten me?'

The following week dragged. Olivia felt emotionally drained, robbed of any sense of optimism about the future. And, although the atmosphere in the house was infinitely more cheerful, now that her father had agreed to approach the bank for a loan, Olivia couldn't see herself staying there any longer than it took to find a place of her own.

It was a situation that had been reinforced by the conversation she'd accidentally overheard Linda and Martin having one evening after they'd thought she'd gone to bed. But she'd been thirsty, and when she'd gone downstairs for a drink she'd heard Martin mention her name.

She hadn't intended to listen. She knew eavesdroppers seldom heard good of themselves. But what she had heard had confirmed her earlier suspicions about her brother-in-law's apparent change of heart where she was concerned.

Martin hadn't changed his mind about her. He hadn't wanted her to stay on at the farm because she was family.

It appeared he'd invited her to stay because he'd been hoping to persuade her to use what little money she had to finance the redevelopment of the cottages, after all. He'd reasoned that without the expense of an apartment, she'd have had no excuse for needing extra funds.

What hurt Olivia the most was that Linda had gone along with it. Obviously her father hadn't known anything abut Martin's manipulations, but Linda had been party to his plans all along. If it hadn't been for her father, Olivia was sure she'd have packed up and gone back to London, the sense of betrayal Joel had awakened only strengthened by her sister's deception.

That was why, a few days later, she found herself in Newcastle again, checking out the estate agents. It served the dual purpose of pricing possible apartments and asking about job vacancies.

She didn't have her CV with her, of course, and it was a very unorthodox way of introducing herself to possible employers. But her experiences in London had taught her that having confidence in her abilities was worth a handful of good references.

Even so, the day was a bit of a disappointment as far as finding herself an apartment was concerned. Those she did view were usually too small or too expensive. The one she did like on the riverside was already spoken for, and she'd had to content herself with leaving her name and phone number just in case the present buyer pulled out of the deal.

Still, she did have a couple of interviews lined up for the following week. She'd have to take a trip to London before that to arrange to have the rest of her belongings couriered north. She'd also check out of the small hotel where she'd stayed when she'd first returned to England. The manager there had offered to keep a room free for her until her return.

On impulse, when she left Newcastle she drove back to Bridgeford via Millford. She assured herself she wanted to see the village again, but the truth was she wanted to drive past Joel's house one more time. She didn't expect to see him. It was the middle of the afternoon and he'd probably be lecturing. In any case, there was no point in pursuing their relationship. Whatever excuses he came up with, she'd never forgive him for not believing her.

She slowed as she reached the green. If Joel's car was at his gate, she was prepared to do a U-turn. But it wasn't. As anticipated, the house looked deserted. Well, what had she expected? But it proved how much she was deceiving herself.

She was driving round the green when she saw Sean. He wasn't on his own. He was walking beside a tall, lanky individual who, despite the fact that he wasn't wearing his cassock, was unmistakably the vicar of All Saints Church.

Olivia hesitated, slowing behind them, not sure what she intended to do until she'd pulled alongside. Then, rolling down her window, she said, 'Hi there,' including them both in her deceptively casual greeting.

'Olivia!' Sean recognised her at once, leaving his relative's side to put both hands on the rim of the open window. He gave her a wistful look. 'I've missed you, Olivia. Have you missed me?'

Olivia wasn't sure how to answer that one. Of course she'd missed the boy, but saying so wasn't going to help anyone. However, Brian Webster saved her the dilemma.

'Oh, it's you, Livvy,' he said without enthusiasm. 'What are you doing in Millford? Joel's not here.'

Olivia could have said that she hadn't come to see Joel, but she didn't. Instead, she turned her attention to the boy. 'Does your mother know you're here, Sean?' she asked, with a swift glance at Brian. 'I thought it was only weekends that you spent with your dad.'

'You're right. He shouldn't be here,' agreed Brian, without giving the boy time to reply. 'He evidently expected to find Joel at home, but he was disappointed. Fortunately, I'd seen him getting off the bus, so I intercepted him before he found somewhere to hide.' He sighed. 'I mean, he could have been hanging about for hours.'

'That's true,' said Olivia, giving Sean a disapproving look. She was remembering what had happened the last time he'd run away and she knew Joel wouldn't be pleased at his reckless disregard of his mother's feelings.

'Well, it is Thursday,' Sean protested. 'And I am supposed to be spending the weekend with Dad. What does it matter if I come a day early?'

Olivia and Brian exchanged glances, and then she said, 'You know the answer to that as well as I do. You're supposed to wait until Friday so your dad can collect you.'

'And let's not forget your mother!' exclaimed Brian. 'She must be out of her mind with worry by now. I'm going to go straight into the vicarage and ring her to let her know where you are. Then I suppose I'll have to drive you home.'

'I don't want to go home,' muttered Sean stubbornly, but Olivia steeled her heart against him.

'I can take him back,' she said instead, immediately regretting the impulse to get involved again.

'Oh, could you?' Brian's face cleared for the first time since she'd met them. 'That is kind of you, Livvy. I've got a wedding rehearsal at five o'clock and I was thinking I'd have to put them off.'

'But I don't want to go home,' said Sean again; however, Brian had no sympathy.

'You don't have a choice,' he said briskly. 'Come along. Get into the car.'

Sean looked sulky. 'I don't have to. Mum says I should never get into a car with a stranger. I can get the bus back. I'm old enough.'

'Get in,' said Olivia warningly, leaning across the passenger seat and pushing the door open. 'Now.'

Heaving a sigh, Sean obeyed her, flopping into the seat beside her with evident ill grace. Brian slammed the door, raising his hand to both of them, and then Olivia put the car in gear and drove away.

'Dad isn't going to like this,' said Sean eventually, apparently deciding to take a different approach. 'He said we wouldn't be seeing you again. Ever. I think he's angry with you. Have you done something to upset him? He wasn't in a good mood all last weekend.'

Olivia gave a brief shrug of her shoulders. 'I'm sure in this instance he'll be glad you're not spending another night in the barn, don't you?'

'I wasn't going to spend the night in the barn.' Sean was indignant. 'I was just going to go and play football on the lawn until Dad got home.'

'And what about your mother?'

Sean sniffed. 'Dad would have rung her when he got back.'

'But what if he had an evening lecture? It could have

been eight or nine before he came home. Your mother would have been frantic by then.'

'No, she wouldn't.'

'Yes, she would.'

'She wasn't before.'

'That was different. She thought you were at your Dad's.'

'But I wasn't.'

'No. But she didn't know that. And as that's where you'd gone before…' Olivia sighed. 'You know I'm right, Sean. You can't keep running away like this.'

Sean hunched his shoulders. 'I wish I could live with Dad.'

'Yes, I think we all know that. But you can't.'

'Why can't I?'

'Because your father isn't married. He doesn't have a wife to look after you when he's not there.' She took a breath. 'If he was married, it would be different. But he's not.'

Sean looked thoughtful. 'You like my dad, don't you?'

Olivia knew where this was going. 'Yes. But I don't want to marry him.'

And how true was that?

'Why not?'

She hesitated, and then, deciding it was now or never, she said, 'Because I was married to him years ago. Before I went to America.' She gave him a rueful smile. 'It didn't work out.'

Sean gazed at her in amazement. 'You were married to Dad,' he said incredulously. 'He didn't tell me that.'

'No, and probably I shouldn't either,' murmured Olivia uneasily. 'But—well, it's not a secret.'

Sean was thinking hard. 'So you must have liked him once,' he said at last, and Olivia stifled a groan.

'It was all a long time ago,' she said quellingly. 'I'd rather talk about why you keep running away from home.' She paused. 'What's wrong? Jo—your dad said you seemed happy enough in the beginning.'

Sean shifted in his seat. 'It was all right, before—'

He broke off and Olivia glanced quickly at him. They'd been here before, too. 'Before—what?' she prompted. 'Go on.'

Sean cast her a look out of the corners of his eyes and then he seemed to slump lower in his seat. 'Before—before the hulk told me they were going to have a baby,' he muttered in a low voice, and suddenly everything he had done made a peculiar kind of sense.

Olivia sought for an answer. 'Well—that's wonderful,' she said at length. 'You're going to have a brother or sister. You should be pleased.'

'So why hasn't Mum told me?' demanded Sean, startling her by his vehemence. 'She hasn't even mentioned it and I don't know if Stewart's lying or not.'

Olivia was beginning to understand a little more. 'Oh, I think it's true,' she ventured gently, remembering Louise's sickness and how pale she'd looked that morning Olivia had called at the house. 'Perhaps she doesn't know how to tell you. Perhaps she's afraid you'll be angry. And what with you running away and all, she probably thinks it's the last thing you want to hear.'

'But—' Sean stared at her. 'But that's why I've been running away. Well, partly, anyway. I'd still rather live with my dad, but that's not going to happen, is it?'

'Not yet,' said Olivia, forcing a smile, wondering how she'd feel if Joel found someone else. Hearing about his marriage to Louise had been painful enough, but at least she hadn't been around to witness it.

Sean frowned. 'So—do you think if I told her I knew she'd be pleased?' he asked consideringly.

'I'm sure of it.' Olivia spoke firmly, wishing her own problems could be solved so easily. 'I think you've got to be grown-up about this, Sean. You're not a baby, are you?'

'No.'

'So, show your mum that you love her; that you'll go on loving her even if she has half a dozen babies!'

The following morning, Olivia was in her father's room, helping him into his wheelchair preparatory to wheeling him to the car, when Linda appeared in the doorway.

'You've got a visitor,' she said without preamble. 'Can you come?'

'A visitor?'

For a heart-stopping moment Olivia wondered if it was Joel, come to thank her for taking Sean home, but Linda soon disillusioned her. 'It's Louise Web—I mean, Barlow,' she said irritably. 'Do you know what she wants?'

Olivia could guess, but she only shook her head. She'd dropped Sean at the end of the road, allowing him to explain where he'd been to his mother if he wanted to. She'd thought it would be easier if he wasn't forced to say what he'd been doing, but if Louise was here it looked as though he'd told her the truth.

'I won't be a minute, Dad,' she said, settling the old man in his chair with an apologetic grimace. 'You can come through, if you like.'

'No, you go and talk to her, Livvy. I'll have another look

at the crossword. And don't worry about me,' he warned her. 'If there's one thing being confined to a bed teaches you, it's patience.'

Linda had put Louise in the living room, and, although she hovered in the doorway for a moment as if she'd have liked to know what the woman wanted, eventually common courtesy forced her to withdraw.

Olivia looked at Louise a little warily when they were alone. 'Linda said you wanted to see me,' she said, gesturing towards the sofa. 'Why don't you sit down?'

As she did so, Olivia noticed that Louise looked much better this morning. There was colour in her cheeks so whatever this was about, it couldn't be all bad.

'I hope you don't mind me coming here,' she said, apparently understanding the situation with Linda. She waited until Olivia had seated herself on the armchair opposite, before she continued, 'First of all, I want to thank you for bringing Sean home yesterday afternoon.'

'That's OK.' Olivia was relieved. 'I'm glad he told you.'

'He had to anyway.' Louise pulled a wry face. 'Brian called me just after you left Millford.'

'Ah.'

'But that wasn't all he told me,' Louise went on, smoothing a hand over the knee of her trousers. 'He told me he knew about the baby; that Stewart had told him without mentioning it to me.'

Olivia nodded. 'I see.'

'It was because he'd talked it over with you, wasn't it? Why is it that he always seems to find it easier to talk to someone else and not to me?' She sighed. 'Still, I suppose I have been pretty wrapped up in myself since I started this morning sickness. I didn't have any with Sean, you see, so I've taken badly to it.'

Olivia didn't know what to say. She and Louise were hardly likely to be friends. 'And was he pleased?' she asked, choosing the least controversial option. She didn't even want to think about how it was when Louise was expecting Sean. That was much too much information.

'I think he is pleased, yes,' Louise said now. 'He thought I didn't want him to know.'

'Well, I'm glad it's turned out so well,' said Olivia, wincing at her choice of vocabulary. 'He's a really nice boy. And a credit to you.'

'Yes, he is. A nice boy, I mean.' Louise blew out a breath. 'Does Joel know? About the baby?'

'Not from me,' said Olivia flatly.

'You don't think Sean might have confided in his father?'

'I think he was worried about you,' said Olivia carefully. 'Staying with his father allowed him to put it out of his head.'

'Well, I appreciate what you did.' Louise bent her head. 'Particularly after the way I behaved.'

'Like you said, you had other things on your mind,' said Olivia, wishing this conversation was over. She made to get to her feet. 'But now, if you don't mind—'

'Wait!' Louise put out a hand, making Olivia stay in her seat. 'I haven't finished.' She wet her lips. 'When I said after what I'd done, I wasn't talking about Sean, Livvy. I was talking about Joel.'

'Joel?'

Olivia was totally confused. What on earth was Louise saying? Unless… The bile rose in the back of her throat.

Unless Louise was about to tell her that the child she was expecting was Joel's.

'I'm not explaining myself very well,' Louise went on uncomfortably. 'But this isn't easy, Livvy.'

Olivia frowned. 'What isn't easy?'

'It was me,' said Louise quickly. 'I was the one who told Joel you'd had the abortion. Maureen—my cousin Maureen, that is—used to work at the clinic in Chevingham. She knew how I felt about Joel, how jealous I'd always been of you. She couldn't wait to tell me that you'd made an appointment and then changed your mind at the last minute.'

Olivia's throat felt dry. 'But you knew I hadn't gone through with it.'

'Yes, but when I heard about your miscarriage, I told Joel that you had.' She hurried on, trying to excuse herself. 'I hated myself afterwards, Livvy. When you two split up and everything. But it was too late then.'

Olivia blinked. 'You destroyed my life because you were jealous!'

'I was totally, totally ashamed of what I'd done.'

'But that didn't stop you from marrying Joel when he came back to Bridgeford, did it?' exclaimed Olivia bitterly. 'My God, Louise, I don't know how you could do such a thing.'

Louise sniffed. 'I know, I know. I was a bitch. And I've paid for it. But—well, I didn't have to tell you,' she added defensively. 'And like I said before, Joel still loved you. So lying to him didn't do me a bit of good.'

CHAPTER FOURTEEN

JOEL emptied his glass and reached for the bottle sitting on the low table in front of him. He upended it into the glass and then scowled when only a few drops of the amber liquid emerged to cover the base of the crystal tumbler. The whisky was all gone. He'd swallowed almost half a bottle of the stuff. Even so, he thought irritably, he should have called at the pub on his way home and bought another. But at that point, he'd still been kidding himself that this wasn't going to be another lousy night.

He flung himself back against the cushions of the sofa, staring unseeingly into the empty grate. It wasn't cold enough to need a fire, but right now he could have done with one. He felt chilled, through and through.

He'd been feeling this way for days, ever since he'd had that phone call from Louise. He'd suspected something was wrong when he'd gone to pick up Sean on Friday afternoon, but he'd assumed she and Stewart had had a row. And then Sean had told him that his mother was expecting a baby, which had seemed to explain her agitation. He knew from the first time she was pregnant that Louise didn't take kindly to losing her figure.

But the call that had come on Sunday evening had been totally out of the blue. After all, it had only been a couple of hours since he'd dropped Sean off, and his first concern had been that there was something wrong with his son. But it had soon become apparent that the reason for Louise phoning him had nothing to do with Sean. What Louise had to say, she hadn't had the nerve to reveal to his face.

To say Joel was devastated by her confession would have been an understatement. He'd wanted to get in his car and drive to Bridgeford and confront Louise personally with her lies. Only the knowledge that Sean would be there, that he might be frightened and not understand his father's anger, had kept Joel from making a scene that night.

However, he had gone to see Louise the following morning. He'd cancelled a lecture and driven straight to his ex-wife's house. He'd been so angry, but she'd been tearful—even though he knew she could turn them on to order—and pregnant, and although he could blame her, the person who was really to blame was himself.

He'd been so stupid. Accepting Louise Webster's story instead of believing his wife. No wonder she'd run away to London. She'd had to suffer the after-effects of the miscarriage without anyone to support her. They'd all believed she was lying. Even her father.

And now, he'd only compounded the offence by showing he still believed she'd had an abortion. That evening they'd spent together had been so perfect until he'd opened his big mouth. He'd thought that by telling her he'd forgiven her, she would be grateful. Instead of which, he'd destroyed their relationship all over again.

He had gone to the farm after seeing Louise, hoping

against hope that Olivia would agree to talk to him. But she
hadn't been there. Linda had said her sister had gone to
London and she didn't know when—or even if—she'd be
back. She had been looking for an apartment in Newcastle,
she'd added, but Olivia hadn't found anything she liked.

Which had been the final straw. Joel hadn't slept the
night Louise phoned him and he hadn't had a good night's
sleep since then. His smug little world had been shattered
and he was afraid it was going to take more than a university degree to put it right this time.

When the phone rang, he practically leapt from the sofa
to answer it. It might be Olivia, he thought. She could be
back from London and Linda would have told her he'd
called at the farm.

But it wasn't Olivia. It was his mother, calling from the
airport in Newcastle. 'Can you come and pick us up,
darling?' she asked. 'The plane was delayed or I'd have
rung you earlier. But we wanted it to be a surprise.'

Joel stifled a groan. 'I can't, Mum.'

'You can't?' Diana Armstrong sounded put out.

'No. I'm afraid I've been drinking,' Joel admitted, knowing
how that would be received. 'Sorry, Mum. It's good to hear
from you, but you should have warned me you were coming.'

Diana mumbled something about thoughtless sons, and
then Patrick Armstrong came on the line. 'It's OK, Joel,'
he said. 'We can easily take a taxi. It was your mother's idea
to ring you. I guessed you might have company tonight.'

Joel frowned. 'Company?'

'What your father's trying so unsubtly to say is that we
heard Olivia was back home again,' put in his mother
tersely. 'She's not there with you, is she?'

'No.' Joel's tone was cooler now. 'More's the pity. She's not even staying in Bridgeford any longer. Her sister told me she's gone back to London.'

'Well—' Diana was obviously trying not to sound too delighted. 'Well, it's probably all for the best, Joel. After what she did.'

'But that's the point,' said Joel grimly. 'She didn't *do* anything. Louise told me a couple of days ago that she'd been lying when she said Liv had had an abortion. She hadn't. She really had had a miscarriage. And nobody—but especially me—would listen.'

He thought he might feel better when he got off the phone, but he didn't. He'd thought that telling his mother she'd been wrong about Olivia all along would give him some relief. But he was mistaken. The hollowness inside him seemed greater if anything. A great gaping hole of nothingness where once he'd had a heart.

He was in the kitchen, checking for beers in the fridge, when the doorbell rang. He'd just discovered he had two bottles of a German brew and he put them down on the counter with a distinct lack of patience. What now? he thought. Someone selling double-glazing? Or perhaps Sean had run away again. Surely not, now that he knew why his mother had been feeling so unwell.

He hoped it wasn't anyone from the university. He was only wearing drawstring black sweatpants and a black T-shirt. He'd intended to go for a run earlier, but intermittent rain and the bleakness of his mood had deterred him.

It was still light out and when he pulled open the door, he had no difficulty in identifying his caller. Olivia stood outside, slim and beautiful in a red slip dress and incredibly high heels, a loose wrap of some gauzy material floating about her bare shoulders.

'Hi,' she said, sheltering under the lee of the overhang. 'Are you going to invite me in?'

Joel stepped back abruptly, almost losing his balance in his haste to get out of her way. And then, still staring at her as if he couldn't quite believe his eyes, he said stupidly, 'I thought you went back to London.'

'I did.' Olivia moved into the hall, shedding her wrap into his startled hands. Then, glancing thoughtfully at him, she said, 'Are you drunk?'

Joel was taken aback. 'Me?' he said. 'Drunk?'

'You're acting as if you are,' she declared, sauntering past him into the sitting room. Then, turning, she pressed one finger delicately to her nose. 'It smells like a distillery in here.'

Joel tried to pull himself together. 'You're exaggerating,' he said, following her into the room and snatching up the empty bottle and his glass, stowing them away in the drinks cabinet. 'I was having a quiet drink, that's all.'

'A quiet drink?' Olivia faced him, her hips lodged carelessly against the back of the sofa. 'All alone?'

'No, my harem dashed upstairs as soon as you rang the bell,' said Joel shortly. And then, just in case she thought he was serious, 'Of course alone. Who else would I be with?'

Olivia moistened her lips. 'I don't know. What was that girl's name? Cheryl something or other. You could have been with her.'

'No, I couldn't.' Joel took a steadying breath. 'Why are you here, Liv? Have you come to say goodbye?'

'Goodbye?'

'Linda said you might stay in London.'

'Did she? Well, actually, I was arranging to have the rest of my belongings sent to the farm.' She paused. 'Sorry to disappoint you.'

Joel swore. 'That doesn't disappoint me, for God's sake! But what was I supposed to think?'

'Oh, I don't know.' Olivia shifted and the silky bodice moved sensuously against her body. 'You could say you were glad to see me.' She paused. 'You could even say you like my dress.'

Joel groaned. 'You look—fantastic,' he muttered shortly. 'But what is this, Liv? A crucifying mission? Have you come to see how much more pain I can take?'

'No.' Olivia turned then, walking around the sofa, trailing long nails that matched her dress over the soft leather. 'Why should I want to hurt you, Joel? Haven't we hurt one another enough?'

Joel sucked in a breath. 'Then you know—'

'About the lies? Yes, Louise told me.' She glanced his way. 'I assume she's told you?'

Joel nodded.

Olivia moistened her lips. 'And how did that make you feel?'

'Stupid! Devastated! Angry!' Joel raked back his hair with a hand that shook a little. 'God, Liv, I knew Maureen Webster worked at that clinic. And I had no reason to suspect that Louise might be lying.'

'Except that I'd told you it wasn't true!' exclaimed Olivia unsteadily. 'It never occurred to you that I might be telling the truth, did it?'

'Of course it did.' Joel swore again. 'Didn't she tell

you? I phoned the clinic. I wanted proof that you'd actually had an abortion.'

Olivia stared at him. 'And what happened?'

'I got some empty-headed receptionist who said she couldn't give out confidential information about the patients.' He groaned. 'All she would tell me was that, yes, you had had an appointment. She said nothing about you cancelling it.'

'Oh, Joel!' Olivia trembled. 'You should have had more faith in me.'

Joel shook his head. 'Do you think I haven't tormented myself with that ever since Louise decided to tell me?' he demanded. 'I've gone over every minute of those days with a fine-tooth comb and, whatever I do, I can't forgive myself for being such a fool. I should have listened to you. I should have realised you wouldn't have been so upset if it was what you'd wanted. Instead, I could hear the receptionist telling me that you had made the appointment in one ear and Louise whispering that you'd never wanted my baby in the other.'

'Oh, God, Joel—'

'No. Don't feel sorry for me, Liv. I was twenty years old. I should have known better.'

'We were both just kids,' said Olivia huskily, gazing up at him with brimming eyes. 'I wonder if I hadn't run away if we might have learned the truth.'

Joel made a helpless gesture. 'Do you think I haven't considered that, too?' He sighed. 'It would be so easy for me to say that you running away settled the matter. That it proved you'd been lying all along. But I was the real culprit, Liv. I blame myself totally. I moved out of the farm. I let you think that, as far as I was concerned, our marriage was over.'

'Our marriage was over,' whispered Olivia, but Joel only shook his head again, coming towards her, his face dark with emotion.

'Do you honestly think that if you'd stayed in Bridgeford, I'd have been able to keep away from you?' he asked hoarsely. 'For God's sake, Liv, I love you. I've never stopped loving you, dammit. Louise knows that. Maybe that was why she decided to be generous for once in her life.'

Olivia's lips parted, but, although she was tempted to tell him why Louise had had a change of heart, she decided that could wait. Evidently his ex-wife hadn't told him the whole story and Sean wouldn't be too eager to confess that he'd run away again.

'So—what are you saying?' she breathed, running the tip of her finger along the roughened edge of his jawline.

Joel flinched at her touch, but he didn't move away. 'Look at me,' he said instead, gripping the back of his neck with agitated hands. 'You've been back—what? Barely a month. And already I'm a nervous wreck. I can't eat; I can't sleep. And any illusions I had that I was content with my life have all crashed and burned. Does that answer your question?'

Olivia gazed at him. 'You mean that, don't you?'

'Damn right, I mean it,' he declared savagely, and, abandoning any further attempt to restrain his actions, he slid his hands over her shoulders and pulled her against him. 'You know I love you,' he said huskily. 'You must know I want to be with you.' His eyes darkened. 'Does your being here mean that you might forgive me, after all?'

Olivia uttered a breathy little laugh. 'It might,' she said tremulously. 'I'm thinking about it.'

'Well, don't take too long,' said Joel unsteadily, burying his face in the scented hollow of her throat, and Olivia trembled all over.

Her fingers clung to his shoulders, glorying in the taut strength of the arms that encircled her so possessively. Even now, it was hard to let herself believe this was actually happening. She'd been so depressed when she went to London, so unsure of what to think, what to do.

But this was Joel, she thought incredulously, the man she loved and who loved her. Had loved her for fifteen long years, years they'd wasted because of a jealous woman's lies.

And like a dam breaking, emotion flooded her body. There was no need to keep him in suspense. She loved him too much to let this moment slip away. 'I've thunk,' she said huskily, pressing herself against his hard body. 'The answer's yes.'

Their journey up the stairs was only punctuated by moments when Joel divested himself and Olivia of what they were wearing. Her shoes barely made it past the first stair and her dress slipped silkily off her shoulders a few moments later.

The fact that she wasn't wearing a bra caused a few minutes' delay as Joel's hands found her breasts and stroked them into painful arousal. But when she slid her hands beneath his T-shirt, he was compelled to discard it and go on.

She found the drawstring of his sweats only seconds later. The soft fabric skimmed down his narrow hips and he had to kick himself free of them before he tripped. However, her lacy thong did make it to the landing, where it adorned the newel post, like some erotic symbol of their desire.

Their lovemaking was hot and urgent at first. They were hungry for one another and there was no time for foreplay before Joel spread her legs and plunged into her slick sheath. Her moan of satisfaction was stifled by his mouth, and Joel's head was swimming as the blood rushed wildly into his groin.

He felt Olivia climax only moments before his own release, the instinctive tightening of her body engulfing him in flames. 'God, I love you,' he groaned, when he lay shuddering in her arms, and Olivia stroked the damp hair back from his temple with a trembling hand.

'I love you, too,' she whispered. 'So much. As soon as I saw you again, I knew I'd just been kidding myself that I'd got you out of my life.'

They made love again then, gently this time, sharing every delicious moment, stroking and caressing each other in an emotional demonstration of their love and renewal.

But then, Joel propped himself up on one elbow and looked down at her. 'Tell me about Garvey,' he said, not wanting to spoil the moment but he had to know. 'Did you love him?'

Olivia gave a rueful smile. 'Yes, I loved him,' she said. 'But not like I love you,' she added huskily. 'I couldn't understand why at first. He was young and very good-looking and I don't deny I was flattered when he asked me to marry him and move to New York, but there was no real—connection, if you know what I mean?'

'I'm trying to,' said Joel gruffly, and Olivia giggled.

'You've no need to be jealous,' she assured him gently. 'Our relationship was anything but passionate.' She paused. 'I must be incredibly naïve. When he insisted on waiting until we were married before consummating our relationship, I thought he was doing it for me, because he knew I'd had one disastrous relationship—ours—and he thought I wasn't ready for another.'

Joel's brows drew together. 'What are you telling me? That he was—gay?'

'See, you got it in one,' said Olivia ruefully. 'Yes, he was gay. But it took me months before I found out. And because he convinced me that we were good for one another, that it wasn't necessary for a relationship to be a sexual one to work, I went along with it. For what seems like such a long time now.'

Joel turned her face towards him. 'God, Liv, if he hurt you—'

'He didn't.' Olivia sighed. 'I hurt him, I think. But it took me some time to realise that, although I was living this celibate life, Bruce wasn't. I was just his cover, the wife he could escort to functions and display on any occasion when a wife was needed.'

'Hell!'

Joel stared down at her with impassioned eyes and she reached up to press her lips to his. 'Don't look like that, darling. It wasn't all bad. Bruce was a generous man. He was kind. Selfish, perhaps, but kind. I had my own bank account, a string of credit cards. He liked me to spend his money. He encouraged me to fill my wardrobe with expensive clothes, expensive accessories. There was nothing I couldn't have—financially, at least.'

'And then?'

'And then I discovered that he was leading a double life. The nights he was supposed to be working late—he was a merchant banker and they often work late into the evening—he was visiting his lover. Well, a series of lovers, actually,' she appended, her cheeks turning pink. 'He was a member of this club and—'

Joel laid his finger across her lips. 'You don't have to go on,' he said. 'I get the picture.' He paused. 'So you told him you wanted a divorce?'

'Mmm.' Olivia's lids drooped. 'He wasn't pleased.'

'I can believe it.' Joel snorted. 'You were in danger of exposing his deception.'

'Right. And all our friends—*his* friends, and work colleagues, all thought we had an ideal marriage.'

Joel nuzzled her cheek. 'So, what happened?'

'I moved out of our apartment. I got myself a small walk-up in Brooklyn and started divorce proceedings.'

'I gather they took some time?'

'You better believe it.' Olivia nodded. 'Bruce fought me every step of the way.' She bit her lip. 'He—he even went so far as to tell anyone who'd listen that I'd moved out because he wanted children and I didn't. I'd been stupid enough to tell him about—about the miscarriage, and he chose to use that against me, too.'

'But God, you could have made him suffer. Not to mention taking him for every penny he had.'

'I didn't want his money. I didn't want anything from him. OK, maybe I was stupid, but I just wanted to be free.'

'Oh, Liv!' Joel gazed at her with agony in his eyes. 'I wish I could take back every one of those years and make it up to you.'

Olivia looked up then, a smile tilting the corners of her mouth. 'Hey, this is going a long way to achieving it,' she assured him huskily. 'We all make mistakes, Joel. Me more than most.'

'And now?'

She wet her lips with a nervous tongue. 'I suppose that's up to you.'

'OK.' Joel didn't hesitate. Getting up onto his knees beside her, he said, 'Marry me. Marry me, Liv. Again. As soon as I can get a licence.'

'You really want to marry me again?'

'How can you doubt it?' Joel groaned, taking one of her hands and raising her palm to his lips. 'I'm crazy about you, Liv. Say you'll give me a second chance.'

Olivia didn't hesitate either. She wound her arms around his neck and pulled him down to her. 'Oh, I'll give you another chance,' she whispered. 'And I will marry you. Whenever it can be arranged.' She hesitated. 'I want to have your baby, Joel. We can't replace the one we lost, but we can ensure that Sean has more than one brother or sister, hmm?'

They were both sound asleep when the doorbell rang.

Olivia, her bottom curled spoon-like into the curve of Joel's thighs, was the first to hear it. The sound echoed unpleasantly through her subconscious, and, although she didn't want to move, she was obliged to open her eyes and shift a little restlessly against him.

Joel, getting exactly the wrong impression, pressed closer, and she felt the unmistakable stirring of his erection. 'Hey, you're insatiable,' he muttered huskily, parting her thighs, but Olivia pulled away from him, turning onto her back as the doorbell rang again.

'Hear that?' she said, unable to prevent the smile that

touched her lips at Joel's obvious disappointment. 'You've got a visitor.'

'Shit!'

Joel scowled, but when the bell rang for a third time, he had no choice but to slide out of bed and reach for the dressing gown hanging on the back of the bedroom door.

As he wrapped its folds about him, Olivia pushed herself up against the pillows. 'Who do you think it is?' she asked, unknowingly exposing dusky pink nipples to his urgent gaze, and Joel groaned.

'My mother and father?' he suggested flatly, seeing the look of dismay that crossed her face at his words. 'They phoned from the airport earlier. They wanted me to go and pick them up, but, as you know, I'd been drinking. I had to refuse.'

'I'm glad you did,' she murmured, barely audibly, but Joel had heard her.

'So'm I,' he said, pausing to bestow a lingering kiss at the corner of her mouth. 'Hold that thought, baby. I won't be long.'

The bell rang again, more insistently this time, as he went down the stairs, and, although he'd been attempting to pick up all the items of clothing strewn around, the summons was too urgent to ignore. Abandoning his efforts, he dropped the clothes he had rescued onto the chest at the foot of the stairs and strode barefoot to the door.

'Are you aware that it's raining, Joel?' demanded his mother, brushing past him into the hall. 'So much for us being concerned about you. You certainly took your time answering the door.'

'Are you aware that I was in bed, asleep?' retorted Joel,

giving his father an apologetic look as he followed his wife inside.

'In bed?' Diana Armstrong took off her jacket and shook a spray of water over the floor. 'It's barely ten o'clock, Joel. How much have you been drinking, for heaven's sake?'

'It's none of your—'

He didn't finish. His mother had been about to deposit her coat on the chest when she saw the jumble of clothes Joel had dropped there. Without hesitation, she picked them up, saying with obvious distaste, 'You've got a woman here, haven't you? Your father was right.'

Joel took the garments out of his mother's hands and returned them to the chest. 'Not *a* woman,' he said tersely. '*The* woman. Liv arrived just after you'd called. Does that explain the situation?'

Diana's mouth dropped open in disbelief, but Patrick Armstrong was much less perturbed. 'I wondered how long it would be before you two got together again,' he said warmly. 'I hope it works out this time, son. I really do.'

'Thanks, Dad.'

Joel shook the hand his father offered, but Diana wasn't finding it so easy to come to terms with what she'd heard. 'You mean—you were in bed with Olivia Foley?' she said incredulously. 'Oh, Joel, is that wise? What if—what if she hurts you again?'

'I won't.'

The voice came from above their heads and Joel turned to find Olivia coming down the stairs towards them. She was wearing an old rugby shirt of his that barely covered her thighs, a momentary peek of scarlet lace proving she'd rescued her thong from its perch.

His heart leapt into his chest as he went to meet her. She was so adorable, so beautiful, and she was his. He could hardly believe that fate was being kind to him at last. He wanted to take her in his arms and howl his satisfaction to the moon.

'Olivia!' Diana recovered quickly, moving towards the pair of them with a practised smile on her face. 'You must forgive me for being anxious. It's a mother's privilege, you know?'

'Well, it's a wife's privilege to defend herself, Diana,' responded Olivia smoothly, realising that the intimidation Joel's mother had once represented was all gone. 'Hello, Patrick,' she added, accepting his warm hug. 'Did you have a good flight?'

'Well, it was delayed—' Joel's father was beginning, when Diana broke in.

'What did you say?' she demanded. 'A *wife's* privilege?' She turned blankly to her son. 'You two haven't got married again while we were away, have you?'

'Not yet, Mum,' said Joel comfortably, putting a possessive arm about Olivia's shoulders and pulling her close. 'But it's only a matter of time. I've asked Liv to marry me and she's said yes.'

'Well, congratulations!' Once again, it was Patrick Armstrong who made the first move. 'It's long overdue, if you ask me. There should never have been a divorce.'

'I agree.' Joel bent and bestowed a warm kiss on the top of Olivia's head, and no one watching them could be left in any doubt that he meant it. He looked at his mother. 'Aren't you going to give us your blessing, Mum?'

Diana's lips tightened for a moment, but then, as if the

realisation that she couldn't fight against her whole family occurred to her, she came to give them both a kiss. 'What can I say?' she exclaimed, and there was reluctant defeat in her eyes. 'I hope you'll both find the happiness you deserve.'

EPILOGUE

'CAN I go in the pool again, *please*?'

Sean dragged the word out and his father and step-mother exchanged a knowing glance.

'You've spent half the afternoon in the pool,' Olivia pointed out, deciding to play the bad cop for a change. 'Didn't your father suggest you needed a rest? If you want to come with us this evening, you need to have a sleep.'

'Well, just five minutes more,' said Sean wheedlingly. 'Then I'll go and rest for a while, I promise.' He gave Olivia a beaming smile. 'I know you don't mind, really. And after all, in a year or so you'll be wanting me to teach Natalie to swim.'

Olivia patted the baby digesting her feed on her shoulder and pulled a wry face at Joel. 'That is true,' she conceded, feeling a quiver in her insides when she met his disturbing gaze. She knew what that look meant and he was getting impatient.

'OK,' Joel said abruptly. 'Five minutes, and then you go to your room. And I don't want to hear you playing that electronic game when you're supposed to be resting. Or you'll be keeping Marsha company tonight.'

'OK, Dad.'

Sean grinned at both his parents and then dived smoothly into the water. Since coming to the United States, his swimming skills had improved tremendously. But then, having a private pool in their garden was such an advantage. Something they would seriously have to consider when they got back home.

It was just over a year since Olivia and Joel had married again, and so much had happened in those twelve short months.

Their wedding had been a quiet affair, with just their families present. Olivia had worn an oyster silk dress, which swirled about her knees, and carried a bouquet of roses and white baby's breath, that had proved to be quite prophetic in the circumstances.

Sean had acted as both pageboy and best man, his own delight enhanced by the new arrangements that had been made for his care. His mother and father had agreed to share custody from now on, Louise admitting she'd be grateful for a little time to get used to having their new baby.

Meanwhile, Olivia had found part-time employment with an estate agency in Chevingham. It meant she didn't have so far to travel and she could easily collect Sean in the afternoons when he was living with them. It worked really well, satisfying both her need to do something useful and her desire for motherhood.

The fact that Sean got on so well with his stepmother was an added bonus. And Joel, who'd been accustomed to working late into the evenings when he was living alone, found himself leaving the university as early as possible, eager to spend time with his new wife and family.

Then, towards the end of the summer, Joel had been offered a year's sabbatical in the United States. He'd be attached to a prestigious American university, and it would enable him to study their technology as well as giving him the opportunity to lecture to a different student faculty.

It had been a wonderful offer, and Olivia hadn't hesitated before encouraging him to take it. His wife and family were expected to accompany him, of course, and a house in a small town just outside Boston had been put at their disposal for the duration of their stay.

Naturally, Sean had wanted to go with them, but Joel had explained that it wouldn't be fair to his mother to take him away for so long. However, a compromise had been reached: Sean had joined them at Easter, flying the Atlantic on his own, to the envy of all his friends.

Olivia's own news had had to wait until they were settled in Massachusetts. The revelation that she was expecting a baby had filled them both with excitement and apprehension. But, in the event, their fears were groundless. Olivia had had a perfectly normal pregnancy. Their baby daughter, whom they'd called Natalie, had been born in the hospital in North Plains, instantly gaining the love and attention of both her parents and her brother.

Their year in the United States would be over in October, and, although Olivia would be sorry to leave, she was looking forward to going home. They had still to show off baby Natalie to both her grandparents and her aunt and uncle, and, despite Sean's dismay at leaving the swimming pool and the friends he'd made at his school in North Plains, he was full of excitement at the thought of telling all his English friends of the experiences he'd had and the places he'd seen.

His swim over, Sean went to take his shower and to have a nap, and Joel lifted Natalie out of his wife's arms and cradled the little girl against his chest. Natalie was three months old and thriving, and Joel had just watched Olivia feeding her, an experience he found both distracting and stimulating.

The baby reached for the finger he held in front of her, gripping it with amazing strength for her age. 'You must be tired,' he said, touching her soft cheek with amazing gentleness. 'Your mother's fed you and changed you, and you should be ready to give us a few minutes' peace.'

'Babies are unpredictable,' said Olivia, with the knowledge gained from mixing with other mothers at the baby clinic. Her eyes twinkled. 'Perhaps you ought to be honest with her and tell her you want to take her mother to bed.'

'Is it that obvious?' Joel grinned, his teeth very white against the tan that had deepened all summer long. It was much hotter in Massachusetts than it was in the north-east of England. Olivia thought he looked well-nigh irresistible in a black vest and cargo shorts, and she couldn't wait until they were alone together either.

Half an hour later, Joel rolled onto his back beside her, giving a groan of satisfaction that Olivia shared. 'I wish we weren't going out tonight,' he said regretfully. 'I'd rather stay here with you. Alone.'

Olivia looped one hand behind her head. Her hair was damp from the humidity in the atmosphere and she had no idea how tempting she looked to her husband at that moment. 'We have to go,' she said. 'Or you do, anyway. They're giving the dinner in your honour. A kind of send-off to say they'll be sorry to see you leave.'

Joel turned onto his side to face her, his fingers stroking one swollen nipple into an instantaneous peak. 'I know,' he said, his voice thickening as he bent to suckle from her breast. 'I guess I'm just feeling possessive, that's all. When we go home, I'm going to have to share you with your family again.'

Olivia tried to steel herself against what he was doing. 'I'm looking forward to seeing Dad,' she said a little breathlessly. 'According to Linda, he gets about in his new wheelchair a lot. He's even talking about getting a car with hand controls only. It's wonderful that he's feeling so much better about himself.'

'Thanks to you,' said Joel, his fingers straying down over her ribcage to her navel. His hand dipped between her legs and Olivia felt the sympathetic flood of heat his tongue and lips had engendered. 'Your coming home was the best thing that happened to all of us. Me, particularly. I can't imagine what my life was like before you came.'

'Well, I suppose I have Linda to thank for that,' she murmured weakly. And then, trying to be sensible, 'I must remember to leave a bottle of milk for Marsha to give Natalie if she wakes up while we're gone.'

Marsha had proved to be a godsend. An elderly black woman, she'd answered their ad for a housekeeper when they first arrived. Olivia had been grateful to her for so many things, not least being there when she'd gone into labour. It was Marsha who'd driven her to the hospital and made sure Joel was there when their baby was born.

'Marsha's had half a dozen children of her own. I think you can rely on her to know what to do in all circumstances,' said Joel drily. His mouth sought hers and Olivia gave up the fight to keep her head.

With a little moan, she turned onto her side and wrapped one leg over his hips, bringing his semi-aroused sex close to her throbbing core. 'OK,' she said, 'I'll stop talking. But you're wasting time now. We've only got about twenty minutes before Sean will start wondering where we are…'

HARLEQUIN®

Mediterranean NIGHTS™

Tycoon Elias Stamos is launching his newest luxury cruise ship from his home port in Greece. But someone from his past is eager to expose old secrets and to see the Stamos empire crumble.

Mediterranean Nights
launches in June 2007 with...

FROM RUSSIA, WITH LOVE
by *Ingrid Weaver*

Join the guests and crew of *Alexandra's Dream* as they are drawn into a world of glamour, romance and intrigue in this new 12-book series.

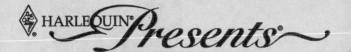

HARLEQUIN *Presents*

RUTHLESS

Men who can't be tamed...or so they think!

Meet the guy who breaks the rules to get exactly
what he wants, because he is...

HARD-EDGED & HANDSOME

He's the man who's impossible to resist.

RICH & RAKISH

He's got everything—and needs nobody...
until he meets one woman.

He's RUTHLESS!

In his pursuit of passion; in his world the winner takes all!

Billionaire Sebastian Armstrong thinks he knows his
housekeeper inside out. But beneath Emily's plain-Jane
workday exterior there's a passionate woman trying to
forget she's fallen in love with her handsome boss.

THE RUTHLESS
MARRIAGE PROPOSAL

by Miranda Lee

On sale June 2007.

REQUEST YOUR FREE BOOKS!

2 FREE NOVELS PLUS 2 FREE GIFTS!

PASSION GUARANTEED SEDUCTION

YES! Please send me 2 FREE Harlequin Presents® novels and my 2 FREE gifts. After receiving them, if I don't wish to receive any more books, I can return the shipping statement marked "cancel." If I don't cancel, I will receive 6 brand-new novels every month and be billed just $3.80 per book in the U.S., or $4.47 per book in Canada, plus 25¢ shipping and handling per book and applicable taxes, if any*. That's a savings of close to 15% off the cover price! I understand that accepting the 2 free books and gifts places me under no obligation to buy anything. I can always return a shipment and cancel at any time. Even if I never buy another book from Harlequin, the two free books and gifts are mine to keep forever.

106 HDN EEXK 306 HDN EEXV

Name	(PLEASE PRINT)
Address	Apt. #
City	State/Prov.	Zip/Postal Code

Signature (if under 18, a parent or guardian must sign)

Mail to the **Harlequin Reader Service®:**
IN U.S.A.: P.O. Box 1867, Buffalo, NY 14240-1867
IN CANADA: P.O. Box 609, Fort Erie, Ontario L2A 5X3

Not valid to current Harlequin Presents subscribers.

Want to try two free books from another line?
Call 1-800-873-8635 or visit www.morefreebooks.com.

* Terms and prices subject to change without notice. NY residents add applicable sales tax. Canadian residents will be charged applicable provincial taxes and GST. This offer is limited to one order per household. All orders subject to approval. Credit or debit balances in a customer's account(s) may be offset by any other outstanding balance owed by or to the customer. Please allow 4 to 6 weeks for delivery.

Your Privacy: Harlequin is committed to protecting your privacy. Our Privacy Policy is available online at www.eHarlequin.com or upon request from the Reader Service. From time to time we make our lists of customers available to reputable firms who may have a product or service of interest to you. If you would prefer we not share your name and address, please check here. ☐

HP07

Mediterranean Brides

**Two billionaires, one Greek, one Spanish—
will they claim their unwilling brides?**

Meet Sandor and Miguel, men who've taken all the prizes
when it comes to looks, power, wealth and arrogance.
Now they want marriage with two beautiful women.
But this time, for the first time, both Mediterranean
billionaires have met their matches and it will take more
than money or cool to tame their unwilling mistresses—
try seduction, passion and possession!

Eleanor Wentworth has always been unloved and
unwanted. Greek tycoon Sandor Christofides has wealth
and acclaim—all he needs is Eleanor as his bride.
But is Ellie just a pawn in the billionaire's game?

BOUGHT:
THE GREEK'S BRIDE
by Lucy Monroe

On sale June 2007.

Surrender To The Sheikh

**He's proud, passionate, primal—
dare she surrender to the sheikh?**

Feel warm winds blowing through your hair
and the hot desert sun on your skin as you are transported
to exotic lands. As the temperature rises, let yourself be
seduced by our sexy, irresistible sheikhs.

Ruthless Sultan Tariq can have anything he wants—
except oil heiress Farrah Tyndall. Now Tariq needs to
marry Farrah to secure a business deal. Having broken
her heart, can he persuade her to love again?

THE SULTAN'S VIRGIN BRIDE

by Sarah Morgan

On sale June 2007.

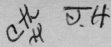

Sara hadn't
to eavesdrop

She'd heard Jane's voice quite clearly through the open door.

"I wish you weren't so involved with Sara, Con. She worries me."

Then Sara couldn't avoid hearing Conrad's answer, tender, comforting.

"It's all right, Jane—really it is. She's harmless. Just a passing holidaymaker. What could she possibly do to us?"

Then there was silence, and Sara felt an unfamiliar and sharp pain stab her as she imagined Conrad embracing Jane.

She hurried on her way. She had managed to forget the job she was here to do, but Conrad's words—so blatantly untrue, had he realized it—had reminded her forcibly of who she was and why she was on the island. . . .

Dear Reader:

We hope our December Harlequin Romances bring you many hours of enjoyment this holiday season.

1989 was an exciting year. We published our 3000th Harlequin Romance! And we introduced a new cover design—which we hope you like.

We're wrapping up the year with a terrific selection of satisfying stories, written by your favorite authors, as well as by some very talented newcomers we're introducing to the series. As always, we've got settings guaranteed to take you places—from the English Cotswolds, to New Zealand, to Holland, to some hometown settings in the United States.

So when you need a break from the hustle and bustle of preparing for the holidays, sit back and relax with our heartwarming stories. Stories with laughter...a few tears...and lots of heart.

And later, when you get a chance, drop us a line with your thoughts and ideas about how we can try to make your enjoyment of Harlequin Romances even better in the years to come.

From our house to yours, Happy Holidays! And may this special season bring you a lasting gift of joy and happiness.

The Editors
Harlequin Romance
225 Duncan Mill Road
Don Mills, Ontario, Canada
M3B 3K9

A SECRET TRUTH

Alison York

Harlequin Books

TORONTO • NEW YORK • LONDON
AMSTERDAM • PARIS • SYDNEY • HAMBURG
STOCKHOLM • ATHENS • TOKYO • MILAN

Original hardcover edition published in 1987
by Mills & Boon Limited

ISBN 0-373-17052-1

Harlequin Romance first edition December 1989

CHAPTER ONE

IT was the last, hot, lazy day of her fortnight's holiday when Sara saw the man she had given up all hope of tracking down.

She was sipping her second *citron pressé* slowly, making it last, revelling in the baking heat of the afternoon sun. This time tomorrow she would be heading for noisy old London and city grime and, most probably, grey skies. Her shorts and cut-away top would be exchanged for a suit—and her beautiful bronze would suddenly seem a waste of effort. Not that acquiring it had called for much effort: the smooth olive skin she had inherited from her Italian mother took care of that.

At first, the thirty-three-footer inching its way into a berth among the other boats, its wash setting their rigging tinkling, was just a part of the scenery. A dominant part, because it was a sleek, expensive-looking, powerful creature, the purr of its engine hinting at reserves of speed not needed for slow quayside manoeuvres.

The man matched the boat. Tall, broad-shouldered, his movements as he moored economical and sure. He was wearing a white T-shirt and navy shorts that anyone could have worn, but on him they took style from a body that was magnificently proportioned and in peak form. Against the white, his arms were deeply bronzed, and no doubt his legs—which were at present hidden below the level of the quay—would be equally impressive. He was stooping over the ropes, and Sara could see that his light brown hair, sun-

5

bleached on top, had enough crisp movement in it to be interesting without tipping over into the slightest trace of femininity.

He straightened up and glanced in both directions, up and down the quay. That was when Sara first thought there was something familiar about him. Surely she had seen that firm jaw and strong-featured face before? But where? The image she was struggling to pin down wasn't linked to sun and casual clothes.

It was as he began to walk across the cobblestones towards her that she saw his eyes clearly for the first time, and his identity exploded into her mind like a shell-burst. They were amazing eyes—there no other word for them: an intense blue, with a startling clarity of gaze that made a casual glance significant to the one who was on the receiving end of it—and set under dominant brows that were straight and dark, much darker than the hair he was brushing back.

Conrad Blake. It was incredible—but it was true. She was looking at him now, as surely as she had been when Fran showed her the TV shots of him and set her on his trail for the profile the magazine wanted to do of him. *Where Are They Now?* the series was to be called, its subtly disparaging title meant to reflect the meteoric rise and fall of the high fliers featured.

He's right here, that's where he is, Sara thought in bemused disbelief, watching him come closer and closer to where she sat.

The *patron* of the Café de la Marine had strolled out to look around and, as if to confirm what she already knew, he called out a greeting.

'*Salut, Monsieur Blake. Ça va? Libéré sur parole aujourd'hui?*'

The eyes flashed with answering amusement.

'*Ça va bien, Gaston. Et Les Genêts n'est pas une prison, salaud! C'est un paradis, comme vous savez bien.*'

He exchanged a brief handshake with the café owner and went on his way round the corner of the café, while Sara watched him over the rim of her glass. Her heartbeat, which had quickened ridiculously as he came towards her, slowed down now that the danger was over. What danger? she asked herself. Conrad Blake didn't know her. There was no reason to have reacted as she had done.

His voice had been deep and firm, completely at home with his easy French. But Conrad Blake was a man who would never be out of his element. He would make himself master of any situation. She had felt that when she'd seen him dominating the screen. Fran's snide remarks had not diminished him then, and in the flesh he certainly lived up to the promise of the screen image. He did not for a moment look like the 'yesterday's man' the series wanted to feature—and yet he had disappeared. No one at Blake Enterprises had been either willing or able to say where he was. Loyalty? Or ignorance?

In any case, why was she sitting here? Sara counted out her francs on to the table with the two little dockets the waiter had left, and went quickly along the quay to the nearby telephone kiosk, using her last remaining change to get through to the magazine office. After that only traveller's cheques remained and she didn't want to change any more of those.

'*Spica.* Can I help you?' That was Gina in reception, bored with the week and wanting to be off.

'Gina—Sara here. Listen—there's no time to waste. Get Fran to ring me back at this number. Ready?' She read out the box's number and Gina repeated it, perking up a little.

'Where are you? Home?'

'No. In Brittany still. Gina, I haven't any more——' The little light had been flashing and now she was cut off.

Sara turned her back on yet another of the quayside hopefuls who was ogling her through the glass, and tapped her fingers on the receiver, willing it to ring. If Fran was out, or Gina hadn't got the number down clearly, that was it. She couldn't stay on here without authorisation, or without the necessary cash filtering through, and as this was latish on Friday afternoon there was only now to sort things out.

The phone shrilled and Sara snatched it up.

'Now what? Lost your passport?' Fran's blasé voice sounded amused.

'Hi! No—on the contrary, I've found something. Someone, rather. Conrad Blake, in fact.'

'You've *what*?' Fran's voice sharpened. 'Where is he? I don't believe this.'

'Neither did I, but it's definitely him. He walked right past the café table where I was sitting.'

There was an explosion at the other end of the line.

'Then why the hell aren't you after him? What's the good of letting him disappear again, you mutt!'

'Calm down, Fran. His boat's right opposite me. Sooner or later he's got to come back to it.'

'Thank the lord for that. You're still wet behind the ears when it comes to this job.'

'Not that wet—but thanks a lot! Well, what do you want me to do about it?'

'Do? You ask that, after all the blind alleys we chased up trying to find the man? You stay on, of course. You get your aristocratic little nose to the ground and you sniff out that story, my girl. Did you ever think otherwise? Wait a minute . . . you said "boat". That sounds pretty elusive to me. You're not going to let him slip from between your fingers, are you?'

Sara grinned at Fran's obvious agitation. 'Not to worry. I heard him say where he was staying. It's one of the smaller islands, and he thinks it's paradise. Les Genêts, the name is. I don't know much about it.'

'You've been there a fortnight, for heaven's sake!'

'Fran—there are three hundred and sixty-five islands in the Golfe du Morbihan. It takes more than a fortnight to know them all.'

'"Miracles are our everyday achievements",' Fran was quoting from the plaque some joker in the editorial office had brought back from holiday.

'This particular miracle's going to cost money,' Sara said. 'I shall have to hire a boat to get me to and fro. And I shall need somewhere new to stay. After tonight I'm out on my ear. They've got a whole new intake coming in at the sailing-centre, so that's out.'

'Get organised, then. Do the necessary. Where's your initiative?'

Sara felt suddenly apprehensive. She was so new to *Spica*, and working out here on her own was vastly different from having Fran just behind her shoulder.

'Got any tips on how to go about it, Fran?'

'Heavens, woman! Just work on the man. Charm the story out of him. I don't have to give you lessons on male/female chemistry, do I? And this had better be the good one, Sara. I've been going through the other five in the series, and they're a pretty tame bunch. So get digging, and dig deep.' She paused, listening to the silence. 'Are you still there?'

'Yes. I'm thinking.' Sara had been caught by a not

unfamiliar stirring of distaste. She might not have been long on *Spica*'s payroll, but already she had found that a lot of the strong feminist work went against the grain. She had known she wanted to write, and journalism had seemed the answer. But so often it wasn't *what* she wanted to write. Did she really want to keep on ferreting out something juicy, as Fran put it, and have *Spica* edit it into the sort of copy that boosted the magazine's sales?

'Listen, you.' Fran cut into her thoughts impatiently. 'This call's costing too much for meaningful silences. I'll get some expenses transferred to your account. Don't book in at the local Ritz—that's an order. And ring me when you're settled. Are you listening, Sara?'

'Yes, I am—really. I'll phone you on Monday if I've anything to report.'

'Whether or not you've anything to report. I can't contact you at the moment, remember. So keep in touch every two days or thereabouts. Right?'

'Yes. Right.'

Fran's tone changed to a growl. 'Then stop having cold feet and get moving!' The line clicked then went dead.

The man who had been ogling Sara through the glass deliberately brushed against her as she came out of the kiosk.

'Get lost!' she told him in English, the venom in her voice unmistakable in any language. Apart from her qualms about the job she was about to embark on, she had good reason to be 'off' men right now, and men who treated girls as easy push-overs, especially.

Keeping a look-out for any sign of Conrad Blake returning, she went over to look at the big map of the Golfe near the landing-stage.

Les Genêts wasn't far away—just beyond one of the

larger islands close to the mouth of the estuary, in fact. It wasn't one of the standard stopping-places for the boat tour—and, in any case, there wasn't another departure due until six. If she took that to the Ile d'Arz and then tried to get a small boat to go over from there to Les Genêts, it was getting a bit late and risky. And finding just where on Les Genêts Conrad Blake was living might not be easy.

She walked along the quay, looking down on *Câline*. She was a big boat, her cabin invitingly and carelessly open, probably with other cabins beyond it. Sara's pulse quickened. Dared she?

It was the wedding-party that decided her. They came round the corner, a riotous procession led by a laughing bride and groom, and all eyes turned to watch their approach.

Sara slipped down the damp green steps and in seconds she was in *Câline*'s cabin, her heart knocking against her ribcage, surrounded by gleaming wood, polished brass and the bright royal blue of the linen seat-cushions.

A folded-back door leading to the forward area of the boat confirmed what she had thought. There was a galley, a shower compartment and loo, and beyond them another open door into a cabin in the prow.

The safest place without a doubt was in here, Sara thought, going right through into the far cabin. He might go into any of the other areas, but this was unlikely to be needed on such a short trip. But the door had been left open, and she dared not close it and risk the change being noticed.

The right-hand locker had a pile of sleeping-bags in it, and they squashed down sufficiently under her weight to accommodate her. Now a folded end of a bag to wedge the lid a little open, like this . . . She lay down, closing the lid. Shades of *The Mistletoe Bough*—but possible. If she piled the bags up at one end, she could lie back against them and be high enough to see out through the gap.

She arranged herself as comfortably as possible, and then left the lid open. She would hear Conrad Blake stepping down on to the deck, and he would have to unhitch the ropes before he came round to the wheel end. Then all she would have to do would be control her claustrophobia for a short time and that would be it.

It wasn't long before a firm tread on the deck alerted her. In her dim hiding-place Sara held her breath until she saw first the long, bronzed legs, then the rest of Conrad Blake, coming down the steps into the cabin. He gave her a worrying moment by standing still and looking round with his brows drawn together into a frown, but then he unfastened the top of his shorts and dragged his shirt off over his head. Heavens! Sara gulped. What was the man going to do next? But he merely tossed the shirt on to a seat, re-fastened the belt of his shorts across his flat stomach and went up into the steering-well.

The engine roared into life and Sara breathed again, able now to relax into an interested appraisal of the man at the wheel.

Stripped, he was even better than clothed. Smooth, rippling bronzed muscle and spare, compact flesh, the hair that tapered down to his waist and beyond glinting gold in the sunlight. His legs, braced on the boards for balance, were strong and straight. The wind, now that *Câline* was picking up speed, was blowing the hair back from his forehead, and his keen blue eyes, narrowed against the sun, stared ahead in concentration.

He had matured and strengthened tremendously since that first film-clip Fran had shown her, Sara reflected. Now he was all man. Then he had been a raw graduate about to join the family firm, at that time just on the brink of nationwide expansion as Blake Enterprises. He had been full of eager, pioneering enthusiasm as he talked of the company's aim to bring design, colour co-ordination and originality in household furnishings within the reach of the average family. It was not the altruistic business he had made it sound—for it had turned him into a millionaire by the age of thirty. Pleasing average families was lucrative. Maybe it had also made him dissatisfied by his mid-thirties. Who knew? That was what she had to find out.

As *Câline* purred through the water, Sara thought over what Fran had said as they watched all the library film available on Conrad Blake.

'Bet his mother loves him!' That was at the end of the first clip. 'All that eager young oomph boiling over! Come to think of it, Sara—not just his mother, either. Our Mr Blake has certainly packed a lot into his tender years, according to the tabloids.' She pushed a folder of newspaper clippings across to Sara as she switched on the light. 'Annabel's . . . Ascot . . . St Tropez plus boat . . . skiing at St Moritz—and as many girls as we've had hot dinners, you've noticed? But never the same one twice. Safety in numbers—or afraid for his money? See how he's grown in this next one . . . and I don't mean in height or width. This is at the World Trade Fair.'

Sara spoke her reactions out loud. 'Much more mature, isn't he? Harder, but you'd expect that. The jaw's toughened, and the eyes. The way he speaks is different: more sure of himself. A bit blasé, even. Super-sophisticated.'

'The empire's expanded by this time,' Fran said. 'He's running it jointly with his father and it's spreading into

Europe. He's Mr Big. And quite a hunk, if you like that sort of thing.' Her eyes narrowed. 'Now—do you, Sara? Like that sort of thing, I mean? We don't hear much about what goes on in your life beyond the old office door, do we?'

She was looking at Sara in the way that was common on *Spica*, where the nature of everyone's sexuality was the subject of speculation.

'In theory, yes. In practice, *at this present moment*,' Sara replied, with emphasis on the words 'he and every other man leaves me singularly unmoved.' She grinned. 'You could say that I'm lying fallow, as a friend of mine used to say between involvements.'

'And could that mean—to carry on the metaphor—that you've suffered from a patch of bad husbandry?' Fran drawled.

That was enough. 'That's my business,' Sara told her coolly.

'So's he. So make sure you get him for us,' Fran retorted instantly.

Realising that she was still staring, fascinated, at the unconscious magnificence of the man at *Câline*'s helm, Sara couldn't help grinning. If Fran could see her now . . . tune in to her thoughts . . . she wouldn't have any need to question likes and dislikes and sexual attitudes.

The sound of the boat's engine had changed, she realised: throttled back, but also contained and amplified by steep banks that she could see through the opposite porthole. They must be going to land on Les Genêts.

Her pulse quickened again as Conrad Blake disappeared from view and she heard his footsteps overhead, then felt the boat lurch as he jumped ashore. He didn't come back into the cabin, much to her relief, and, squinting sideways from her coffin-like hiding-place, Sara saw him running lightly up the steep steps cut in the rock-face.

She stayed put for a minute or two longer, then warily opened the lid and stretched her stiff limbs. Not to be recommended as a form of travel, she decided, massaging the threat of cramp from her calf muscles.

In the main cabin, the T-shirt Conrad Blake had been wearing was on the seat. The sun had been shining on it through the window and when she tentatively put out a hand to touch it, it felt warm, almost as though it had only just been stripped off and still retained the body heat of its owner.

The idea, false though it was, disconcerted her and she withdrew her fingers sharply. The movement disturbed the shirt, and she saw that underneath it was a wallet. Sara picked it up. There were far too many crisp, high-denomination notes in it to be left lying around in invitation. Impossible, though, to return a wallet left in a private boat without giving away the fact that you had been snooping. She tucked it back.

She knew, the second the cabin doorway darkened, that Conrad Blake had come back, though she had not heard a thing.

Sara felt all the little hairs on her skin stand upright, and her heart seemed to have leapt up into her throat where it was trying to batter a way out. It took all her self-control to turn calmly towards him and give what she hoped was an attractive little gamine shrug.

'Oh dear! Caught!'

Annoyance had sharpened his features, emphasising the high cheekbones and the slight hollows slanting between them and the firm line of the jaw. A film of sweat glossed his forehead, as though he had been running, but the eyes were cold steel under the frowning brows.

'Like hell you're caught,' he agreed smoothly. 'What the devil are you doing on my boat?'

Sara widened her eyes. 'Oh! You're English! That's good.'

'If you think shared nationality makes for shared possessions, think again, lady. I said, what are you doing on my boat?'

The exchange, brief though it was, had given her time to concoct a story of sorts.

'I was simply dying with thirst. I thought—just a tiny little drink of water . . . no one could mind that, surely?' She was using what Tessa, her flatmate, called 'the Murillo Virgin' look, but it didn't move Tessa, who knew her far better than to believe it, and it didn't work on him, either.

'Is that so?' he said sceptically. There was an odd expression on his face, a deepening of suspicion. 'All the same, I think precautionary measures are called for, don't you?' He came down the last two steps and his sudden movement made Sara's eyes, so dark a velvety-brown as to be almost black, blink in involuntary apprehension. 'Turn round. *Round*,' he repeated, giving her arm a little push, the touch of his fingers, so very warm and alive, in startling contrast to the coldness of his manner.

She turned her back towards him, unsure of what he wanted her to do, and again felt that disturbing touch to make her complete the full circle.

His eyes were raking her from head to foot.

'Hardly the sort of gear to hide anything,' he said shortly, commenting ambiguously on her skimpy cotton top and shorts, his eyes coming up to hers to make sure she knew both his meanings. 'All the same . . .' one finger reached out to hook the wallet out from where it lay partly hidden under the T-shirt, '. . . I think we'll take no chances. You're not in a hurry, I presume?'

He slid his long legs under the table and pulled out the wallet's contents, his eyes on her to note her reaction.

She didn't disappoint him. She felt like a shop-lifter, and a guilty flush coloured her cheeks as her eyes fell away from the questioning accusation in his, because, after all, she had handled his wallet.

As he slowly and deliberately counted every note, the cabin seemed to grow warmer, as though all that firm muscle and smooth, sun-tanned flesh had pushed up the temperature up by several degrees.

'All there—or maybe you just hadn't got round to it.'

She gave him cold look for cold look. 'I told you—all I wanted was a drink.'

'Ah, yes! The famous drink of water.' He got up suddenly, and strode past her into the galley, making her instinctively flatten herself against the folding door behind her. He turned the tap full on with an extravagant gesture that brought the muscles of his arm and bare back into relief. Nothing happened. Not a drop of water.

'I drained the tank this morning,' he said flatly.

'That was my bad luck.' She had only hesitated for the merest fraction of a second, but he noticed and snorted with impatience and disbelief. 'Oh, yes?'

As he was about to pass her again, he stopped abruptly, then scared the living daylights out of her by suddenly reaching out and grabbing her by the shoulders, thrusting his face close to hers, the intentness of his expression highly alarming.

'Let me go!' She squirmed uselessly as his hands tightened on her shoulders.

'Beautiful!' he growled, his grip not giving way a jot, his

expression contradicting the word.

'Vicious—if you don't stop this!' Sara panted.

Suddenly she was free again and he was leaning against the cabin side, looking scornfully at her.

'Not you. Your perfume. Estée Lauder's *Beautiful*. I noticed it the minute I stepped into the cabin over on the mainland, but told myself I was imagining it. You've been here all the time, haven't you? You hitched a lift across without the least idea where you'd end up. I've heard of girls like you—but I still find it hard to credit how stupid you are.'

'I just wanted to go to an island. Any island,' she said defiantly.

'Without paying for it—yes. Well, consider yourself lucky that you're not being asked to pay for it in a way you didn't anticipate.'

Again his eyes moved slowly over her, stressing his meaning, and she was made burningly aware of the inadequate protection the few items of clothing they wore between them would give her if he chose to be difficult.

Moving so fast that she had no time to dodge the blow, he gave her a resounding slap on the bottom.

'On your way, you silly creature! And don't let me catch you nosing around my property again. The whole point of an island is seclusion.'

He followed her undignified scramble up on deck, laughing as she slipped and almost fell back into the gap between *Câline* and the stone steps, and she was humiliatingly aware of his eyes boring into her back as long as she was in view.

Just before she turned the corner round a huge outcrop of rock, he called, 'And while you're exercising your legs round the island, exercise your tiny mind as to how you'll get off it. You might have got a free lift across—but there's no boat service, paid or free. Think about that ... Beautiful!'

Fool! Sara panted to herself in angry rebuke. How could she have been such an impulsive idiot as not to think of that for herself? What had Fran said? Wet behind the ears ... And how! That whole busines on *Câline* had been an object-lesson in how *not* to make first contact with a man you were supposed to charm a story out of. To judge by that little episode, he didn't seem to be a person who had even a nodding acquaintance with charm, for that matter.

Anyway—whatever the outcome, she was here on Les Genêts now, and she was jolly well going to have a good look round. If she had to eat humble pie to Conrad Blake to get off the island again, so be it. No doubt it would suit his over-inflated ego to be able to pour a bit more scorn on her. But he'd get his come-uppance in the end. This was going to be one story she would enjoy writing!

She was following the path clockwise round the island, and after a little while she saw the first sign of habitation. Past habitation, if the dilapidated appearance of the cottage, with its encroaching weeds and firmly closed shutters, was anything to go by. It was close to the sea in its own little bay, huddled against the steep side of the cove.

Sara followed the path up the slope through broom and trees, glad of her rope-soled espadrilles, for the going was rough. But, once on top of the cliff, the view was breathtaking across the Golfe. Strung across the luminous haze of water, golden in the sunshine, islands seemed to hang like emeralds, drawing her attention for a long time away from her immediate surroundings.

What a place Conrad Blake had chosen to escape to! You didn't really need a reason to want to stay here ... but, all the same, a man in his position must have a pretty strong one. Finding out what that reason *was* was going to be—a little shiver ran through her at the remembrance of his touch, and at the way those devastating eyes of his had looked her all over—it was going to be quite an experience.

And spending time here would serve a dual purpose. She had been speaking the truth when she'd said she wanted to come to an island—any island. On a publisher's desk back in London were the opening chapters of a novel—not her first, but the others had been bouncers—and an island was going to feature strongly in the latter half of the book. That was why she had chosen the Golfe for her holiday. But always there had been people around, masses of activity to take part in. A sailing holiday had seemed like a good idea, especially for a girl on her own, but it had allowed no thinking-time. Already on Les Genêts she was feeling the stirrings of ideas.

She tore her eyes away from the view at last, and concentrated on her purpose. There were cliffs along the curve of the east coast, with the raucous chatter of sea-birds coming from their nesting-places on hundreds of ledges.

Towards the centre of the island the land went on rising to a high plateau crowned by a circle of standing stones— no unusual sight in this part of France—and in the middle of them a lower, more solid mass that invited investigation, but there was no time for that now.

She was beginning to think she would never find any other signs of occupation, when the whinny of a horse alerted her. As she drew nearer, she saw a fence encircling a field, and a friendly dappled grey horse nodding over it, eager to follow her along.

It was not until Sara reached the trees at the far end of the field that she saw the house. Long and low, built of rough grey stone with an open veranda bedecked with lush green creepers, it overlooked the Golfe across an uncultivated stretch of wild land, as though nothing should be allowed to distract from the breathtaking view. She felt instinctively that this was Conrad Blake's place. Over the door, in the shade at the back of the veranda, was a bleached name-plate on which she could just make out the carved words 'La Domaine'. The name seemed appropriate, she thought sarcastically.

Beyond the house and partly hidden among trees, Sara could see two smaller buildings—cottages by the look of them—beyond which the ground shelved sharply up to a rocky headland ablaze with golden broom.

Warily she picked her way through the trees and alongside La Domaine, while the horse patiently tracked her other side of the fence. From the back the house was not so low, the ground dropping sharply to allow for another storey beneath the two of the seaward side, and there was a well kept garden sheltered by steep banks thick with shrubs.

Movement beyond the open door made Sara shrink back behind a tree, just in time. Conrad Blake strolled out, a glass in one hand, saying something over his shoulder, that she couldn't quite catch, to a person who remained indoors. He had changed into pale grey trousers and a crisp white open-necked shirt, and as he stood on the terrace surveying his territory he reminded her ludicrously of the painting *Monarch of the Glen*.

Obviously, he wasn't giving her and her plight any consideration. He had his pre-dinner drink, a meal someone else had prepared in the offing, no doubt, and if a passing thought focused on her it was probably no more than 'to hell with trespassers'.

Knowing where he was now, Sara went back round to the front of the house and boldly crossed the open land she had been reluctant to traverse when she was unsure who might be watching. The idea of maybe having to go back and ask for help bugged her. No doubt he would make her stand like a schoolgirl in the head's study, and have her watch him finish his meal before he condescended to take her back to the mainland. He would take her, in the end, she was sure. He wouldn't want strangers hanging round his valuable privacy . . . but he wouldn't make it easy.

It was an imagined ordeal that she never had to face. One of the cottages was obviously lived in, but the old woman shelling peas on the doorstep certainly didn't look capable of moving herself far, let alone a boat. The second cottage was shut very tight, though it looked neat and tidy and might have someone living there. If nothing turned up, she would give it a try before resorting to crawling to Conrad Blake, she decided.

Then the path veered towards the shore, and she saw him—an old man down below, emptying lobster pots on the edge of the rocks, with a boat . . . a blessed boat!

Sara began scrambling down over the rocks. *'Monsieur!'* she called when she was near enough to be heard above the noise of the waves, *'Pouvez-vous m'aider?'*

Once she had broken through the barrier of his deafness, it was plain sailing. He was willing and able to help her, he said calmly. It would only be a matter of fifteen minutes or so to take her across and up to town. If *mademoiselle* would wait until he had checked the last pot—and if she didn't mind keeping her toes out of reach of his lobsters—nothing would be easier. He would have had to go across in any case to deliver his catch to the Miramar in the morning. They could have them tonight at no extra charge.

He was philosophically unquestioning about her predicament, and Sara didn't attempt to explain. She was just
thankful that she didn't have to go on hands and knees to
Conrad Blake for help—or spend a foodless, sleepless night
on an island she sensed could change character with the
fading light.

She sat in the prow of the boat, looking back on Les
Genêts while the old man coaxed his motor up to top speed.

The sun was low now, and a golden nimbus seemed to
shine round the island's green, rocky silhouette. As they
drew further away, Sara saw La Domaine for a brief
moment, before the lie of the land hid it from her again, and
she wondered what Conrad Blake was doing now. Waiting
for her abject appearance at his door, no doubt. Well, let
him wait.

But let him look out, too. She'd be back.

CHAPTER TWO

WHEN Sara first opened her eyes, she wasn't sure where she was. The break and sigh of waves registered to begin with, then through the open door she saw the curve of the little bay and the skiff beached on the sand, and remembered.

She sat up and looked round with a sleepy half-smile. She had said she would be back, and she was. She was also waking up in the cottage she had first thought unfit for human habitation—and that was just what it was, really, but she couldn't afford to be choosy.

When she'd started her hunt for accommodation, she was told at the Syndicat d'Initiative that every room in every hotel and boarding-house in the area was booked, and that there was nowhere to rent available until the next month when school holidays were over. Disbelieving, she had tramped the streets asking for herself, but with no success.

It was only as a last resort on the following morning that she tried the estate agents, and drew an equal blank with them until she came to the last one on her list.

'I deal with long-term lets, you understand, *mademoiselle*,' the man behind the counter told her, not unkindly. 'The short holiday trade is quite a different matter.'

'But haven't you *something* empty *somewhere*?' she pleaded. 'It would only be for a week—two at most, and it would mean income for the owner.'

'I really am sorry. I would have liked to oblige you, but there is absolutely nothing.'

It sounded final enough, and she was about to turn away

24

when he suddenly added, 'Unless . . .'

'Yes?'

'But no. It was a stupid thought. Of course it wouldn't do. You couldn't possibly want it.'

'Try me, please!' Sara's velvety-brown eyes pleaded with him, her expression eloquent. 'I'd take a spot on a pinhead if you offered it, really I would.'

He laughed. 'If you really are so desperate—there's a cottage on Les Genêts—empty because it's due for renovation this summer, but the builders are running behind schedule. It's pretty primitive. Cold water only . . . a Camping Gaz stove . . . no electricity . . . and the——' he shrugged fatalistically, '—the facilities are in the garden. Not what you would want at all. It was foolish of me to mention it.'

Sara couldn't believe her luck. 'I'll take it!' Her reply was enthusiastic enough to be convincing, but he still looked doubtful.

'I really don't know, *mademoiselle*. The cottage is structurally sound . . . and equipped, you could say—but only in a very rudimentary way.'

'Look—you haven't attempted to deceive me about its condition at all, and I'm perfectly willing to take it as I find it,' she said. A little more discussion convinced him, and eventually they got round to signing the necessary agreement for the following week with an option on the subsequent one.

Boats were in equally short supply at high season, and Sara found herself having to go to a yard that didn't fill her with confidence, where she had to take an unreliable looking has-been, but at least it had managed to get her here.

By the time she had bought a few provisions and paraffin

for the lamps—an apologetic afterthought reminder from
the estate agent—it had been dusk when she chugged across
to Les Genêts, no time of day to cope with unpacking and
lighting unfamiliar lamps, she had decided; so, after a
scratch supper of bread and Brie eaten outside on the beach,
she had made up the bed with the sheets bought in the
Casino supermarket, and not even bothered to unpack a
nightdress. None of the windows would open to her
repeated bashings, so in the end she had left the door open,
preferring to risk moths and mosquitoes rather than
suffocation: hence this morning's sweet awakening to the
noise of the sea.

She got out of bed and, rejecting the idea of a wash in the
sink where a spider had taken up residence, ran out and
into the sea in the flimsy bra and pants in which she had
slept.

The water was glorious: clear and green, and beautifully
warm from the dual efforts of the sun and the Gulf Stream.
Sara swam out a little way and floated, looking back at the
cottage. Already, with its door and shutters wide open, it
looked a more-alive place. By the time she had cleaned it,
and got her things unpacked and arranged, it would do
very well. And what better way to start the day than this?

Feeling fresh and exhilarated, she did a showy, splashy
crawl back to the shore and went indoors to dig out a towel
and clean clothes. An hour later, the two rooms that
comprised the cottage were clean, and the musty sense of
having been long closed had given way to the smell of
coffee. Round the back there was an outdoor shower that
worked, after a fashion, and now, wearing a fresh white
cotton-knit sun-dress with her hair tied back with a yellow
scarf, she took her coffee out on to the beach and sat on the
side of the boat to drink it and eat the couple of *biscottes* that

were passing for breakfast. With no refrigerator, food shopping would have to be done daily. Already she was aware of gaps in her supplies that yesterday's hurried shopping had left, but she would make do until tomorrow.

Today was for settling in . . . for another swim or more in that delicious water . . . and for getting to know the island.

Sara sat up suddenly. She was acting like a holiday-maker, in danger of lotus-eating on Les Genêts and forgetting the true purpose of her presence here. She would allow herself another hour to get rid of the nettles by the door that threatened her legs every time she went in and out. She would master the windows . . . then that was it. She must really give her mind to the question of how she could make fruitful contact with Conrad Blake.

Direct approach in her true capacity as journalist was unlikely to achieve anything, that much was clear. She could watch him, she supposed, find out who else was at La Domaine with him . . . talk to the people in the other cottages and find out what they knew about him . . . but that wouldn't be enough. Somehow she must make acceptable personal contact so that she could get the man himself talking.

Not easy. She shelved the problem and set about the nettles, using a kitchen knife to hack them down awkwardly, and then closing the cottage door while she swept up, to prevent the dust spoiling her earlier indoor efforts.

That done, she took the knife to the windows, hoping to release the stuck paint with its sharp blade. It wasn't easy, and she was going at it with all her strength and concentration when a voice made her jump and sent the knife clattering to the ground.

'What the hell are you up to now?'

She spun round to see Conrad Blake, not at something near eye-level, but high above her on the grey horse. He must have come across the sand, for she had heard no sound of hooves.

His expression tightened. 'Yes . . . I thought I recognisd the hair. Could you be suffering from overwhelming thirst again?'

Sara's stunned reaction was not so much to what he said; at first that didn't register. What flashed through her mind was the thought that he could have caught her scampering around in her bra and pants—even less, in fact, for the idea had entered her head at the feel of the silky water that she could bathe in the nude in complete privacy here. It hadn't ocurred to her that he would come this way at all. The track leading to the inlet had seemed his direct link with civilisation . . . but she should have remembered the horse. It was frisky, and he reined it in hard so that it reared in impatience to be off.

'Whoa, Clouzot!' He leapt easily down, slapping the horse's neck while Sara tried to rearrange her features more intelligently.

'Good morning. You surprised me,' she said, pulling herself together.

'I'm sure I did.' He looked steadily at her. 'Now, cut the formalities and tell me how you explain this particular trespass.'

'Trespass?' For the first time she realised how it must look to him. The closed door—locked, for all anyone could tell—and her hacking away at the windows. That, plus their previous encounter.

'I wouldn't bother acting the innocent,' he went on before she could speak. 'You got away with it once, but don't imagine you'll do it again.'

She started to reply. 'I really wasn't trespassing. I'm——'

He stooped and picked up the knife from the ground, holding it under her nose.

'Would you say this was a normal means of access to a house for a law-abiding citizen?' He gave a sceptical laugh.

Sara protested, 'I can see how it looks to you, but this is all a big mistake.'

'As far as I'm concerned, the mistake was in not seeing what you were up to the first time we met. It stands out a mile. You're after a cheap holiday, aren't you? If I hadn't come back the other day, you would have had a nice, comfortable night on *Câline*. Now you think you can go one better and hang out in this place.'

'If you would only let me speak!' Sara said hurriedly. 'I saw the agent and——'

'Which agent? What's his name?'

The blue eyes, staring so accusingly into hers, made her mind go an absolute blank. The agent might never have had a name. Her mouth stayed open for a moment, then she closed it and swallowed hard.

'As I thought,' he said with grim satisfaction. 'But just to give you the benefit of the doubt, *mademoiselle*, you shall come back to my house while I phone this mysterious, nameless agent. I know who handles the Les Genêts property; his name's no mystery to *me*. I'll go through the motions of checking up on your cock-and-bull story, then you can have the pleasure of listening while I really get down to business and phone the police.'

Sara's opportunity dazzled before her eyes like a revelation. Why argue with him? Let him put himself firmly in the wrong . . . accuse her to the agent, who would, of course, vouch for her. Then, when he was squirming with the knowledge of what a false accusation he had made, she would have a superb advantage over him. But she would not scold him. She would be gracious, understanding and magnanimous in her forgiveness. And he would have to be pleasant and apologetic. Some kind of relationship would have been established.

She let her eyes fall away from his and allowed him to go on.

'I see you realise how little point there is in arguing,' he said. 'That at least saves time. You'd better get on the horse.' That took her by surprise, and her eyes flew to his again in real alarm.

'I don't ride. I never have.'

'I think you'll find you do—as of now. You don't imagine I'm doing to give you the chance to scuttle off to that boat of yours and make a run for it, do you? You'll be quite safe on Clouzot.' The grey horse danced sideways at his name, and Sara moved back hurriedly.

'I can't do it. I won't!'

'All you have to do is sit up there, damn it!' He was losing patience now. 'Put your foot in the stirrup. Here—like this. Now, up!'

She found herself soaring upwards to land, with a small yelp, in an undignified face-down heap across Clouzot's back.

'I see you have a nodding acquaintance with the truth in some matters,' he said, addressing the remark to a view of her that didn't bear thinking about. 'At least there's no mistaking the fact that you don't ride. Put this leg over. This one.' Impatient hands shoved her leg in the right direction, and Sara struggled upright, holding on to the saddle for dear life. Her white dress, little more than an elongated T-shirt, rode up to the tops of her thighs and resisted all efforts to pull it down.

'I'm not dressed for this,' she said coldly.

'Don't worry. I'm quite immune to temptation,' he answered with equal coolness. Then he took the horse's bridle and strode off across the bay.

As they reached the firm ground beyond the sand, Clouzot skittered sideways again and Sara clutched the saddle convulsively.

'I hope you're not going to let this horse start running away,' she said nervously, watching Clouzot's ears flatten menacingly as she spoke.

'They don't run. They canter or gallop. And nobody—animal or person—does what I don't want him to do,' Conrad Blake threw over his shoulder. She believed him.

They went on in silence and, as the feeling that she was not going to fall off grew stronger, Sara watched her captor instead of the horse's head. He was wearing a white cotton shirt and khaki riding-breeches, and even someone as immune to the opposite sex as she was could admire dispassionately his tall, broad frame. There wasn't an ounce of surplus flesh in the tell-tale area above the tightly cinched leather belt. She thought that he, too, might have been swimming, because his hair, especially in the nape of his neck, was quite wet. That was another reminder not to take privacy in the water for granted.

He glanced out to sea as she looked at him, giving her a glimpse of that firm chin and brow, with the unruly, vigorous hair lifted by the breeze, and she took pleasure in thinking of the fall that his pride was heading for. He little knew that he was taking her right where she wanted to be—inside La Domaine. Everything was going well so far, she exulted, schooling her face to calm blankness as they turned into the sheltered garden.

Parting company with Clouzot was as ungainly as the

mounting, and she thought she caught a flicker of amusement in Conrad Blake's eyes as he loosely knotted the bridle on the fence up near the house, but he was quite serious when he turned to wave her before him into La Domaine.

Through a wide doorway on the left of the cool, shady hall she could see what was obviously the kitchen, with a big pine table and bunches of herbs hanging from the ceiling beams. A flickering glow reflected in the quarry tiles showed that somewhere out of her line of vision there was a fire, probably a wood-burning stove, she thought, detecting the unmistakable, lovely smell of it.

In the big, low-ceilinged salon, without waiting for an invitation, she sat on one of the antique, carved pine chairs with their small-print upholstery, and primly folded her hands in her lap while she watched him at the phone.

The window embrasure where he stood was deep, showing the thickness of the walls which were plastered unevenly and colour-washed a soft, warm peach. The pinkish-brown of the floor-tiles carried through here, but in this room they were polished to a fine gleam, and there were rugs in a blend of cool greens and blues and white before the ornate stone fireplace and at each side of the huge table. Someone had done a clever arrangement in a gleaming black bowl with dried flowers and grasses. Sara recognised hydrangea heads shading from dark, coppery red to pale brown, and thistles, and something that looked like a delicate beige version of Queen Anne's Lace. But of the person whose hands were responsible there was neither sight nor sound.

'*Allo? Landal?*' Conrad Blake had got through to the agent, and had turned round to face her, obviously not wanting to miss any of her expected discomfort while he explained what he had found her doing. Sara smiled at him, and waited and listened.

When he finished, there was a volley of explanation from the agent, and Conrad Blake's expression changed from angry certainty to reluctant doubt. He covered the mouthpiece.

'What's your name?'

'Sara Lawrence.' Her wide brown eyes looked steadily at him, her oval face innocent and calm. He turned his back on her, drew breath, and proceeded to tell the agent at length and in detail that communication between them would be a good thing. He was not a mind-reader, he went on. If he saw what had all year been deserted property being attacked by someone, what was he to think? He then listened to what was, presumably, a long apology, and eventually, with a curt '*d'accord*', put down the receiver.

Sara waited, hiding her glee, and he slowly turned round.

'It seems . . .' he said slowly, '. . . that I owe you an apology. Apparently, I jumped to the wrong conclusion.' He shrugged. 'What can I say? I'm very sorry.'

It was straight and dignified. She tested him a little further.

'I can hardly blame you. Appearances were against me. And precedent.'

That was his chance to seize on the occasion when he had been in the right—but he didn't take it, and she admired him for it.

'This time I was wrong.'

She gave him the full benefit of her dazzling smile. 'You're forgiven—though not for the horse.'

Amusement softened his face, and Sara realised as she saw the changed expression that he could charm as well as command. When he was not making clipped, professional comments or conveying disapproval, his mouth had sensuality: the upper lip a wide, perfect bow, the lower full. When he smiled, as he was doing now, one corner of his mouth rose higher than the other in a teasing, attractive way. For the first time in months, Sara thought fleetingly of kissing and being kissed, surprising herself, and banishing the thought quickly before it reached her eyes.

Conrad Blake looked down at her slim brown legs, and his smile broadened.

'If you can't forgive the affair of the horse—then I certainly won't forget it. And I find it hard to apologise for. Quite an experience—for both of us.' He looked up at her face again. 'Well—since I now know your name, Sara Lawrence, I'd better introduce myself. Conrad Blake.' He held out his hand and she put hers into it. He had nice hands, she noticed. Long, capable fingers, the nails short but well manicured, and on his wrist an ultra-modern square gold watch with a black face and no numerals on it.

Thinking quickly, she decided to react to the name.

'Conrad Blake? That's funny. It's the same name as the man who designed my cane suite back in London.'

It was as easy as that. 'The very same,' he said. 'Style Atticus—choice of three fabric patterns, four colour-ways. You probably bought it last spring. Right?'

'Right! And I chose the cream.' Sara's expression of surprise was genuine, but what he took for surprise at the coincidence was surprise at the easy way he came out with information about himself.

'This is extraordinary!' she went on. 'Fancy being on holiday in the same place as my furniture-designer!'

'Even furniture-designers have lives to lead,' he said

dismissively. 'Will you have a drink? It's the least I can do to make amends.'

Gently . . . Sara told herself, sensing a slight withdrawal.

'I'd love a fruit juice,' she told him. He disappeared into the kitchen and that gave her time to think about her next move. When he came back, she was looking out of the window at the seaward view.

'Isn't it wonderful?' She took her glass with a murmur of thanks. 'Like an illustration out of a fairy-tale. All that golden water . . . I wonder what it looks like in winter, though.'

'Slightly less magic. The islands seem to disappear almost when the sea's rough. They're all quite low-lying. This one has more height than most, hence the megalith, I suppose.'

'You've seen it in bad weather, then?'

'I spent last winter here. It was quite an experience.'

She sipped her orange juice, feeling her way tentatively. 'Isn't it difficult, running a business like yours from here?'

'Businesses get to the stage when they can almost run themselves. As long as the staff selection has been well done, and the planning's good, that is. In any case, it doesn't take long to get to London if you have a plane available.'

He was looking out thoughtfully over the water, and she was close enough to see the little laughter lines at the corner of his eyes, pale against his tan, and smell a clean freshness—not quite strong enough to be identified as any particular male toiletry. Maybe whatever he used had been all but washed away in the course of his swim, but there was a lingering, appealing wholesomeness about him.

He changed the subject. 'Come and sit out on the terrace while you drink that. I'll just go and let Clouzot into the field, then I'll join you.'

He took her back into the hall and showed her the door beyond the stairs, opening on to the terrace. There were deckchairs, solid Atlantic-crossing types with comfy, long leg-rests.

Legs. He had shown definite interest in what she knew was one of her good features, so Sara arranged herself to advantage, smooth brown limbs well in evidence, remembering Fran's crude advice when they were after one particular story from a susceptible male: 'If you've got it, flaunt it—then whip it away.'

Her strategy failed, however, for when he came out after a little delay he was carrying a tray with cold meats and pâté, French bread and salad, a bowl of rosy peaches and a carafe of white wine, beaded with moisture from the fridge.

'It's midday, so I thought we might as well have this just to reinforce my apology for misjudging you,' he said, summoning her over to join him.

So much for flaunting, Sara thought wryly as she tucked her legs away beneath the oilcloth-covered table.

'This is lovely.' She helped herself from the offered dishes, 'But you shouldn't have gone to so much trouble.'

'I didn't.' His reply was matter of fact. 'It was left ready and there's plenty. Since I don't go in for socialising, it seemed a good idea to do it now when circumstances dictated.' A broad enough hint that she needn't expect anything to develop from a mere courtesy gesture, Sara thought.

'I saw you in town, didn't I?' For a moment the question disconcerted Sara, then she realised that he couldn't possibly know she had been following him. He would assume that she had been at the start of her search for somewhere to stay.

'Did you?' she said. 'Maybe. I've been here two weeks on

a sailing holiday in Sainte Anne d'Auray.'

'So why come here? Les Genêts hasn't a lot to offer someone of your age, and the cottage you've taken is so neglected I really thought it was a write-off.'

She was prepared for that, and she had decided to stick as close as possible to the truth.

'Actually this is just the sort of place I was looking for in connection with something I'm writing. I've never lived on an island, and I needed to know just what it would be like.'

'So you write, do you?'

Dangerous ground, her mind warned. 'Try to. Been trying for years.' That was his lead to patronise her, and this time he took it.

'I thought the island thing had been done to death. Didn't some woman produce a tome about her experiences as a castaway?'

'Yes. I read it. But that was factual. I want background for fiction.'

He smiled in a slightly superior way. 'Love on a coral reef? Women's stuff, is it?'

'Sort of.' His eyebrows would rise much higher if he knew the sort of 'women's stuff' *Spica* would expect her to write about *him*, she thought.

'You won't get much inspiration for the romance here.' Was he warning her off again? 'There's much more scope for someone your age in town.'

The repeated mention of her age annoyed Sara, and she was tempted to say more than she intended.

'I don't need to research romance. I've gone through that stage and come out decidedly wiser, thank you.'

'That sounds pretty world-worn for someone——'

'Someone my age?' she finished tartly for him, adding, 'Which, incidentally, is going on twenty-four, not fourteen, as you seem to think.'

'All of twenty-four!' he said with gentle mockery. 'And already you've given up romance. Is that because some man didn't come up to scratch?'

'He was romantic enough as long as it suited him,' she said steadily. 'And still is, no doubt, with anyone who has enough money to make it worth his efforts.'

'That sounds like a big story condensed into a very few words,' he said, quite genuinely and softly.

'An *old* story.' Sara watched him carefully as she prepared to tell him more on a sudden impulse. She had found that confession laid bare the soul of the listener more often than not. 'I was at college with the man in question. He was older than me, and ambitious—very. He set up his own advertising agency and I was besotted enough to go in with him. Not as a partner, you understand. I was the female bait on reception until Jonathan got himself nicely involved with a client's daughter—a very rich client, need I say? Then I was given to understand that my time was up—in his life as well as in his business. It wasn't just my romantic aspirations that suffered. He'd held up my career by a good twelve months.'

Her words were flippant, but something of the pain she had felt must have come through, because he said quite genuinely again, 'I'm sorry. Really sorry.'

Her eyes slid away from his and lingered a moment on the broad strength of his shoulder. It would be a good shoulder to cry on, she thought foolishly, if you happened to be the kind of person who indulged in tears over spilt milk, that was.

'Men can do inexplicable things,' he went on. There was silence for a moment while she tried to sort out the implication of that remark. Men in general? Some men?

Himself? Had he done something he wanted to escape from?' 'What it all boils down to, of course,' he went on, stretching his legs out and leaning back, 'is personal honesty. I presume you were taken for a ride all along the line?'

'Not quite all along. Towards the end I knew what was coming, but I wouldn't let myself believe it. Self-deception as opposed to being deceived.'

'If a man puts his cards on the table and the girl still wants to go on with the game, it's different, of course,' he said, looking at her somewhat speculatively, she felt, the brief moment of what had seemed like real sympathy over. 'That's the principle I've always stood by. No promises I didn't intend keeping. No false idea of either the present or the future. That way, no one gets hurt.'

No one? Sara wondered silently. Hadn't a single one of that harem of nubile females Fran had shown her been deluded into hoping for a permanent relationship with this very attractive man?

He seemed to dismiss the subject then, throwing his napkin on to the table. 'I'll get coffee. It should be ready. More wine to go with that peach?'

'No, thanks.' He was beginning to want to get rid of her now, she sensed. A pity, just when she had detected something she wanted to follow up, but better to keep a grip on her curiosity and keep things sweet between them. When he brought the coffee she had walked to the end of the veranda and was looking towards the two rooftops almost hidden among the trees.

'You have neighbours, I see,' she said casually, coming back to sit down.

'An elderly couple who've always lived on the island in the first cottage. He's retired, but still potters around with his lobster pots and oyster beds—scares his wife half to death getting down to them. Their daughter helps out here and keeps me ticking over.' Me, not us. So he was alone at La Domaine, she noted.

'And the other cottage?'

'That's lived in, too. Sugar?' She shook her head, and before she could ask anything else he picked up the wine carafe and quite neatly, she thought, diverted her. 'Did you like the wine? I get it through the old couple. They've got relatives in the trade and I'm working my way through all the best slopes.'

'It's good.' Sara filed the second cottage for future investigation, since he obviously didn't want to say anything about it. 'My mother has connections in the wine trade, too. She's Italian.'

'I wondered.' He looked at her through narrowed eyes. 'There's something about you that suggests more than straightforward English. You have a certain style.' His eyes ranged frankly and appreciatively over her and again Sara felt unfamiliar thoughts gathering at the back of her mind. His hair had dried now, and in the nape of his neck she could see one curl, a particularly tight one, which—when he saw it—he would no doubt brush fiercely to straighten it. She had an overwhelming urge to slide a finger into it, pull it out, and let it spring back again. What was it about this man that gave her such crazy ideas?

His inspection over, his eyes met hers again, and this time some kind of unspoken message flashed between the two of them, quickly extinguished on both sides.

Sara hastily drained her cup and stood up. 'I must get back,' she said abruptly. 'Thank you for lunch.' Then mischief made her add, 'As a matter of fact, I've met your old man. He took me back to the mainland the night before last.'

'Did he, indeed?' He wasn't at all abashed. 'I wondered what had happened. But you looked like a girl with initiative.' His eyes flickered with devilment. 'How are you going to get back to the cottage today? I could offer you a return lift on Clouzot.'

'Which I would emphatically refuse. '

'No other transport, I'm afraid.'

'None needed.' She smiled at him. 'We're close neighbours, after all.'

That was a mistake. His face closed and he turned to lead her to the door, where he stopped and looked down at her. 'As far as being neighbours goes, I wouldn't want you to get the wrong idea. Lunch was to reinforce my apology. I really don't socialise. My time is fully occupied and, as I told you, I do value my privacy.'

It was like a slap in the face. Sara's Italian blood, which seemed to have skipped her mother's generation to flow at double strength in her, inflamed her reply.

'And, as I told *you*, I had enough trouble with one businessman to put me off wanting any involvement—even neighbourly—with another. So I think we understand each other quite well, Mr Blake. Goodbye.' She gave him a smile of dazzling insincerity and turned away.

She had only gone a few steps, cursing herself already for her hasty tongue, when he called her name. She spun round, hoping that he had had second thoughts, because there was nothing to be gained from the destruction of the tenuous link between them. 'Yes?'

'I should perhaps warn you in case Landal hasn't—the bank behind your cottage is pretty unstable. The rains earlier on washed away a lot of topsoil, and the rocks are loose in places. Don't try to take any short cuts to the top. Stick to the path.'

'Thank you. I will.'

He raised a hand in dismissal and she walked on until she was beyond the trees and bank that edged the garden. Incompetent twit! she muttered savagely to herself, kicking at a stone. Without that short-fuse reaction of hers, there would have been at least a chance of casual encounters being turned to profit. She wasn't usually so thin-skinned—especially when it was in her interest not to be.

Her behaviour had been totally unprofessional. She had reacted like a huffy woman, which was both surprising and mortifying, since she claimed to be—at present, at least—someone who had no interest at all in the opposite sex.

CHAPTER THREE

THE motor coughed, spluttered, picked up again, then cut out altogether.

Sara swore. She'd known this would happen sooner or later. The wretched boat she had hired had 'disaster' written all over it. She unscrewed the cap and checked the fuel, though she knew very well that the amount the yard had put in should last for several crossings, and this was the first trip over to the mainland that she had attempted. She pulled savagely at the starter.

Nothing. Not a peep out of it. It was as dead as a dodo.

She looked round helplessly. She was half-way between Les Genêts and the Ile d'Arz, and there wasn't another living thing in sight. It was too far to swim in either direction, even if she could have contemplated leaving an unmanned boat drifting around for others to crash into.

There was bound to be some kind of craft along sooner or later. The Golfe was buzzing with boats of all kinds all day long . . . except now, when she most needed one.

She resigned herself to a long wait, and tried to give her mind to an appreciation of the beauty of the morning. There was a faint, milky haze hanging over the water, and the islands rose from it as though conjured up by some magic hand. It was no good, though. A poor night's sleep had made her little inclined to rhapsodise over the joys of nature.

Yesterday had turned into a rather aimless day. All that

action crammed into the morning, then nothing to do but reproach herself and wander round the island, achieving absolutely nothing for the rest of the daylight hours.

She had found a path going beyond *Câline*'s inlet round the cliffs and past the second cottage, the one Conrad Blake didn't want to talk about, but there were no signs of life there. Then she'd concealed herself in the vantage point overlooking the garden of La Domaine, but in the two solid hours she had spent there she had seen not one single thing. Whatever Conrad Blake was doing, he wasn't doing it in public. Nor in the privacy of his garden, for that matter. And there was a nasty, persistent variety of ant on Les Genêts, she'd discovered to her cost.

Even the session she'd had in the evening with her cassette recorder, trying to clarify her thoughts on him so far, had been frustrating. One of the buttons kept jamming, so she'd been forced to keep starting again and she had ended up with the most incoherent mess of ifs and buts and maybes.

This morning she had got up, determined to make a fresh, businesslike start. She would do the necessary shopping trip to the mainland, make the promised phone call to Fran, and from somewhere—*anywhere*—get inspiration as to what she could do next. Maybe Fran would have ideas. Something would happen. It had got to.

She pulled a face. It had—right here, half-way between two islands.

Suddenly she sat up, realising that the Ile d'Arz was further away than it had been and Les Genêts quite a bit nearer. Of course! The tide. What a stroke of luck. It was going to take her back to Les Genêts, and that was better than hanging around waiting to be rescued.

While the boat drifted slowly, wearisomely back towards the island, she tried to assess where it would land her. The current tended to sweep round between the two islands, and there wasn't much chance of being returned to her own little bay. But the tide hadn't reached full strength yet, and with luck she would not be carried out beyond the oyster beds. She leaned over the prow and paddled with both hands for all she was worth, and managed to get herself carried into the creek where *Câline* was moored.

When she straightened up, confident of being washed slowly along towards the jetty, it was to find that *Câline*'s owner was on board, poker-faced, watching her.

Let joy be unconfined ... she thought, then called clearly, 'Before you breathe a word—especially the word "trespass"—let me say that I had no choice in the matter. I would have preferred to be nearer my own place, but the tide thought otherwise.'

'What happened to your motor?' He caught the side of the boat with a boat-hook, conveying by his attitude that, but for his intervention, his precious, immaculate paintwork would have been damaged, and edged her along more quickly towards a free bit of the landing-stage beyond *Câline*.

'Conked out on me,' Sara said shortly, preparing to make fast.

'I expect you're out of fuel.' The boat rocked as he stepped down into it, forcing her to sit back quickly.

'I'm *not*,' she stated crossly. 'The tank's nearly full. This is just a bad boat. I knew it from the start, but it was the only one I could get.'

'They must have seen you coming.' His efforts were producing no more response from the motor than hers, and he was not pleased. 'Your jaunt will have to wait, by the looks of things. I don't suppose repairs are quite your scene, and I'm in too much of a hurry. I've an appointment in half an hour.' He shot back his immaculate cuff to glance at his watch and frowned in annoyance. 'I can't waste time on you today.'

The injustice implicit in the word 'today' rankled.

'Any time wasted yesterday was certainly not my fault,' she said pointedly. 'And I'm not "jaunting". I have some very necessary shopping to do.'

He had the grace to look, if not sheepish, at least a little less aggressive at the mention of yesterday.

'I suppose you can come over with me,' he said reluctantly. 'But that means coming back as well, and I can't hurry back to suit you, nor can I hang around all day waiting for you. I shall be two hours on my business. If that suits you, fair enough. Otherwise the only thing I can do, I suppose, is look at this for you when I get back.'

'I wouldn't dream of it,' Sara said stiffly, considering that the ungracious offer didn't merit a 'thank you'. 'The man from the yard can jolly well come over and put his own boat right. So——' She stood up and jumped on to the landing-stage before him so that she had the advantage of height for a moment, '—I'll accept your offer of a lift across and try not to inconvenience you any more than that.'

Two strides of his long legs reversed the position, taking him into *Câline*'s cockpit.

'Don't let's hang around, then,' he said briskly, giving her a brief tug aboard. 'Sit there.'

He was up at the prow, casting off, before he had finished speaking, then he pushed them along with a boat-hook until they slid away from the jetty.

'I suspect that thing of yours could fall apart if it got *Câline*'s wash against it,' he said in sardonic explanation as he jumped down into the cockpit and started up an engine that purred immediately into life, its note soaring to a throaty roar as they swept out of the inlet. 'Which yard did you go to, for goodness' sake?'

She told him, and he greeted the name with a sceptical, 'Oh, them. I might have known.'

The rest of the way he was silent, and Sara equally so while she wondered how she could turn this course of events to her advantage. Nothing could be done now, with him in this grumpy mood, but maybe she could get him a bottle of something or other as a thank you for the lift . . . catch him in a better frame of mind, though heaven knew when that would be!

When they were safely berthed in the port, he shrugged on his jacket then looked at his watch and relaxed a little.

'Good. I shall be on time.' He shot a rather more friendly look at her. 'I can't bear to be late for an appointment. It makes me very edgy if I think I'm going to be.'

The hand he gave her to step ashore was more gentle, and this time she was conscious of the pleasant, firm warmth of his fingers.

'Thank you,' she said, smiling up at him, unaware that her inward softening was reflected in the curve of her lips and the look in her eyes. 'I'm sorry to keep inflicting myself on you.'

For a moment, blue eyes held brown. 'Not too painful an infliction, when all's said and done,' he said. 'If you have problems, wait at the Café de la Marine, over there. I'll check before I go back.'

Then, with a little nod, he strode off along the quay. Sara

watched him go, thinking that, dressed as he was for a business call, he was much more like the man she had first known through the media. He had stepped down into the cabin before coming ashore, and brought out a brown-paper-wrapped box, slightly larger than a shoe-box. It didn't seem to be intended for posting, for there was no address on it.

She toyed with the idea of following him again, but decided against it. It was too risky now. First, she would go to the boatyard to arrange for someone to take her back over and deal with that montrosity of a thing they had hired her, then she would call *Spica*, and leave the shopping until last.

The first project fell through immediately. The boatyard gates were closed and padlocked, and there was a little handwritten notice, '*Fermé le vingt-quatre d'août. Mariage de famille.*'

Sara was almost pleased. It solved the problem of further contact with Conrad Blake. She would have to go back with him, let him look at the faulty motor ... then she would have definite reason for doing something to show her appreciation. Maybe she would cook him a meal. Surely, under the circumstances, he couldn't refuse? At the right time of day, and with plenty of wine to relax him, then he might talk more indiscreetly than he had done so far.

Feeling more light-hearted now that she had a course of action planned, Sara made for the nearest telephone booth to call Fran and went through the usual reverse-call procedure.

'So what have you got to report so far?' Fran's brisk question, put without the indulgence of a greeting, pierced the booth like a gunshot.

'Not a lot, I'm afraid. It's all a bit vague, really. One thing I do know for certain is that he's been here all last winter.'

'Why? Was he ill? Do you think he had a breakdown or something?'

'I'm sure not. He's still involved in Blake Enterprises—flies over when necessary—but he seems to be thinking of staying on.'

'Hardly enthusiastic boss-man behaviour.'

'I think maybe he's a bit bored with it all. I'm guessing, but he did say something about the company running itself.'

'So who's he got tucked away there to pass the time with?' The suggestive note that Sara knew well was in Fran's voice.

'As far as I can discover—nobody. And he doesn't seem to want company of any kind—especially the feminine variety, judging by the brush-offs he keeps giving me. It's all done fairly politely, but the meaning's clear enough.' She told Fran about the break-in misunderstanding, and the meal from which she had been dismissed with a flea in her ear.

'I feel a bit at a loss, Fran,' she went on. 'I've not done this kind of thing before—interviewing without seeming to interview. I wish I could just say who I am and ask what I want to know.'

'And get an even bigger flea in your ear,' Fran replied drily. 'No chickening out, little Sara. This is your test. If you're going to get anywhere on *Spica* you'll have to learn to cope with such situations. If I could have chosen who to send it might not have been you just yet, but since you're on the spot, you'd better get on with it.'

'There is one thing to follow up,' Sara said slowly. 'There's a cottage near his place, and he's not keen to talk about whoever's taken it. He changed the subject smartly when I asked. Though if it's someone he's involved with, why the separate house? There's room enough at La Domaine for half a dozen girlfriends.'

'Maybe he's gone off girls. Hey! Perhaps he's got a fella stashed away there. Do you think he could have turned into that sort?'

'Definitely not.' For some reason this made Sara's hackles rise. She had only to remember the way he looked at her legs. No, there was nothing of that about Conrad Blake, however much it would make Fran's day and *Spica*'s story if it were true.

'Well done . . .' Fran purred. 'It sounds as though you've at least discovered which way the wind blows. Hope you enjoyed the experience.'

'You're disgusting!' Sara spoke half-jokingly, but she was conscious that at the bottom of her she really did find the constant flow of innuendo at *Spica* distasteful. She wanted to put an end to the conversation. 'Well, if there's nothing else, Fran, I'll go and get on with my shopping.'

'Not so quickly, sweetie. Macho man can wait a bit longer, can't he? I've still got the most important thing to say, so make sure you take it in. You have the rest of this week to get somewhere with your story, then at the weekend you're going to have a visit from a friend.'

'A friend?'

'Yes. As far as anyone else is concerned. Actually, it's Dave Becker. He's shooting a fashion feature in Biarritz this weekend, and I've persuaded him to make a slight detour on his return drive. He couldn't get to Vannes at a respectable hour on Sunday, so you're to pick him up at the Post Office—will that do?—about midday on Monday. He likes to sleep late.'

The idea of someone else being brought in on the story panicked Sara. 'But what's he going to do? If you want shots of the island, couldn't I have done those? And where's he going to stay?'

'I've booked him in somewhere outside town on his route, but he's going to doss down with you while he's working. And don't worry about what he's to do. He's got enough sneaky shots of celebrities to prove that however much the subject's privacy is guarded, he can get the stuff. I don't think your Mr Blake will be proof against Dave. If the worst comes to the worst, though, and there's no real meat in the story, we'll run it as a "Lost in the Outback" feature. But I'm counting on there being more than that, Sara. Right?'

'Right,' Sara said dully. 'I hope Dave knows what he's in for. This place of mine is like a rabbit hutch. It'll be the lumpy old settee in the living-room for him.'

'He'll survive. Monday the thirtieth, then. Midday. And if you've come up with the goods by then, you can hitch a lift back with him. If absolutely necessary, stay on longer, but let there be good reason.'

Sara began her shopping, feeling distinctly depressed about Dave Becker's visit. She had met him on several occasions. He had done a lot of freelance work for *Spica*, and though he was a talented photographer he was not a pleasant person. The underhand nature of his work had left its mark on him, or maybe he did that sort of work because of the kind of person he was. Whichever way round it was, she didn't like him, and his involvement made an awkward job more of a worry than it already was.

She forced herself to shake off the feeling and concentrate on thinking up the meal that was going to unlock Conrad Blake's tongue. The sooner this business was over, the better.

A fiendishly expensive tin of whole chicken in wine and herbs was the best she could do for meat—nothing fresh would survive a possible day or two, since the date was uncertain. Firm, huge tomatoes and peppers for a salad would be fine, as would glossy purple aubergines. Meringue cases were the best she could do for dessert—nothing else would survive the primitive storage conditions on Les Genêts, but tinned wild strawberries and fresh peaches would make an exotic filling. She chose a bottle of Château-Lafite, and as an extra extravagance a half-bottle of Courvoisier. Conrad Blake looked like a man who would enjoy a glass of brandy. The crockery at the cottage was dire, but if she made it a sort of picnic ... maybe on the beach with a driftwood fire ... she could cover up a multitude of sins. The idea of the beach at dusk and the flicker of flames reflected in water appealed to her, and as she waited with her purchases at the Café de la Marine she felt moderately cheerful again. It was only a job, after all. She would look back on it and have a good laugh, no doubt, one day.

As he approached her, Conrad Blake seemed reasonably pleased with his morning's work, judging by his expression, which was several degrees warmer than it had been.

'Still here? I take it you had no luck, then?' he asked.

'They were closed for a family wedding. So I'm afraid I shall have to take up your offer to look at the motor. I'm sorry.'

He took the shopping-bags from her. 'No problem. These outboards are pretty simple. It won't take long.'

She noticed that he no longer had the parcel with him, and wondered again what had been in it.

He actually whistled cheerfully to himself while he took off his jacket and started up the engine to take them down the estuary to the Golfe. As they picked up speed, Sara shivered in the movement of air. She hadn't noticed how much the day seemed to have changed while she was in the shops. It was dull, now, and much cooler.

When they came out into the Golfe she saw there was no view to speak of. The earlier haze had thickened with the drop in temperature, and she could actually see a white, rolling blanket sweeping towards them, awesome and spectacular as it spread across the water. From somewhere beyond it, a big boat's muffled foghorn boomed.

'Are we going to make it?' she asked Conrad Blake.

'Just about. The Met men must have got today's forecast wrong. There was no mention of this.' He was straining to see ahead, and he had throttled back the engine so that *Câline* was chugging slowly ahead. He saw Sara shiver. 'If you want to go into the cabin, you'll be warmer.'

'No. I'm all right. I'll stay here, in case you need another pair of eyes.'

He was keeping an eye on the compass, she noticed, making sure of his direction, and although she didn't particularly enjoy the situation she felt quite safe.

'In that case, you can keep an eye out to starboard and sing out as soon as you spot the Ile d'Arz. It should be coming up in a minute or two.'

Sara stared hard into the whiteness, hearing muffled hooters sounding all over the Golfe and glad that they were away from the main bulk of traffic.

'There!' she exclaimed suddenly. The island loomed quite close, changed into something indistinct and mysterious.

'Good.' He glanced at his watch. 'Another ten minutes at this speed and we'll be there. Can't say I'll be sorry. But if we hadn't pressed on we could have been stuck on the mainland all day—all night, for that matter.'

Chances, chances! Sara thought wryly. Too bad they hadn't been delayed. She could have used it to good effect, maybe.

Les Genêts materialised at last, and Conrad Blake cut out the engine to let *Câline* slide gently along the inlet. Even here in the shelter of the steep banks, the fog had penetrated, blurring shapes and dulling sound.

'Well done!' Sara said thankfully. 'Now all we have to do is follow our respective paths home.'

'Not yet.' He was making fast, fore and aft. 'I can't let you go off into this. We'll hang on here until it lifts a bit. We can make ourselves moderately comfortable in the cabin.'

Sara followed him below deck, secretly rejoicing in the weather's co-operation. She was getting her chance, after all. As he lit the lamps, she saw that Conrad Blake's hair was beaded with tiny drops of moisture, and she put up her own hand to find that her hair, too, was damp.

'Give it a rub.' He pulled a towel out of a locker and tossed it to her. 'Then you'd better put this on. You look frozen.' A sweater of his, big and white, followed the towel.

The ivory clip holding her hair back had an obstinate clasp and Sara struggled with it for a moment until he noticed.

'Let me.' He unfastened it in seconds, then as a matter of

course took the towel from her. 'Turn round.' He rubbed her head, quite firmly, pressing her forehead against his chest as she remembered her father doing when she was a child. Only then she had clasped her arms round his waist for support . . . and it wouldn't do to go to those lengths now.

'Thanks,' she said as he pronounced her dry. She felt a little embarrassed, and ferreted in her bag for her comb to hide her face. It had been such an intimate thing for him to do.

He gave his own head a perfunctory rub, watching as she restored her hair to smooth, silken order with rhythmic strokes.

'How long is it since you had it cut?' he asked.

'Seven or eight years, I should think. Do you think I should?' She paused, fingering the dark swathe that fell over her shoulder and clung to his white sweater.

'Not at all. It's charming. Most distinctive. The ultimate in femininity—or does that displease you? One never knows with today's woman.'

'Oh, I think you can take it that we all like a compliment, despite appearances to the contrary, Mr Blake!' she smiled.

'It had better be Conrad if we're going to be bumping into each other in here for the next little while. Now—did you eat in town?'

'No. I never gave it a thought.'

'So we may as well see what *Câline* can come up with.' He squatted down and looked into the cupboard beside the tiny sink. 'Would you like beans . . .?' He moved tins around. 'Beans . . . or beans?'

'I think I'd like . . . beans,' she said with mock solemnity, and they both laughed.

'But I can elevate them with a drop of Mâcon Rouge. How about that?' He reached across and put a bottle on the table, while Sara remembered her shopping.

'I've got fresh bread here. No butter, but the crust's lovely. And grapes.'

He unearthed a familiar jar. 'Coffee for afterwards, if you don't mind it black and instant.'

'A feast.'

'A beanfeast!'

Why, he's really very nice, Sara thought as they got the simple meal ready. He's easy to talk to, and if I'm to call him Conrad he must be relenting on his hard-line no-fraternising policy. Conrad . . . Con . . . She tried the name over, but didn't feel quite ready to come out with it yet.

They settled in enforced knee-to-knee proximity at the table and tackled the food. Then Sara found herself asking quite naturally, 'You said you were here through the winter. Didn't you find it lonely?'

'I wasn't alone all the time—though when I was, I discovered quite a taste for solitude. Surprising in my case, because all my life I've been surrounded by people—boarding school, Oxford, the business merry-go-round. But when I was jolted into seeking my own company, I found it . . . acceptable. Does that sound insufferably big-headed?'

'No. Just factual.' And she should be picking up leads and drawing out more facts, but she couldn't bring herself to say, '*Who* gave you companionship when you wanted it?' and '*Why* did you suddenly develop a craving for solitude?'

It was too late, anyway. The opportunity was gone, and he was saying, 'But I want to know about you,' pushing away his empty plate and leaning back, his blue eyes speculative. 'Do you make a living from this writing of yours?'

'No best-sellers as yet—just little things here and there. I work in an office for my daily bread.' The almost-truths came out quite easily.

'I thought you'd changed course after Jonathan?'

'There are offices and offices. Look—I've thought about it since. I shouldn't have gone on at length like that about Jonathan. I should have realised what he was like. He was fairly transparent about his priorities, now that I look back on him. But at the time I thought he was wonderful—thought it was worth doing anything to be with him. He never really promised me a future—not a definite one.' Her eyes grew momentarily darker as she remembered, then she looked up at Conrad with a shrug and a quick smile that was touching in its bravery. 'It wasn't really love, or it would have hurt more than my pride. I just enjoyed being swept along by someone as glamorous as Jonathan. Even when he was giving me the push he was quite devastatingly . . . *winsome*!' The smile became stronger.

'But did it affect you?'

'It made me——' she risked an allusion, '—satisfied with my own company, too.'

He didn't rise to the bait with denial or acceptance of the similarity in their cases, just looked steadily at her.

'And is that still the case?'

With his eyes holding hers, looking deep into her thoughts, it seemed, she couldn't find a flip answer and the silence extended until she suddenly became aware of the mist swirling past the cabin windows, brighter now with the promise of sunshine trying to break through.

'I do believe it's clearing,' she said, standing up.

He got up slowly, the hint of a smile playing round his mouth.

'And I do believe you're dodging the question, Sara Lawrence.'

For a moment he looked down at her with a quizzical expression, then, taking her completely by surprise, he leaned forward, put his hands on her shoulders, and very gently kissed the tip of her nose.

Sara blushed. 'What—what was that for?' she asked naively.

'It was because you're rather a nice person—and because I'm glad that the winsome, faithless Jonathan didn't manage to put you off men for life. And also it was because I understand very well how much it hurts to find that your trust in someone has been misplaced.' That was too serious, too close to his own experience in some way, maybe, because she saw him make a deliberate switch in mood. 'And if you want more reasons—it was because with that sweater of mine drooping down to your knees and swamping you, you look like a kid dressing up in grown-up clothes. So off with it, and we'll see if it's clear enough to venture forth.'

While she stripped off the sweater in some confusion, he went up into the cockpit and called down to her.

'Yes—I can see the sun and almost to the end of the inlet. You'll be all right now.'

She washed the pan and plates quickly, leaving them to drain, and when she appeared on deck with her shopping-bags he was already down in her boat, investigating the innards of the motor.

'Shall I wait?'

He didn't look up. 'Lord, no! I can't promise instant miracles.'

'Thank you very much, then. And sorry to be a pest.'

He might have grunted something in reply, but he was so busy with a spark-plug spanner that she heard nothing. She hovered there awkwardly for a moment and finally said, 'Well—goodbye for now, then.'

'Yes . . .' he said absent-mindedly, lost in mechanics.

So that's it, Sara thought as she set off up the path. He couldn't get rid of her quickly enough. Obviously he'd regretted that uncharacteristic moment of friendliness. And she hadn't even got round to suggesting her thank-you meal. Maybe she would manage it when she collected the boat.

She rubbed the tip of her nose reflectively. Fancy Conrad Blake suddenly kissing her like that . . . and drying her hair.

What you ought to be thinking of, she told herself sharply, is who spent last winter with him, and what made him realise he had misplaced his trust in someone. She had a job to do . . . a fact that tended to recede into the background when Conrad Blake . . . Con . . . was around.

CHAPTER FOUR

HE MUST have spirited the boat back after dark, because when Sara went out next morning, there it was, hauled up on the far side of the bay with a scrap of folded paper held down by a stone on the seat.

> Wrong petrol/oil mix. Changed it and cleaned off the spark plug. Should be fine now. Fill her up yourself, rather than those idiots. C.B.

He could easily have come and told her himself, rather than write it down. The obvious inference was that he hadn't wanted to. Sara felt piqued, and consequently all the more determined to get the wretched story done.

She swam out much too far in annoyance and, by the time she reached the shore again, aching all over, she still had not worked out how to go and invite Conrad for a meal without feeling that she was forcing herself on someone who had no desire for her company.

She spent a lazy morning, and after an early lunch set off with the intention of having a close look at the cottage beyond La Domaine. But she was in no mood to hurry, and let herself be side-tracked into climbing up to the high point of the island where the megalith was.

The stones were much larger than she had thought, towering away overhead, their broader bases going no one knew how far into the earth. The group in the middle of the ring was different, and when Sara drew close enough she

60

saw that they formed the entrance to an underground chamber.

The site was very exposed, and commanded views all around the Golfe. How had those early people with primitive resources managed to get these great stones upright? Sara wondered. And why had they done it? What had happened here through the years? Having created such a place, for what dark purpose had they used it? She could see that the chamber was empty now, but surely it had not always been so. Her imagination started to run riot. The table-like rock construction that formed the entrance had the appearance of an altar, and who knew what sacrifices might have taken place there once when gods were angry tyrants who had to be appeased . . .

She shivered, in spite of the warmth of the day. It wasn't the bright, sparkling warmth of yesterday before the mist, but a heavy, oppressive heat that made her think longingly of the sea again. But she had wasted enough time. She ran swiftly down the hill and rejoined the path.

Clouzot greeted her like an old friend when he saw her coming, and Sara stopped to pat the velvety nose he thrust into her face, then took the back way round the field, not wanting to go across the open stretch in front of La Domaine.

She was in luck, she saw as she came up to the cottage. Someone was lying out on the turf beside a plate on which lay the remains of a salad—female, and young, her head resting on her arms.

Sara bent down hurriedly, untied the bow of one of her espadrilles, and gave the ribbon a sharp tug to break its stitches. Then she went nearer to the sleeping woman, one shoe flapping as she walked.

'*Pardon, madame* . . .' She waited until the blonde head

lifted then went on, '*J'ai un petit problème*,' holding out the ribbon and lifting her foot from which the espadrille dangled.

'*Mademoiselle* . . .' the blonde corrected drowsily. 'And I'm as British as you are by the sound of things. What's the trouble?'

'Oh, good. That makes the explanation easier. I've broken a strap. If you could lend me a needle and thread—or a pin, even—it would make the walk back to the far side a lot easier.' Sara thought her dilemma quite neat.

'The far side?' The blonde's sleepiness disappeared. 'You must be the person in the old cottage. I saw it was opened up from the boat.' She sat up and surveyed Sara with interest. 'Here for long?'

'A week or so. Maybe more. What about you?'

The girl shrugged. 'As long as I want, basically—or as long as I can take it. So far, it's not been exactly a hardship.'

That told something, but not a lot. She seemed to have been here long enough to get to know Conrad Blake, but whether she was here *because* of him was another matter.

'Sit down.' The girl patted the turf by her side. 'We may as well introduce ourselves. Jane Cameron. And you are——?'

'Sara Lawrence.'

The girl was looking at Sara, her head on one side. 'I don't know you from somewhere, do I? You look vaguely familiar.'

'It's my fairly ordinary face, I expect. I've never been to Scotland.' Sara had detected a slight accent.

'I do leave the place sometimes, as now. Never mind. I'm pretty good at remembering people usually, so I've either slipped up with you or it will come to me eventually.' She got up. 'I'll fetch that repair kit. Would you like a drink?

I've got ice-cubes—and I don't expect you run to those in your place.'

'Too right! Something cool and fruity would be lovely.' Sara watched her go indoors. She was slim and shapely in her white bikini. Thirtyish, maybe ... and attractive enough to have rated more than a second glance from Conrad Blake.

There would never be a better chance to push for information, she decided, and prepared for action as she saw Jane returning with two glasses of what looked like Orangina.

'Thanks. Quite a little English colony here, aren't we?' Sara gestured with her glass towards La Domaine.

'I suppose we are.' Jane sipped her drink calmly, waving away an inquisitive wasp.

'Have you met Conrad Blake?' Sara was glad of the sewing, which meant that she need not look at the girl while she questioned her.

'Several times.'

So far, non-committal was the word that sprang to mind to describe the answers.

'Do you know,' Sara persevered brightly, 'I actually have some of his furniture? Can you beat that for coincidence? You knew he had a colossal business empire, did you?'

'Who hasn't heard of Blake Enterprises?'

This wasn't much good, but Sara was determined to go on.

'I can't imagine why he's here, can you? Not with a business like that to run. All last winter, too, he told me. It's very strange.'

'I expect he had his reasons.'

'Damn!' The needle had slipped, but the exclamation came as much from frustration at the fruitless conversation as from the sharp pain in Sara's finger. Was she imagining it, or did Jane Cameron's voice grow cooler with every reply?

'I should have brought you a thimble,' the girl said.

'I'm fine. I've nearly finished.' Sara racked her brains. She must make a final effort to get something out of this oh-so-discreet Scot. 'I've met Conrad Blake a couple of times,' she said, biting off the thread. 'But he hasn't been over-friendly, I must say.'

Jane Cameron took the proffered needle. 'Perhaps you got off on the wrong foot.'

Sara looked up sharply, wondering if this was just a chance remark, or if Conrad had told the girl about finding her on his boat—maybe even issued a warning against her as a nuisance to beware of. But the blue eyes looking reflectively at her were neutral.

Staring straight at the girl, so that she could detect the least flicker of reaction, Sara made one more attempt.

'What do you think of him?' The question was blunt and the answer equally so, in spite of the slight smile.

'I don't. Sorry to rush you, but I must get back to work. Are you going to finish that?' She gestured towards the Orangina.

Sara drained her glass, tied her espadrille back on and stood, throughly snubbed.

'Thanks for the drink, and for your help.' Damn all help where I really wanted it! she thought furiously.

Jane glanced up at the sky, still sunny overhead, but clouded over and lowering in the west. 'It looks as though there's trouble brewing up there. I should get back quickly. Once the weather starts changing here, it does it quite spectacularly.'

'I will.' Sara hesitated. 'Maybe I'll see you around?'

'Maybe.' The girl nodded a goodbye, and turned away.

Hardly promising for future contact, Sara thought as she hurried back across the island. The girl had seemed quite friendly to begin with, but then she had clammed up and brought the curtains down in no uncertain fashion. If she had such pressing work to do, why offer the drink? No . . . she just hadn't liked the direction of the conversation.

Did she work for Conrad Blake? It was quite possible that he would need letters typed—but why the secrecy, if so? Unless . . . maybe the working relationship was not entirely innocent. The girl was attractive enough. And so was he, Sara's mind added, unbidden.

The first drops of rain fell, and Sara made a dash for the cottage, getting there just before the skies opened and it poured down.

She got out her cassette recorder and settled down for a recording session, wiping the tape clean of her first abortive effort and lying on the bed with the microphone in her hand.

'Wednesday, August the twenty-fifth. Conrad Blake,' she began. 'He's here for an indefinite stay on Les Genêts, though he still seems to have control of the business—goes back by plane when necessary. The house he's in—La Domaine—is big enough for a family, but he's alone in it. Local domestic help comes in daily.

'Why is he here?' She switched off for a moment and thought, then resumed. 'He might be disillusioned with his job. What he said about the business running itself implied a lack of challenge. But, if so, what challenge does he find here on an almost uninhabited island?

'Relationships—so far I'm not sure what kind, could have given him problems. It might be a man. "Men can do inexplicable things" were his words, I think. That could have referred to himself, I suppose, not someone else. There was no further explanation. He also talked of knowing how it feels to find that trust in someone has been misplaced—so obviously someone's let him down at some stage. No indication who, so far.

'What is he like? Charming, when he wants to be. Autocratic when it suits him. Wants privacy—a strong one, that. Quite determined not to be forced into social involvement, though if it comes about for a genuine reason he can be a very good host. Variable in mood, swinging from one extreme to the other. For instance——'

She stopped. She had been going to mention the kiss on the nose and the subsequent total withdrawal, but she didn't want that on record, she decided. Fran would know what she meant, anyway.

'There may be some involvement between him and someone else on the island,' she resumed. 'He's very uncommunicative indeed about her, and she's not giving anything away either, though she does know him.

'She's Jane Cameron, Scottish, attractive, thirtyish. Has the cottage beyond La Domaine for as long as she wants it. Doesn't want to discuss C. B. at all. Refers to work that she's doing. Maybe——'

Sara pressed the pause button. She should have waited and watched, of course; found out exactly where Jane Cameron did this hypothetical work. Rushing off just because she had been dismissed had been both stupid and careless. She switched on again and concluded her report with the words, 'Maybe she works for C. B.', resolving to check up.

It was still pouring down and the cottage felt very claustrophobic with the doors and windows closed. She re-read a letter she had received at the sailing-centre from her mother, feeling pleased again at the reference to a pleasant theatre-outing with a male friend. Her mother had lost so many years . . . it was good to see her starting to live again, getting back into the mainstream.

When Sara was in her teens, her father had got involved with a much younger woman—a temporary affair, Sara and Mrs Lawrence had thought, quite mistakenly as it turned out, for he had never returned to his family. Mrs Lawrence was already vulnerable—she had given up her country and her strong family ties for the man who was now rejecting her. Four years of waiting and hoping reduced her to a shadow of the woman she had been with Sara fiercely protective and caring, but powerless to help. It was not until her husband died from a massive coronary that she began tentatively to look to the future again, rather than wait hopelessly for the chance to resume her past life. It had taken more years for her to place her shattered trust in any other man.

Sara wrote an affectionate reply, then a brief note to her flatmate, who must have been wondering where on earth she was. Rain was still sheeting down, so she went on to do a bit of washing and, after checking on her food supplies, decided that the aubergines had ripened far too quickly and would have to be used up in a ratatouille for supper. By the time she had got this on to cook she felt that she knew just what a prisoner in solitary confinement must feel like.

What an unsatisfactory day this had been! No advance made, and no sign of Conrad Blake. All this time on her hands, and not the least inclination to get on with her book, even. A dead day.

She clattered the dishes in the sink, trying, as she vented her frustration on them, to banish the thought that if she were really honest she would have to admit that not seeing

Conrad Blake affected her far more than making no progress with the *Spica* story. She had felt so comfortable with him on *Câline*. He had been more than friendly, it had seemed; then he had dropped her like a hot potato. She needed to see him again to correct that unpleasant feeling.

After a brief appearance the sun went down and the light began to fade. Sara resigned herself to supper and early bed, and the writing off of this day with the fervent hope that tomorrow would be better.

She was coming back from braving the horrors of the loo in its spidery cabin, when a crashing and splintering from the steep bank startled her only a yard or two from the end of the cottage. Sara realised at once, thanks to Conrad's warning, that it was a rock plunging down through the vegetation, and her reflexes were good, enabling her to spring forward to the shelter of the wall, out of reach of that particular hazard.

But she had counted without the rain-soaked grass, and her foot shot sideways from underneath her, bringing her crashing heavily to the ground while the rock rolled harmlessly on to the sand.

Sara sat up groggily and looked at her knees first—both grazed—before examining the part of her that was really hurting: her ankle.

Warily she attempted to get up, realising at once that she had badly wrenched it, if not worse. It was agony to put any weight on it at all, and by the time she had hopped, limped and leaned her way back into the cottage it was already beginning to swell.

She bathed it in cold water and, having no bandage, improvised a bulky substitute from a pair of cotton socks. She felt sick with the pain, and eating was out of the question, so she turned off the gas, leaving the ratatouille for next day. Great! she thought bitterly, biting her lip as she struggled into the bedroom and sat on the edge of the bed to undress. This was all she needed. A fat lot of chance she had of doing anything with a foot out of action. And who would care? Who would look after her? Not a soul.

She thumped the pillow and got another stab of pain in her ankle as a reward. Lousy, lousy day . . . and with her ankle hurting like this—lousy, lousy night ahead.

'Anybody there?'

The voice and the background hammering on the cottage door penetrated the sleep she had at last fallen into well after dawn. She looked at her watch with bleary eyes and saw that it was ten o'clock.

'Yes——' she called groggily, reaching for her long cotton kimono that had seen better days. 'I'm coming.'

It was Conrad's voice, she realised, and pleasure at the thought of seeing someone—anyone—made her stand with reckless haste on the bad ankle. It was still painful, and it took her a worryingly long time to get to the door and open it.

'Hello!' she said breathlessly, self-consciously pushing back her untidy hair. 'You caught me oversleeping, I'm afraid.'

'Is that all? I wondered what was going on with the cottage shut up like Fort Knox and the beach looking as though it's undergone a bombardment. I needn't have disturbed you, but I thought I'd better check that you were still in one piece.' His expression was quite neutral, and Sara wondered if he would have shown any stronger reaction if she had been lying out there among the fallen rocks. Probably not. He would most likely have shrugged and told himself that that was another problem solved.

'As you see—they missed,' she said drily. 'That was a timely warning you gave me, though. If I hadn't been half expecting something to happen, things might have been different.'

'Good. That's all right, then.' He nodded dismissively and seemed about to depart in response to Clouzot's impatient whinny and tug.

'By the way,' she said quickly, 'thanks for doing the boat. If you'd come to tell me it was ready I'd have thanked you more promptly.'

'What on earth for? It was no great shakes. Merely a civilised bit of assistance, the sort I'd have given my worst enemy. In any case, I wanted to get back home.'

Sara stared fascinated into his eyes, and decided she knew just why they were so compelling. Apart from the clear, bright blue, there was a dark rim edging the iris that gave unusual definition to an already strong colour.

She realised that he was waiting for some response, his eyebrows raised questioningly at her silence.

'I could have given you a drink or something,' she said. 'Actually——' she had remembered the dinner, '—I wondered if——'

'Forgive me if I appear rude,' he interrupted smoothly, and she knew that he didn't care a toss whether she thought him rude or not, 'but I don't want to hang around. I seem to have wasted rather a lot of time recently. There's a lot of work waiting, so as long as you're all right . . .?' He nodded briskly again and turned, ready to remount.

Sara had a strong, overwhelming urge to thump the back he'd turned on her. The superior, autocratic, snubbing pig of a man!

'And by the way,' he said over his shoulder, a gleam in his eye that suggested there was nothing 'by the way' about what was coming, 'don't waste your efforts quizzing Jane Cameron about me. She's really quite unlikely to be indiscreet and satisfy your curiosity. Heaven knows why you're such a prey to it. Nosy women are a terrible bore, don't you think?'

The knowledge that Jane Cameron had seen through her and reported on her, but above all the scorn in the last words of his, took Sara's breath away. She stepped back in embarrassed reaction, and all her weight went on the bad ankle. Her face contracted and a little moan of pain escaped her.

Conrad paused, one foot in the stirrup, impatience in his voice.

'Now what?'

'Nothing!' she muttered savagely, hanging on to the door. 'Don't waste any more of your precious time, *please*.'

He saw the ankle, bulky in its wrapping of socks.

'Don't be stupid. You *have* hurt yourself. Why didn't you say?'

'Because I wasn't hit by the damned rocks. I fell.'

'How ridiculously pedantic. Let me see it.'

'The hell I will!' said Sara crudely. 'Go away.' She was being utterly childish now, but she couldn't stop herself. She hobbled across to the nearest chair and flopped on to it, conscious that she was scruffy and unwashed, with last night's mud still on her battered knees, and that her behaviour matched her disastrous appearance.

He took no notice of her words. He was hot on her heels, then kneeling down to unpin and remove the socks, with an upward glance of eloquent amazement that they were the best she could do as a first-aid measure. Her ankle emerged in swollen splendour, all shades from brown to purple.

Conrad's fingers were surprisingly gentle as he manipu-
lated her foot.

'You can move it?'

'Yes, but it's no picnic.'

'That's obvious.' He sat back, looking at the foot, then he
held up the socks. 'Are these the best you can do in the way
of support?'

'I wouldn't be wearing them if I could do any better,
would I?' she snapped.

'Where's the bathroom?' He looked round, probably
convinced he could find a first-aid stock she had completely
overlooked.

'There isn't one.'

'No bathroom?'

'Only that.' She waved a hand in the direction of the
sink, and he went over to it and stared into its murky stone
depths, then began to wash his hands with the unspoken
implication that handling her scruffy person made it
necessary for him to use even such primitive washing
arrangements as these.

'No hot water, either,' he commented.

'Only if you heat it on that thing.'

He looked at the Camping Gaz stove for a moment, then
back at her.

'Dare I enquire about the loo?'

'At the end of the garden.'

'Good God!' He looked as though it was her fault, then
threw the towel down impatiently. 'Well, that's it, then.
You'd better come up to La Domaine.'

Sara was flabbergasted at the sudden suggestion. 'What
on earth for?'

'Isn't it obvious? This place is bad enough for a fit person.
In your state, how can you cope with mod cons down the

garden? And if you lose your balance near that stove, heaven knows what you might do to yourself. Besides, you really are going to have to rest that foot, and you'll never do it adequately here.'

She was outraged by the blend of annoyance and reluctant charity in his voice.

'It's out of the question. I don't want to come, and you don't want to have me there. You can't deny it.'

'Life's full of things we don't want. There's no point being foolish about the inevitable. Having you under my nose might not be desirable, but if it's necessary I suppose I can put up with it.'

His whole attitude, and in particular the unfortunate reference to 'nose', pushed her over the top.

'You called me a nosy woman.' Her voice had a most unattractive whinge, and she could hardly believe she was speaking in this childish way.

'So don't give me cause to do so again and it won't need to be repeated. Look——' He stepped towards her impatiently. 'You're wasting time. You've got to dress. I can't take you up to the house in that thing.'

Suddenly she was swept up in his arms, stiff as a ramrod, making herself as unyielding as possible against his broad chest while he carried her through to the bedroom and placed her carefully on the bed.

'Clothes . . .' he said, looking down distastefully at the tatty pile of them on the floor, where she had dropped them the night before. 'Are these what you want?' He poked a toe disdainfully at them.

'Don't touch them!' she practically shrieked, feeling like a wild-eyed witch on the bed. 'They're yesterday's. I can get my own.' She reached for the drawer, then stopped, refusing to have him watch her sort through her underwear. 'If you must stand over me, you could pass the blue shirt and the skirt with it from that cupboard,' she added ungraciously, waving a hand towards the far corner of the room.

'These?' He held up the rainbow-coloured skirt and the blouse, and she nodded assent. 'What else? You'll need a change of clothes.'

'No, I shan't. I shan't be there long enough.'

'This will do, and this ... and this.' He ignored her completely, taking garments at random and stuffing them into a holdall from the bottom of the cupboard. 'Now, are you going to put the rest in, or shall I do it for you?'

'You insufferable, pompous, unbearable——'

'For the love of heaven, stop wasting time and get dressed,' he said in an objectionably bored voice, reaching out to undo the sash of her kimono.

'Take your hands off me!' She clutched the shabby garment to herself, and tugged the sash out of his fingers.

He folded his arms and stood looking down at her.

'You seem to have something of a rape-fixation. Let me assure you that taking you up to the house is a decision I reached with the gratest reluctance. In fact, I'm looking forward to nothing so much as your being back here again. And I don't want to touch you for any reason other than moving you from A to B. Has that sunk into your tiny mind?'

'Oh, get out!' she snarled, and he did so calmly, saying just before he closed the door with ostentatious quietness, 'Give me a call when you're ready.'

Once rid of his presence, she calmed down and tried to view the situation objectively. I should be glad about this, she thought as she struggled into her clothes—unwashed, but what option was there with him in the room where the sink was? He was going to take her into his house, let her stay there, even if only on sufferance. She should be giving three muted cheers about the opportunity that had fallen into her lap. But she wasn't.

Nosy woman . . . that was what had touched her on the raw, because it was too close to the truth. She worked for a nasty, nosy magazine, and nobody was forcing her to do it, so why was she? This assignment was definitely going to be her last. It wasn't her scene, this prying into private lives and looking for whatever unpleasantness you could find under the stone of the public image. If Conrad knew what she was really up to, he would let her rot here and gladly. Besides, this morning had proved beyond doubt that there was a connection between him and Jane Cameron . . . and suddenly Sara had no desire to discover just what it was.

Leaning against the bed, she tucked a few extra things into the tote bag then hobbled over to the door and opened it.

'You silly, stubborn woman,' he said as he picked her up carefully. 'Hang on to the bag and I'll hang on to you.'

Maybe it was the sudden swinging aloft into the saddle, or just nervousness at being up there again. It could even have been as simple as the fact that she hadn't eaten since before noon the previous day. Whatever the reason, as Conrad was getting the key from inside the door and locking up, Sara felt the blood drain from her face and the world begin to swing alarmingly around her. She hung on to the saddle with a strangled 'Please', then was aware of him by her side, holding her steady while she drooped over his head and hung on to his crisp hair as though he had no feelings in his scalp.

'Steady does it,' he murmured. 'Just keep your head down and don't try to move. I'm holding you.'

Awful though she felt, Sara was comforted by his voice and by the reassuring firmness of his arms. Gradually the world stilled and her eyes cleared, and she slowly lifted her head to gulp in air.

'If you could release my hair some time, when you're quite ready,' he said calmly, and she transferred her grip to the saddle again with an embarrassed apology.

'What was all that about?' He was inspecting her face carefully. 'Is your foot so very painful?'

'No, I think I'm maybe a bit short of food. I didn't want to eat after the fall. I'm all right now.'

'All the same, I don't think we'll take any chances. Keep your feet well forward, especially the bad one.'

Before she had time to realise what he was going to do, he had sprung into the saddle behind her.

'Not over-comfortable for either of us, but safe,' he said in her ear, reaching round her for the reins. 'Now, just lean back. You can't fall. My arms will stop you.' He made a noise that the unprotesting Clouzot evidently understood, and they set off.

Sara was beyond speech. She did as she was told. It was impossible to keep either her dignity or her distance with his thighs against hers, his body tightly pressed to her own, and his chin resting on her head.

'Comfortable' was not the word she would have used. Nor 'uncomfortable'. Strange, rather. The feel of his reassuring firmness around and behind her, warm and solid, did the most odd things to her. She still felt light-headed from the attack of faintness—that must be why she had this peculiar feeling, like a minor and not at all painful electric shock. She let her arms relax down over his as he reached round her to hold Clouzot's reins. Lean back, he had said. Gradually she did so, her head against his shoulder. She had been right about that shoulder, it was the most reassuring place ... and she could hear the strong, regular beat of his heart. It was a primeval sound, and in counterpoint was the clip-clop of Clouzot's hooves over the stony path.

'I'm sorry to be giving you so much trouble ...' she said, feeling drowsily kind towards him.

It was snub time again.

'Don't worry,' he said coolly. 'Marthe will do all the looking after you that's involved. In fact—I shall probably quite forget you're there.'

CHAPTER FIVE

WHY did Conrad have to do that? Sara thought crossly as she watched Marthe bustling around in the bedroom, putting her few possessions away. Why lull her with kindness and friendly words, then—wham! slap her down like an importunate schoolchild? She ought to be prepared for it by now, but each time it took her completely by surprise.

He had carried her upstairs when they arrived at La Domaine, flinging instructions over his shoulder to Marthe as she trotted after them. Then he disappeared and, through the window which overlooked the garden at the back of the house, Sara saw him set off on Clouzot again, no doubt intending to complete his interrupted morning's exercise and at the same time begin the process of forgetting that he had an unwanted temporary lodger.

Well—*tant pis*! At least she would make the most of the facilities while she was here. Through an open door Sara could see her bathroom, all pine and pale blue tiles, and enormously inviting after days of hurried washing under a cold outdoor shower, whose public position made a bathing costume essential while she used it.

'More than anything I'd love a bath,' she told Marthe.

The little birdlike woman nodded. 'Yes—good for the swelling. And afterwards I bandage for you. Wait for the water, then I shall help.' Her few words of English and Sara's fairly adequate French made conversation of a sort possible, but Marthe was a quiet little person whose beady

78

dark eyes seemed to see all and give nothing much away. She had accepted Sara's presence with a discreet lack of comment or question. Now she disappeared into the bathroom, and soon scented steam began to drift out to Sara.

Once she was safely in the bath, Marthe left her, issuing firm instructions that she was not to attempt to get out without help. Sara lay back in dreamy bliss, the water soothing to her foot and doing wonders for her spirits until she noticed that there was a decidedly female-slanted selection of bottles and jars around on the glass shelves. So Conrad Blake was not quite the recluse he made himself out to be! Hot on the heels of that discovery came the niggling afterthought that maybe it was only herself that he had this overwhelming urge to repel. A little of the pleasure went out of the bath.

The bed that Marthe helped her into was a fantastic creation with an ornate metal frame painted pale lemon, patterned with leaves and flowers, its head and foot panels curving over in scroll fashion. It could have come from one of Marie Antoinette's playrooms at Versailles, but the mattress was comfortable and modern, and there was a blue-and-white-check summer duvet. Beside the bed, a round table had a fringed cover of the same fabric, and on it were grouped pieces of antique porcelain and a brass lamp with a graceful, arched stem and fluted glass shade.

I match the décor, Sara thought with satisfaction, smoothing down her pale blue cotton nightshirt as she held out her foot for Marthe's attention.

'*Oh—ça alors!*' The elderly face wrinkled in sympathy as she applied evil-smelling and unpleasant-looking dark green ointment with gentle fingers.

'What on earth *is* that?' Sara exclaimed, pulling a face.

The string of ingredients defeated both her French and Marthe's English, but the overall idea seemed to be that it would work miracles.

A little later Marthe reappeared with a loaded tray which she carefully put on Sara's knees.

'Better than the ointment?' she smiled, indicating the dish of *poulet chasseur* with its accompanying warm, crusty *flûte* and the basket of apricots. 'Eat it all, *mademoiselle*, and make sure you drink this.' She indicated a glass of pale amber liquid. '*La spécialité de mon père*. It will relax you.'

Relax her it certainly did. The afternoon was an unknown quantity, drifting by in sleep and contented half-sleep, and the sun was low in the sky when Sara surfaced fully to find Marthe again by her bedside with another temptingly loaded tray.

Conrad, true to his word, had not put in an appearance. She had half thought he would at least pay a brief courtesy visit, but it began to appear that not even that slight civility came into his scheme of events. Marthe vouchsafed that *monsieur* was not having dinner at home that evening, and after she had eaten Sara resigned herself to settling down early.

She was hobbling back from the bathroom, smelling of minty toothpaste and with her hair in its customary loose plait for the night, when there was a brief tap on her bedroom door.

'*Entrez!*' she called, expecting Marthe.

But it was Conrad, smoothly elegant in pale grey trousers and crisp matching shirt, smelling faintly of some expensive male toiletry and giving every impression of being on his way out to impress someone.

'Oh!' Sara halted, holding on to the dressing-table, annoyed at being caught in her short nightshirt that left far too little of her person to the imagination. 'I didn't expect it to be you.'

'Just a flying visit. Are you comfortable?'

'Perfectly, thank you.' He was looking at her in the assessing, impersonal manner of a doctor who was obliged to look in but didn't really want to know.

'How's the foot? More adequately bandaged, I see.'

'And treated with Marthe's magic ointment.' She looked coolly at a point just over his left shoulder, and put no more effort into the conversation than he was doing.

'Pain's bad for the temper, isn't it?' he said smoothly, not letting his face slip when her eyes darted to his at that. 'I've brought you these to take your mind off it.' He showed her the spines of a couple of books—a new Margaret Forster and a Julian Symons. 'Have you read them? There are others, if so.'

'Thank you. They're fine,' she told him stiltedly.

'And this might pass the odd moment, too.' He took a company brochure out from underneath the books: black, with gold lettering and border, very expensive-looking. *Blake Enterprises—A Venture in Design*, Sara read, and a surge of anger swept away her control.

'Just because you've brought me here under your roof, very much against my wishes, I might add,' she said hotly, 'there's no need to keep reminding me of your opinion of me. You made the position quite clear earlier on.'

She took the books ostentatiously and put them on the dressing-table, leaving the brochure still in his hands.

'Don't be so touchy.' He threw the booklet on the bed. 'This was intended as a peace move, not an insult. I'm *volunteering* a bit of information, not having it wheedled out of me. I thought if I did that, perhaps you might manage not to glower at me with those dark, threatening orbs of yours whenever you see me. I don't want my evening out spoiled by thoughts of you festering here—so read all about me, and forget about *this*.' He reached forward and gave her nose a gentle tweak.

Sara twisted her head away and her plait swung out at the sudden movement.

He caught it and held her captive by its thick rope. 'Do you always to do this with your hair at night? Very fetching! It makes you look every day of fourteen years old. Or is that the wrong thing to say again? One never knows quite when one is stoking up those fires of annoyance in you.'

'I just wish you wouldn't *treat* me like a fourteen-year-old,' she said with ill-concealed impatience.

'A nice fourteen-year-old, though,' he answered, still teasing, and giving her plait a little tug. 'The kind who wouldn't object to a little avuncular goodnight kiss.'

He leaned forward, aiming for the side of her face, but some spiky little devil in Sara made her turn her head so that her mouth was there to meet his, instead of her cheek. The same devil urged her to go on and show him she was all woman, made her lips part and cling to his with velvety softness, and sent her warm, scantily clad body swaying towards him. She felt his sudden tensing at the touch of her rounded femininity against his solid male firmness, and was aware of the kiss becoming more dynamite-packed than either he or she had anticipated, before she took the initiative and stood back.

'I'm not a child,' she said, rather superfluously, and was triumphant to see that at last she had managed to disconcert him instead of it being the other way around.

He stared at her, surprised arousal lingering in the depths of his eyes.

'No . . .' he said thoughtfully, and the disturbance she had deliberately engineered was there, too, in the huskiness of his voice. 'No—you're no child, Sara. On that point we are in full agreement.'

'Good.' Still her eyes held his defiantly, and there was tension in the air, almost tangible between them.

His next remark cut it abruptly. 'You are not, however, above indulging in childish tricks.' Then he seemed to click back into control of himself and the situation. 'What am I thinking of, keeping you standing here when you are obviously on your way back to bed?' He looked briefly at his watch. 'And indeed—why am I here when I'm expected elsewhere at this very moment? Enjoy your books and sleep well. Good night.'

Who had won that round? Sara asked herself, gathering the books together and climbing into bed when the door closed behind him.

She sat up in bed for quite a while in a thoughtful daze, and when she did at last turn to reading, it was the brochure that she opened.

There was a studio portrait of Conrad Blake, his face serious, calm, incredibly handsome. The photographer had used lighting cleverly, to accentuate the bone structure, and he had caught the penetrating quality of those stunning eyes by taking the shot from slightly above, so that Conrad was looking up from under his strong brow.

Sara traced the shape of the lips she now knew in a way no glossy studio portrait could convey, remembering. I know why I have no enthusiasm for this story I must do, she thought with sudden illumination. It isn't just because of moral scruples. It's because I don't want to bring *you* under *Spica*'s rotten magnifying glass.

The eyes seemed to burn into hers from the page, but it

was an illusion. The portrait didn't see her any more than the real man saw the real her. She was to him a troublesome juvenile, to be cared for when she couldn't care for herself, but to be relegated 'out of sight, out of mind' as quickly as possible. Right now he had most certainly completely forgotten her, because if he said he was going out for the evening on this island, what choice was there? Who could he be spending it with but Jane Cameron—the cool, self-possessed, decidedly attractive and definitely adult Jane Cameron?

That was a great thought to go to sleep on, she reflected gloomily, asking herself immediately why she should care. But she did.

Next morning, when she took her bath, the ankle both looked and felt better.

'Where do you get this stuff?' she asked Marthe, as more of the green ointment was generously applied.

'We make it. My mother gathers the herbs, as her mother and grandmother did before her. How does the foot feel when you stand on it today?'

'Better, but still a bit painful and weak.' That was hardly true at all, but Sara didn't want to leave La Domaine.

She was punished for her deceit. Conrad was conspicuous by his absence, and the morning dragged. Then when Sara looked out of the window after lunch, she saw him walking across the lawn with Jane Cameron. The girl was talking animatedly, her head turned towards him. As Sara watched, she saw Conrad laugh and then put an arm round the slender silk-shirted shoulders and pull the girl to him, resting his head on hers with the affectionate ease of people who were well used to each other.

A pain, unfamiliar and sharp, stabbed and spread in

Sara's chest as she watched them, then she let herself slide down in the bed so that she was too low to see any more. Dinner last night. Lunch today. No wonder he was too busy to spare time for anything and anyone else!

It was six o'clock before she saw him. He came into her room after a brief tap and pause, and she saw that he didn't appear to intend dining out today. He was still wearing the jeans and fine white sweater she had noticed at lunch time and, as he lifted his arm to close the door behind him, Sara saw again the image of him pulling Jame Cameron towards him, and the memory froze her face in peevish solemnity.

'You're looking pretty gloomy,' he said.

'I've had a pretty gloomy day.'

'Is it bad?' He pointed to her foot, misinterpreting her attitude.

'The ankle? No, much better. Well—quite a lot, anyway.' She remembered her act rather belatedly.

'Bored with staying in bed, are you? And I've been too busy to offer much in the way of company.'

'Yes,' she said sceptically. 'I saw how busy you were at lunch time.'

Marthe's tap on the door removed the need for any reply.

'Oh, *monsieur*—I didn't know you were here,' the older woman said with a hint of disapproval. 'I want to know if *mademoiselle* would like ham or an omelette this evening.'

'Oh—ham, please, Marthe,' Sara said with scant enthusiasm.

'Make that for two. I'll have mine up here,' Conrad said surprisingly, and Sara's cheeks flushed at the unexpectedness of it.

Marthe pursed her lips. 'If *mademoiselle* wishes . . .?'

Conrad rocked back on his heels, hands in the pockets of

his jeans, enjoying the two women's reaction with male egotism.

'And does *mademoiselle* wish it?'

'Does that really enter into it?' Sara said, switching to English. 'If fancy dictates my direction at the moment, what can I do about it?' For Marthe's benefit, she sugared the acid of the words with a smile.

'*Mademoiselle sera enchantée,*' Conrad said, looking at Sara with amusement playing round his mouth. 'We must make sure there's a good, very sweet dessert,' he added as he turned and followed Marthe out of the room. 'See you in a little while.'

He needn't think I'm going to get excited about his charity, Sara told herself crossly, then rushed into the bathroom to wash and scent herself and do just that very thing, quite forgetting to limp.

She couldn't help noticing that Conrad had changed into 'dining-out' clothes again, this time navy blue trousers and a dark blue shirt of some dull, silky material that showed every movement of the muscles beneath it in a very touchable way. He took his tray over to the chair by the window, while Marthe placed Sara's carefully in her lap, then he told Marthe she could go over and see her parents if she wished; he would take the trays back to the kitchen when they had finished.

Sara had resolved to be calm and even a little distant, but over the excellent asparagus soup followed by *jambon de Paris* and *frisée* salad with tomatoes sliced in olive oil and fresh herbs she found herself thawing out completely and finally thoroughly enjoying herself.

When they had finished the last of the Normandy apple tart, Conrad put the trays on the floor and sat back, long legs stretched out indolently, still apparently disposed to stay on and talk.

'Did you read the brochure?' he asked.

'Yes.' She was suddenly wary.

'Do you think it impressive? All those branches, factories, production lines?'

'Very impressive.'

'Then you're wrong, and I shall tell you exactly why I'm here.' Sara's heart rocketed.

'No, please don't. I really don't want to know.' Fran's training, her professional curiosity—everything went overboard in her sudden panic. What she didn't know, she couldn't reveal, could she?

'You're being paranoid again. I'm *offering* to talk to you.'

'No, you're not. It's Marthe's father's wine talking. Lord knows what proof it is! I'm a stranger, remember. Why should you want to talk to a stranger about your private business?'

His eyes glinted with amusement. 'How can you sit there in bed in your ridiculous nightdress, after dining with me in your sleeping-quarters, for heaven's sake, and maintain that we're strangers? We're not, Sara.' His face grew thoughtful, surprised. 'Were we ever?'

He didn't give her time to work out exactly what he meant by that. He leaned forward, quite determined to go on with what he wanted to say.

'Have you ever known what it is to feel totally dissatisfied with what you are doing? To feel it's not worth the effort ... think it's incomprehensible how you came to be doing it in the first place?'

He had caught her reluctant interest quite dramatically. Oh, yes, she could agree with that far more fervently than he would ever know!

'We all have moments of disillusion,' she said, resorting to a safe cliché.

'I'm not talking about moments. I'm talking about days, weeks, months, a lifetime stretching ahead of you.'

'But how can you feel like that? You're a household name. Everything you do turns into an overnight success.'

He looked dispiritedly at her. 'It depends how you rate success. Do you know that last year we produced twenty thousand red plastic mixing-bowls—all exactly the same, all with pouring lips and rubberised non-slip base rims. I don't speak of the blue and the coral and the lemon ones.' He ran a hand through his hair. 'My God! Can't you see them all coming off the production line one after the other ... piling up ... forming a plastic equivalent of the Common Market food mountains? Do you know, I got to the point of having nightmares about them?'

Sara gave an involuntary gurgle of laughter. 'Don't tell me you've withdrawn to an island so that you can make one limited-edition mixing-bowl—white, no lip, no rubber-base rim? A mixing-bowl to shatter the world?'

He grinned. 'Not quite. And yes—I can laugh about it now. But when that first terrible sense of disillusion was triggered off in me, I didn't feel like laughing. Of course, it took something pretty big to bring me to that point, and I'm not going into that. For a long time I'd felt to be on a sort of production line myself. I'd worked hard, always intended coming into the family busienss, felt excited about it to begin with. In some ways, I still find it satisfying. I know, for instance, that the vast quantities of mass production that threaten at times to annihilate me are sources of individual pleasure for millions of people. I do know that. But I feel a need to find my own identity again. Can you understand that? I've been a public figure for far too long. I've had a succession of almost production-line girlfriends, all beautifully designed and presented, all passed perfect! Where was the reality in it all? I started to ask.'

'And have you found it, this reality you want?' Sara was serious now, crossed legs drawn up under the duvet, her elbows resting on her knees, her hands cupping a face dominated by wide, thoughtful brown eyes.

'I'm getting there.' He fell silent, looking out of the window.

Had he found reality with Jane Cameron? Was she the one to give meaning to his life? Sara's head drooped forward and she felt strangely drained of vitality. He heard her sigh.

'You're tired. I've stayed too long.' He stood and came over to the bed, lifting the fall of dark hair that was shielding her face from him, weighing it for a moment on his hand and then letting it slide slowly through his fingers.

'No plait tonight?'

She smiled. 'That comes later.'

'And how unbearably solemn we've been, haven't we?' he said.

With a lightning change of mood that took her completely by surprise, he sat on the bed and, cupping her face with his warm hands, he turned it up to him. Then, watching her all the time with eyes that now glowed with wickedness, he claimed her unsuspecting mouth with lips that teased and caressed her own.

At first it was a deliberately light, experimental affair, and while she was still too much taken by surprise to react he pulled away from her for long enough to say mockingly, 'Just checking that what happened yesterday wasn't a figment of my imagination.'

Then he was kissing her again, and this time not as a spectator of his own actions. This time it was for real, and Sara's blood leapt from shock to wild, answering excitement. His hands moved down over her shoulders to pull her towards him, crushing her against the silken smoothness of his shirt and the sensual warmth of flesh and blood beneath it. The seductive teasing of the first kiss had deepened into a wildfire of demand and response that was in danger of consuming them both in its fierce flaring, turning them into something different, something too hot to handle. For burning seconds Sara was without shame, clinging to him and discovering with fevered hands the contours of his exciting body. Then those same hands were pushing him away and she was hunching up against the bedhead, eyes blazing.

'What do you think you're doing?'

Conrad, his eyes glittering and his chest rising and falling rapidly, let out a frustrated exclamation.

'I should have thought that was pretty obvious. You did say you wanted treatment appropriate to your age, I thought?'

'And appropriate to your position as my host. Fine words you spoke back at the cottage, Conrad Blake, about only touching me in order to get me from A to B.'

'And didn't I?' His eyes smouldered tauntingly down at her. 'It seemed to me that you were progressing from A to B very satisfactorily indeed. What stopped you?'

It wasn't the sneer in his voice that hurt, it was the fact that all through the meal they had eaten together he had been straight, solid, deeply interesting, talking with what she was sure was sincerity. But now he had swung right back to playboy status, and she resented the change in him, the diminishing of him, more than she was capable of putting into words.

'I shall be leaving tomorrow,' she said with icy determination.

'If you're fit. We'll leave decision-making until the cool of the morning.' He went towards the door, still angry, but she saw that the sarcasm had faded from his face when he turned to look at her briefly.

'Don't forget that you started that. If you can't take the consequences, I suggest you let sleeping dogs lie. Aroused, they call for more handling than you seem to be capable of. I heard Marthe come in a moment ago. I'll send her up.'

She stared at the closed door when he had gone. He'd heard Marthe come in—and she certainly hadn't. So had he known all along that what he was doing wasn't going to lead to anything? All the time—had he been only teasing? And there she had been, taking him seriously, falling right into the trap and proving herself to be the panicky, immature kid he thought her.

Sara frowned, thinking back. All the same, whatever he said, there *had* been a difference between what he had begun and what it had turned into. Of that she was certain, in spite of his scorn.

She hugged her knees, resting her chin on them. A fine muddle it all was! When she had been wanting his story, he had disappeared and everybody had clammed up. Now that she didn't want his story, he seemed determined to force it on her. And now, too, there was this far more dangerous thread running through their relationship: a thread that had shown itself capable of snaking around her, tangling her in something as treacherous as any under-water weed to a drowning person.

'No little problems?' Marthe said suspiciously as she

came into the bedroom.

'Problems?' Sara realised that the older woman's ideas of correct behaviour were shaken by the free-and-easy bedroom association between two comparative strangers. 'No, Marthe,' she lied, imagining the woman's severe face had she walked in a few moments earlier. 'No problems at all. In fact, I think I'm quite cured.'

Oh yes? taunted a little demon in her mind.

Next morning, the ankle, though still discoloured, was back to normal size and quite comfortable to walk on. Sara took a last luxurious bath and put on her blue shirt and rainbow skirt, then for the first time she left her bedroom and ventured downstairs, through the quiet house.

'You really are safe to go back to that little *cabine?*' Marthe asked, looking up from the pastry she was rolling at the kitchen table.

'Quite safe, Marthe. And thank you a million times for all your care. Is Monsieur Blake around?' She half hoped that he had already gone across to the mainland on some business or other. A note of thanks would have been easier than a personal confrontation, but she was out of luck.

'He's in the studio,' Marthe said. 'Shall I get him?'

Studio? The reporter in Sara was not as dead as she thought.

'No—I'll go to him,' she said quickly. 'Which way?'

'Round the corner, at the end of the veranda. You can't miss it. But take care with the foot, *hein?*'

The room Marthe called a studio was an outbuilding, attached to the main house, but not visible until Sara had rounded the corner. Expecting some cradle of design for Blake Enterprises, Sara was surprised to find a functional workshop, with rows of small tools, shelves on which were stacked abrasive papers, and where there were blocks of wood piled up against the wall.

She stood quietly in the doorway, looking round. The flagged-stone floor was littered with shavings, and the air was fragrant with the smell of them. There was a strong light switched on over the workbench, and the barred small window above, quite inadequate, seemed to indicate that the room had once been a dairy.

There was a murmur of voices through the partly open door of a further room opening from the back wall, but Sara was in no hurry to have her interested look round cut short.

Her eyes, up to now taking in a general view of the room, suddenly sharpened as she saw the object in the pool of light on the bench. It was a wood-carving of a sea bird—a tern, she thought, its wings raised, caught to perfection at the point of flight. She stepped forward and picked it up carefully. The dark cap of the head looked like ebony. The body wood she couldn't guess at, but the carving was done incredibly skilfully, using the grain to suggest the lie of the plumage. The feet were of a more golden wood, as was the beak, the joints invisible, and the whole wood sculpture was mounted on a rough, natural piece of rock.

She went impulsively over to the back door, excitement too powerful to damp down spurring her on.

'Did *you* do this?' she burst out excitedly. Conrad and Jane Cameron were sitting at a table, examining something under a powerful Anglepoise lamp. Conrad turned, his face freezing in displeasure as he saw what she was holding. His hair was peppered with wood dust, and there were smears of it down the front of his shirt.

'Who told you to come in here?' he said shortly.

Sara was too wound up to stop.

'Oh, don't start all that again!' she said impatiently, caring about nothing except the perfection she was holding. She looked down at the bird, her fingers touching it, curving round its wings, its head, its breast, in an excess of tactile pleasure. 'This—this *beautiful* thing . . . Did you do it? Really do it yourself?'

'What if I did?' He was watching her with hooded weariness.

Jane Cameron was slowly standing up, but Sara didn't care about her. Conrad as a person of integrity was being reinstated in her mind through this wonderful creation of his that she was holding.

'It's terrific! It can't be the first. You must have done more.'

'A few.' She could have shaken him for his reluctance to answer.

'Why didn't you tell me about them last night?'

'Why should I have told you? I've told precious few people.'

Jane touched Conrad's arm briefly. 'I left something on the stove, Con. I'll be back in a few minutes.' She gave Sara a token smile as she passed. 'Glad you're better.'

That could be taken in more than one way, Sara thought, as she stood back to let the girl get by. Glad she would now be leaving La Domaine was the most likely meaning behind the words. But keen interest in this new facet of Conrad's life quickly took over again.

She turned the figure over and found a word roughly carved in the rock.

'There's a name on it, I see. Genista. Why that? Why not your own name?'

'One "why" at a time. Genista is because of the island— Les Genêts. It's the botanical name for broom. And I haven't used my own name, because this is something that I want to stand on its own merits, not within the protective aura of Blake Enterprises.'

'I see. How long did it take to do this?'

'It took the sycamore quite a number of years to reach its mature height of seventy feet, then the cut wood another year to season, then——'

'Stop being deliberately obtuse. *You.* Your part of it.'

'Well, there you have the real joy of it. No time and motion study. No delivery dates. No rapid mass production.'

Sara looked at him, her head on one side, a smile stealing across her face.

'In other words, this represents that unique, world-shattering, white mixing-bowl?'

He nodded, smiling at her at last. 'Right!'

'I tell you something——' she put the bird carefully down on the table, '—those twenty thousand or whatever red plastic mixing-bowls did a damn good job if they caused you to give birth to one of these.'

'You really do like it, don't you?' he said, his tone making her realise just how much this work meant to him.

'I do. Surely someone has told you how good you are?'

'Yes. A gallery over on the mainland. I approached them for an outside opinion, but they insisted on sending a couple of figures to Paris.'

'And?' she prompted.

'I'm afraid people wanted to buy them. For a great deal of money.' He looked at her with almost comic despair. 'I don't seem to be able to get away from making money but, believe me, it's only a side-effect of this.'

Sara nodded. 'I know. What grabs you is the making of

one, beautiful, perfect thing. Making it with love and care.'

He picked up a block of wood from the end of the bench.

'See this? It's American redwood.' He turned it on its side. 'I know that in here there's an otter, very sleek, with its head half turned just here.' His fingers were smoothing the wood while he imagined what he would do with it. He caught her smiling at his enthusiasm. 'I know. I'm hooked!' He put the block down. 'Well—since you've seen this, and you're obviously interested, you may as well see what Jane does.'

'Jane? Is she a craftsman, too? Is that why she's here?'

He hesitated. 'Partly. Come on.' He took her arm to draw her nearer the table, then stopped. 'Your foot. I'd forgotten.'

'So had I. It's functional now, really.' She raised her bag to show him. 'I came to thank you and say goodbye.'

He shot a wry glance at her. 'A woman of your word, I see.' Woman, not child, she noticed. Then he picked up two pieces of jewellery he and Jane had been examining and handed them to her.

There was a silver bracelet with an almost bark-like finish and a pattern of random holes that seemed to form naturally in the metal. A delicate thing, deceptively heavy. And there was a gold pendant, again with a rippling, textured surface, but this time with a fall of tiny diamonds like a sprinkling of dew tumbling down one side. Both items were beautiful, with the same cool, detached beauty that marked their creator, but neither held the same enchantment for Sara as did Conrad's breathing of life and love into a piece of wood. There was another dimension in his work, a dimension that went beyond surface beauty.

They talked for a moment or two longer, then he walked to the door with her.

'You're sure you're fit now?' he asked.

'Quite recovered.' They exchanged glances, acknowledging without words that she was not merely referring to the state of her ankle.

Jane was coming back to the studio, and the sun gleaming on her golden hair made Sara feel sombre and dull in comparison.

'Have you warned Sara about tomorrow?' she called as she drew near.

Conrad hesitated. 'No—I'd forgotten about it, to tell you the truth.' He turned to Sara. 'We're going over to the mainland. There's a fête—quite a big one—along the coast, and we're meeting up with friends and staying with them for the night. I'm sure they'd welcome you, too. Marthe and her parents are going—staying with relatives—so it will really be a bit desolate here.'

Jane Cameron's silence spoke for her.

'Thank you,' Sara said, 'but I think I'd be wiser to take it easy for a couple of days. I don't really want to do much standing around yet, you know.'

There was a flicker of relief in Jane Cameron's eyes as she hurried to approve this decision.

'I'm sure you're right. There'll be crowds of people jostling around, and there's always dancing in the streets. Con—could I have a word with you now?' A hand on his arm made sure he didn't go with Sara.

She thanked him again, and went on her way. Definite hostility there, she reflected as she stopped a short distance along the path to shake a tiny pebble out of her shoe. The air was very still, and she heard Jane Cameron's voice quite clearly through the open studio door.

'I wish you hadn't got so involved with her, Con. She worries me.'

Then Conrad's answer, tender, comforting.

'It's all right, Jane—really it is. She's harmless. Just a passing holiday-maker. What could she possibly do to us? Don't worry, love.' Then there was silence, and Sara's face burned as she imagined the comfort of the voice, reinforced by arms and lips.

She hurried on her way, more quickly than wisely. In the past hour's excitement she had managed to forget the job she was supposedly here to do, but Conrad's words, so blatantly untrue did he but know it, had reminded her forcibly of who she was and why she was on the island.

The bright day dimmed with the knowledge.

CHAPTER SIX

THE cottage looked more depressing than ever after the light, attractive rooms at La Domaine. Sara flung open the windows and took the pan of decidedly 'off' ratatouille down the garden to get rid of it, thinking that it stank as badly as her next task—which was to update her findings on Conrad.

She hated the job. She knew exactly what *Spica* would do with the facts: how they would be twisted, distorted, changed into something hideously different from the simple truth Conrad had given her.

They would portray him as a neurotic playboy who had gone through all the pleasures money could buy, and found nothing but boredom. They would sneer at his island. Take apart his relationship with Jane—the first girl to share his interests—and imply that the only thing she shared with him was his bed. And they would broadcast to the world the skill he had keep secret ... take away his pride in achievement, his anonymity, his pleasure in creation.

Nevertheless, she thought miserably, she was still working for the magazine. She was here at their expense, and in no time at all Dave Becker would be arriving to take his pictures. There was no getting away from it.

She recorded her findings in a tight, quick monotone. At the end of the recording she stabbed at the off button and then buried her head in her arms with a moan of sheer misery. This definitely had to be the last thing she did for *Spica*. She must get out now, while she could still feel ashamed of what she was doing. The misery was such hell that she could see only too easily how the blunting of reactions, the anaesthetising of emotions would follow and be welcomed.

The gloom hung on, and she went to bed early, lonely after her two days of being cosseted. Tomorrow night, with no one on the island, would be lonelier still. The next night, with Dave Becker in the cottage, didn't bear thinking about.

The morning dawned bright and sunny again, and the first thing to be done was a trip over to the mainland to get in some food. There were the overdue letters to her mother and flatmate to post, and she really ought to speak to Fran. The thought of the latter task was so unwelcome that Sara set off in the boat very early so that she would be able to do no more than leave a message on the answering machine in the *Spica* office.

On impulse, after she had done that, and while she was still in the phone box, she dialled the flat, intending to ask Tessa, who was a Fleet Street secretary and well placed for picking up information, to keep an eye and an ear open for news of suitable jobs.

She had forgotten the difference in time, and it was a sleepy voice that croaked, 'Yes?'

'It's me . . . Sara. Sorry if I woke you, Tess.'

The voice sharpened miraculously.

'About time I heard from you! Are you home?'

'No, still in France. A job came up. Listen, Tess——'

'No, *you* listen. I've been dancing with impatience here. There's a thing from your favourite publishers . . . or should I say non-publishers?'

'Oh, I'm not wasting my precious francs listening to yet

another variation on what they don't want. Tessa, will you——'

'No!' Tessa squealed forcefully. 'It isn't the big manila job with a rejected manuscript. It's small—a letter.'

Sara's heart lurched. Once before, a letter in the post had meant a turning-point in her career. While Jonathan's interest had been so patently waning, she had entered a competition to find the young freelance journalist of the year. She had won it—the letter announcing her success arriving right on cue, the morning after Jonathan had jilted her. That letter had offered her three months' working experience in an editorial office, and had led indirectly to the job on *Spica*. Could fate present her with a second such stroke of luck? Surely it wasn't possible. But why would they write otherwise?

'Read it,' she said tersely.

'What if it's not what we think?' Tessa's voice was suddenly nervous.

'Oh—read it, for heaven's sake!'

It was no miracle. Nothing was certain, but there was definite encouragement. They liked the chapters and synopsis she had sent in ... wanted to see the rest, but couldn't make a firm decision, of course, until the book was completed. It was enough, though, to give shape and momentum to Sara's future plans.

'Tessa,' she said, when the excited dialogue that had set the wires buzzing had died down, 'I'm going to leave *Spica*.'

'On the strength of a "maybe"?' Tessa's sensible feet were firmly back on the ground.

'I'm not so daft. No, I want part-time work—nothing too demanding. I'm going to write. This has made up my mind for me. Will you look out for something?'

'"Starving author needs job to maintain garrett"?' Tessa teased.

'Something like that.'

'Well, as long as you can pay your half of the rent and not drive me round the bend with temperament ...' The warning light brought the conversation to a rapid close, and Sara went off to do her market shopping, if not walking on air, at least considerably easier in mind. Knowing what she was going to do would surely help her through the next few days.

On the way back to the island *Câline* swept past her little boat, not close enough for speech, but near enough for Sara to see that Conrad raised his hand in greeting and Jane didn't. She was standing beside him in the cockpit, fresh and attractive in a pale pink flying-suit, looking straight ahead with her blonde hair blown back by the wind. Through the cabin windows the dark, sober-clad figures of Marthe and her parents were visible.

A momentary pang of disappointment that she had turned down the chance to be one of the party was soon banished. Given the way Jane Cameron felt, it would have been impossible, and Sara told herself that the time would be much more profitably spent in working out the least amount of harm Dave Becker could do with his camera.

When the shopping was put away, Sara set off for a walk round the island with this in mind, intending to turn back the moment her foot began to protest. But in the end it was her mind that made her give up, not her ankle. She had never noticed before, but if you watched the stones of the megalith as you followed the cliff path, the shifting viewpoint made it seem that the stones themselves were surreptitiously moving, changing place and re-forming like a huddle of people gathering in unspoken disapproval. It's because you feel guilty, she told herself, unable to take her eyes from them. You're seeing condemnation in everything and everybody.

The feeling of unease was so strong in her, though, that in spite of all her self-admonition she hurried back to the little bay from where the silent watchers couldn't be seen.

She put fresh coffee on the stove as soon as she got in, working almost by touch alone as her eyes struggled to adjust to the cottage's dark interior, and it was as she turned from the cupboard, a mug in her hand, that she saw a shadowy figure silhouetted against the brightness of the doorway.

It was enough, in her state of mind, to make her cry out and drop the mug which shattered spectacularly on the stone floor.

'I'm sorry. I obviously startled you,' said Conrad's voice.

Sara leaned in shaky relief against the table.

'I'll say you did. I thought you were miles away. What happened? Did you forget something?'

He didn't answer her immediately.

'Here, let me pick this mess up for you.' He stooped and gathered together the broken pieces of pottery. 'That's the worst of it. If you have a brush for the rest?' He finished the job, then stood up, and she could see him clearly now. 'Is that coffee I can smell? Got enough for two in the pot?'

Sara got more mugs from the cupboard and filled them.

'I must have given you as much of a shock as I got with that little performance,' she said. 'I've been up looking at the megalith and my imagination was doing crazy things. It's quite a place.' She told him something of her fancies.

'Just as well I came back, then,' he said. 'If you'd got to that state by mid-morning, what would you have been like this time tonight?'

She stared at him, not quite sure what he meant. She was going to be alone here tonight in any case, so the fact that he had turned up again briefly wasn't much consolation.

'I'd better explain,' he said, putting his mug down on the table and leaning against the wall, looking, she thought, as out of place in the shabby cottage as a peacock in a back-street chicken-coop. 'I decided that since your calamity-rating was pretty high—high enough to tip the scales towards some dire disaster or other happening while you were on Les Genêts on your own, at any rate—it would be as well for you to have a bit of supervision. So here I am.'

Sara stared disbelievingly at him. 'You mean, you've actually come back—come back *deliberately*—for that very reason?'

He nodded. 'The very same.'

He looked smug and was obviously expecting thanks, but her reaction was not that at all. She felt quite despairing that this man who had nothing to gain from association with her, and so much to lose, persisted in doing things for her. Every time she steeled herself to get on with her job, he compounded her difficulties with his damned gentlemanly consideration!

'I don't need permanent supervision,' she said shortly. 'I've been taking care of myself for a long time—and quite adequately. You must go and join your friends. I *chose* to stay here, remember?'

'Don't worry! You're not being a nuisance,' he said blandly. 'It's all arranged. All taken care of. We're going to have a picnic.'

'Is that so?' Sara said with dangerous quietness. 'You think you can organise my day without any reference to me, do you?'

He exerted his charm. 'I'm referring to you now—a little late, admittedly.'

'You're telling me. It didn't sound anything like referring.'

'Well, all right, then. Telling, if we're picking our words so carefully.'

'And *I'm* telling *you* that I've got my own plans for today. You probably mean well, but you can't just walk in here and start dictating what I'm to do.'

'Oh, don't be so stuffy, Sara.' He looked down at her with confident amusement, so sure that she was going to drop into his hands like a ripe peach. 'Look at the sun! There's a lovely day ahead of us. You know you'd enjoy it.'

Sara's annoyance boiled over. 'It seems to me that you've got all the enjoyment lined up for yourself. Could it be that you fancy your chances alone on the island with me? If so, I can disillusion you right now. I've no intention of being any playboy's playmate.'

She was through to him with that gibe, and no mistake. His stance didn't change; he was still leaning indolently against the wall, but icy shutters seemed to close over his eyes. When he spoke, there was no trace of the rather superior humour that had marked his words so far.

'Why don't you admit the real truth—that you're just plain scared of men? What makes you assume I'm such a threat to you? Isn't that rather conceited, Sara? You've lost the facts somewhere in that flat panic of yours. The facts are quite innocent. You've twisted them into something dictated by what goes on inside you.' He straightened up suddenly. 'Yes ... that's more like it, isn't it? It isn't really men and me in particular you're scared of. It's something in you, isn't it? You have thoughts ... ideas you can't quite cope with. And you're scared they'll run away with you, aren't you?'

He had moved over and taken hold of her by the shoulders as he spoke. Now he was forcing her to look at him, and the combination of his touch and his penetrating words and look reduced her legs to jelly.

Yes!—she wanted to shout. Yes—you do something to me that I've never experienced before. You touch me, and my defences aren't there any more. You look at me, and I forget what I'm saying.

For long, hot seconds the truth flowed unspoken between them, then he let her go with a satisfied half-smile and she was able to find words again.

'That's not worth answering. But never mind me, then. What about Jane? I don't understand how you can arrange to do something with her and then just drop everything for some crazy notion. What about leaving Jane alone?'

'Jane's with the friends she arranged to spend the day with. Not alone.'

'And how pleased is she about that?' Sara went on doggedly.

'That doesn't concern you.'

'Oh, yes, it does—since you've managed to make me the unknowing cause of her displeasure.'

He shrugged, then let his arms drop down with an exasperated slap against his sides. 'I can see I'm wasting my time. I might as well leave. This conversation obviously isn't going anywhere.'

Sara gave a satisfied nod. 'So you'll go back to Jane?'

'And make myself look a complete fool? I'm already halfway to that in the Kerjeans' opinion, after arriving and departing almost simultaneously. No, I'll go and get on with some work.' He slanted a cool blue look at her: a this-is-your-loss-not-mine look. 'If you're in trouble, just let me know.'

'I'm glad to say that won't be either necessary or possible, since we've no means of communicating,' she said with childish smartness.

'Just call out at the level you've been speaking most of the time now. Hearing you from across the island should be no problem.'

Her bravado died the minute he walked out after that uncappable last word, and Sara sat down glumly at the table. At least she had got rid of him and his do-goodery, however questionable the means, and that was some consolation. The trouble was, she didn't feel consoled. She had gone much too far in what she had said, and in doing so she had only managed to betray herself. Those eyes of his saw right through her, and he played with her like a cat with a mouse, damn him!

The cottage still seemed full of his presence, and after a few moments she went outside, stopping short when she saw that Conrad was still there. He was sitting on the side of the boat, arms folded, legs stretched out in the most relaxed way possible.

'Why are you still here?' she asked abruptly.

'This is the way I see it . . .' he began conversationally. 'You had a shock, on top of whatever weird ideas the megalith conjured up. Shock produces odd reactions. So I'm starting again from scratch. Forget everything—what was said, what was planned, anything you felt.' He gave her a smile that knocked down her pathetic remaining defences. 'Hello, Sara.'

'Hello,' she said slowly, knowing that she was being deliberately subjected to a mega-dose of charm, and half opening her mouth to swallow it, her opposition melting.

'Since I'm here and you're here, and today is, after all, a fête day, I thought we might possibly—if the idea appeals to you—have a picnic somewhere.'

'Did you?' She was looking at him wonderingly, and all sorts of thoughts were going round in her head. He could be so very nice. Why not let herself pretend, just for one day, that they were friends? Surely she was entitled to one day's pleasure to remember out of all this? Could she do it? Forget the magazine, forget Jane Cameron, just spend one happy, uncomplicated day? Take a positive step to balance the scales with something nice? Could she?

'Well?' He was smiling at her, sensing her weakening. 'I was all set for a day off. It seems a pity to forfeit it.'

'And Jane really doesn't mind?'

'Jane isn't unreasonable. She understands quite well why I came back.'

A strange relationship when reason and understanding took precedence over more powerful emotions—but that was their business.

'All right. Let's have a picnic,' she capitulated, marvelling helplessly that she coud make such a complete turn-around.

'Good.' His approval dazzled her. 'I'll wait outside while you get your bathing costume and any bits and pieces you may need. No food. That's all prepared.'

'You were really sure of getting your own way, weren't you?'

'Just a great believer in the power of reason. Come on, now. No slipping back.'

So he had planned it all in advance—and that explained why Jane Cameron had not waved this morning. I don't blame her, Sara thought. I wouldn't understand if he hared off after some other woman. The intensity of her feelings at the imagined prospect surprised her.

She slipped on her yellow bikini, covering up with white cut-off trousers and a yellow baggy shirt. Forget everything, she told herself. This is a day out of time ... anything you want, anything you like ... anything goes, just for this day.

Conrad's mood seemed to match her own. He took her first for a fast, exhilarating ride in *Câline*, out of the Golfe and along the coast, parting the water like a knife, past the Ile de Groix, and letting her take the wheel when there was a clear stretch ahead of them.

The speed, the wind that sent her hair flying like a dark flag in their slipstream, completed Sara's detachment from reality.

'Where are we going?' she shouted over the roar of the engine, turning an exultant face to Conrad as he leaned on the cabin roof beside her.

'Just going!' he shouted back, and they laughed with the sheer joy of living.

He took the wheel again, and she was content to sit back and watch him, thinking how well he matched the sleek, strong beauty of the boat. It was unfair of nature to invest so much in one man ... so much physical beauty, brains, success, artistic talent. Her eyes moved slowly down from his face, over the balanced poise of his body, braced against the surge of the boat. The fingers of one hand were curved lightly round the wheel, lean, sensitive ... the other hand hung close to her. She wanted suddenly to lace her fingers with his, feel them tighten on her own. She forced her eyes up to his face again and saw that he was looking at her, reading something of what she was thinking and amused by it, but he made no attempt to cash in on his advantage.

'No clues as to where we're picnicking,' he said. 'In a

minute I shall want you to close your eyes so that you're completely surprised.'

Câline cut a curving white arc back into the Golfe.

'Now!' Conrad ordered, and Sara obeyed, sitting listening for the changing note of the engine that would indicate they were slowing down. It came at last, then silence as the engine cut out, then the rolling sound of the anchor dropping.

'Keep them shut, still,' Conrad told her. 'I'm going to carry you ashore.' Before she could object, she was swung aloft and transported over uneven ground, sometimes with the sound of his feet splashing through water, until eventually he put her down on soft sand and said, 'Now look.'

They were in a narrow bay, rocks studded with gorse enclosing it on each side, and a sheer cliff rising up behind them. The sand was smooth and fine, the water shading from turquoise in the shallows to dark green, and the sun shining in directly on them, its heat trapped by the protecting walls. Moored to their left, *Câline* scarcely moved, so still was the water.

'It's beautiful. Where are we?' she asked Conrad, who was watching for her reaction.

'On a desert island,' he said seriously. 'Nothing but the sun and the sand and you and me. We're the last people in the world.'

It was ridiculous how that set a shiver of excitement beginning at the base of her spine and creeping up her back.

'But, fortunately, the next-to-the-last people in the world left us a barbecue.' He grinned at her, and went over to a pile of stones near the foot of the cliff. She followed him and saw that he was taking a metal grill from its hiding-place and balancing it between two rocks, carefully matched for height.

'You've been here before!' she accused.

'I'm very prone to shipwreck. There's driftwood in that crevice, if you wouldn't mind handing it over.'

The fire burned up quickly, the smell of the wood tangy and pleasant. 'Now—just time to prepare these,' Conrad said, taking a newspaper-wrapped bundle out of a plastic bag and opening it up on the sand. Small silvery fish, quite complete, lay there with scales glinting all the colours of the rainbow in the sunlight. He handed Sara a knife. 'You cut along here ... open them up, then remove the backbone and any superfluous bits.'

'Must I?' Sara looked apprehensively at the way he was setting about it.

'You'll never survive on a desert island unless you can do this,' he told her firmly. They worked away in concentrated silence on what seemed to Sara like a whole shoal of fish.

'What are they?' she asked, when she could bring herself to speak again, the last fish dealt with.

'Sardines, and if you've never eaten them fresh before, you're about to start living!'

Some time later, a time of delicious smells and sizzlings, of burned and licked fingers, of popping corks from sparkling wine cooled in a shady, watery crevice, Sara lay back on the sand, her limbs glowing golden in the sunshine. In one hand she had an end of a crusty loaf which she was nibbling idly, and in the other a glass, empty for the second—or was it the third?—time. She squirmed into a more comfortable position.

'That, I'd have you know, was the most superb meal of my life!' she said in a very stately way to Conrad. 'You caught them yourself, of course?'

'Naturally. With a bent pin and a piece of string.'

She nodded. 'I guessed as much. How does that thing go? "A Jug of Wine, a Loaf of Bread—and ..."'

'And?' he prompted managing with difficulty not to laugh at her.

'I've forgotten,' she lied, looking at him owlishly, balking at the words she well knew should follow. 'I do believe I'm a little bit sloshed.' She waved the glass, then put it down carefully. 'And you haven't told me where we are.'

'Beneath La Domaine,' he told her, enjoying her surprise.

'Then why haven't I seen this bay before?'

'Because of the overhang. It's absolutely secret.'

'It's absolutely magic!' She wriggled around, trying to get comfortable, until Conrad put a rolled-up towel under her head; then she gave him a drowsy smile and promptly fell asleep.

Sara woke much later to find him propped up on one arm, looking down at her.

Caught at the moment of waking when what is true seems more true, and the striking of attitudes is impossible, she just stared up at him, her wide eyes darkening. The sound of the sea became lost in a stillness that was so intense it seemed to run in her blood.

'Thou ...' he said softly. 'That's the missing word you couldn't remember. "Thou beside me singing in the Wilderness."'

Sara's heart was racing. 'I ... I think I had too much wine,' she said.

'You've had plenty of time to get over it.' His eyes held hers, and all the blue of the unclouded sky seemed to be concentrated in them.

'Don't——' she whispered, pleading against something intangible.

'I'm not doing anything.' He raised his free hand in demonstration, but his eyes were caressing her even as he denied it. 'We were talking about poetry,' he continued softly. 'An academic discussion.'

'No, we weren't . . .' Still she lay there, prisoner of his eyes.

'What, then?' He rested his hand gently on her bare waist and she gave a convulsive little movement at his touch, so that he smiled, knowing his power over her.

'Con——' she murmured, her eyes on the lips that were so near her own. Her breath caught in her throat, and then with a little murmur that held all the longing she could feel rising up in her she slid her arms round his neck, and it was she who closed the gap between them, pulling him against her, feeling his hand move slowly up over her body, as her flesh sprang into exultant life in response.

The world spun away into space, taking with it all her resolution never to give herself easily to any man again. There was nothing but the rough, urgent demand of his lips, the sweet pain of her flesh crushed beneath his, the overwhelming force of their desire. All the things that marked them as a man and woman to whom this could never happen disappeared in the whirling vortex of her mind. They were primeval man and woman, needing each other, wanting each other, meant for each other.

He drew away from her for a second, his eyes burning with the ultimate question, and suddenly Sara's mind jolted back on the rails again. This was Conrad Blake, the man she was here to deceive and to betray. The man who, if he knew her for what she was, would despise her.

Somehow she found the strength to drag herself out from beneath him, to scramble up and sit back on her heels, rapidly adjusting her bikini.

'That got out of hand,' she said breathlessly, avoiding his eyes.

There was stark disbelief in his voice. 'Correct me if I'm wrong, but I was under the impression that you were making at least your fair share of the running.'

'You caught me unawares. I was still half-asleep.'

His derisive laugh brought her eyes to his face to see the scorn written on it. 'You seemed very wide awake indeed to me.'

She got up, scattering sand over him in her hurried scramble.

'There's no point in arguing. It's over now. Let's have a swim.'

'The classic remedy? Nearest thing to a cold shower? I don't believe this!'

She couldn't bear to stand there looking at him any longer, feeling his frustration and anger. She turned and began running over the big flat rocks alongside which *Câline* was anchored.

'Sara!' His voice was sharp with command. 'Sara!' He was coming after her, and his tone scared her. She couldn't struggle with him. If he touched her again she was lost.

She skidded on a mossy rock, regained her balance, looked over her shoulder as she passed the boat. He had almost caught up with her.

Sara hurled herself towards the water in a running dive, only knowing that she had to keep distance between them. He must have moved with the speed of light, because before she broke the surface he cannoned into her in mid-air, sending her over sideways to land with an ungainly, painful splash feet away from where she had intended, the breath quite knocked out of her.

She surfaced, gasping and blinking, pushing wet hair from her eyes.

'Are you all right?' He was swimming towards her, his face anxious.

'Of course I'm not!' she spluttered. 'What was that for?'

A fit of coughing prevented further angry words, and it was all she could do to keep afloat. He touched her then, firm hands on her waist supporting her until the coughing stopped.

'It was the only thing I could do,' he told her. 'You were diving straight for the rocks. You took off like a missile.'

'Couldn't you have warned me?'

'I tried. You weren't disposed to listen.'

'I don't see any rocks.' She trod water, peering down, but unable to see for the disturbance she was creating.

'They're pale—don't show up against the sand. Jane christened them *Les Trompeuses*. It means deceivers.'

'I know what it means!' she said crossly. He had released her now, and they were facing each other. So this was their place, his and Jane's. The thought created a new kind of discomfort. 'Well, thanks for nothing. If you knew the place was dangerous, you could have warned me in advance and saved all that.'

'The trouble is,' he said with heavy meaning, 'we don't always realise just where danger lies, do we?'

Sara swam out away from the beach and its reminders, the earlier easy mood quite gone between them. He followed her at an unfriendly distance, and it wasn't long before she turned back, telling him shortly that after such a winding she didn't feel like going far.

He turned too, passed her, and reached the rocks first, heaving himself up easily and turning to stretch down a hand to help her out.

It was only then that Sara saw the deep scratches scoring his side, and realised that he had saved her from injury at his own expense without saying a word about it in the face of her ungraciousness.

'Oh, Con!' she said, her voice shaking with remorse, and all her peevishness gone in an instant. As she watched, blood that the coldness of the sea had prevented from flowing began to ooze in slow drops from the gashes and run down his glistening body.

'O-o-o-o-h!' She reached out with wet hands to touch him, as though she could stop the bleeding with her fingers. He caught her hands in his and pushed them impatiently aside.

'It's nothing. A couple of scratches. Yet another of the day's minor inconveniences.'

He helped her back to the safety of the sand with cold politeness, and it was help that she needed while she fought to control the tears that threatened.

'You must go back to the house and get those cuts bathed and disinfected,' she told him diffidently.

'Please, there's really no need to fuss,' he said dispassionately. But Sara was already pulling on her clothes and packing away the remains of the picnic. He shrugged and dealt with the ashes of the barbecue and the grill, not bothering to attempt to dissuade her from leaving.

Câline made the short circuit of the island to the landing-stage, the sound of her engine covering the silence between them. Sara refused to go straight back to the cottage, insisting on going up to La Domaine to treat the cuts, and telling him shortly that it was the least she could do.

Once there, she worked with gentle thoroughness, her head bent over so that he couldn't see her face.

It was only gradually that Conrad became aware that

the drops of warm moisture he could feel falling on his skin were not from the pad of cotton wool soaked in disinfectant, but from Sara's eyes.

'Sara!' He put his finger under her chin and raised her face, warmth creeping back into his voice again at last. 'What's all this? Why are you crying? There's absolutely no need.'

'Isn't there?' she choked, the tears coming faster. It was the awful symbolism of the fact that Conrad had been physically hurt through her that was tearing her to pieces. It was a visible representation of the deeper hurt she was destined to do him—the hurt she couldn't bear now to think about. It had been such a short reprieve today while she lived her childish dream of a day out of time, but reality was back now.

'Sara . . .' Heedless of his cuts, he drew her into his arms. 'No, don't pull away.' He held her firmly, and for a precious moment she allowed herself to be held, her face pressed against the rough warmth of his chest while he stroked her hair, comforting her as one would comfort a child.

Why did it have to be you? she cried out within herself, knowing at that moment that he of all men was the one she could grow to care for. The one day out of time she had allowed herself had turned from a consolation into a torment: a torment doubled by Conrad's present tenderness that encouraged the painful flowering of a love that could never be.

'Why are you so afraid of your feelings?' he murmured into her hair.

Because nothing is what it seems to be, she thought wretchedly. Then, knowing she could never explain, she moved away, picking on the one barrier that could be safely spoken about.

'I'm not afraid. I do what you should do. I remember Jane.'

'Jane?' The name seemed to puzzle him, then his face cleared. 'There's nothing there to make you hold back. Really.'

She couldn't understand him. She had seen him, heard him with Jane Cameron. Was he really a man of such easy morals as this? And did he assume her to be the same?

She looked at him, her eyes full of misery. 'Do you really think I'm the sort of person to be a push-over for someone else's man?'

'But——' He stopped, frustration flickering over his face. 'Hell! I could easily set your mind at rest—quite easily. But I must speak to Jane first, damn it!'

'How—set my mind at rest?' The despairing lethargy was giving way now to real anger at his persistence in maintaining he could arrange his cosy little life so that everyone was kept happy. 'Are you trying to tell me that you have the sort of understanding relationship with her that allows each of you the odd lapse, as long as it's not too meaningful?' she asked. 'If so, you can count me out of that sort of set-up. When I get involved with a man again, I want it to be with someone who believes sex has to have a basis in love and loyalty.'

'Do you realise how damned offensive that is?' he asked, dangerously quietly.

'Just think of the facts.' She was riding high now on her trumped-up outrage. 'You make social arrangements that ensure there's only me left on the island. You come back because you're "concerned" about me. When I question your motives, you do all in your power to smarm your way around me. I give you the benefit of the doubt—and look how it ended. You even cash in on this injury you've done yourself.'

'Don't talk such utter rubbish! Do you really think I would go to the length of doing this to myself as some move in a stupid game?' He gestured impatiently to his side.

'Oh, believe me, I know very well to what lengths people will go,' she said dully, brought back to the painful truth of her own purpose again. 'I'm going now. I've a friend coming tomorrow. There are things to do.'

She threw the cotton wool she had been gripping unconsciously in her hand on to the dead ashes in the fireplace, unable to bear looking at Conrad any longer.

Through the kitchen, through the hall, and out of the house she went in a silence that seemed to echo around her. He, at the almost tangible, pulsating heart of that silence, made absolutely no attempt to speak again or to try to stop her.

CHAPTER SEVEN

SARA's night was restless, and she was both glad and sorry that the morning would bring Dave Becker to the island. Having to share the cottage with him would be dreadful, but it would stop any further painful involvement with Conrad, and the undesirable prospect of a protracted stay under the same roof as Dave would mean that somehow she would find the courage to get this business over quickly. The sooner she ruled a line under the Conrad Blake story, put this ill-fated island behind her, and got down to serious work on her book, the better.

After breakfast she prepared a not-very-appetising lunch. There was no point in making Dave too comfortable: he had to be keen on a quick result, too. She put a blanket and pillow ostentatiously on the lumpy settee in the living-room. With someone like him, it was as well to spell out conditions in words of one syllable!

She was going out to the boat when some sixth sense made her aware of being watched. She looked up to see Jane Cameron standing on the path coming from the direction of *Câline*'s mooring-place, looking down at her.

Sara's hackles rose, and she spoke brusquely. 'Yes, I'm here. Where did you expect me to be? Did you have to make it so obvious you were rushing back to check?'

Jane's fair skin coloured slightly. 'As a matter of fact, I had no thought of you in my mind at all when I came this way. It was always my intention to come back this morning. And I'm here because I just happened to want a brisk walk round the island to blow a headache away.'

They looked at each other in mutual hostility.

'I didn't ask Conrad to come back, you know. I didn't even want him to,' Sara said defensively, then went on the attack again. 'And for heaven's sake—why do you keep staring at me like that?'

Jane came on down the path. 'I told you when we first met that I felt I knew you from somewhere. I still have that feeling every time I see you. I have it now.' She threw her head back in sudden resolution. 'Yes—you do worry me, Sara. I admit it. Sooner or later I shall remember whatever it is about you that bugs me so much. I'm never wrong about these things.

'If you've got second sight——' Sara said, knowing how ungracious she was being but too tired, confused and grumpy to care '—I wish you would use it at a distance. You make no secret of the fact that coming face to face with me gives you no pleasure.'

'Can you wonder? You've meant trouble since the first moment you set foot on Les Genêts, in one way or another. You've insinuated yourself into everything—my house, my work, Conrad's house in a big way, his business, his work——'

'You needn't go on,' Sara cut in angrily. 'I shan't be here much longer.' Then the smart of Jane's bluntness stung her into going further. 'So whatever it is between you and Conrad that gives you the jitters so badly need worry you no more.'

She was unprepared for the alarming effect her words had on the older girl. Jane's colour drained away, leaving her face white and her eyes scared.

'What has he told you?' she said, her voice strangled in her throat.

'Nothing,' Sara said, watching her warily. The girl looked as though she could pass out any minute. 'Nothing at all—truly. We had a picnic lunch and a swim—and that was it. You've——' she had been going to say 'nothing to worry about', but sudden awareness that she was crossing the bounds between truth and falsehood made her falter.

Jane looked at her for a moment longer, then without speaking she turned and almost ran off along the path past the cottage, while Sara, faced again with her own distasteful purpose, started up the boat's motor with a savage tug that ought to have broken the starter.

Dave Becker was late.

'Twelve, we said, I think?' Sara greeted him coldly, shifting the big loaf and heavy bag of fruit she had been holding for the past half-hour to the other hand.

'And "hello" to you, too, sweetie!' He was quite unmoved. 'Where is this dump you're hanging out in, then?'

'A boat-ride away.' She eyed the small canvas bag slung over his shoulder with his camera. 'Have you got everything you want? There's no point in getting across there and finding half the stuff you want is still in the boot of your car.'

He patted the bag. 'All present and correct. I travel light. Helps me to take advantage of local offers.' His eyes ran insinuatingly down the length of her, making her feel that her blue and gold striped sun-dress was transparent.

'No local offers on Les Genêts,' she said with clear double meaning. 'You have to shop around on the mainland for anything you want.'

He grinned, and she remembered from previous occasions how totally unsnubbable he was. '*Touché*, Sara, dear. Lead on.'

On the boat, he sat facing her and quizzed her about

Conrad. Finding it even harder to talk about him to this man than she had anticipated, Sara gave him a rough outline of what she had discovered, avoiding his knowing eyes by staring over his shoulder and making a great show of concentrating on the steering.

'Bit downbeat about it, aren't you?' he asked shrewdly when she had finished.

Sara shrugged. 'It's a job. I want it over now. I've been here long enough.'

'What's he like, then?'

She couldn't embark on a description. 'You'll see for yourself.'

'I don't mean appearance. What's he *like*? Sexy— hunky—all the words you girls bandy around? Has he tried to make it with you, for instance? Would the idea appeal? Come on, Sara! Give!'

'Don't try to reduce everything to your level,' she told him coldly. 'I told you—it's a job. We're almost there. You can see the cottage now.'

Successfully diverted, he looked over his shoulder.

'My God! Is that the best you could do?'

'So you'll get on with the work quickly, I take it?' she asked him sweetly.

'Too right, I will.' In the cottage, he looked round with comic despair for the few seconds it took to see everything, then he picked up the pillow and dropped it back on the sofa. 'What's this, then?'

'Your quarters. And don't blame me—blame Fran. This is her idea.'

He walked over to the bedroom and stared in. 'It's a nice, big bed, Sara.'

'And I occupy all of it, so don't waste your time.'

'You're a hard woman . . .' He gave her another lazy, uncomfortable inspection. 'Despite the soft exterior!'

'Oh, shut up, Dave, and come and eat.'

He eyed the charcuterie and salad and uncut bread. 'You really shouldn't have gone to so much trouble,' he said solemnly, then grinned at her, and for a moment she was almost deluded into a faint feeling of liking for him. It didn't last.

In spite of his throw-away manner, Dave Becker seemed to have picked up all the pointers that Sara had not tried too hard to give him.

'Draw me the layout of Blake's place,' he asked her when they had finished eating. He watched her rough sketch take shape. 'Where's the workshop? And does he lock it?'

'Here,' she pointed. 'I don't know if it's locked or not. The window's too high to be any use—and there's a housekeeper you'll have to look out for.'

'Quite a harem he's got there.'

Sara thought of Marthe's sober little figure. 'You won't want any pictures of the housekeeper, that's for sure.'

'So which cottage is the girlfriend's?' Sara showed him, and he nodded. 'Right. Well, no time like the present. We'll have a little walk and see what turns up for the book, shall we?' He got up, stretching.

Every step they took seemed to Sara to diminish the loveliness of the island. She dreaded seeing Conrad again, and if she could have decently got out of going anywhere with Dave she would gladly have done so. Sneaking up on La Domaine in company with somebody else seemed so much worse than when she had been alone—and that had been bad enough.

'Must we run?' Dave called after her, and she stopped impatiently, not realising that she had got so far ahead of him.

Dave wanted to see the cottages first, so they passed the

big house and turned right towards the headland. Dave stopped.

'The sun's in the right position now. Go and see if there's anybody home. Get the girl to the door and I'll take a few shots of her.'

'I can't do that. I'm not on those terms,' Sara protested.

'You're not a social caller, you're a feature-writer— remember? Get on with it.' He gave her a little push, and she found herself walking forward, trying frantically to work out something plausible to say. An anxious glance over her shoulder showed that Dave had drawn back into concealment.

Maybe Jane would not be there, she hoped fervently. She knocked and moved to one side to give Dave the clear shot he needed, marvelling that she could think of such a thing, feeling as nervous as she did. There was only the shortest of waits before the door was opened. Remembering how strangely frightened Jane had been at their earlier meeting, there only seemed one thing to say.

'I'm sorry about this morning,' Sara began awkwardly. 'I was rude and aggressive. I'd had a bad night—and it was nothing to do with you, really.'

Jane looked levelly at her, composed now. 'I didn't exactly pull any punches myself, so let's take it that we each gave as good as we got.' There was a little pause while Sara felt herself again under that close scrutiny. 'As a matter of fact,' the girl went on drily, 'just so that you don't work too hard on the apology—I'm wondering right now what it is you really want.'

That was too close to the mark, and any glib words Sara might have countered with dried up.

'Remember that I apologised . . .' she said, turning away. Apologised for what was past, but also for what was to come. Perhaps when Jane saw the *Spica* article as she most surely would—there was always some 'kind' friend to make sure of these things—she would remember the words and perhaps believe that Sara had not enjoyed what she was doing.

The door closed as she walked away and waited for Dave to come and join her. When he didn't appear, she stopped and looked back. Maybe he had gone to get a picture of the rocks from the headland. He had mentioned that on the way up.

A sudden whinny made Sara spin round, heart in mouth. So there was to be no easy escape. Conrad was coming out of the field on Clouzot. He saw her, inevitably, and instead of turning left he cantered back across the rough ground before La Domaine.

'Were you looking for me?' he asked, his face as smoothly sculpted and expressionless as a statue's.

'No. Just walking round the island.' As always, the sight of him was having that weakening, melting effect on her.

'I thought it hardly likely, after the forthright opinions you expressed yesterday.'

'Which I stand by,' she said with a show of defiance.

'A woman of resolution . . .' He stared at her, then added after a perfectly timed pause, 'However misguided.'

'I think not, but there's no point in talking about it.' Her eyes went to the left side of the denim shirt he was wearing. 'How is your side?'

That was a mistake. For a dangerous second, memory of yesterday flared between them, then was quickly extinguished.

'*That*'s fine.' The emphasis was very slight, but sufficient to imply that much was left over from yesterday that was not at all fine.

'This isn't your usual time for riding, is it?' she hurried on, not wanting to pursue the subject.

'No—but there's a storm coming up. You hadn't noticed?'

She followed his pointing arm and saw that the blue sky was being rapidly veiled in the south-west by ominous clouds. She seized the chance to escape.

'Goodness—I'd better head for home.'

'I thought you were expecting a friend today?'

'Yes. We've got separated.'

'How very careless,' he said with light sarcasm.

Sara shot an anxious look over her shoulder and at the same time Conrad followed the direction of her glance. Together, they saw Dave approaching. Conrad's expression changed as he looked back at her, suddenly tinged with contemptuous accusation.

'When you said "a friend", I assumed a girlfriend.'

'Why should you assume anything?' she countered defiantly.

'Because after yesterday, the idea of your actually inviting male company seems bizarre, to say the least.'

Sara's cheeks were flaming as Dave sauntered up and heightened her colour even more by putting an arm possessively round her shoulders and stroking her neck with his fingers.

'Hi!' he said casually, patting Clouzot's flank and looking up at Conrad with his beady little eyes. 'I take it you're one of the permanent residents?'

'Conrad Blake—Dave Becker.' As she reluctantly introduced them, Sara wanted desperately to knock Dave's arm away, but that would have given the impression that Conrad's taunts were justified.

Conrad reached down to shake hands briefly, his face schooled into a mask of social politeness.

'Good morning. Are you here for the day?'

Dave widened his eyes. 'Oh, heavens, no! A couple of days at least. Maybe longer.'

'Staying on the mainland, are you? The Miramar's pretty good.'

'No. Just squeezing in with Sara here. She's finding the cottage a bit lonely, she tells me, aren't you, love?'

Sara felt to be nearing explosion point with stifled rage.

Conrad studiously avoided looking at her as he answered. 'How sad to be lonely on holiday. Fitting two people into that tiny cottage should make it positively cosy, though.'

'Cosy, indeed,' Dave agreed blandly, playing along with the game.

Sara saw Conrad's knuckles had whitened on the hand that held the reins, confirmation that the surface sociability was indeed just that—no deeper than the skin that was betraying it. Underneath lay dislike of alarming intensity.

'I won't keep you,' he said, speaking directly to her this time. 'I'm sure you have lots to talk about.' He turned to Dave. 'Get her to discuss her philosophy of life some time. Love and loyalty, for instance. She has very amusing views on both.' His heels dug into Clouzot's flanks, and they made off in a thunder of hooves towards the path down to *Câline*'s cove.

'Well, well . . .' Dave began, then, changing from reflection to protest as Sara viciously knocked his arm away, 'Hey! What's that for?'

She directed all the frustration of the two encounters on him.

'Don't ever try mauling me about in public again! Keep your hands to yourself—and don't play games, Dave.'

He registered the angry whiteness of her face, but was

unmoved by it. 'Is that the go-ahead for doing it in private, by any chance?'

'Dave, I swear I'll hit you if you go on in that vein.'

'Just testing a theory, love, that's all.' He gazed thoughtfully after Conrad. 'I always maintain that if you give people something to react against, you find out more about them. Now, there was quite a bit of reacting going on there. You say that you regard this Conrad Blake business as just a job.' He eyed her speculatively. 'I'd say that was pretty debatable, myself. But as far as he's concerned there's no debating about it. The gentleman has decidedly warm feelings towards you. Yes, decidedly.'

'Don't talk such rubbish. We couldn't disapprove of each other more if we tried.'

His head on one side Dave grinned his monkey grin at her. 'What's approval got to do with anything? Since when did a bit of disapproval put the stoppers on a real gut fancy for someone?'

He was too close to the truth, and Sara had to switch his attention away from herself. 'Did you get your picture? I'm not going to Jane Cameron's door again if you didn't.'

'Ah—Jane Cameron ...' Dave's antennae were still picking up and analysing. 'Now there's a lady who has no warm feelings for you at all. I wonder why, Sara? Does she see the same signs as I do between you and the Lone Ranger there, I wonder?'

Sara set off at a spanking pace along the path, and he ran after her.

'All right, stroppy. Pax it is. This is "just a job", like you say. I want to get a few shots of Blake now, if we can. Is it possible to cut across and get above him anywhere? You're the expert on the topography of this place.'

'If we keep on the way we're going he's bound to pass us

soon. He always goes round clockwise and comes back this way.'

'So, if I'm pointing the camera at the scenery, I can get him? OK. Pretty low on interest, but it'll do for starters. Lead on.'

They walked on in silence until they reached the point where the megalith was first visible.

'Now that's something!' Dave enthused. 'If he'd only go up there . . . get his damned horse to rear up against those storm clouds . . . with those giants towering over the pair of them . . .' His voice sharpened. 'Hey! Where is the man, by the way? Shouldn't we have passed him by now?'

'Maybe he changed his mind and turned back the way he came for once.' Sara fervently hoped so. She had no desire to come face to face with Conrad again.

A muffled exclamation made her look round. Dave had wandered over close to the edge of the cliff and he was crouching down now making backward silencing gestures with one hand. Sara went softly over, quite unsuspecting, thinking that nothing more than a vulnerably close seabird's nest had caught his attention.

What she saw, though, almost stopped her breath and froze her to the spot.

Conrad was down there, out at the end of one of the fingers of rock, his hands on his hips, his head thrown back as he breathed in the freshening wind from the sea.

As Sara watched, he raised his arms slowly and rose on his toes, poised to dive. He was naked, and he was beautiful . . . lean, bronzed male perfection. He cut through the air and slid into the restless water with hardly a splash, then reappeared, striking out away from the island with a powerful crawl.

It had been a moment of such irresistible beauty that

Sara had to swallow hard to get rid of the lump in her throat. So powerful an impact had the sight of him made on her that it was only then, too late, that she realised she was not alone and that Dave's camera was in his hands.

'Oh, boy!' he whistled softly. 'I'll never do better than that.'

'You can't!' The cry was torn from her, too late by heaven knew how many silent takes.

'I already have, sweetie.' He was grinning, still looking out after the figure cutting through the choppy waves.

'It's totally unfair.'

'How unfair? Taking a picture of someone who strips off in a public place? It *is* public, isn't it?'

'They won't use it.' Her vehement assertion was wasted and she knew it. *Spica* would love the picture. She could see the caption already ... *Going Wild* ... *Nature Boy* ... whatever corny banality they would come up with.

'What made him do it, do you think?' Dave was going on chattily. 'I mean, he knew we were around, so he must have been half-aware that we could come across him. All of which seems to indicate that we have a pretty relaxed, uninhibited person in our Mr Blake.'

Sara pounded on in ashamed, furious silence. She knew only too well why Conrad had had that irresistible urge to plunge into the Golfe. The encounter with her and Dave had made him feel dirty. Dave made *her* feel dirty, so she understood only too clearly the impulsive tearing off of clothes, the lungs snatching at the wind, and the body crying out for the cold, cleansing touch of the sea.

She passed Clouzot, stamping and tossing his head impatiently, tethered to a bush further along the path. The horse whinnied, but Sara didn't stop.

'I'm going up to the standing stones,' Dave called after her.

'Go where the hell you like—and stay for ever. That would suit me fine!' she shouted back, putting as much distance between them as possible.

The cottage looked sordid, with the remains of lunch left on the table. Sara cleared the dishes into the sink and got rid of the food left-overs. She stuffed the pillow and blanket under the settee, and kicked Dave's bag savagely through into the bedroom while she swept the crumbs from the living-room floor, finding any reminder of his presence unbearable at that moment.

It was growing darker and darker, and there was an ominous rumble of thunder in the distance. She could hardly see what she was supposed to be doing, but didn't want to light the oil lamps and add to the stuffy heat in the cottage.

Between two rolls of thunder, Sara heard the slither and clank of Clouzot's hooves on the path and tensed, shrinking back from the window until Conrad had gone past. He was doing nothing according to routine today. He never came back this way and she was scared.

Justifiably so. He didn't go by, and Sara's heart raced as footsteps—swift, angry footsteps—approached. He walked straight in and stood just inside the door. Even in the shadows he was aware of the colour that flooded into her face, but he didn't—she thanked heaven—know that it came from the memory of the superb body she had seen silhouetted against the sea as the wind whipped up the waves.

'Do I offend your sensitivity?' he asked cuttingly, rapping belatedly with his knuckles on the door. 'I thought this was the place of cosiness and friendship. Do forgive me.'

Sara swallowed. Her legs felt woolly, as though with the aftermath of flu. 'What do you want, Conrad?'

His shirt clung damply to his chest, and his hair was sea-tamed into unfamiliar dark sleekness. But it was his eyes, a frightening blend of hot anger and cold contempt, that drew her own.

'No—it's not a question of my wants, but yours, Sara,' he said, his voice like a lash. 'What do *you* want? Surely not that contemptible little runt I've just seen poking around the megalith? You wanted quality, you told me. Love and loyalty. Surely you can't delude yourself that you'll get either from him?'

Somehow she found a voice. 'You don't know him.'

He snorted with contempt. 'One look's enough. He's trash! And yet you don't shrink away from contact with him, do you? You don't hesitate to welcome him into your house—into your bed, it seems—so why not me? What's the pretence about, Sara?'

'That's a totally unjust accusation!' she said hotly.

'Is it? Is it?' He strode into the bedroom, stared round, then seized Dave's bag, emptying its unmistakably male contents disdainfully on to the bed. 'What about this, then? And this? And this?' He brandished Dave's intimate belongings in her face before flinging them contempt-uously down again.

'Get out of my room!' she shouted, suddenly finding a voice again and rushing towards him, but she came to an abrupt halt as he rounded fiercely on her.

'Your room? *Your* room? Shouldn't that be *our* room? Yours and that creature's? Yours and anybody's, it seems. So why the hell not yours and mine? Where do I fall short of the mass acceptability?'

There was unbearable threat in the way he reached out for her. Sara knew she had to move—to break the tension that was crackling between them. If he let his anger tip him over the edge now, she was sure that he would never forgive himself, and that she would never get over it. But she was rooted to the spot by the sheer animal hypnotism of his blazing eyes. It was Dave who saved her.

'Don't let me interrupt anything.' He spoke with heavy humour, and he was leaning against the doorpost, his eyes sliding greedily from one face to the other. 'If I can just get the clean shirt I brought with me, Sara dear, I'll go and have a shower under that splendid contraption you showed me in the garden, then you two can get on with your little chat. Now ... where did I put my things?'

Conrad strode out of the bedroom and Sara fell back before him into the living-room. He made a grandiose gesture towards the bed, looking murderous.

'You'll find them in the bedroom, I think.' His chest was rising and falling rapidly, and Sara could sense that he was a coiled spring of fury, ready to lash out at the least provocation.

Dave raised his eyebrows and gave a lascivious smile in Sara's direction. 'Of course. Stupid of me. Where else would they be?'

He strolled past Conrad and, just for a second, before her fury erupted, Sara had to concede that it took a kind of courage to pass so close to the menacing figure that towered over him.

Then something snapped in her. She flew at Dave's back.

'Get out! Get out of my room! Stop your rotten act!' She pounded at him, beat on him with her fists so that he stumbled forward on to the bed, and when Conrad grabbed her wrists to stop her, she rounded on him and tore herself away from his grip with superhuman strength, lashing out at him too with equal fury as the Latin blood in her blazed its way through all restraint.

'And you!' she sobbed. 'You with your conclusions and accusations. Who do you think you are? Get out! Get out, both of you. Just leave me alone.'

The sight of their two faces, Dave's rising from the bed, Conrad's close to hers, with the beginnings of awareness of how awful the scene had been spreading over it, was too much to endure. It was she who ran out of the cottage into the stormy darkness, past the bewildered Clouzot, slipping and lurching up the path.

She was a wild creature, and it was the wild place on the hilltop that drew her through the huge drops of rain that were falling, shining silver in the intermittent snick and flash of lightning.

She was half-aware of a voice calling faintly behind her, but the wind tore it away and flung it into the turbulent air. Then there was nothing but darkness, split by fierce arrows of brilliance and the sound of the thunder rolling round the deep purple sky. And there was the pull of the terrifying, sacrificial, ancient place towards which her frightened spirit was compelled.

CHAPTER EIGHT

THE madness that had driven Sara up to the megalith in such conditions had exhausted itself by the time she had reached the circle of stones.

She stood struggling for breath and shivering, half from the primitive fear the place roused in her, half from reaction to the scene she had left behind. What was she going to do now that she had scrambled up here? Stay and frighten herself half to death with wild imaginings? Turn back and creep home to the cottage again like a drowned rat—and a foolish one at that? Neither prospect attracted her.

She had fled to the highest spot on the island in a storm, the spectacular strength of which she had never seen equalled. Lightning forked and sizzled its path across the sky, and in the intensified darkness afterwards, the after-image of the standing stones glowed red before her eyes. The crack of thunder that came almost simultaneously made her whimper and cover her ears instinctively, looking frantically round for shelter. Another flash showed her the dark entrace to the burial chamber in the centre of the stones, and her shivering intensified. Not there—no matter how fierce the storm.

She forced herself to reason. The wind was coming strongly from the south-west, driving the rain slanting before it. In the next flash, she picked out the standing stone whose angle offered most shelter, and waited for another blinding second of light to dart over to it and lean against the modicum of protection it offered.

As her breathing quietened, Sara was almost against her will caught up in the fascination of the tableau nature was presenting, the solidity of the stone against her back helping to foster a small sense of security.

The sight of the Golfe, now that she could allow herself to be distracted from her own immediate predicament, was spectacular. The other islands had disappeared into the darkening steely-grey and white-lashed turbulence, and when the squalls of rain eased off periodically, the faint flashing of the lighthouse was a telling reminder of man's feebleness in the face of angry elements.

It was while her ears were ringing from the next thunderclap that she heard her name, the call eerily disembodied in the echoing darkness and the voice thin on the howling of the wind.

Sara craned fearfully to one side to look round the sheltering stone, and gasped as the next lightning flash showed her what appeared to be a figure on the table stone of the burial chamber, glistening with rain, tense and watchful.

Unbelievably, her frightened cry was heard and when the figure moved she saw that it was only an optical illusion. He was at the other side of the stone circle, and the uneven ground level had seemed to project him on to the table stone.

He called her name again and came leaping across to her, no apparition, but Conrad: warm, solid, and very much of the present.

'You crazy idiot! Are you out of your mind?' He grabbed her by the arms and shook her to emphasise the words.

'Let go of me—and leave me alone!' Her voice shook as she shrank back against the stone.

'Do you realise how utterly irresponsible that was?' he went on angrily. 'I'd no idea which direction you'd taken. I tried *Câline*, La Domaine—everywhere.' His face was running with water, as was her own. Drops of rain slid from his eyelashes while he looked down at her.

'Nobody asked you to follow me. I don't want you here. And I'm not going back down there until I'm good and ready!' She let herself slide down until she was sitting on the wet grass, her arms wrapped round her knees, stubborn and stupid and soaked to the skin.

He saw her involuntary start at the sudden crash of thunder.

'Well, you don't look to be enjoying it much!' he shouted over the prolonged, dying rumble.

'I don't like storms.' She threw her head back and glared up at him. 'But there are other things I like less—and the sort of thing you were implying about me back there in the cottage comes pretty high on the list. So do grown men who brawl like randy tomcats.'

He stepped closer and crouched down beside her.

'You have an elegant turn of phrase, lady.' Lightning flashed and held long enough for her to see him clearly.

A squall of wind blew a fiercer sheet of rain over them. 'Hell!' He slicked back his soaking hair. 'This is no place to make conversation. Come on.'

He seized her arm and hauled her to her feet, ignoring her protests. When she realised that he was forcing her towards the burial chamber, Sara's struggles intensified.

'I'm not going in there!'

'Yes, you are. At least it's dry.' Thunder crashed around them again. 'And you can hear what I'm saying with a bit of luck!' he shouted in her ear.

'I don't want to listen to you. I've heard enough of your opinions.'

'Look——' He spun her round with another angry shake, holding her so that she was forced to face him. 'I

apologise for what I said back at the cottage. I didn't believe
it even when I said it.' His next words spoiled that
sentiment. 'Nobody could fancy that creep. And I certainly
don't believe that you do. I was rude—OK? I was offensive.
I behaved like a randy tomcat. I'm sorry. Is that enough?
Now will you get in there?' He gave her another push.
'Sara—it's a space. A dry, empty space. That's all. I'm with
you. There's nothing to worry about.'

As he was speaking he was guiding her down the short
slope and under the table stone into the chamber. 'Mind
your head,' he said with calm practicality, drawing her
attention away from the imaginary to the real. 'Now turn
round. You can sit down. There's a widish ledge facing the
way we came in. Got it? And in a minute, when your eyes
have adjusted, you'll see that the entrance looks quite light.'

His voice, which had been half drowned by the noise of
the storm outside, was strong and comforting now.
Surprisingly, Sara felt herself growing calm, reassured. He
seemed to have filled this place, which up to now she had
only associated with death, with his warmth and life.

That's how it's going to be for some woman with him, she
thought with a pang of sudden regret. Fears dissipated,
darkness dispelled, everything made easy. Lucky, lucky
Jane . . . if she was that woman.

'All right now?' his voice asked in the darkness.

She slid away from him to the end of the cold stone ledge.
'More or less.'

'Don't worry—I'm not going to touch you,' he said
smoothly. 'I only want to talk to you. And by "talk", I mean
unburden you of some of the crazy ideas you seem to have
in your head. First of all, about Jane.'

'My thoughts about Jane aren't crazy,' she interjected
adamantly. 'And you're not going to change them.'

'Will you *listen*?' he said impatiently. 'Half the awkwardness between you and me seems to stem from your conception of where Jane fits into the scheme of things. Right?'

'Certainly.' Sara said stiffly.

'You think that she's important to me, and that I let her down by anything remotely approaching friendship with any other woman?'

'Friendship!' Sara's voice was scornful. 'That's a bit of a stretch of the imagination, isn't it?'

'So how does it affect your thinking——' he went on, ignoring her interruption, 'if I tell you that Jane is not my girlfiend, not my fiancée, not even a passing romantic interest for me, and never will be. She's my sister.'

There was a stunned silence. Then, 'Your sister?' Sara said disbelievingly.

'Stepsister, to be precise. Different mothers, the same father.'

'Then——' she paused, trying to make sense of it. 'Why the mystery? I don't understand.'

'You will, when I've told you quite a long story. Willing to listen?'

'Yes ... Yes, I am!' The storm was, if not forgotten, firmly relegated to second place.

'Perhaps the secrecy will be more understandable if I tell you that for thirty-two of my thirty-three years I hadn't the faintest idea of Jane's existence. My mother, I have been assured, right up to the end of her own life, five years ago, knew nothing of it either. So you see, secrecy has featured quite largely all along.'

'Do you mean that your father had a prior marriage that he never told either of you about for some reason?'

'Jane is twenty-nine,' he said with telling dryness.

'Twenty—oh, I see.' She broke off. Born four years after

Conrad, while his father and mother were well and truly married.

'I wonder if you do, fully. Not yet, I think. You see—my parents were, to me, a completely happy, united couple. There were no unpleasantnesses, no quarrels, no poisonous air of suspicion. They had the sort of marriage I always, at the back of my mind, even at the height of my wild-oats period, thought I would one day embark on myself. I went on believing this right up to the death of my father last year.'

'He never told you?' Sara strained to see his face in the darkness but she could only make out the glitter of his eyes, veiled now as she watched by the slow closing of his lids as though to shut out painful memories.

'No, never. I had to find it out from his papers when he died. Can you imagine that? I had lost a father whom I loved very much ... but I found that, in a way, I had lost someone I'd never know. And I'd also lost my whole life. Everything seemed a sham, suddenly. Everything had to be questioned, doubted ... It was a bad time. Very bad. It shook my entire world.'

Sara remembered the Conrad she had seen in the newsclip of that time. She had found the change in his outward assurance hard to understand then. Now she knew why he had seemed such a devastated man. She swallowed to clear the lump that had suddenly grown in her throat.

'Did he leave you an explanation, then? Did he tell you why? What had happened?' she asked huskily.

'No. I had to find out all that from Jane's mother. All I got from my father's papers was the bare information that a sister existed whom he had been supporting for almost thirty years. There was just a brief note saying he had kept quiet about Jane for my mother's sake and, by the time she'd died, the secret had become so much a way of life for him that he couldn't face the inevitable publicity if he revealed it. He added a postscript saying that Jane, unlike me, had always been aware of my existence.'

'And did that help when you eventually met?'

'Not really. In a way it seemed to separate us even more. She had been entrusted with knowledge and I hadn't. On the other hand, I had been cherished, protected from reality, publicly acknowledged as my father's child. She had been hidden away, unacknowledged. There was a lot of stress on both of us.'

'Is that why you brought her to Les Genêts? To give you time to get to know each other?'

'Yes. And, in a sense, I had to get to know my father, too. That was strange ... difficult to accept. Margaret, Jane's mother, came along for a while at first. She's a good woman—very independent, but very loyal. She told me everything. They met at an art exhibition in Edinburgh. Strange ... I never knew my father was interested in art, or anything creative for that matter, apart from building up Blake Enterprises. He seemed to keep that side of him for the time he spent with Margaret and Jane. It's true it wouldn't have interested my mother at all, darling though she was. But to go back to the meeting: someone took him along, and Margaret was there. She'd modelled for several of the portraits on show, and she was introduced to him, and they talked. It was a difficult time for my mother and him, apparently, through which I lived with a child's blissful unawareness.'

'How old were you then?'

'Three, or thereabouts. My mother and I used to go abroad on business trips with him. He liked us to do that always before I reached school age. What passed completely over my head was the fact that she was seven months pregnant with the child who would have been my legitimate brother or sister. Things went wrong unexpectedly and the medical help was inadequate. She lost the child, and worse—she was told that there could be no more. You can imagine the circumstances. My mother, desperately unhappy, maybe feeling a kind of twisted resentment that it was through Dad's business that her hopes were lost. My father guilty about the part he had so innocently played in the tragedy. No doubt their personal life had its problems. Margaret helped him through. She says she was never deluded that she was anything more than a willing consolation. Her pregnancy was a shock to both of them. One of the tricks nature plays to show her supremacy, I suppose. Neither of them thought of terminating it, though. From then on my father saw them fairly frequently and Margaret says she always thought of him as her best friend. He was always going away on business, and the flights to Edinburgh were easily lost among the rest, I presume.'

'And of course, he couldn't possibly let his wife know that another woman had borne his child . . .' Sara said with poignant understanding of the situation. 'The child she would so much love to have had . . .'

'It was out of the question. Somehow he managed to care for both families. I know that he loved my mother and protected her to the best of his ability. In the same way, he protected Margaret and Jane. His will ensured that they would in no way want for anything in their lifetime.'

'So your life wasn't really a sham at all, was it?' she questioned gently. 'It was all done for love, it seems to me. For love or the temporary lack of it. Don't you see that?'

'Yes, in time I came to realise it, but it took the breathing-space I've had here to get to that stage. I think it would never have come about at all if I'd had the eyes of the world on me . . . and I'm sure Jane and I would never have managed to work through to the sort of relationship we have now if we'd had the world breathing down our necks.'

Sara nodded in the darkness. 'I can appreciate that. It's quite a story . . .'

Story. Her innocent use of the word cut through her spellbound fascination with Conrad's account. Oh, how Fran would love this one, she thought with sudden bitterness. How she would lick her lips! She had wanted something sensational to spark up the series. Well, here it was: all the ingredients of a Grade One *Spica* revelation.

If I wrote this up, Sara thought, I'd never look back. My reputation would be made in far bigger fields than *Spica*. No . . . and I'd never *dare* look back, she told herself contemptuously, because I wouldn't want to see what the uncaring, greedy touch of the Press could do to two lives that had touched mine.

It was at that moment that she knew her decision to leave *Spica* couldn't wait. She had to leave now, before this story was written.

She realised, with a sudden wild leap of the heart, that Conrad had moved closer to her. She could feel the length of his thigh against hers, his hands, with compelling firmness, taking her shoulders, turning her towards him. The whole atmosphere between them changed and pulsed into vibrant, dangerous life. The time for explaining was over, the mood had undergone a metamorphosis into something that set her skin creeping with half-fearful, half-excited anticipation.

'So, Sara . . .' She heard the alteration in his voice, in the new, throaty sound of it, the catch that followed her name. 'So there's nothing between us, is there? No barrier to make either of us deny the feelings we both know we have.'

Help me . . . She made a silent appeal to whatever spirits lingered in the place, to whatever strength there was in her own will to resist the tide of emotion that was threatening to sweep her into unthinking response.

Her hands spread against his chest, feeling the strong, aroused beat of his heart, wanting to slide round the back of him and pull him into her arms, but managing—*just* managing—to remain braced against him, gently holding him at a distance.

'But you can't leave your story there——' she said breathlessly, snatching desperately at the last words she had spoken. 'You haven't finished. You're still here on the island, living in a sort of limbo. That can't go on. What's going to happen to you?'

'Still resistance?' he reproached, but not, she was thankful, forcing her.

'I *care*,' she emphasised. 'I know you now. You've shown me your beautiful work. You've just told me how you feel. I don't want to think that you'll go back to being swallowed up in Blake Enterprises.'

'Not one hundred per cent, as before. I shall go on being involved, but at least now I know what I'm going to do with the profits. It's simple. I'm going to fund Art Galleries and the talent that can supply them. I'm going to buy time for other people to find the satisfaction I have now. There'll be a point to what I'm doing, don't you see? The Blake Enterprises money will be doing something worth while at last, not just piling up.'

'But that's wonderful!' she exclaimed, delighted into near forgetfulness again. 'Perfect!'

'Wouldn't it be?' he said significantly. 'Wouldn't it just be . . . if I had someone to share my enthusiasm?' His voice was demanding again, his hands urgent, and danger was electric in the air. But it was a danger that drew her with the same deadly fascination as the living flame draws the moth.

Sara cast a desperate look round, and saw that the sky

through the entrance was lighter and the canopy of cloud was parting here and there, with faint stars appearing.

'It's over! We can get out of here!'

She sprang thankfully to her feet, but he kept his iron grip on one of her hands and when they were out in the open again he forced her to stop and face him again.

'So you're still refusing to grow up, Sara? Is that it?'

The hardening of his voice and the scorn in the words cut into her emotional tension and confusion, stinging an equally hurtful response from her.

'Grow up into what? One of your production-line girlfriends? There for a moment, then moved on to make room for the next? Don't try to steamroller me into gratifying a sudden whim, Conrad. I've been there before, remember? I'm streetwise to those tactics.'

His grip slackened, and she thought he was letting her go, but it was only a move towards pulling her savagely into his arms, his mouth hard on hers, his arms crushing her against him. For a second she was rigid with shock, then, against her will, pleasure welled up in her, softening her limbs, her body, her lips against his so that she clung to his kiss, utterly captive to the desire she had so vehemently denied.

For an eternity, all the complications that surrounded them ceased to exist and they were two people bound by a force strong as life itself, borne on a tidal wave of passion that set the stars whirling in their courses.

When at last he drew away she opened her eyes, to see his expression in a last distant flash of lightning ... triumphant, tenderly mocking, every inch the dominant male.

'Streetwise, Sara?' he said softly, teasingly, then he was raining kisses on her face, her wet hair, her eyes, and her senses were swimming again, betraying her.

'No!' The cry was torn painfully from her against his

lips, startling him after her helpless passivity. 'No . . .' she repeated, more steadily, her will-power strengthening. 'There's something I have to settle—first.'

He pounced on the word. 'First? So you see some kind of future in which I play a part?'

She stared at him hungrily, knowing that she would be unable to deny herself some flowering, however brief, of the passion she was struggling to control. She would free herself of *Spica*'s bonds, then she would tell him who she really was and what she had been sent to do. She would put herself at his mercy . . . test what he claimed he felt for her, and find the truth of it.

No . . . Thoughts were whirling through her mind at the speed of light. No, I can't bear that risk! First I'll let him make love to me. Then, if what I tell him is unacceptable to him—and her heart thudded and missed a beat at the prospect she was so afraid of—then I shall have something to remember: a night, an hour, whatever it is, to feed on for the rest of my life.

'Well—do you?' he pressed.

'I can see as far ahead as tomorrow night,' she said, flooded with sudden calm. 'Dave will be gone by then. I'll see to it. I—I shall be alone in the cottage.'

She had done it. Offered herself to him in a way that, even as she spoke, she marvelled at.

'And I promise you,' she went on, 'that he means nothing to me. He's a colleague who found out where I was staying and inflicted himself on me. I despise him.'

Conrad lay his fingers on her lips.

'You don't have to say all that. I believe you. Tomorrow night we'll talk—seriously. No reservations. No holding back.'

Sara nodded slowly, her eyes on his in the faint light of moon and stars. An involuntary shiver ran through her.

'You must go and get out of those wet things,' he said, beginning to lead her down the slope. Still the sense of peace persisted in her. The scents of the island were heavy after the rain, making the surrounding darkness voluptuous and velvety with richness.

'I shan't see you until the evening,' he said. 'I have to fly to London for a meeting, but I'll be back. We'll picnic on the beach—it's always fine after a storm like this.'

'Yesterday's beach?' she asked, her limbs melting with languorous warmth as she remembered.

He tightened his fingers on hers. 'No. It will have to be yours. The tide's wrong for the La Domaine beach. We couldn't get the boat round. I want Jane to be there—we can wait, can't we?—so that you can meet her without all the undercurrents that have been there. But afterwards . . . just you and me.' His voice was full of firm promise.

At the cottage, he glanced at the light showing through the part-open shutters. 'You're not scared to go in?'

'Not at all.'

He kissed her once more on the forehead, as though he too felt the peace that filled her. 'Tomorrow,' he said softly.

'Tomorrow.'

Sara watched him go off into the darkness, then turned to the cottage door and the uninviting prospect of what lay beyond it. She sighed. Before tomorrow came tonight and the resolving of the problem of Dave and his pictures, because he couldn't be allowed to leave the island with those.

He was sitting at the table, doing nothing, and apparently just waiting for her to come in. He had lit the oil lamp and in its glow Sara saw that his face bore a smug, self-satisfied smirk. All the dislike she felt for him and what he stood for hardened her voice and made her say exactly what she felt.

'I want you out of here first thing tomorrow. It would be this very night if I felt I could cope with taking the boat across in the dark.'

'Fine by me. All I need still is to get into that studio. I'll be off and gladly with everything I want and more in the can.' He was fiddling idly with the strap of the camera as he spoke, still smiling and looking at her in a way that made her feel uneasy. She had spoken hastily and that wasn't wise. She needed to take things very, very carefully.

'Dave . . . I sounded bitchy, I know. But this place really is too small. You saw what impression it gives other people, too, didn't you?'

'I did.' He slanted a foxy look up at her. 'And we don't want certain people *in particular* getting the wrong impression, do we?'

'I don't want anyone running away with the wrong idea about my morals,' she said sharply, and he laughed outright at that.

'Come off it, Sara. After what went on up there just now, you're not going to fool me.' He tipped his chair back, watching her closely. 'Kinky types you go in for, I must say. He certainly chose a very way-out spot to have his wicked way with you.'

Sara's heart skipped a beat then started to thump and race.

'You were up there?'

'You bet I was! Always follow the main contender—that's what I was taught—and it pays dividends.'

'You were listening? Eavesdropping?' She could hear panic in her own voice. This was terrible. If Dave had got wind of what she had just been told by Conrad, there would be no stopping him.

'Unfortunately not.' She breathed again. 'Though I'm sure it would have been very educational,' he went on mockingly. 'I had to toss up between sight and sound. I wanted a picture, and if I'd come close enough to hear I wouldn't have got what's in the box.' He tapped the camera with a smug grin. 'Don't expect you did much talking, anyway.'

'Picture, you say? In the dark?'

'Of course you were too busy to notice at the time, but not all the lightning was quite what it seemed. Ever heard of flash, Sara? You can do wonderful things in the dark with it, and on a night like this one's been the subjects never even notice, bless 'em. In here——' he tapped the camera, '—I've got another hot little number featuring Nature Boy Blake and friend.' He licked his lips suggestively. 'Friend with a lot of curves and a very clinging dress. Very clinging nature, too. You were closer to him than a second skin, sweetie. Nice!'

Sara forced herself to show the minimum of reaction, her voice steady and calm. 'Now that one you just can't use, Dave. You weren't assigned to get pictures of me.'

'By the time I've finished with it, it'll be Woman with a capital W, not one recognisable woman, delectable though she may be.'

'That's good news.' Her voice was still even, though she wanted to kill him.

'Black and white ... very shadowy,' he mused. 'Just the odd highlight on the curve of a hip, the line of a thigh ... And the focus on what the flash really showed up to perfection: the look on his face. Sara, my love, he looked as though he'd got a ten-course feast of the gods right there in front of him. Magic!'

'Glad I was of service,' she said with forced smoothness. 'And speaking of feasts, we'd better think of food ourselves.' That gave her a chance to hide her feelings in movement. Dave sat there, watching her, not offering to help,

continuing with his half-sniping, half-self-praising mono-
logue while she thought savagely of how much she would
like to choke him.

She switched off mentally from what he was saying, but
she was very aware of where he was putting his camera. It
was down beside his bag, just under the settee. Tonight she
would have to make sure somehow that the film in it was
dealt with—but in such a way that Dave wouldn't know
until it was too late. If he found out that she had damaged it
or taken it, he'd only stay on and get more pictures. So
tonight Dave Becker was going to have to sleep very
soundly indeed. She toyed with the idea of offering her
comfortable bed and taking the settee herself, but that
would be so out of tune with the nature of their relationship
that he would be bound to smell a rat at once. And if he took
the camera in there with him, there would be no desirable
way to explain why she was creeping into his room in the
night if she happened to disturb him. No, there must be
some other way.

'I think we'll have this tonight—just to show there are no
hard feelings,' she said brightly, getting out the wine and
brandy she had intended for the softening-up of Conrad.
What a long time ago that seemed! A few short days . . . but
a long, long personal journey.

Dave's eyes brightened and he showed signs of life.

'Got a corkscrew? We could get going on that plonk
while you're busy. What is it you're making?' He looked
over her shoulder, sniffing appreciatively.

'Paella. Mostly tinned stuff, of necessity, but it should be
all right, I think. And there's a treat for dessert, too.' The
meringues and wild strawberries joined the sacrifice.

It was not at all difficult to make sure that most of the
wine went Dave's way. At the end of the meal, Sara
pretended to have run out of coffee, and gave him two

brandies—large ones—instead. After that, he was very mellow, very sleepy, and very prone to try a last attempt at sharing her bed.

She managed to dissuade him, hiding her distaste, and after the sketchiest of tidying up in the kitchen, she shut herself away in the bedroom.

She heard him blundering about clumsily for a short while, then there was a string of complaints as he tried to settle himself on the settee.

Sara undressed. If by some awful chance she roused him in the course of her attempt to get the camera, then she must at least look as though she had been to bed. She could always make the excuse of needing a drink or a trip up the garden.

'Sara?' a sleepy voice called. 'You're a hard, hard woman.'

'And you're a very trying man!' she punned. He guffawed, then there was silence.

Sara sat in the darkness, having put her lamp out, waiting until the rise and fall of Dave's breathing reached snoring proportions. Then, heart in mouth, she carefully began to open her door. Did it creak? Why hadn't she thought to notice? She held her breath. No. So far, so good.

Her bare feet were silent as she moved across the floor. The open shutters allowed enough light for her to see the camera case. The buckle tinkled on the stone floor as she moved it, making her heart thud dangerously, but Dave slept on.

Back in her room there was another bad moment when she scraped a match on the emery, the rasping sound magnified by her fear into something tremendous. Then there was the 'phutt' of the flame on the lamp, and the click of the camera case as it sprang open to her fingers' pressure. But still Dave's breathing reassured her.

She part-closed the case again, to check which number was showing in the little window, then took out the film. She turned the lamp up to full brightness, and carefully unwound the film and held it close to the glow. She was an amateur in such matters, but light harmed film, and what was there would go. Anything further taken would be equally doomed, she was sure.

Which of the tiny frames held Conrad? she wondered, remembering the beauty of that special moment. It seemed wicked to destroy it ... but not as wicked as the use that would be made of it if she allowed its continued existence.

The film carefully re-rolled and put back at the appropriate number, Sara replaced the camera and silently shut herself in her room again.

When she was at last in bed she heaved a trembling sigh of pent-up relief. Now she could sleep. Now she could begin to believe that she would work it out.

CHAPTER NINE

IN SPITE of all he had had to drink, Dave was moving around early next morning. Jolted into wakefulness by the noise he was making, Sara groped sleepily for her watch and saw that it was only six o'clock. She got out of bed, pulled on her kimono and gave a discreet tap and pause before opening her bedroom door.

'Dave—what are you up to?' He was already dressed and busy with a battery shaver.

'You wouldn't ask if you'd spent the night on that thing.' He nodded graphically at the settee. 'I'm off up to the house in a minute. I'm going to get shots of those carvings while the coast's clear.'

'But how do you know it will be?' she asked nervously.

'Because Blake's on his way out somewhere. I saw the boat go half an hour ago, at least, while I was trying to get the creases out of my legs. If you hadn't been sleeping so well in your comfortable bed you'd have heard him, too. That boat of his has certainly got some engine!'

Sara was distinctly uneasy. 'But what if his workshop's locked? He can hardly have bothered going out there to open it up so early in the day.'

Dave gave a derisory laugh. 'I've yet to encounter the lock that beats me. Want to come and act as look-out?' He saw her expression. 'OK. Forget it. Stay purer than the driven snow to the end, if that's the way you want it. Just get the coffee going, eh, love? See you soon.' He slung his camera over his shoulder and let himself out.

Sara started on last night's washing up—any job to syphon off some of the nervous tension she felt. Let him get in and out without being seen, she prayed fervently. Don't let anything go wrong now, please! Maybe Jane had been roused by the sound of *Câline* . . . Maybe Marthe had gone over early to get breakfast before Conrad left . . . Maybe— *Stop it!* she told herself firmly.

She put coffee on to percolate and went out to have a shower. Conrad had been right about the storm clearing. The sky was a deep, dense blue and looked incapable of changing.

She was dressed and the coffee was ready by the time Dave came back.

'A doddle!' he said, blissfully unaware of how the word fell like magic on her ears. He sat at the table and hacked a chunk off yesterday's bread, which had gone in the way of French bread from sublime to regrettable. 'The door was locked, but it was an easy one. I got the tern or whatever it was that you told me about. Pretty special, as you said. That guy has more than his share of talent.' The admiration in his voice was genuine. 'And there was something else started—an otter, I think. Still rough, but you could tell it was going to be good.'

Sara remembered the enthusiastic, sensitive keenness of Conrad's fingers as he'd handled the wood whose destined shape he could so clearly see, and a wave of love flooded through her. She brought herself back to Dave and the present with difficulty.

'So you're satisfied now?'

'Fully. And you can ship me over whenever you like, sweetie.' He threw the bread down in disgust. 'Stuff this! I'll get a decent breakfast over there before I set off for England, home and sprung mattresses.'

The sea was like a millpond again, all last night's violence spent. Sara felt so pleased to be seeing the back of Dave that she went to the length of sharing his coffee and croissants at the Café de la Marine so that she could give herself the added joy of actually seeing him drive away. He was chirpy to the last.

'No good offering you that lift,' he said as he started up the engine. 'Too much research still to do, eh, sweetheart? *Ciao!*'

Sara felt a great slackening of tension as she watched the car grow smaller, bearing its still-undiscovered damaged film. So far so good. Now for Fran and *Spica.*

It was cowardly to use the office answerphone for a resignation, she supposed, but she intended there to be no argument about it. The row of kiosks near the post office was empty and Sara shut herself in the middle one and arranged a supply of francs on the ledge, then stood for a while, thinking out what she must say. In the end it took three separate diallings, since the space for leaving a message was nowhere near long enough to get everything in. One call to say there was not going to be any Conrad Blake story and convey her distaste for *Spica's* policies; a second to say that obviously she was resigning as of now, and apologise for leaving them in the lurch; a third to add that of course she understood that she was forfeiting all her rights, both financial and testimonial, by behaving as she was.

When Sara let herself out of the box she felt lighter than she had done for months. The market traders watched her pass, a dark, glowing girl walking on air. 'Some lucky man ...' they murmured to each other, but she was unaware of the stir of nostalgia for lost youth that spread in her wake. She sang all the way back to the island, not caring who heard her, only knowing that it was wonderful to have *Spica* out of her life. She was free to be herself, listen to herself and not *Spica*'s earpiece, give herself, if she chose, for no other reason than that she wanted to with all her heart.

Tonight ... The word rang like a chime of bells in her mind, flowed like cognac in her veins. Wonderful tonight! And if a small warning voice at the back of it all queried, 'And tomorrow?' she stifled it.

Cutting herself off from *Spica* seemed to unblock all the channels of her mind. Back at the cottage she found herself brimming with ideas for the book she had hardly thought about since Tessa had told her it was approved. She took her thick pad and pen out to the overgrown garden behind the cottage and wrote and wrote: her hero Conrad, her heroine herself, her own love leaping from the page. She forgot lunch, forgot tea, forgot everything until the shadow of the house falling across the page told her how far the day was spent.

With a cry of dismay she flew indoors. Six o'clock! Whatever had she been thinking of? And she must be lovely for tonight. A late picnic, Conrad had said. How late was late? It had better be late enough!

She showered again and put on a bikini she hadn't yet worn—royal blue, with a matching blue and white sarong skirt. Each time she looked in the mirror it was as though a new person looked back at her with dark, dancing eyes, smiling, eager. She brushed her hair until it shone with a blue-black gleam that was almost oriental, then knotted the sidepieces on the crown of her head, tucking in a white wild rose from the bank behind the cottage as a frivolous afterthought.

'You're mad!' she told her reflection, and the happy

stranger smiled back at her and mouthed, 'I don't care!' with soft, eager lips.

She was just ready when she heard voices, one of them Conrad's, and excitement fizzed up in her like champagne bubbles. It was as though she was going to met him for the very first time as she stepped out on to the beach.

Clouzot was there with two baskets strapped to his back, and Conrad and Jane were unloading a hamper and boxes and rugs. Conrad looked up and saw her, and she felt the caress of his eyes move slowly over her, coming back to hold hers with such warmth and promise that she felt herself colouring like a schoolgirl, though the flutter of desire that the sight of him awoke in her was an all-too-womanly reaction.

'I haven't prepared any food . . .' she said with sudden realisation as he came towards her, though food was the furthest thing from her mind.

'Don't worry.' Conrad's eyes glinted as he lowered his voice, his hands sliding possessively over the golden satin of her shoulders. 'I shall just eat you, instead. You look . . . absolutely *à point, mademoiselle*.'

Jane, coming slowly over to join them, was still hesitant in manner.

'Meet my sister!' Conrad drew her forward with an affectionate glance.

'I hope you don't mind that I know,' Sara said diffidently.

The girl shrugged. 'Conrad thought it was time to tell you, so . . .' She looked as though she had not been so sure herself, and Sara noticed that she had not given her own opinion, only Conrad's.

'It's a wonderful story. Too wonderful to be a total

secret.' She reached out impulsively and touched Jane's hand.

'It's certainly not for general distribution,' Jane said quickly, adding, 'But, of course, you realise that.' The warning was clear: watch your step—and the ice had definitely not melted, it seemed.

'Of course,' she said reassuringly, before turning to Conrad again. 'What can I do?'

'You can gather as much driftwood as possible while the light's still good.' He was crouching down, stacking sticks in a little pyramid. 'I've brought enough to start the bonfire, but we need more to keep it going.'

'I'll come with you.' The quiet offer from Jane seemed like an olive branch, and Sara accepted it as such with a smile of thanks.

When they came back, arms full of bleached, twisted wood, the fire was blazing well and there were candles placed around on the rocks to form a glittering circle of light, each flame protected by a clip-on glass shield.

Sara dropped her load of wood and stood, hands on hips, laughing.

'Oh, my! When you picnic, Mr Blake, you certainly do it in style.'

'I have a well developed sense of occasion,' he said, with a look that set a tingling running up her spine and made the breath catch in her throat.

Jane had thawed out during the wood-gathering.

'Come and sit down,' she told Sara, making herself comfortable on one of the rugs. 'There's no point in unpacking the food until we're absolutely ready. Tell me what you've been doing today, Sara.'

Sara sat hugging her knees. 'Working, would you believe? Inspiration struck when I got back from the mainland, and I've actually been scribbling almost non-stop ever since. If only I'd had my typewriter here I'd have romped away.' She spread out her fingers and mock-typed a few words in the air.

When she glanced at Jane, it was to find her motionless, staring most disconcertingly, as though at a ghost.

'Didn't you know about my writing?' Sara asked, a little uncomfortably.

'Yes, I did ...' Jane said slowly, and there was an alertness about her now, a kind of peculiar awareness spreading over her face, but of what? 'Con told me. But I hadn't thought about it until now.' She gave herself a little shake as though to wake herself up. 'Tell me about it. What do you write?'

She listened with surface attentiveness while Sara talked of the precious first encouragement she had received, and made all the right appreciative noises, but it was as though all the time her mind was somewhere else.

Her distracted air vanished when Conrad began unpacking the delights Marthe had prepared. There were little pots of lobster in a delicious cream sauce, home-made paté and freshly baked bread, boxes of different salads, a flan like an artist's palette, and a basket of glowing peaches, apricots and purple grapes with the bloom still on them. Bottles of the delicious local wine from Marthe's family's vineyard were already cooling in the sea.

As the meal progressed, Jane seemed more animated than she had ever been, and the atmosphere grew effervescent as the fire glowed red and the sky rewarded them with a spectacular sunset that spread a kaleidoscope of colours across the horizon. The moon was high and silver in the sky when Conrad stood and brushed the sand from his legs, the firelight flickering on his bronzed skin, turning him into a figure of pagan splendour.

'Who's going to swim up the path of the moon? Jane, I don't suppose I can tempt you?'

Jane stretched lazily. 'I don't think I will, thanks. You know I'm no swimmer. I'll stay and clear up.'

'Sara—you'll come.' It was a statement, not a question, and Sara unfastened her skirt and stood, slim and long-legged, dusky in the soft light, taking the hand he offered. She felt her excitement intensify with a thrill of fear. So far this evening they had played romantic games. Now, the way Conrad looked at her said that the games were over: he had waited the promised day and the time to talk was almost here.

Once in the water he told her to make for the Pointe d'Ankou on the right of the bay, and matched his strong stroke to her weaker one as they swam through the silver-surfaced calmness like people in a dream landscape, with only the gentle ripple of their movement breaking the silence.

At the Pointe Conrad climbed out and offered his hand to pull Sara on to the rocks with him. Though she was cold from the water, the instant he touched her her veins seemed to run with molten fire, and the movement out of the sea became a movement into his arms.

Sara knew that she was borne towards the ending of this night with an inevitability she was powerless to resist; she was intoxicated with anticipation, ready to give him a lifetime but unable to deny him a second, if that was all he wanted.

Where their wet bodies touched and clung, coolness turned to warmth. Little runnels of water streaming from their skin joined course, only to be flung off into the darkness by eager hands, catching the moonlight like a shower of pearls. For a long moment Sara felt only a fierce hunger that crushed all other thoughts in an explosion of sensation, then Conrad's lips released hers and he buried his face in the satiny hollow of her neck with a shuddering sigh of satisfaction.

'What a trial of strength this evening has been! Why was I so stupid as to think we could indulge in social platitudes? All I've been wanting to do ever since I saw you is this.'

He crushed her to him again, his hands sliding down the silken wetness of her body, tightening on the dark rope of her hair, dislodging the rose in his eagerness.

They slipped suddenly on the uneven surface, lurched, clung to each other laughing as they regained their balance, and the tidal wave of passion subsided and allowed reason to re-establish itself precariously.

'The wrong time and the wrong place, it would seem, Mr Blake,' Sara murmured teasingly into his ear.

'But the right people?' There was real seriousness in his question. 'Sara? Sara?'

He held her away from him, scanning her face in the moonlight. 'You said you had to sort something out. A day for thinking, you said.'

She pressed her lips to his again, stilling his urgency.

'How can we talk here . . . now?' she said, then, 'Jane's waiting. We can't even begin, can we?'

'Witch!' He pressed her to him again, raining kisses on her face. 'Temptress! Torturer! Tell me one thing, then. Does anyone else—Jonathan or whatever his name was . . . or anybody at all affect your thinking?'

She rested her head on the broad strength of his shoulder, so that she could almost taste the salty freshness of his skin as she spoke.

'No one. Only me.'

'And your job? How important is that?'

'What job?' she murmured dismissively, her hands moving over the muscles of his neck, feeling the tension in them ease at her touch.

'How have you done this to me in so short a time?' His arms tightened convulsively round her. 'So many girls before you, there have been—and now . . . who were they? Meaningless passers-by. It's as though they never existed. The only eyes I can see are your eyes. The only touch I remember is your touch . . . and the feel of you in my arms.'

'Oh, Con! And yet, you don't really know me at all, do you?'

He cradled her head against him, his fingers moving gently on the nape of her neck. 'I know you better than anyone I've ever met. I had only to look at you to know you with a knowledge that takes no account of the world's time. If we were Buddhists, I'd say we'd loved in every existence prior to this one. Every existence *but* this one,' he added with emphasis.

Sara sighed. 'Jane will think something has happened to us.' She took his hands in hers and kissed them, the lingering of her lips softening her action. 'Be patient.' Another kiss. 'Be practical. We must get back.'

'Damn!' The explosive curse startled her, but it wasn't directed at her, she realised, as he stooped and peered at the water which was murmuring against the rock on which they stood. 'You're right—and not just because of Jane. This wasn't such a clever choice of place. The tide's turned. We must go before the current reaches full strength. Quickly! Let me get in first.'

He lowered himself into the water and lifted her down, pressing her against the lean strength of his body for another irresistible moment, then he swam behind her, back along the path of moonlight towards the glow of the bonfire, low and dying now.

'I'll see Jane home, and then come back,' he said softly as they got out of the water and walked towards the bonfire.

'Promise?' Now she was the impatient one.

'I promise.' He squeezed her fingers in return before letting her go.

Jane was standing near the fire, very still, watching them approach. When they were near enough Sara saw that though her face was impassive, her eyes were savage.

Why? What had happened to change her mood again? Was it just anger at being kept waiting? The laughter, the teasing, the apparent enjoyment of each other's company had gone and now Jane seemed full of resentment. Had she seen them in each other's arms out there? Could she be jealous of her new-found brother's affection? Sara glanced back over her shoulder, but the place where she and Conrad had been was no more than a hard black outline. When she looked at Jane again, the girl seemed more in command of her feelings.

'Did you have a good swim?'

'Wonderful.' Conrad was too honest to say he wished she had come along, and the look he slanted at Sara would have given the lie to the words if he had spoken them.

'I've packed everything except the candles. I was waiting for the glass to cool down.' As she spoke Jane was dismantling the little lights and stowing them in the baskets. The picnic was definitely over.

'You should have come with us. The water was lovely,' Sara said as she fastened her skirt over her wet bikini.

'Oh . . . I wasn't idle.' Jane spoke in an oddly self-satisfied voice.

'I'm sorry about the packing up. I would have helped.'

Sara spoke placatingly, wondering if a sense of grievance over this was bugging Jane.

Jane stood up briskly. 'It took no time at all. Actually, I went for a short walk. It was very ... interesting.' She laughed, a high, unnatural sound. 'Unplanned things often are, don't you think?'

Sara picked up her towel and looked around. Conrad was dealing with the fire, raking its still-glowing embers. Everything else was stowed away. 'Well ...' she said awkwardly, 'I'll go and get out of these wet things if there's nothing else I can do.'

'Nothing. Do go and get warm.'

'It was a wonderful picnic. Thank you—and goodnight, Jane.'

'Goodnight.'

As Sara passed Conrad, his goodnight had a soft 'for now' added, in a voice that was too low for Jane to hear.

With the cottage door standing open, Sara heard Clouzot whinny with pleasure to be moving towards home again, then came the slow fading of his hooves against the murmur of Conrad's and Jane's voices. Maybe it was understandable that Jane should be a little strange, Sara thought. Her life had been unusual, to say the least.

She lit the lamps and put coffee on to brew, then hesitated a long time over what to change into. Remembering the first bitter-sweet awareness of her feelings for Conrad, she took out her white jeans and yellow baggy shirt she had worn on that day. The love that she was allowing to blossom now had seemed so impossible then.

The hands of her watch crawled slowly, tantalisingly. Restlessly keyed up, she tried to improve the appearance of the cottage while she waited, but all the time her mind was impatiently crying 'when?'

At last she heard the sound she was waiting for—footsteps, their urgency indicating that Conrad too was impatient for the moment that was now finally here.

The door was flung open, crashing back against the wall, and Conrad strode into the room as Sara rose to her feet, her eyes aglow, her arms reaching out to him. Then, as she saw his face, they froze and fell slowly, awkwardly to her sides again.

This was a stranger, not the Conrad who had pressed his love with such urgency only a short time ago. White of face, his eyes blazing and a nerve twitching at the corner of his mouth, for a moment he stared at her as though his eyes would penetrate her soul.

'What's wrong, Conrad?' she faltered.

He shut the door with exquisite, exaggerated care that was more scaring than any violence, then came over and with contemptuous, ironic courtesy indicated that she should sit, before taking a chair opposite her and folding his arms, his eyes never leaving her face for a second.

'Why, nothing!' he said, his voice tight and scornful. 'Nothing's wrong. I've come to talk, as we arranged. What else does one do but talk—with a *journalist*?'

Prepared, as she had been, to tell him the truth in her own time, Sara felt the colour flood her cheeks at his devastatingly unexpected accusation and the implication in his voice. Then the tide of hot blood receded, leaving her as white as Conrad. She swallowed hard, her initiative deserting her, the words of love she had been brimming over with turned to a hard, bitter lump in her throat.

'Why—why do you say that?'

His eyes were ice-cold, vindictive. 'Ah—now there's an interesting thing. By referring to you as a journalist, I happen to be speaking the truth—a commodity completely unknown to you. I was completely taken in by you. I must hand you full marks for that. But women are more clever, as you, of course, know. Jane wasn't taken in one little bit.'

So it was Jane who had found out. But how? Sara closed her eyes against the almost tangible hostility in his.

'She always mistrusted you, right from the start,' he went on. 'But she couldn't quite recall what it was that had sown the seeds of her mistrust until tonight.'

Sara remembered the strange reaction when she had spoken of her book.

'You mean, when I talked about writing?'

'Not even the talk, Sara.' Slowly he moved his long fingers over the surface of the table as though on a typewriter. 'One little gesture. And it gave you away instantly. You'd been pictured in some magazine she'd read—won a competition for budding journalists, she says. You were shown sitting at a typewriter . . . just like this.' He repeated the taunting gesture. 'And there was a blurb saying that your prize had led to permanent work on a magazine.'

Maybe that was all he knew. Maybe it wasn't too late. Sara attempted to pull herself together.

'Yes, I did win a competition. And yes—the office I work in is a magazine's office. But what's so very dreadful about that?' Fear put bluster into her voice, making it obvious that she was covering up when she ought to have been giving the honest explanation she had intended. Even as the words fell on the air, she knew they were hopeless.

Conrad rocked back on his chair, his eyes seeing through her.

'There's honest journalism, about which there is indeed no call to be ashamed. And there's gutter-press work that maybe even a proportion of those who indulge in it aren't too proud about. We know which category your work comes into don't we, Sara? We know why you haven't been at all eager to come clean about your job. You were cunningly oblique about it. "I work in an office for my daily bread." So innocuous. And what a good job you did on me, Sara.' His voice was bitter, despising her, despising himself. 'No doubt you're well practised in charming the dirt out of people. Your big, brown eyes to soften a man up . . . and your pathetic little contrived accidents to arouse his chivalry. It worked on me.'

'I didn't contrive anything!' she said hotly. 'Any more than you contrived to scrape your side on the rocks. I even told you that I didn't want to know about you—quite clearly, when I was at your house. I tried to stop you. I hated what I was doing.'

'Oh!' His eyes glittered with triumph. 'So it was my life you were sent to dig into, was it?'

She stared at him, wretched with despair and shame, incapable of a shred of further defiance. It was no good. She was condemned unheard.

'You know it was.'

'And the proof's here in the cottage, as Jane found.' His eyes went to the top of the cupboard where her tape recorder was, and now he stood up abruptly and brought it down, placing it on the table between them. 'Very thorough proof, Jane says. I must hear you at work, Sara. Coldly efficient, Jane found it—but not the sort of efficiency one truly admires, of course.' He looked at Sara's white, stricken face, his own expression iron-hard. 'Yes . . . she intruded in your cottage, Sara, while we were having that misguided little chat on the Pointe d'Ankou. But you can hardly object to intrusion, can you? You've done so much of it yourself. Shall we listen?'

'No! Please! I can explain. *Please* don't switch it on.'

But he had already done so and her cool, recorded tones cut into the distress of her live voice. Sara clenched her fists, forced to listen in an agony of shame, her head turning from side to side as she heard herself listing speculation and discovery with cold, methodical objectivity.

Conrad stabbed at the button and released the cassette. 'Enough of that. I'll hear the rest in private.' He slipped it into his pocket. 'One thing Jane didn't find was the writing you were so assiduous about today. I must have that, I think, Sara. The finished article, I presume? Get it, please.'

She ran to fetch her pad from the wardrobe in the bedroom, putting it into his hands in silence. It was a small thing for him to be wrong about, and he wouldn't change his attitude about it, but it was *something*.

He didn't even read it. Before she could stop him, he ripped out the pages of hurried scribble and tore them in half, in quarters, in eighths. The ferocity of the gesture went ill with the cold control of his voice.

'The ashes of the bonfire will take care of these,' he said as he crushed the pieces in his palm.

'But that wasn't——'

'Don't!' he thundered, his taut self-possession snapping at last. 'Don't say another lying word to me. All I want from you now is the name of the filthy rag that sent you here.'

She told him, and saw by the curl of his lip that he knew the nature of the magazine.

'Remember this,' he told her, in such a way that she could not doubt his word for a second. 'My solicitors could destroy *Spica* and you. They'll find a way of doing so if a word of what you know appears in that paper's sordid pages.'

She watched him go to the door, dumb with anguish. She

couldn't find the strength to make any attempt at an explanation and exoneration of her actions. He wouldn't listen, she knew. His mind was flint-hard against her. It was too late. There was a world of difference between confession and discovery ... a world that ranged from darkness to light, and she was lost in the shadow of darkness.

In the doorway, Conrad paused and looked once more at her.

'I can't think what else you were hanging on here for ... what it was that you were working up to. Curiosity about what it's like in bed with the head of Blake Enterprises, was it? Well, that's something you'll never feed into your pernicious little machine, isn't it? And something you'll never be able to mull over with your seedy associates. Thank God for preserving me from that experience, at least.'

His face looked years older, and his eyes seemed drained of all their colour as he looked bitterly at her.

'You know what "Pointe d'Ankou" means?' he went on heavily. 'It's a nice irony. "Ankou" is Breton for "death", Sara. And something did indeed die there tonight, didn't it?'

The door closed silently behind him.

CHAPTER TEN

OVER and over in Sara's mind the scene replayed itself, torturing her as she wondered how she could have halted the awful tide that had swept Conrad away from her. If she had said this . . . told him that . . . protested . . . let the whole story come tumbling out the second she was aware that he knew.

But she hadn't. She'd done everything wrong, every single step of the way. The thing was, though—how else could she have done it? She'd acted guilty because she *was* guilty. Apart from the suggestion that she had contrived the accidents, every single thing she had been accused of, she had done. What hadn't been dragged into the open was the fact that she did truly love Conrad, and had grown to do so all the time she was preparing the wretched material for *Spica*. There was no falseness about that.

But Conrad would never see it now. If she had told him everything herself, voluntarily, it would have been different. Dangerous still, because how could she expect him just to pat her on the head and say 'There, there! It's all right!' when it was obviously not so. It wasn't an 'all-right' business she had been involved in. But she would have made him understand—if she had told him herself.

She had been found out, though. Discovered. Raked out from under *Spica*'s stone. Now anything she said would seem to come from that, not from the deep, the true feelings she had. It could look as though she was trying to save her own skin: maybe even as though what had begun as gutter journalism had turned into something worse. He might even think her an opportunist who had seen which way the wind was blowing and taken advantage of it. If she told him of her resignation and the destroying of the film, both actions could be seen as fitting in with a sudden decision to ditch *Spica* and look for greater personal gain.

There really was no way out of the horror, no way that would lead her back towards Conrad. The only thing to do was get away as soon as possible. Spare him the sight of her, spare herself the pain of seeing him.

She stretched her cramped limbs and glanced at her watch for the first time. Almost two o'clock. At least four more hours before it would be light enough to cross over to the mainland. Four hours to pack and clean up the cottage—because there was no way she could bear to lie in bed thinking of all she was losing. And the 'all'—no matter what Conrad might think of her—was not the rich head of Blake Enterprises, but the love of a man who had looked at her so eloquently with those wonderful eyes of his, who had melted away the traces of disillusion and disappointment in her and replaced them with a happiness, the absence of which now would leave her haunted to the end of her days.

And she couldn't cry. There were no easy tears to let the pain flow out of her. It was hard and wounding inside her, that pain; beyond crying, beyond words.

She forced herself to concentrate on the packing first. Each garment she folded and put away recalled some moment shared with Conrad. Nothing she had worn when she was with him could she bear to put on again. The memories would be too vivid. When she caught sight of the yellow shirt she was wearing in the mirror, she took it off at once and pulled on an old blue sweatshirt, unable to bear the sight of it. Yellow—the colour of sun, the colour of sand, the colour of happiness. She left it lying on the stripped bed, because she had been wearing it when she had first realised she was in love—but now it was associated with tonight and Conrad showing her how much he despised her. Always from now on yellow would be the colour of misery.

She worked on mechanically, washing, polishing, cleaning like a zombie until there was not a single thing left to do to fill the long night hours.

Five o'clock. Time *was* passing. She pulled a chair over to the window and threw wide the shutters, then turned out the lamps and sat staring into the darkness, waiting for the dawn.

It began with a faint lightening in the east along the line of the horizon, spreading pearly fingers slowly outwards and upwards. Pale, shell-like colours tinged the sky, deepening and changing, becoming stronger as the first tip of the sun's circle appeared. In the trees behind the cottage a solitary bird started to sing, its music full of a heavy sweetness and poignancy that tightened Sara's throat and gripped her heart. She sat there for a long time, watching the brightening day. How many sunrises? How many sunsets? How long would life go on without Conrad? She rubbed her forehead on her arms, then stood. No point in looking back—or forward into a desolate future, for that matter. Today she had to leave here. Tomorow—all the tomorrows—could take care of themselves.

Before she left, she took her yellow shirt out on to the beach and dug a deep hole with her bare hands. Then she thrust the bright garment in and covered it, stamping down the moist sand to bury it. Let it lie here with her dreams, not taunt her with memories. She needed no reminders of what had happened on Les Genêts.

The shutters fastened, the cottage locked, Sara picked up

her things and took them over to the boat. It was low tide, a tricky time to negotiate the channels . . . but what would it matter if she never reached the mainland?

She was putting the last bag in the boat when she heard the voice she had never thought to hear again.

'Running away? I guessed you'd do just that.'

Conrad was there on the path, leaning against the bank, wearing the jeans and shirt he had pulled on over his trunks last night. He was unshaven and his hair was tousled, as though he had run his fingers through it time after exasperated time. And he looked as though—like her—he hadn't slept at all.

Sara stared at him and a deep, unbearable yearning gathered in the pit of her stomach. She wanted to brush his hair back, smooth away the shadows under his eyes, see the brightness return to them. But that was not to be.

'There's no point in talking,' she said hopelessly. 'Yes, I'm going. And right now.' She pulled on the starter, then again, desperately, as no answering cough and roar responded.

'This is almost where we came in.' He straightened up, but made no move to come down and start the boat for her. 'This time it's very convenient, however, because I haven't finished with you yet. You might as well save your efforts— it's not going to go.'

She looked up from another useless tussle with the starter to see his face expressionless as he waited for her to do what he told her, and resentment at the boat's conspiring with him spilled out.

'Wasn't last night enough? Do we have to go over it all again?'

'We do. I thought I'd taken care of everything once I'd got the tape and script—but then I realised that there was something else. The friend, Sara. The inexplicable working colleague who just happened to call in on you. Was he involved in your little venture as well? That would be the logical assumption.'

Her heart sank as she imagined the further sordid details that would be dragged from her, and he read the answer in her eyes.

'I see we *do* still have things to talk about. You'd better come up to the house. Leave your things here. Nobody's going to be around.'

She hung back. 'You don't have any reason to worry about Dave——'

His raised hand silenced her. 'Oh, but I do. He's gone. I must know what's gone with him.'

Miserably she climbed out of the boat and splashed through the shallows, then pulled on her canvas shoes.

'I assure you——' she began again.

'At the house,' he said implacably. 'Assure me there—if you can.' He gave her a contemptuous glance and set off along the path. Sara followed, and he didn't speak again until they were in the sitting-room at La Domaine.

The whisky bottle and empty glass on the table alongside two used coffee-cups were silent witnesses to the way the night had been spent. He gestured for her to sit down and took a seat facing her.

'So what was his function?' he began without delay.

Sara swallowed. 'He's a photographer.'

There was a momentary silence, while Conrad digested the implication of this. 'I wasn't aware of any pictures being taken. You'd better tell me what he did.'

She couldn't look at him. 'He—he took shots of the scenery, and your house, and——'

'And *they're* not going to sell extra copies. So let's have the real scoops he got, Sara.'

'Jane—but just standing in her doorway, that's all he took of her,' she hurried on to add before her voice dried up on her.

Conrad leaned forward, his eyes burning into hers. 'Go on. What else?'

'You . . .' she said miserably. 'You diving into the sea, just after I'd introduced you.'

His voice was ominously quiet when he spoke.

'And where were you when he was doing his keyhole photography? Right there with him? Stooping as low as he was?'

Her silence was answer enough.

'I suppose there's more?' he said icily.

'One more . . . of that kind.' She gulped in a shaky breath. 'The night of the storm. He was waiting up at the megalith for us to come out. You know what happened.'

'Oh, I do! And I know how well it was timed. You were very reluctant to be kissed before we came out, weren't you?'

'No!' She shouted her denial. 'No, Conrad. Accuse me of what you like, but not that. I had no idea Dave was there— no idea the picture had been taken. Do you really think me as low as that?'

He looked steadily at her, cold and calm in the face of her heated response. 'Tell me what I'm supposed to believe, then.'

Sara subsided into her chair. Should she try to explain? Was it worth the effort, the humiliation of seeing him grow more sceptical, more scornful as she stumbled through her reasons? But she must at least dispel any fear he had that Dave had left the island with his film intact.

'You can believe this,' she said at last. 'When I found out

what Dave had done, I wasn't going to let him get away with it. The other shot—the one of you diving—that wasn't my fault, either. He saw you, and he was too quick for me. Oh—I knew why you couldn't wait to get into the sea. I knew how you felt——'

'Never,' he cut in sharply, 'never presume to tell me you understand my feelings. You don't. It's as simple as that. So cut out the psychology and stick to facts. What did you do about the film?'

'I took it out of the camera during the night and held it—all of it—close to the lamp. He never knew.' She shot a quick glance of defiance at him as she prepared to make her last revelation. 'So when he broke into your studio yesterday morning and took pictures of your work he had no idea that it was a total waste of time. '

'My work, too?' His jaw tightened.

'But I destroyed the film,' she stressed.

His expression sharpened. 'You were on it. You were protecting yourself. Why should I think you were concerned about me?'

His reaction didn't surprise her. She had known all the time she was speaking that he would make the most unfavourable interpretation.

'Think what you want,' she said dully. 'The fact remains that the film's non-existent.' She looked at him, forcing herself to speak calmly. 'And even if you hadn't found out about me, there would have been no article about you. I don't expect you to believe me, but once I knew you, I found the whole underhand business nauseating. It was my job, but it was impossible in the end. Yesterday, after Dave had gone, I rang the office and told my senior that I wasn't submitting a story, and I resigned.'

He locked his fingers together, staring at her over the top

of them. 'I don't know you've done that, do I? You could be spinning me any kind of yarn to make yourself look better.'

'That at least I can prove.' She jumped to her feet and ran impetuously over to the telephone, then realised that Fran wouldn't be in the office for ages yet. 'No, I can't,' she said miserably. 'There won't be anyone in the *Spica* offices yet.'

'Then we must give them time to arrive.' He was all calm, cool reason, addressing her with the politeness reserved for strangers. 'I hear Marthe in the kitchen. We'll have breakfast while we wait. There's no point in being uncivilised. And in view of the kind of night it's been, perhaps you'd like a bath first? I know I would.'

He guided her to the kitchen doorway, one hand on her arm as though she might run away.

Marthe looked up from the stove. 'Oh—*mademoiselle*! So early. What a surprise!'

'She's a very surprising lady,' Conrad said with smooth sarcasm. 'We've had a somewhat disturbed night, Marthe. Could you prepare breakfast for two in the sitting-room? Give us twenty minutes or so to freshen up.'

Marthe's eyes darted from him to Sara and she was obviously unsure what to make of the situation, but discreet as ever.

'Very well, monsieur.'

Sara shook his hand off angrily as he marched her upstairs. 'You're insufferably sure of yourself. What makes you think you can organise my every movement? Why should I have a bath and eat on your instructions?'

He shrugged. 'Please yourself. You have to do something until the office opens, don't you? I hardly imagine your thoughts are entertaining enough. And you could certainly use a bath. You have dust on your face and sand under your nails. There's no reason to let the outside match what's beaneath the surface. Use the room you're familiar with for whatever purpose you choose.' He walked on to his own room, leaving her smarting from the sting of his cruel words.

In her old bedroom Sara looked at herself—scruffy, as he had implied, but blanched and strained too, which he had chosen to ignore. The eager, joyful girl of last night was gone. She seemed to belong to another lifetime. How many more deaths will he make me die? she asked her jaded reflection.

She took a bath, after all, and it revived her a little, making her feel more up to lasting out the rest of the inquisition Conrad seemed determined to put her through. She was a virtual prisoner on the island until he chose to help her to get away, in any case, so there was no question that he was master of the situation. If his intention was to reduce her to even more abject shame than she already felt, all she could do was stick it out with as much dignity as possible.

He was strangely calm through breakfast, passing her food she didn't want and couldn't eat, while he ate a hearty meal himself, his eyes sliding away from their impersonal contemplation of her whenever she looked up. Sara broke up a croissant on her plate, but couldn't eat a crumb, though she drank cups of Marthe's strong black coffee.

'I'm an idiot!' she burst out at last into the silence. 'Why didn't I think before? I can ring Fran—my senior—at home. I have her number. Let me try now.'

'Go head.' Conrad came over to the phone with her and stood close while she dialled the number: close enough for her to be achingly aware of the hollow of his neck where she longed to bury her face. Just in time to stop the build-up of tears in her throat, she heard Fran speak.

'Fran——' she said nervously. 'It's Sara.'

The explosion was instant. 'And about bloody time! What the hell are you playing at? Have you got an overdose of sun out there? What do you mean—*no story*? You're paid to get a story. And what's this garbage about resigning? You can't—and in any case, did no one ever tell you about working out notice? Why, Sara? *Why?* Sara? *Sara?*'

Sara had been holding the receiver towards Conrad, but brought it back to her own ear again.

'I'm listening. I meant everything I said, Fran, I'm afraid. I'm not coming back to work on *Spica*, whatever you say.' She shot a glance at Conrad's impassive face. 'Just one thing, have you seen Dave yet? He must have got back some time yesterday.'

'Oh, he's back all right. Back and gibbering with rage! I had him on the phone at midnight. What did you do to his film, Sara? He got in last night, itching to develop it— didn't even eat first—and what did he find? Not a thing! It had been tampered with—exposed to light, he says, and he's ready to swear you're responsible. We could sue you for this, Sara. I'm damned if I'm putting up with——'

Conrad had taken the receiver and put it down with a bang. He walked towards the fireplace, hands in the pockets of his jeans, stretching them tautly over his slim hips, then he turned round and looked at Sara.

'Of course, all that proves nothing, does it? When did all these noble gestures of yours occur? Let me see . . . It would be the morning after you were made aware that my future wasn't tied up with any other woman. Could it be that you scented brighter prospects for yourself than *Spica* offered?'

Pain grew in Sara until it seemed to fill her completely, but she wouldn't let him see her break down.

'If that's what you want to believe, there's no point in going on talking. Nothing I can say will destroy such determination to think the worst of me.' The total unfairness of it all overwhelmed her suddenly and, in spite of her resolution, her voice rose in an impassioned plea. 'Why are you doing this, Conrad? Why don't you just help me to get out of your life? For God's sake, let me go!'

'Sit down.' For the first time she sensed that he was near to losing his cool. 'One more thing, and then it's the end. You're going to listen to something.' He switched on the cassette recorder, and Sara shrank back in her chair as, once again, she heard her own voice.

It was the last recording she had made, when she had gone back to the cottage after her two days at La Domaine. He made her listen right to the end, through all the descriptions of his carvings. At the time she had done them coldly and quickly because she had hated what she was doing, could hardly bear to go on with it, but to him it must seem as though even her expressed admiration for this work had not been genuine. At the end he let the tape run on, and Sara suddenly jumped as her own recorded voice cried out. It was a long-drawn-out cry of anguish that she remembered uttering so well as she had plunged her face into her hands. She hadn't the least idea then that the faulty machine was recording everything still.

Conrad rewound the tape and played the sound again. 'Why?' he said, his voice thick with passion, his eyes piercing hers. 'Why did you cry out like that?'

Knowing his attitude, she couldn't bear to lower the last flimsy layer of pretence and strip herself down to the naked truth before him. She had gone far enough. She refused to give him a second more of satisfaction, no matter how much the feelings of that moment tugged at her heart.

'Because——' Her mind thrashed around feverishly for a reason. 'Because I was exasperated with the stupid machine. It's on the blink and I'd tried to switch off but the button wouldn't work.'

He leapt to his feet, his eyes blazing.

'Liar! Liar, liar, liar!' He was towering over her now, gripping her shoulders with iron fingers that felt as though they were meeting through her flesh, shaking her and then dragging her up on to her feet. 'Tell me the truth, damn you!' he shouted into her face. 'Why that cry? What did it mean?'

A desperate anger swept through her, an anger to match his own, because he wanted to squeeze every drop of blood out of her before he sent her on her way.

'All right!' Her voice matched his, its harsh violence making a mockery of the words she spoke. 'All right. I'll tell you. It was because I hated what I was doing. Couldn't bear it. I couldn't bear it because I loved you. *Loved you.*' Her breast was heaving, her eyes glittering with unshed tears. 'Will that do? Am I low enough now? Am I hurting enough to satisfy you?'

He was the one who cried out then, not in despair but in exultation.

'At last!' The words rang out so unexpectedly that Sara froze, her mouth open on a further protest that never came. 'At last ...' he repeated softly, his voice vibrant with emotion, and the pain of his grip on her shoulders eased as his hands slid down her back to pull her against him. 'Oh Sara!' His voice was muffled in her hair, warm on her skin. 'Sara ... why couldn't you just tell me that hours ago? It was all I needed to hear.'

She couldn't ... she dare not believe him. It was another trick, another punishment ... And yet, his hand was smoothing her hair, cradling her head against him, and his heart was pounding against her breast with the same eagerness as her own.

'Don't torture me, Conrad,' she began brokenly, her voice almost too faint and strained for him to hear. But he *did* hear, and he spanned her vulnerable, slender neck with his hand, then slid his fingers up to cup her chin and tilt her face up to his.

'Is this torture?' he said softly, kissing the tears brimming from her eyes. 'And this? And this?' He rained kisses all over her upturned face until she couldn't do anything but believe him, cry out with joy that came from the very depths of her soul, and respond.

But still a tiny doubt lingered.

'How can you do this, after all that you know?' she cried when they paused momentarily for breath, her lips bruised by the exquisite pain of his passionate kisses.

'How can I not love you, knowing you?' he returned swiftly, his eyes blazing into hers. 'Something as strong as life itself drives me towards you, urges me to listen to my heart, not to my dented male pride. What does pride matter beside love, Sara, my sweet, my only one?' This time his kiss was deep and tender and long, and Sara felt that not only their bodies, but their hearts and souls were made one by it.

Marthe's voice suddenly spoke drily from the doorway, falling like a stone into the emotionally charged air through which it came.

'I did knock . . .'

They turned their faces towards her, still clasping each other tightly, their eyes reflecting other worlds.

'I wondered if you needed more coffee,' she went on, 'but . . .'

Conrad smiled. 'Yes, Marthe—"but". We have other

things on our minds, as you see. Mademoiselle Sara is going to marry me.' He looked down at Sara. 'You are, aren't you?'

Sara's face was flushed with a rosy glow. 'It seems I have little choice. But even if you'd asked me privately, I'd have said yes. Oh yes! And soon!'

Marthe was forgotten again as he gazed intently, burningly into Sara's eyes, his hands moving possessively down to draw her close to him while love swelled to fever pitch in her.

'*Félicitations, monsieur, mademoiselle!*' Marthe added a few more words in a tone that, for her, came close to humour, but Sara couldn't quite catch their meaning before the closing of the door behind the little Breton woman.

'What did she say?'

Conrad was shaking with laughter. 'She said it was just as well—in view of the speed things were moving at. Come and sit down.' He pulled Sara on to his knee and settled her comfortably against him, with his arms round her.

'Last night I thought this was impossible.' Sara sighed happily as she moulded her softness to Conrad's hard strength.

'Last night was last night. Oh, I was angry: angry to have been taken in in such a way, angry that my privacy should be invaded by a rag like *Spica*, angry that you, of all people, should work for them and come here with such a purpose. I wanted to lash out, and I did. But then when I left you I thought, "What are you doing, you fool?" I began to see that your experience with Jonathan could explain the temporary attraction *Spica* had for you ... and I couldn't believe that everything that had happened between us— spoken and unspoken—had been an act. Even if you'd come to Les Genêts with the intention of getting a story, you must surely have changed your mind. I couldn't bear to think that there had been no sincerity between us all the time.'

'Oh, Con! It was so awful. There was Dave coming—*they* arranged that, not me—and I couldn't stop him . . . and it got more and more complicated, and more and more painful. I wanted to tell you so many times—and last night I was really going to. I couldn't have gone on deceiving you, even when I'd opted out of the job I was supposed to do . . . and then you——'

'I know. I flew in with my accusations and knocked the words back down your throat.'

She nodded. 'Yes . . . But everything you said was true, that was the trouble. I *was* guilty, and having you find out like that instead of my telling you . . . Oh! It was the worst night of my life.'

'For me, too. I went over everything we'd said and done, wanting to find something to prove that you really had had a change of heart, but nothing seemed to convince me absolutely. It could all have been done for a purpose, it seemed, until I heard that despairing little cry.' He kissed her. 'It was the most wonderful sound in the world to me then. But still something in me needed to have you tell me yourself—expand that sound into the meaning I thought I read into it . . . and it seemed today as though you never would.'

'Did you sleep at all?' Sara ran a soft finger tip under his eyes, eyes that, however tired they might be, had regained the brightness she so loved.

'How could I sleep? I came over to the cottage before it got light, and I spent the rest of the night where you saw me this morning. I watched the light in your cottage, scared to death that you wouldn't agree to speak to me again, but determined that you were not going to slip away unseen.'

'You were out there all the time?' Sara thought suddenly of the sunrise they must both have been watching together, utterly miserable, and desperately wanting a solution. How different the beauty of that dawn would have seemed if only she had known that he was there.

'Sara——' His voice was curious as it broke into her thoughts. 'Tell me—what were you doing out there, digging a hole in the sand?'

She blushed, feeling stupid. 'I—I was burying my shirt. And don't laugh like that, Conrad! It was a—a very poignant moment!' She too could laugh at it now, she found.

'Go on. Tell me.' He let his head lie back against the chair, slanting a shining, teasing look at her from under half-closed lids. 'I've got to know if you often feel compelled to bury a shirt at moments of high stress. I mean, I feel it's something a man should know about his wife!'

She butted her head against his chin, then grew serious again, tightening her arms round him.

'That particular shirt saw a lot of our relationship growing. Do you remember? I was wearing it when I bathed your poor side, and that was when I first realised how much I loved you and couldn't bear what I was meant to do to you. And I was wearing it last night when I was convinced I'd lost you. I never wanted to see it again.'

'Oh, my love!' He kissed her again, not the wild, passionate kisses of earlier on, but a long, slow, comforting kiss that healed her wounds and drove away the last traces of that early-dawn desperation on the beach.

'You really do forgive me?' she asked.

'And you me?' There was no need for either of them to answer with words. 'Besides——' he said with a sudden change of tone, 'if it hadn't been for that abysmal magazine, we would never have met. Now, there's a thought—and one that doesn't bear dwelling on.' He straightened up. 'Let's go and dig up your shirt! Shall we?'

Sara nodded happily. 'And there's the boat to see to—not that I have the least desire to use it, as long as you want me to stay here.'

'You'll go on writing, of course? So it doesn't matter much where we live? I'm buying this place ... but we'll need to be back in England most of the time, for all sorts of reasons. You don't mind?'

'As long as you're there,' she said, her eyes eloquent.

A little time later, he returned to the question of the boat.

'It won't take long to get it going,' he said, a little sheepishly. 'All it needs is the petrol put back in it.'

'Conrad!' Sara looked accusingly at him. 'Was that what you did?'

'We couldn't have an undignified scuffle on the beach, could we? And if you'd once managed to start the damned thing ...'

She sat up and gently cuffed his cheek with the back of her hand.

'So, Mr Virtuous! You *contrived an accident*, did you?'

'I did ... but from now on, everything I do—everything *we* do—will be with deliberate, open, delicous intention!'

The heat of his gaze made her melt back into his arms. It was the perfect answer, and it deserved and got the perfect reward.

HARLEQUIN

Coming Next Month

#3025 ARAFURA PIRATE Victoria Gordon
Jinx had been warned about Race Morgan, skipper of the boat taking her
scientific research team to Australia's northern coast. But she's confident she
can handle it, as long as he keeps their relationship professional.

#3026 GAME PLAN Rosemary Hammond
Jake Donovan, so everyone says, has an infallible plan that makes the women
fall at his feet. However, when it doesn't work with reserved Claire Talbot, he
finds to his surprise that he can't forget her....

#3027 SPELL OF THE MOUNTAINS Rosalie Henaghan
Sophie is determined to make a success of her motel—and has no intention of
selling out to the powerful, dynamic hotelier Jon Roberts. Her refusal only
sparks his determination, for Jon isn't used to women who say no!

#3028 JINXED Day Leclaire
Kit soon discovers that playing with toys all day can be a dangerous
occupation, especially when working for a man like Stephen "The Iceman"
St. Clair. The normally cold and stern owner of The Toy Company behaves
more like a volcano whenever Kit is around.

#3029 CONFLICT Margaret Mayo
Blythe's first priority after her father's death is to make the family business
pay—and especially to prevent it from falling into Coburn Daggart's hands.
Years ago, Coburn hurt her badly, and Blythe makes up her mind to pay
him back.

#3030 FOOLISH DECEIVER Sandra K. Rhoades
Allie has learned the hard way that men don't like intelligent women. So, on
vacation at an old girlfriend's, she conceals her genius IQ. Her scheme
backfires when Linc Summerville believes she is a dumb blonde and treats her
like a fool!

Available in January wherever paperback books are sold, or through
Harlequin Reader Service:

In the U.S.
901 Fuhrmann Blvd.
P.O. Box 1397
Buffalo, N.Y. 14240-1397

In Canada
P.O. Box 603
Fort Erie, Ontario
L2A 5X3

Especially for you,
Christmas from
HARLEQUIN HISTORICALS

An enchanting collection of three Christmas
stories by some of your favorite authors captures
the spirit of the season in the 1800s

TUMBLEWEED CHRISTMAS by Kristin James

A "Bah, humbug" Texas rancher meets his match in his
new housekeeper, a woman determined to bring the spirit
of a Tumbleweed Christmas into his life—and love into
his heart.

A CINDERELLA CHRISTMAS by Lucy Elliot

The perfect granddaughter, sister and aunt, Mary Hillyer
seemed destined for spinsterhood until Jack Gates arrived
to discover a woman with dreams and passions that were
meant to be shared during a Cinderella Christmas.

HOME FOR CHRISTMAS
by Heather Graham Pozzessere

The magic of the season brings peace Home For
Christmas when a Yankee captain and a Southern heiress
fall in love during the Civil War.

**Look for HARLEQUIN HISTORICALS CHRISTMAS
STORIES wherever Harlequin books are sold.**

INDULGE A LITTLE SWEEPSTAKES
OFFICIAL RULES

SWEEPSTAKES RULES AND REGULATIONS. NO PURCHASE NECESSARY.

1. NO PURCHASE NECESSARY. To enter complete the official entry form and return with the invoice in the envelope provided. Or you may enter by printing your name, complete address and your daytime phone number on a 3 x 5 piece of paper. Include with your entry the hand printed words "Indulge A Little Sweepstakes." Mail your entry to: Indulge A Little Sweepstakes, P.O. Box 1397, Buffalo, NY 14269-1397. No mechanically reproduced entries accepted. Not responsible for late, lost, misdirected mail, or printing errors.

2. Three winners, one per month (Sept. 30, 1989, October 31, 1989 and November 30, 1989), will be selected in random drawings. All entries received prior to the drawing date will be eligible for that month's prize. This sweepstakes is under the supervision of MARDEN-KANE, INC. an independent judging organization whose decisions are final and binding. Winners will be notified by telephone and may be required to execute an affidavit of eligibility and release which must be returned within 14 days, or an alternate winner will be selected.

3. Prizes: 1st Grand Prize (1) a trip for two to Disneyworld in Orlando, Florida. Trip includes round trip air transportation, hotel accommodations for seven days and six nights, plus up to $700 expense money (ARV $3,500). 2nd Grand Prize (1) a seven-night Chandris Caribbean Cruise for two includes transportation from nearest major airport, accommodations, meals plus up to $1,000 in expense money (ARV $4,300). 3rd Grand Prize (1) a ten-day Hawaiian holiday for two includes round trip air transportation for two, hotel accommodations, sightseeing, plus up to $1,200 in spending money (ARV $7,700). All trips subject to availability and must be taken as outlined on the entry form.

4. Sweepstakes open to residents of the U.S. and Canada 18 years or older except employees and the families of Torstar Corp., its affiliates, subsidiaries and Marden-Kane, Inc. and all other agencies and persons connected with conducting this sweepstakes. All Federal, State and local laws and regulations apply. Void wherever prohibited or restricted by law. Taxes, if any are the sole responsibility of the prize winners. Canadian winners will be required to answer a skill testing question. Winners consent to the use of their name, photograph and/or likeness for publicity purposes without additional compensation.

5. For a list of prize winners, send a stamped, self-addressed envelope to Indulge A Little Sweepstakes Winners, P.O. Box 701, Sayreville, NJ 08871.

© 1989 HARLEQUIN ENTERPRISES LTD.

DL-SWPS

INDULGE A LITTLE SWEEPSTAKES
OFFICIAL RULES

SWEEPSTAKES RULES AND REGULATIONS. NO PURCHASE NECESSARY.

1. NO PURCHASE NECESSARY. To enter complete the official entry form and return with the invoice in the envelope provided. Or you may enter by printing your name, complete address and your daytime phone number on a 3 x 5 piece of paper. Include with your entry the hand printed words "Indulge A Little Sweepstakes." Mail your entry to: Indulge A Little Sweepstakes, P.O. Box 1397, Buffalo, NY 14269-1397. No mechanically reproduced entries accepted. Not responsible for late, lost, misdirected mail, or printing errors.

2. Three winners, one per month (Sept. 30, 1989, October 31, 1989 and November 30, 1989), will be selected in random drawings. All entries received prior to the drawing date will be eligible for that month's prize. This sweepstakes is under the supervision of MARDEN-KANE, INC. an independent judging organization whose decisions are final and binding. Winners will be notified by telephone and may be required to execute an affidavit of eligibility and release which must be returned within 14 days, or an alternate winner will be selected.

3. Prizes: 1st Grand Prize (1) a trip for two to Disneyworld in Orlando, Florida. Trip includes round trip air transportation, hotel accommodations for seven days and six nights, plus up to $700 expense money (ARV $3,500). 2nd Grand Prize (1) a seven-night Chandris Caribbean Cruise for two includes transportation from nearest major airport, accommodations, meals plus up to $1,000 in expense money (ARV $4,300). 3rd Grand Prize (1) a ten-day Hawaiian holiday for two includes round trip air transportation for two, hotel accommodations, sightseeing, plus up to $1,200 in spending money (ARV $7,700). All trips subject to availability and must be taken as outlined on the entry form.

4. Sweepstakes open to residents of the U.S. and Canada 18 years or older except employees and the families of Torstar Corp., its affiliates, subsidiaries and Marden-Kane, Inc. and all other agencies and persons connected with conducting this sweepstakes. All Federal, State and local laws and regulations apply. Void wherever prohibited or restricted by law. Taxes, if any are the sole responsibility of the prize winners. Canadian winners will be required to answer a skill testing question. Winners consent to the use of their name, photograph and/or likeness for publicity purposes without additional compensation.

5. For a list of prize winners, send a stamped, self-addressed envelope to Indulge A Little Sweepstakes Winners, P.O. Box 701, Sayreville, NJ 08871.

© 1989 HARLEQUIN ENTERPRISES LTD.

DL-SWPS

INDULGE A LITTLE—WIN A LOT!

Summer of '89 Subscribers-Only Sweepstakes

OFFICIAL ENTRY FORM

This entry must be received by: Nov. 30, 1989
This month's winner will be notified by: Dec. 7, 1989
Trip must be taken between: Jan. 7, 1990–Jan. 7, 1991

YES, I want to win the 3-Island Hawaiian vacation for two! I understand the prize includes round-trip airfare, first-class hotels, and a daily allowance as revealed on the "Wallet" scratch-off card.

Name_____

Address_____

City_____ State/Prov._____ Zip/Postal Code_____

Daytime phone number _____
                        Area code

Return entries with invoice in envelope provided. Each book in this shipment has two entry coupons—and the more coupons you enter, the better your chances of winning!
© 1989 HARLEQUIN ENTERPRISES LTD.

DINDL-3